The Neglected Garden

SUZANNE WINTERLY

Alizester Books

ALIZESTER BOOKS

First published in 2019

Copyright © Suzanne Winterly 2019.

A CIP catalogue record for this title is available from the British Library.

ISBN 978-1-9993168-0-8

Cover Design: Books Covered Ltd.

Alizester Books
Monasterevin
Co. Kildare
Ireland

In memory of my grandparents, AMJ and NRJ,
who loved gardens and reading

Chapter 1

Gilly Townsend slammed the front door and her sister's collection of china birds shuddered on the polished chest in the hall. Vanessa, seated at the kitchen table, looked up as a second door crashed against the wall.

Vanessa still wore her office clothes, a pale blue suit and heels with a gold trim. She smiled at Gilly, her Parker pen poised over another wedding list.

"You're early," she said, pleasantly.

Gilly scowled as she marched towards the fridge. "Vanessa, just wait till you hear what my day's been like."

Her sister glanced at the metal clock on the wall and sighed. Gilly took a can of lager from the fridge and banged the door shut.

"Careful," warned Vanessa. "One of these days it'll come off its hinges."

Gilly snapped off the ring pull and took several long gulps. "That's better." She looked down at the sheets of paper on the round white table. "What's this? Another guest list? How many more people do you plan to invite?" She spotted the Valentine card on the counter by the electric cooker, a large cardboard teddy bear clutching a satin heart. "Hey, look at that! Ken must

1

have got another rise. Those cards are seriously expensive. If you ask me, it's a scandalous waste of money with all the people starving in the world."

Gilly felt calmer now that she'd vented her fury. Nothing like slamming a few doors to get it out of her system. She swallowed another gulp of beer. She knew her sister didn't take her seriously. She rarely did. No one in the entire world took her seriously. That was the problem.

Her sister's fiancé liked to spend money but he wasn't what her father called *flahoolagh*. Only yesterday, Gilly had rebuffed again his advice about getting a grip on her bookkeeping. Reconciling her bank statement was vital, as she couldn't run her business without it, he said, and he would be happy to give her a lesson. Another lesson. No thanks, Ken. Bookkeeping was boring and depressing. It wasn't fun being reminded about the deep hole into which she'd fallen.

A strong, sweet scent made Gilly glance around. The largest bunch of lilies she'd ever seen hid half of the window. Ken certainly doted on Vanessa.

Her sister frowned as she pushed the paper sheets and magazine into a neat pile. "There's no point talking to you when you're in one of your moods."

"I don't suppose there were any Valentine cards for me, were there?"

"Afraid not. Just a letter from the bank." Vanessa nodded towards the new bookshelves, a glass and aluminum construction, which had cost her at least two weeks' salary. A brown envelope lay on top.

Gilly snatched it up and ripped it open. She ran her eye down the contents before she dropped it into the pedal bin. "There's where that belongs."

Why did the bank always choose the worst time to remind her about her overdraft limit?

The frown on Vanessa's brow deepened. "Just look at you, Gilly, you're sopping wet. Take off your coat. It's dripping all over the floor. And your hair... at least you remembered to take your boots off this time."

Gilly looked down at her mud-splattered overalls. She'd left that woman's garden so fast that she hadn't had time to change. Vanessa had always been obsessively tidy ever since they were children. Where did she find the time to keep her house so spotless? Their mother had divided their shared bedroom in half when they were younger and Vanessa's side had been scrupulously neat with a well-hoovered, pink carpet while Gilly's lay scattered with crumpled clothes and abandoned toys.

She took off her wet jacket and flung it over the back of a chair, sat on another chair and stared. Vanessa had had her hair cut, the second time this month. So unfair that her sister was born with straight, shiny hair. Gilly ran a hand through her wet curls. She needed to do something about hers, but she couldn't afford it at the moment. The girls in boarding school had always tormented her about her unruly mop. Fuzzy Wuzzy, little Miss Frizzy, Curly Wurly. And those were the polite names. Most people didn't realize Vanessa and she were sisters when they first met them, their dark brown eyes inherited from Dad being the only similarity.

Should she tell Vanessa about Mrs Reilly? Her sister wasn't always interested in her design work and thought it a dirty, messy job that was unsuitable for a woman. Gilly knew where she'd got that from: their father. He'd never believed landscape design to be an appropriate profession for one of his daughters. Banking, of course, or stockbroking, would have been a different matter.

She watched Vanessa fiddle with the sheets of paper, line them up so that they stacked exactly square. Her lips twitched as she glanced at Gilly and looked back at the table.

Gilly burst out, "Do you know what that bloody woman said to me? Dolores Reilly, the penny-pinching old bat?"

"I hope you haven't had another row with her."

"I've walked out. Ness, I could not... no matter what I said, I could not convince her about that statue. She won't spend money on quality planting, won't pay me for the work I've done so far and yet she wants that. You should have seen the thing... like something from the Italian renaissance in a semi-detached in Sandymount."

Vanessa's frown resurfaced. "You walked out? That wasn't very sensible, was it?"

"And you know why my clothes are soaked? Those two sons of hers sprayed me with the hose. Actually thought it was funny too. I told their mother to keep them under control..."

"What about your overdraft?"

"Do you know what she said to me? She said she'd get a man to finish the garden. That I wasn't able to... well, I just lost my temper and I pointed out..."

Vanessa raised her hand, like someone directing traffic to come to a halt. "I don't want to hear. You'll never learn, will you? It's always the other person's fault. You're never going to get anywhere with that attitude."

"Oh give me a break, you don't know what it's like. You're all set up in that marketing job of yours – a nice, cosy little number, with your fiancé and two salaries. You don't know what it's like to have to struggle."

"You're jealous, I know, that's why you go on about Ken. At least he's not a two-timer."

A flush burnt Gilly's cheeks. She should never have told her about Ronan. Vanessa had guessed, of course. Nobody works every weekend, she'd said, he has to have another woman. It had been going on for two months, two whole months of lies and deception.

"Anyway, I've no time to hang around arguing." Vanessa

stood up. "I'm going to meet Daddy and Ken in the Shelbourne tonight for dinner. I was going to invite you but I don't suppose you're in the mood?"

"No." The last person Gilly wanted to see was her father.

He'd always preferred Vanessa. All her life, she'd lived in her elder sister's shadow. No matter how hard she tried to impress Dad, he never seemed to notice. She didn't care anymore and it only made it easier to avoid him.

Gilly shut her eyes. She already regretted the row with Mrs Reilly, although she wouldn't tell Vanessa that, because the woman had plenty of money to spend. If she'd been under less pressure from the bank, if she'd somewhere of her own to live, she might have felt less stressed and been able to cope with the hideous statue and those unruly boys. Now it was too late. She couldn't go back.

She glanced around Vanessa's white kitchen with its uncluttered counter tops. Her life was a mess. One huge, untidy mess. If it hadn't been for her sister, she wouldn't even have a roof over her head. It was Vanessa who had bailed her out and invited her to stay when her last landlord told her to leave because she couldn't afford the rent. The financial crisis was a disaster. Landscaping companies much bigger than hers were going out of business from lack of work. The construction industry had ground to a halt and this meant no new houses built. No new houses meant no new gardens. Unusual arctic weather had also struck Ireland in December and January, and left the ground frozen for weeks. Minus ten degrees recorded in Kilkenny. Sometimes it seemed like she was being hit by one plague after another and this run of bad luck might not end until her business was completely wiped out.

How many months had she been staying here? Must be at least three and now Vanessa and Ken were engaged and he spent more and more time at her house. There was no way the three of them could live together. She was like an awkward cuckoo in their spotless nest. But how could she move out when she'd no money and nowhere to go?

Vanessa combed her hair in front of the mirror over the bookcase. She pinned it back with a silver slide. "If you ask my opinion, Gilly, you would be better off making an effort to get along with the likes of Mrs Reilly than helping poor old Mary with her vegetable plot. I know she's a friend of Mum's and she's been lonely since her husband died, but... Mary hasn't a cent, we both know that and when I bumped into her the other day, do you know what she told me?"

"What?"

Vanessa sighed. "She told me that you had paid for her last delivery of logs. Five hundred euros worth. You actually paid in cash for her logs."

Gilly shrugged. "Yes, I did. So what?"

"I wish you'd let her son pay for that sort of thing. He has a good job, hasn't he?" Vanessa rolled her eyes and moved towards the door. "By the way," her sister stopped, as if she'd suddenly remembered, "there was a message for you on my landline. Someone looking for a garden designer. Sounds like it might be an interesting job."

Gilly met her eyes. "Oh yes? What is it?"

"An old walled garden that needs restoration. I wrote the number down and left it by the phone. It's down the country... County Kildare, I think. If you decide to look at it maybe Ken and I could drive you down."

"There's nothing wrong with my car."

"Well, no, but we would be interested to see the place. It's one of those country estates that have been modernized. An old rambling house bought by a property developer from the UK and done up for conferences, with apartments in the yard. You know the sort of thing. I read about this one in last Saturday's

Irish Times." She lingered by the door, waited for a reaction and added, "You'll need help with preliminary notes for the plan, won't you? Ken can hold the other end of the tape measure and I can jot down your ideas. Besides, I'd like to see Glanesfort, even if you decide the job is not your sort of thing."

Chapter 2

"I told you to write down the directions, Gilly," said Vanessa as Ken stopped the car at a third crossroads. "You're nearly half an hour late. What sort of impression will that make?"

Gilly placed her hands over her ears. "Vanessa! You were the one who read about this place in the paper. I thought Google Maps would get us here. How can there be no mobile signal only an hour from Dublin? And anyway, you read the newspaper article so can't you remember?"

She forced herself to concentrate. Of course, Vanessa would have written down the directions. She would never have relied on technology or lost her way; her ultra-organized sister would have been ten minutes early. If only she hadn't babbled all the way down about weddings. You would think nobody ever got married except them.

What had that guy said on the phone, the estate manager? She frowned. Left after the village, straight on past the pub?

Gilly leaned forward from the back seat and gave Ken more directions. He was enjoying himself and relished this chance to try out his new car, a smart red Audi paid for by the computer company. He drummed his fingers on the steering wheel, his floppy hair over his forehead, a boyish flush of excitement on his face. Voted Salesman of the Month for February by his company. The perfect match for her perfect sister.

A large entrance loomed up at the end of the road with stone pillars and a cattle grid.

Vanessa pointed at a sign on the left. "Look at that tasteful gold and green lettering. Glanesfort Luxury Homes. Pretty impressive."

Ornate iron gates stretched across the entrance, black, electronic and firmly closed.

Gilly looked at her sister. "What now? I suppose I ring that buzzer?"

Vanessa nodded. Gilly got out of the car and walked over to the intercom, while excuses whirled in her mind. A flat tyre? Terrible traffic? No, no, better to tell the truth and apologize for her lateness. She felt calmer when she saw the old chestnut trees that lined the gravel avenue, huge, sticky buds on the ends of their bare branches. The trees stretched across to touch each other like friendly arms and formed a natural arch.

"Hello?" She held her finger on the buzzer. "Anyone there?"

There was a silence and then a female voice, precise and very English. "Hello, yes, this is Glanesfort House."

"I'm the garden designer. Bit late, I'm sorry, I got lost."

"Your name, please?"

Gilly raised her eyebrows at Vanessa and Ken. "Gilly Townsend. I have an appointment with Fergus Browne."

"Thank you, I'll let him know that you're on the way."

"Probably the secretary." Gilly got back into the car. "Come on, Ken, get a move on."

Ken shot the Audi forwards, tyres churned the gravel, and he received an immediate reprimand from his fiancée.

The avenue stretched like a long tunnel beneath the trees and, after several minutes, it twisted to the left and the house stood before them, a solid grey rectangle of cut stone with a pillared portico balanced on either side by long Georgian windows; small panes that gleamed in the drizzle. Bare stems of a creeper dripped down the front of the house.

Vanessa peered into the vanity mirror and applied pink lipstick. She turned to Gilly. "Here, have some of this." She thrust it towards her.

Gilly waved it away. "Will you and Ken stay in the car... please? Look, I'm nervous enough without you two listening to what I say. Please, will you?"

"Oh, but we... all right, all right, but don't be too long. Keep what you say short and efficient. Don't waffle on about gardening and be sure to tell them you'll email an estimate."

Gilly ignored her and got out of the car. At the top of the stone steps, she took a deep breath as she pressed the bell. No need to be nervous, it was only another client, another interview. Nothing to be scared of.

The door opened more quickly than she'd expected and she saw a tall man with longish fair hair below his ears. When he smiled, she noticed his teeth, even and white. Early thirties, she guessed, about the same age as Ken and Vanessa.

He introduced himself. "Hi there, I'm Fergus. I work for Marc Fletcher, the owner of Glanesfort. Come in out of the rain for a minute while I look for an umbrella." He beckoned her into the hall.

She looked around. The room was wide and painted pale terracotta. An oval mahogany table in the middle displayed a tall flower arrangement in white and green; lime hydrangeas frothed among cream lilies. A collection of home and garden magazines lay beside the crystal vase. A formal room, but warm and welcoming.

Fergus strolled back across the wooden floorboards, a red and yellow golf umbrella in his hand.

Even the faces in the dark Victorian-style portraits staring from the walls seemed formal. A man at one end with a large nose and grey hair looked superciliously at her from a gilt frame. That was probably his wife opposite, stern and disapproving.

"Are they Mr Fletcher's ancestors?" She nodded at the paintings.

Fergus laughed. "You must be joking! They were left here by the guy who sold him the house. Marc decided to keep them... said they provided the right sort of ambience." He handed her the umbrella.

She admired his broad shoulders as she followed close behind him down a path along the side of the house. He wore faded jeans tucked into black wellingtons and a purple Aran sweater. He didn't care about the drizzle and showed no interest in the umbrella that she held over her head.

Laurels bordered the walk and, here and there, snowdrops peeped out of the dead leaves, their little heads bowed. At the end of the path, a wooden door was set in a high wall with a sign on it that read *Private*. A wave of anxiety struck her. What if the work was beyond her and she couldn't cope?

"I don't know what you'll think of this jungle." Fergus stepped aside for her to go in.

The door creaked open, red paint flaking, and as Gilly looked around, the drizzle eased and the lank grass glistened in a watery sunlight.

Limestone walls surrounded the garden, old stones that had stood for over two hundred years sheltering the two acres from the wind. On the left side, the branch of a hawthorn had punched through and a tangle of ivy and briars trailed across the jagged gap. The rest of the wall remained intact, testament to the skill of stonemasons in the eighteenth century.

"Wow! This is wonderful." She smiled at Fergus, who was busy lighting a cigarette. He held out the packet but she shook her head. She stepped across the sopping grass to a cluster of bare apple trees, their trunks gnarled and coated in moss. A beech hedge, russet in the sudden sunshine, ran the length of the garden and the path beside it lay choked with weeds. At least someone had looked after the clipped hedge. Along the left side, a stone shed stood in shadow, its broken windowpanes gaping. She noticed shattered glass and invasive sycamore saplings and recognized the battered remains of a greenhouse that slumped against the south-facing wall.

Gilly stood and inhaled air that was fresh with a hint of sweetness. So neglected but with so much potential.

Fergus yawned and shivered in the damp. "Well, like I said, it's a jungle."

"I love it. It's much bigger than I imagined."

A ginger cat appeared from under the beech hedge and picked its way through the long grass. It trotted towards Fergus, tail upright like a mast, and rubbed against his legs. He bent down and it scrambled onto his shoulder.

"He knows you well," she said.

"He's Anna's cat. Anna's one of Marc's tenants... in the cottage behind the yard.' He switched back to the garden. 'This overgrown mess hasn't been touched for years. I'll need some sort of plan with an estimate of how much it will all cost to show Marc."

It would cost a lot to restore this to some kind of order and she would definitely need help. If she tried to do all the work on her own, it might be a disaster. She needed to sound confident and efficient. "Of course. That's no problem. Do you have a budget in mind?"

"He said to send in your ideas first and then he'll think about it." Fergus led her along what was left of the brick-edged paths. "He's not one to rush into things, not impulsive, I mean." He explained about Marc Fletcher's property business and told her about the tenants on the estate, how his boss felt they needed somewhere to relax. He'd concentrated on renovating the house and apartments in the yard first but now wanted to improve the garden.

"This would once have been a kitchen garden for the house with vegetables and fruit. Would Mr Fletcher prefer something like a public park? I could divide it up into different sections," Gilly asked and he nodded.

How long would a job like this take? Impossible to say yet as she didn't know what she had to do, but a long time. Months. Four months possibly. Still, a regular income for four months would keep the bank off her back for the time being and she could begin looking around for a small apartment to rent.

Fergus grinned at her, a slow, smile that stretched across his wide mouth. His nose was a little too big but he'd a gorgeous voice, a lazy drawl. Like Ronan's in a way.

She asked, "Is there anyone who could help me with the heavy work? I'll never be able to get through it on my own." If she got this job, she would have to be careful. Fergus might be too like Ronan.

He threw the cigarette on the ground and trod on it, his other hand still stroking the purring cat. "The grounds here are looked after by a man from the local town. He's a serious sort of guy and I don't think he would be keen on extra work. He does the mowing and pruning. Don't worry, I'll sort something out. Why don't you send in your estimate and design plan and I'll find out if there's anyone local available to help?"

"I'll need someone with experience for this job." She glanced back at the garden as they moved towards the white door. So sad that it had been abandoned, as if nobody wanted it. An unloved garden. "Didn't the last owner care about this?"

"Nah. You should have seen the house when we first came here. Seriously run-down. Poor man tried to keep it going but the banking crash sent him over the edge. Debt up to his ears."

"How long has Mr Fletcher owned the place?"

"Two years." Fergus pulled out his cigarette packet and helped himself to another. "Don't you smoke?"

"Not for six months. It took me ages to give up so don't tempt me."

His wide smile reappeared. "I won't."

"How many tenants in the yard? The garden is for them, you said?"

"It's for all of us, I suppose, but yeah, I guess Marc is mainly thinking about them. There are five apartments." He inhaled and blew out rings of smoke, a well-practised skill. "And there are also the guests, the people who come to the weddings held here... and also the business conferences. It's all rented out, you see, every last bit of it."

"OK. Any tips on what Mr Fletcher would pay for the restoration of this garden?" She needed some idea of where to start. A blank canvas was good, but she didn't want to price herself out of the job. No doubt there would be other applicants for this contract.

"I can't give you a figure, but don't expect Marc to cough up too much. He may be rich, but he's very careful with his money, if you get my drift. Never happy to spend it."

"OK, I'll be reasonable, don't worry. What's he like?"

"He's a nice man but hard to get to know. Made a wad of cash and he's only thirty-six and we all admire a man like that, don't we?"

Gilly nodded and resisted the temptation to linger. "I'll need to take some measurements and make a few notes, but don't let me keep you waiting out here. My sister and her fiancé will help me."

Did Fergus have a girlfriend? She couldn't imagine him married, but you never knew with men like him.

They walked back along the outside wall where laurels

dripped onto fallen beech leaves blown from a clump of trees on the left. More snowdrops spread in a strip along the edge of the small copse. She couldn't wait to tell Vanessa about the walled garden.

Fergus stopped near the portico. "Would you like to come in for coffee? You can bring your friends. Alice bakes amazing scones and her jam is always home-made."

Gilly hesitated and glanced towards the Audi. Vanessa and Ken were watching and probably dying to get out and ask questions. "No thanks," she said. "We'd better get the measurements done. I can email the plan and the estimate to you if you need to send them on to Mr Fletcher."

"OK," said Fergus. "You'll meet Alice the next time you come."

The next time. That sounded hopeful. How much influence did this man have with his cautious employer?

"I'll give Marc a glowing report about you," Fergus added with a laugh.

"How did he hear about me?"

"I heard about you. I mentioned you to him when he asked me for ideas about the garden. I met a man called Delaney... you did some work for him, he said."

Delaney. Theodore Ignatius Delaney, an Irish-American who owned a chain of pubs in Dublin. A client who had been easy to get on with, mainly because he lived in Chicago. She nodded.

"Yeah," said Fergus, "Mr Delaney recommended you when he was here for a business conference and said you did a fine job."

She smiled. "That's good. I like to hear that." She noticed a stocky fair-haired man who stood to the left of the door as he stared at her without embarrassment.

Fergus followed her gaze. "That's Stefans. He looks a bit

scary but he's harmless." He reached out and shook her hand. "Good to meet you, Gilly. See you again soon, I hope."

"I hope so, too, and thanks for suggesting me to your boss." The stocky man still watched her and a prickle of unease ran through her. He had very short hair and vivid blue eyes. "What does Stefans do?"

"He's in charge of security," Fergus said over his shoulder as he moved towards the steps up to the door.

Chapter 3

The inhabitants of London had woken up to a frost earlier but now, as Marc Fletcher walked along Pumping Station Road, a brilliant sun glinted on the cars that stretched round the corner, like segments of a long metal snake. Gusts of wind blustered through the naked plane trees and hurtled litter in the paths of pedestrians.

He stopped to shake off a plastic bag that had wrapped itself round his trouser leg. He watched it as it flapped like a demented bird towards the cars and clutch at the windscreen of a Ford Fiesta. Only a ten-minute walk so no need for a taxi. A fast stroll was better for his health; he spent too much time sitting indoors.

He liked the wind. It blew away the cobwebs, made him feel alive.

Nearly twelve o'clock when he glanced at his watch. A little early, but Joe Milligan would probably be late. His timekeeping wasn't the best, but he had good manners and was reassuringly courteous.

He soon reached Chiswick Wharf. Joe was the first private investigator he'd ever met and more eccentric than he'd ever imagined.

He hummed as he walked towards the river, a French song

that his mother had sung to him as a child. She used to sing all the time in those days. He couldn't remember if she hummed now in her apartment in Paris. François wasn't musical, but he would only have encouraged her. François worshipped the ground that Maman walked on. At least she'd got it right with her second choice of husband.

The wind whisked the surface of the Thames to white foam and he stopped to admire it. Every time he came this way, it was different. A different picture. Some days it flowed calm and indolent, other days fast and angry. Today the river slapped against the bank in a petulant mood. A row of seagulls clung to the bow of an open-topped barge, dipping and rising in the waves.

His mobile rang and he answered it. "Marc Fletcher." It was Fergus calling to report on his meeting the day before with the garden designer. "Yes, I can hear you perfectly. How did your meeting go?"

"Very well," said Fergus. "She seems competent."

"Did you ask for references?"

"I've got a recommendation from Mr Delaney, the Irish-American."

"Ask her for another reference. How long before we hear from her?"

"I gave her a week to email a plan and an estimate. It's a big project, Marc." Fergus sounded defensive.

"That's all right. Let me know when you receive her email, please. How's everything at Glanesfort? Did the O'Tooles move out of Number Six?"

Fergus hesitated. "Yeah, all done. There are a few repairs to do before the next lot..."

"What sort of repairs?"

"I didn't realize, sorry, Marc. Just small things. A bit of wiring and... well, yeah, the upstairs toilet is broken."

It was ten past twelve. Milligan might be at the pub by now.

"Just get it sorted out immediately, Fergus. I have to go. I'm meeting someone." He said goodbye and disconnected.

He swung his arms as he walked along Chiswick Mall, past the tall, expensive houses on his left that stared impassively across the river. He spotted a figure in the distance, heading away from him. That would be the private investigator. Nobody in his office knew about his meetings with Joe Milligan and he intended to keep it that way for the time being.

He soon caught up with Joe, who was slightly lame after a hip replacement but still tall and upright in spite of being in his early seventies. The older man beamed at him and clamped his hand onto Marc's shoulder as if delighted to see him.

"Hello, my friend, how are you?" His voice was soft with a slight Scottish accent. "It's a beautiful day, thank God." He put his hand inside his mac and felt for the envelope in his pocket. "I'll give you this now, before we go into the pub. Prying eyes and all that, you know." He pulled out a brown envelope and handed it to Marc. "Yes, it's an excellent day, Mr Fletcher. I think we should have a drink before lunch and I'll give you a quick update."

Chapter 4

“Just look at this traffic jam.” Sally turned in the passenger seat to face him. “We're going to be really late. Shall I give the estate agent a call?”

Marc put on the handbrake. “Yes, please call him. There are roadworks round this bend, roadworks everywhere in London these days.”

He'd seen a short write-up about the Victorian terrace house in a newspaper and a photograph of the red brick front with large sash windows. So similar to a house he'd lived in as a child. The property seemed good value at first glance, if the roof was sound.

His personal assistant shook her straight blonde hair back over her shoulders as she lifted the mobile phone to her ear. “Hello. Oh, good, I'm so glad to have reached you. I'm ringing for Mr Fletcher.” She flashed Marc one of her bright smiles. “He's been delayed in traffic, I'm afraid. He'll be another fifteen minutes, I think. Good, yes, I'll tell him. Thank you.” She pressed a button and tossed the phone into her briefcase. “There you are, all done. He says he'll wait.”

Marc smiled at her efficiency.

“Shall I go through today's post and emails?” She reached

for a file on the floor beside her feet. "It'll pass the time in this wretched traffic."

"Go ahead." He listened as she read a couple of letters, but then his concentration flitted away.

A woman stood at a bus stop, her long dark hair blown across her face. She leaned forward and tried to light a cigarette. Something familiar about her slim figure, the way she held herself, even the long cream raincoat. His pulse quickened. Was it her? He glanced around him. Should he park the car, run over to her and...? What would he say? But no, when she stood upright and inhaled deeply any similarity vanished.

Sally tapped his sleeve. "Marc, are you listening?"

"Sorry, what did you say?"

She frowned. "How much have you missed? Look, here's an email from Fergus. He's such a charmer."

"Do you think so?" What was it about Fergus that appealed to women?

"I'd like to meet him and see Glanesfort. I've heard so much about it. What made you buy a place in Ireland?"

"It seemed a good idea to buy a property at that time." He added quickly, "The housing boom over, mortgages difficult for many people to get and places were cheaper..."

Where nobody would know him. Where he would get some peace, but he'd soon discovered that he couldn't purchase peace of mind like a commodity.

The traffic edged forward and stopped again.

She glanced at the letter. "Fergus encloses an estimate for the restoration of the walled garden. He says the garden designer is drawing up a more detailed plan."

"Good, I've been waiting for that. Would you read me the estimate, please?" He drummed his fingers on the steering wheel while she called out the details and figures. "That doesn't sound too ruinous," he said, when Sally finished.

"Shall I tell Fergus to go ahead?"

"Please do. I hope the landscaper can start straight away as it would be good to get the garden finished by the summer."

"Fergus is very amusing on the phone. He sounds so cheerful, even on Monday mornings."

"He's always cheerful when he's talking to good-looking women."

"Oh – do you think he's a womaniser? I would still like to meet him. Does he ever come to London?"

"Not often since he moved to Glanesfort. His parents live near there and his father is elderly. That's why he wanted the job."

He inched the BMW forwards and Sally fell silent. His mind tracked back to the previous Thursday and his meeting with Joe Milligan. The pub had been crowded as usual. The wind drove people indoors after their morning strolls along the river, but Joe found a quieter table near the kitchen. Marc ordered beer and they went through the private investigator's report. Joe had interviewed an old man who used to live a few doors down from Jane in Putney and he said she'd moved to Yorkshire. Or Lancashire perhaps. Unfortunately the old man was a bit forgetful and he hadn't know her very well. Kept herself to herself and rarely had visitors. Joe was making plans to visit Leeds the following week to check this out and he had a few contacts to whom he would show her photograph. Leeds was a big place, he pointed out, a university city and likely to attract young people who might wish to disappear there.

Sally interrupted his thoughts. "There's also an email from Mr Fukuda's office in Tokyo. You and Michael got on well with the Japanese Corporation's European team, didn't you? It looks like they are still interested in your office building."

"Yes, we did. We met the European Finance Director as well when they came over with the HR team and the architects to have a look at the building. I haven't met Mr Fukuda but he's on the corporation's board of directors. What does he say?"

"Apparently the European team have handed everything over to their head office in Tokyo and they've drafted up a shortlist of ten buildings and yours is one of them. They're going to send a global team from Japan to vet the ten."

Marc digested this. "I think that all sounds positive, but unfortunately Japanese corporations are notoriously slow about making decisions."

"Is it a big corporation?"

"Yes. They recently acquired a faded British brand with a plant and offices in East London. Now they've decided to consolidate their UK and European headquarters in a more prestigious location." He looked at Sally. "Luckily for us, our offices are in Central London." If he and Michael could make a deal with the Japanese, it would be a weight off his mind, free up badly needed cash to invest in other projects. "I can thank Michael for this. Did he tell you he lived in Tokyo before I hired him as our accountant? He has a lot of experience working with the Japanese."

"Yes, he sounds like he loved Asia."

At least the Japanese were interested, but what had happened to the Irish company who'd made an offer for his Dublin apartments? No word from them recently. Better give the chief executive a call later today.

"How is your son?" Sally asked. "I haven't seen him for ages. He must miss you."

"He's fine, thanks. He always says he misses me, but he's got Alice, who dotes on him."

"She's much older, though, isn't she?"

"She must be mid to late fifties – I've never asked." It was a pity Samuel's real grandmother lived in another country. Still, he was a bit young for Maman who'd never had much patience with small children. Give him another fourteen years and she'd be taking him out for cocktails in Paris.

"Poor little boy," said Sally. "It's not easy for him without a mother."

Marc didn't reply.

"Nannies just aren't the same," she murmured, with an unusual lack of tact that made Marc glance quickly at her.

She was right, of course, none of the nannies could ever replace Samuel's mother. There'd been three of them in the four years of his son's life: the most recent was Alice. The first one was Claudia, a tall, strong-willed German, who had walked out when he criticised her routine for being a bit strict. Then there was Jane. His hands gripped the steering wheel. He would like to meet her again; he would have plenty to say to her. Joe Milligan had informed him that he was making progress. It was a slow process, he'd warned Marc right from the beginning. People can vanish without a trace in a country of over sixty million inhabitants, especially if they don't want to be found. There were so many to talk to, so many leads to follow. Joe didn't want to admit defeat, though, and Marc had a very good reason not to give up.

Joe had proved remarkably adept on the internet for a man of his age. He'd discovered that Jane was no longer using the bank account into which Marc had paid her salary, but he'd tracked down another one and that had led him to the man in Putney.

Marc liked Joe. He liked his honest blue eyes and the fact that he seemed to care about him. Once, when he'd arranged to meet him in the local pub, Joe had bought him a pint. "Here, have one on me," he'd said, softly. "You look like you need it, my friend."

*

The estate agent was in his early twenties with a complexion that betrayed an acute teenage problem with acne. He yawned frequently as he showed Marc and Sally around the Victorian three-storey house, leading them from one flat to the next, each room more dark and dingy than the last.

Marc followed behind, reading the estate agent's literature, while their guide kept his eyes on Sally and trotted obediently beside her to open doors. While they looked around, he gazed mournfully at her and chewed his nails.

"It's in a good area," he mumbled. "An area that is becoming more sought after nowadays."

The owner, an elderly man, had died six months before and his family put his house on the market. A pity all of them owned it, because it was more straightforward to deal with an individual rather than a group.

The walls glowed with orange-flowered wallpaper, fighting with the swirled pattern on dirty nylon carpets. Windows shut tight for months on end had encouraged damp and several of the rooms smelled strongly of mouse.

"Who in his right mind would have rented a flat in this dump?" Sally muttered and the estate agent, lurking at her elbow, looked nervously at the floor.

Bundles of yellowing newspapers, chewed to confetti at the corners, gave further evidence of four-legged intruders. Naked light bulbs dangled from ceilings, coated in dust.

"It has potential," Marc replied. "A dangerous word, I suppose, because it usually means I need to spend a fortune."

When their tour of the house finished, they inspected the garden, a mass of long grass with a solitary apple tree in the bottom right-hand corner.

"I like this big space," said Sally, "but it might look better if you have it landscaped."

The estate agent fidgeted with his cardboard folder and

looked at his watch. "You can ring my boss if you're interested," he said, as he locked the front door. "Don't delay because there are at least five other buyers keen on this property." He shifted from one foot to the other. Lying obviously didn't come easily to him.

When he'd driven off, Marc stood back and looked up at the house. He imagined what it had looked like before the conversion to flats. It would make a fine private dwelling, but that might not be as profitable, so perhaps it would be better to keep it in flats. A complete overhaul inside and hopefully tenants would queue up for it.

"I like it," he said aloud and turned to smile at Sally. "Right, I'll treat you to lunch. It's early enough to find somewhere peaceful."

He took her to a wine bar that looked out over the Thames, tables and chairs close together in a glass conservatory, with white walls and framed posters splashed with bold, primary colours.

Marc asked Sally to choose their table and she sat on a leather sofa in the corner, beside a vast rubber plant in a ceramic pot.

He sat down on a leather chair opposite her. He must have been six or seven when he'd lived in that house similar to the one he'd just visited. The family hadn't stayed there for long, but the garden at the back felt familiar, especially the swing attached by ropes to the branch of an apple tree. It brought it all back, suddenly triggered off a memory buried for years. Lying on the lawn, the smell of freshly mown grass, as his mother handed him a sandwich. She'd loved picnics on sunny days. Both of them laughing, happy.

The waiter took his order and asked what Sally wanted to drink.

"Tomato juice," she replied.

Marc ordered a glass of sparkling water to go with his steak.

"I won't have time for dinner tonight, that's why I'm having two courses now."

Sally asked for a smoked chicken salad. "I have been invited out tonight by a friend of my flatmate. She's the one who thinks you're good-looking. She likes your French shrug."

"My French shrug?"

"Yes, you know the way you lift your arms when you question something."

He laughed.

"Are you working late again tonight?" she asked.

"I have to get through a lot of paperwork before I go to Glanesfort at the end of next week."

The waiter reappeared with their food and handed a bowl of mussels to Marc, garlic-scented steam rising from the blue-black shells.

"Does Samuel go to school yet?" Sally asked.

"He's four now and will go to school next September. At the moment, he's in playschool three mornings a week so that gives Alice a bit of a break."

Samuel, Alice, Fergus, the other people who lived at Glanesfort. They seemed another world away when he worked in London.

"I spend too much time away from him, but it's difficult to run a business in London when my home is in Ireland," he said.

Or perhaps Glanesfort wasn't his home. Maybe he felt more at ease in the apartment near Chiswick Mall. He missed his son and often ringing him every evening to say goodnight wasn't enough. He would like to have him with him in London, but Alice had been against it and he agreed with her. It was better that she didn't know why he agreed with her as he didn't want to frighten her. Samuel was safer in Ireland where Stefans could keep an eye on him.

The waiter placed his steak in front of him. Yes, that shabby house brought it all back. Memories opened up like cardboard boxes packed away in an attic. Maman was the one who liked moving. She'd do up one house, get bored and want to start again. His father followed her, his mind preoccupied with work, while Marc trotted after them, cared for by a succession of French au pairs.

"I got a letter from my mother last week." He took a sip of water.

"That's nice. You don't often hear from her, do you?"

"It's almost two months since the last one. I phone her, of course, but she prefers to write letters. Her handwriting is worse than ever and she writes mostly in French so it takes me a while to decipher." She'd abandoned her English at the same time as she'd abandoned London.

"How's your French?"

"OK. I suppose when you learn it as a child, you find it easier to remember."

His mother had scrawled the letter with enthusiasm. She'd been away, somewhere exotic – he forgot where – and had met old friends. How fortunate that her husband was on the board of a bank because she could never have adapted to a life without money.

"How long has she lived in Paris?" Sally tucked into her chicken salad. She'd never met his mother.

"About sixteen years," he replied.

She'd been married to François for fifteen. It hadn't taken her long to forget the horror. No, that was unfair, how could she ever forget? She'd just moved on; closed the door on that episode. His father's death and... Marc quickly switched his attention to the steak.

"This is good," he said. "What's yours like?"

"About as exciting as a salad can ever be." She glanced at his plate. "Yours looks excellent."

28

"Jealous, are you?" He felt at ease with her because he knew her so well.

He remembered how he and his mother had grown closer after his father died. A death like that would either throw families together or apart.

Marc dragged his wandering mind back to the present. "I'm looking forward to seeing Samuel."

"You must miss him dreadfully. What's Ireland like in the aftermath of the property crash?"

He sank his knife into the steak and watched the blood ooze across the white plate. "Ireland has quiet countryside and talkative people. I feel sorry for the older ones – the ones who won't find it easy to get another job." He frowned. "And the younger ones who were encouraged to take out mortgages they couldn't afford."

Sally pierced a baby tomato with her fork.

Was he neglecting his son? Would he grow up... what was the word? Delinquent. So far, Samuel was doing all right. A cheerful little lad with a wild sense of fun. He looked forward to seeing him the next week.

They ate the rest of their lunch in silence. Then Sally sprang to her feet, called for the bill, talked about what she had to do in the afternoon. Marc paid with his credit card and followed her to the car park, Glanesfort back in his thoughts. Fergus had sounded enthusiastic about the designer. Restoring the walled garden would add value to the property and please the tenants. It would also be a place for Samuel to play and might keep him away from the lake.

Chapter 5

There was nothing as off-putting as a blank sheet of paper. Gilly chewed the pencil end in her mouth. It would have been easier if Fergus had shown some interest, but all he'd wanted to do was head back to the house as quickly as possible. Hard to forget about Fergus, the amusement that sparkled in his hazel eyes and his wide grin. Would the owner, Marc Fletcher, know more about gardening? It was often easier when clients knew nothing. The ones who had a slight knowledge were usually the most difficult. Always looking up plants on the internet and suggesting unsuitable species that would die off in Ireland's damp climate.

Gilly leaned back on the kitchen chair and yawned. The clock ticked in the silence. Nearly one, time for lunch because hunger pangs made it hard to think creatively. She'd got out of bed at seven when Vanessa went off to work and still hadn't had any breakfast.

She glanced again at the list in front of her and decided to make some sort of start before she allowed herself to switch on the kettle. Her gaze ran down the standard list of garden features that she usually mentioned to clients: water, lighting, hard landscaping, patio areas, shrub borders, semi-mature trees. The words danced in front of her eyes and any ideas for her first detailed plan remained stubbornly elusive.

She groaned and tossed the pencil onto the table. Still in pyjamas and a faded towelling bathrobe belonging to her mother, wool socks protected her feet from the chill of the black and white tiled floor.

Gilly remembered the call from her bank account manager. He'd seemed relieved when she'd told him that she might soon have a big contract and asked her to ring him at the end of the week to discuss progress. She desperately needed this project; it was a chance to get her life back on track, to create order out of chaos. She looked again at the sheets of paper on the table and picked up the pencil. She wrote: keep apple trees and beech hedge.

At least the hedge lent some sort of maturity to the garden. Who had looked after it and kept it pruned to shape? Perhaps the local man Fergus had mentioned. She hoped he would find a capable assistant to help her because it would be a relief not to have to tackle the garden on her own.

Gilly sketched in the existing features, the walls, the shed, the dilapidated greenhouse. Should she keep the greenhouse? Try to restore it? It would be expensive to repair, but would make an attractive feature with its ornate woodwork.

The dinner in the Shelbourne had gone well. Vanessa believed that Dad thought Ken was a young man after his own heart, halfway up the career ladder at the age of thirty-two.

Gilly wondered what her mother thought. She wouldn't say anything to contradict Dad, of course, because she never did. Even when Gilly had furious rows with him, Mum never intervened. She just took herself off to the greenhouse to potter with geraniums and begonias because watering, dead-heading and pinching out growing tips of unruly plants was her only way of restoring order. Gilly could thank Mum for her love of gardening. She'd always encouraged her in her own quiet way and made her feel that her diploma in horticulture was a good idea.

Her eyes came back to the sketch. What did people who lived in rented accommodation need? They might like plenty of benches; a pool surrounded by gravel where they could listen to the relaxing trickle of water. Perhaps a pool with water lilies in the middle of a summer garden? She wrote two lines of notes. A perennial garden for the summer months would be lovely – full of soft, reassuring colours – blues, pinks, purples and white. There would have to be roses, of course. Beautiful, blowsy old shrub roses would require little pruning and would fill the air with their perfume. She might try growing the rambler 'Paul's Himalayan Musk' up one of the old trees along the south-facing wall, where its small clusters of old-fashioned pale pink flowers could scramble unchecked. Private sections in a public garden would be interesting, different areas to walk to, which she could divide with hedges of yew, box and beech. Perhaps she should cut an arch in the existing beech hedge to link with a formal layout of paths. After all, a historic kitchen garden would have been set out in straight lines. She could soften them with the planting.

The door opened and Vanessa's small, neat figure appeared, wearing a cream wool suit. She dropped her gloves and her leather briefcase on a chair and smiled at Gilly.

"Want a coffee?" Vanessa flicked the switch on the kettle. "I've taken the afternoon off to search for the ultimate wedding outfit. I've decided I'd like a suit. I refuse to have one of those flouncy dresses." She walked over. "What are you doing? Oh, the garden plan. Is it going well?"

"Not too bad."

She moved away, opened the bread bin, took out a wholemeal loaf and began to assemble her lunch: bean salad prepared earlier, a slice of goat's cheese, a few lettuce leaves and a quick drizzle of olive oil.

"Have you had lunch yet?" she asked.

"No," said Gilly. "But don't worry about me. I'll just have a coffee for the time being. I'll have a few cream crackers with cheese in a while."

Vanessa waited for the water to boil and spooned coffee into the percolator. She sat down beside Gilly.

"I've decided that my life is like this garden," Gilly said. "A mess."

Vanessa stared at her as she chewed thoughtfully. "Mmn, well, I suppose it'll sort itself out."

"Ness..." She'd avoided asking this question, but it was time to face up to it.

"Yes?" Her sister looked up.

"What about when you get married?"

"What about it?"

"I mean you and Ken... when you get married," Gilly continued awkwardly. "You won't exactly want me hanging around, will you?"

Vanessa sliced her sandwich and said nothing.

Gilly waited. She would have to move out because she couldn't live with Mr and Mrs Right. It wasn't fair on them. "Mum keeps asking me what I'm going to do and Dad wants me to move back home. I don't think I can bear the thought of living under the same roof as him. He's..."

"Don't worry, we won't want you to go straight away," said her sister carefully.

It was her use of the word *we* that made up her mind. "It's OK, I'm not offended." Her words rushed out. "You've been good to me and gave me a bed when I'd nowhere to go. I'll start to look for somewhere else next week."

"Don't worry, there's no hurry." Her sister nodded at the

sketch. "This is the bit I think must be the most fun. Can I help you?"

"OK, thank you." After all, she needed all the help she could get and Vanessa was an expert at creating order out of chaos.

Chapter 6

The elation Gilly felt after Fergus phoned to tell her that she'd got the job faded when she met her assistant, Dean. He stood beside Fergus in the walled garden, barely up to his shoulder, and scowled at the ground when introduced. He had a pale, unshaven face with brown eyes set close together.

She attempted a smile. "Know anything about gardening, Dean?"

Dean said nothing.

Fergus laughed. "Of course he does. You don't think I'd land you with a complete beginner, do you? He's well used to digging and planting, aren't you, Dean?"

There was still no reply so Fergus repeated, "Aren't you, Dean?"

Dean shrugged and muttered, "I've done some digging all right."

"He had a part-time job in the summer with the council." Fergus shot a quick, sharp look at the young man.

Dean looked no more than a boy, although Fergus had said he was twenty-two, with his short back and sides and a gold ring in one ear. The hair left on the top of his head was bleached blond.

"Were you with the parks department?" Gilly asked. Not

what she needed. An assistant as unenthusiastic as him on her first day.

"That's the place," said Fergus. "They were very impressed with him. Now he's here on a work experience programme. I'll leave you both to it and I'll be back later to see how you're getting on."

Gilly watched Fergus stride away before she turned to Dean. "Right." She tried to sound positive. "I'd like you to help me mark out some of the sections. We'll start with the water garden." She picked up bamboo canes and string and pointed at the dilapidated garden shed. "Over there. I'll use a hose to mark where the pool is going."

Dean slouched after her, the collar of his black leather jacket raised against the wind. His wellingtons were new with the price still marked on a white sticker on the side.

If he'd done some digging before, at least he could help with the heavy work, which would allow her more time to sort out the framework of the design.

She made a circle with the hose in the long grass. "The pond," she told Dean, who watched gloomily. She handed him the bamboos and string. "I'll pace out the distance while you push these into the ground."

She would plant the yew hedge in a square around the section, with gravel paths through three gaps, which would eventually become arches onto the main paths that intersected the garden. The fourth path wouldn't lead anywhere but she might use a seat as a focal point, something to catch the eye – a strong design in wood or iron where people could sit.

Gilly looked around at the damp, lank grass and frowned. A lot of work to get through if it was to be finished by July.

At least the bank had extended her overdraft limit and stopped bouncing payments. That was all that mattered for the time being. Besides, she couldn't suppress this feeling of excitement. Just when she'd started to despair, she'd been handed this lifeline and a chance to show people what she could do.

Her sister had lent her a smartphone as Vanessa had received a new company mobile with her recent promotion. She'd also paid Gilly's car tax so she would make an effort to be nicer to Ness – and poor Ken. She must stop giving him a hard time.

Dean pushed the first bamboo cane into the grass and tied on the string while Gilly paced the distance in front of him.

Gilly adjusted one of Dean's bamboos. "Not there, that's crooked. Look down the line, please, because that helps to keep them straight." She would have to find somewhere else to live. Dublin had suited her until now, but this job would mean a lot of driving, at least two hours a day behind the wheel. Could she afford to rent somewhere nearby? She would have to talk to Fergus about some cash on account. Anyway, she would need some to buy plants soon – the box and yew hedging, and the fruit trees planned for the east wall.

Once the bamboos were in place, she sent Dean off with the strimmer to cut the grass. They would let it grow again and then spray it. A knapsack sprayer was heavy so Dean could handle that.

He hadn't said more than a couple of words and she gave up trying to make conversation. Let him be silent then, she didn't care as long as he did what she asked him to do. She watched him as he cut away the grass, a cigarette dangling from the side of his mouth, his eyes squinting to avoid the smoke. Not a big man, but at least he was stocky and had done some digging.

Here was her chance to prove she could succeed, to make her own mark on an unloved landscape. If she closed her eyes, she could imagine the sweet scent of shrub roses and feel the warmth of sunshine on her back. She would reach out and grasp this opportunity.

When she next looked for Dean, he was leaning against a tree, the strimmer abandoned beside him. She glanced at the mobile Vanessa had given her. Eleven o'clock already. She shouted and beckoned. "Over here. Tea break!"

They ate their sandwiches in the potting shed, a sheet of cardboard jammed across the broken windowpane to keep out the draught, while they sat on upturned wooden crates that had held the terracotta pots stacked behind the door. Bare earth beneath their feet and no light from the dusty bulb, which dangled among the cobwebs.

Dean finished his cheese sandwiches and opened a bag of crisps. He glanced at Gilly and held out the packet. "Want some?"

This, at least, was some sort of gesture. Gilly took a few and thanked him. "Well, how do you like this place so far?"

He shrugged, a quick lift of his solid shoulders. "Dunno yet."

"I know it looks a mess at the moment, but it'll improve. It's just that it's been neglected for so long."

"Nan never told me it was gardening." He'd a quiet voice with a Dublin accent.

"You mean your grandmother found this job for you? Fergus said you came through the local community employment office, or whatever it's called. I thought you'd at least know what the job was."

"Is this an interview or what?" Dean scowled.

"This is supposed to be part of your training." A suspicion took shape in her mind. "It's called work experience. You're paid to do this by the employment scheme people, not Mr Fletcher. Isn't that how it works?"

He stared at her, a quick dart from his narrow eyes. "Yeah? I dunno who pays me... don't care, either, long as someone does." He smiled suddenly and she noticed a chipped front tooth.

"Where did you get the name Dean, anyway?"

"Nan always fancied that actor, James Dean, that guy who died in a car crash."

Gilly recalled the famous poster of James Dean in Rebel Without a Cause. Young, tragic and good-looking. She stared at her assistant. Either his granny had a sense of humour or she indulged in fantasy.

"So, did you or did you not work for the parks department?"

Dean shrugged. "Think it was road maintenance... I was... like, filling in potholes."

A lively rap on the door made them both jump.

Fergus pushed it open. "This looks nice and cosy. How's the work going?"

Gilly stood up. "We'd better get back to it, I suppose." She frowned at Fergus. "Can I have a word, please?"

He followed her out into the drizzle and glanced down at her. "Everything OK?"

Dean still sat on the wooden crate, finishing a cigarette, and Gilly moved further away.

"Where did you get him from?" She spoke in a low voice. "I don't think he knows anything about gardening – and he doesn't seem to know about the work experience you mentioned."

"Yeah? Well, he's a bit dopey, I guess. It's Monday morning, after all." He put his arm round her shoulders and gave her a comforting squeeze, then pushed his hands into the pockets of his jeans. "I've got a lot to do so I'd better go, just make sure the place looks like it's under control by Friday. That's when Marc gets back and you can be sure that he'll want to know he's getting value for money."

"I'll need some money soon to buy hedging plants."

Fergus yawned. "Sorry, I'd a late night. I'll talk to Marc about money. You'll have to visit our local pub now that you're here. There's singing most nights." He raised his eyebrows. "Want a drink with me tonight?"

She hesitated. "I'd like that, but not this evening."

He accepted her answer with nonchalance and strolled away. It was difficult to be serious with him for long. He could twist the conversation to suit himself before she realised. He didn't really listen either, just smiled while his eyes wandered.

A small figure stood by the wooden door, a dark-haired boy. He carried a short stick in one hand, which he raised and pretended to fire at her. "Got you, space alien! You're dead!" he shouted and made explosive noises.

"Hi there," said Gilly.

The boy wore a red raincoat with a hood over curls and looked young. Gilly didn't know much about children, but she guessed he was about three or four years old. He lowered the stick and took a step back as his confidence ebbed away.

She waved, but he dodged out of sight. Who was that? She hadn't been told about a child. Hopefully he would be better behaved than Mrs Reilly's two sons.

Chapter 7

Rain swept across the garden on a violent gust of wind, hard and stinging. Gilly gasped and pushed herself back into the beech hedge for shelter, a pruning saw in her hand. She pulled her waxed jacket round her and gritted her teeth as Dean dropped his spade, abandoned the shallow trench he'd been digging and sprinted for the shelter of the potting shed.

It was nearly three o'clock and she knew there would be no sign of him until after his tea break. The squalls didn't last long, but they soaked the soil and turned the trenches into sticky swamps. Wednesday, her third day, and they'd only just started to dig out where the hedging would go. Fergus would be along any minute and wouldn't be impressed by their slow progress.

Her hair dripped down her face as she walked after Dean. She'd almost reached the shed when a wrought-iron gate in the west wall opened and a woman appeared, clinging to a black umbrella that was doing its best to turn inside out in the wind.

"Hello, we haven't met yet. I'm Alice Rogers. This weather... awful, isn't it? I felt sorry for you and wondered if you'd like to come in for a cup of tea?" She blinked behind round glasses. She wore a dark brown raincoat and wellingtons, with a waterproof Barbour hat pulled down over grey shoulder-length hair.

"Oh, thanks. That would be nice." Gilly thought she might be better company than Dean, who'd already caught a cold and had spent the morning blowing his nose. When Gilly asked him to pick up his paper handkerchiefs, which fluttered across the grass, he'd first looked surprised and then offended.

"Can't help it if I've got a cold, can I?" Dean swore as he turned away, his language worsening with the weather.

Yes, this woman looked friendlier than Dean today and she decided to leave him in the potting shed. She followed Alice into the yard and past the brightly coloured doors and pointed stone of the new apartments, where rain streamed down the windows set in slate roofs. Each door had a brass number and was painted a different colour. Gilly thought that they were probably once outhouses or stables.

Alice led the way through another gateway and across a second yard towards the house, paved slabs set in pea-gravel. The rear of the building loomed over them where dark patches of rain soaked into the grey limestone. When Gilly looked up, she saw a face pressed against the glass of a second-floor window. The boy again. He jumped back when her eyes met his.

They discarded their waterproofs in the basement. Gilly kicked off her muddy boots and she followed Alice up the stone stairway, steep and poorly lit, that led from the basement to the kitchen.

"There's another staircase that leads to the hall, but this is a short cut." Alice opened a door and a bright light made Gilly blink.

A smell of baking bread and a blast of heat welcomed them. She looked around the vast kitchen with black worktops and cream units. A pine dresser on the opposite wall displayed blue and white patterned mugs and plates. There was an island in the middle of the room and at it, on a high stool, sat the dark-haired boy, legs dangling as he ate toast and strawberry jam.

"Samuel, say hello to Gilly," said Alice. "Gilly is the lady who is doing up the walled garden."

The boy's dark brown eyes regarded her with suspicion. "Hello."

"Hi," said Gilly.

Alice lifted a lid on the four-oven Aga and pushed a stainless steel kettle onto the plate. "Tea or coffee? You can have either. Or maybe you prefer herbal? I've a good selection because we get so many different requests from guests these days. There's Earl Grey, chamomile, green..."

"Ordinary tea bag will do fine, thanks."

Two long windows on either side of the dresser looked out over the yard and, at the other end of the room to the right of the Aga was another with a wide window seat stuffed with plump red cushions. Gilly walked over and looked out. The view stretched across lawns sloping down to a stretch of water that lay grey and cold in the damp fog.

"Oh, there's a lake. I didn't know – beautiful, isn't it?"

A pair of swans floated on the surface, near a small wooden boathouse, and a gravel path led from the terrace by the house to two large stone balls, which marked the entrance to the jetty.

Alice took two mugs from hooks on the dresser and placed them on the kitchen island. "Lovely in the summer."

"Is it man-made or natural?"

"I assume it was man-made, most of them were, weren't they, in those days? The river flows in and out of it."

The boy slid off his stool and came over to peer out. "There's Charlie and Sonia." He looked up at Gilly and grinned.

"There *are*," corrected Alice.

"There *are* Charlie and Sonia. They're my swans. Would you like to help me feed them?"

"Not now, Samuel. Gilly is on her tea break and it's raining hard. Come over and take a seat at the table, please. Have you got any homework?" She directed Gilly towards the long pine table with a wave of her hand. "He's in playschool, but sometimes they ask him to do a drawing."

"Nope." Samuel regarded Gilly with a serious expression. "Do you like swans?"

"Yes, I do. I used to feed them in the park in Dublin when I was younger."

"Good. You can help me later."

Alice laughed softly. "Don't mind him, he's a bossy boots. Help yourself to scones and brown bread. I made them this morning."

"Fergus told me you're a good cook." Gilly took a scone and asked Samuel to pass the butter. "I wish I could cook, but I'm hopeless."

"I organize the catering for the guests, the conferences, weddings and suchlike, although I have help when I need it... if there are a lot of people."

Gilly glanced at a collection of framed photographs on the cream wall. There were several of Samuel and Alice, pictures of the boy painting with her, one of them feeding the swans at the lakeside. There were also two of a brown-haired man with Samuel, and one of the same man with a fair-haired woman, a close-up of both of them smiling against a backdrop of sand and sea. He had his arm round her shoulders. In her spotted bikini, she looked tanned and happy.

Gilly pointed at the photographs. "Is that Mr Fletcher?" His eyes were hard to define, a mixture of grey and green. The woman had very dark eyes, similar to Samuel's.

"Yes," said Alice.

"My dad," said Samuel, with evident pride. "My dad owns this house."

"Yes, darling." Alice frowned at him.

"And that's my mummy," added the boy, ignoring Alice. "Do

44

you know something? My mummy is in heaven."

Did Alice look suddenly uncomfortable at the turn the conversation had taken? The boy was perfectly at ease, busy spreading jam on a piece of bread and licking his fingers. What had happened to Samuel's mother?

The door opened and the stocky security man, who Gilly remembered from the day of her interview, came in.

"Ah, Stefans, you're just in time for coffee and cake," said Alice.

He shot Gilly a quick glance and nodded in acknowledgement. "Very wet day," he said. "Cold and wet."

"I have fruit cake, too. I know you like fruit cake." Alice replied. "Help yourself. This is Gilly... er, I'm afraid I don't know your surname, dear. I'm not sure if you've already met Stefans."

"Gilly Townsend."

The man glanced again at her. "Good afternoon." He had a foreign accent and pronounced his words slowly and precisely. "Just coffee, Alice. I will take it with me. Busy today."

Alice switched on the coffee machine beside the Aga. "Miserable weather." She put a tall mug under the spout and pressed a button. A loud noise and steam shot from the machine.

"The boss says he's coming on Friday," said Stefans.

"Yes, Friday. We all look forward to that, don't we, Samuel? Daddy's coming home."

Gilly sipped her tea. Friday was only two days away and she hadn't advanced as much as she'd hoped with the garden; the weather had been so bad, Dean so inexperienced and she'd had to make several changes to her plan to suit the layout of the paths. If they walked on waterlogged soil, it would become impacted and almost impossible to dig. Would the owner of Glanesfort expect more progress?

Poor Dean, it wasn't his fault he knew so little about plants. She looked up at the big clock ticking above the dresser. She couldn't delay long because he would be wondering where she was and he needed supervision, but the warmth in the kitchen soothed her. Rain still slanted down outside, drumming on the windowpanes. It wouldn't be fair to ask him to work in that, especially with his bad cold. Five minutes more and then she would go out and offer him a lift to an earlier bus than usual.

She leaned back against her chair and looked again at the photographs on the wall. Marc Fletcher exuded confidence in that photo with his attractive wife. Could she ask Alice what he was like? Alice looked the loyal type and unlikely to gossip about her employer. Samuel might be a more willing informant.

She turned to the boy. "Are you looking forward to seeing your father?"

His bright smile lit up his face. "Oh yeah, he's so cool."

Alice handed Stefans a mug of coffee, a frothy cappuccino. "I think Marc loves being back here with Samuel. His office is in London, you see, so he has to go over most weeks."

"Good boss, works hard," volunteered Stefans as he moved towards the door. "Thank you, Alice." He shut it gently behind him.

"I want to help Stefans," said Samuel. "I want to look at the screens. Do you know what I saw? I saw a big, big fox. Can I get down, please?"

"No, darling. He's busy and he'll take you out for a drive later, remember? He said he'd get you an ice cream." She glanced at Gilly. "Samuel is talking about the CCTV screens. Tea all right? Have a slice of fruit cake. Hardly the weather for ice creams, but he does love them, the little lamb."

"I'm not a little lamb." He laughed, jumped up, bleated loudly and ran out the door. "See you later, alligator."

Alice sighed. "He's so lively. He's been sitting still all morning in playschool so I suppose he needs exercise and it's too wet to take him down to the swans this afternoon. Fortunately Stefans is very patient with him. Stefans is used to boys... has three of his own."

"Do they live here in Ireland?" Gilly eyed the fruit cake and decided to be strong-willed and resist. She had to get her waistline back under control before Vanessa's wedding.

"Oh, yes, in a cottage on the estate. His wife is Lithuanian, too, and works in a hotel in Portlaoise. She's a good cook and helps me sometimes at the weekend."

Gilly looked at the photograph again. "What happened to Samuel's mother? Poor boy, to lose her so young. Was she ill?"

Alice stood up and began to gather the dirty mugs and plates. "No, no, nothing like that. It was an accident." Alice's brow creased. "We don't like to talk about it as it upsets Samuel... and Marc."

"Oh, I'm sorry. How long ago did it happen?"

"Two years ago. Yes, it was shocking for everyone, very tragic." She moved towards the sink.

Gilly looked at the clock again and rose to her feet. She would really have to get a move on, brave the rain and rescue Dean. She hesitated and turned to Alice. "Would you mind... do you think I could have a slice of fruit cake for Dean, please? He's my assistant and he's not feeling well."

"Yes, of course, take as much as you like. I'm glad to hear you have help – Fergus mentioned a young man." She took a small plastic bag from a drawer in the island and put two slices of fruit cake into it.

"Thanks very much and thank you for the tea and scones." Gilly took the bag from her. "They were delicious. Just what I needed on a day like this."

"You're welcome. Do drop in again soon. I'm surrounded by men here, as you can see, so it would be nice to have some female company."

Chapter 8

Gilly stirred the bath water with a foot and sent bubbles foaming round her body. She would enjoy planting the perennial garden and herbaceous borders always went down well with clients. She would plant a lot more of them if they weren't so much work. Hopefully at Glanesfort there would be someone to keep them tidy.

She hummed a song she'd heard on the radio earlier and then stared at herself in the long mirror behind the bath taps. Why did people put mirrors beside the bath? To admire themselves naked? Mirrors only made her feel uncomfortable.

Gilly studied her new hairstyle. She'd stopped off on the way home yesterday to a place Vanessa had heard about. It'd cost nearly seventy euro, much more than she would usually spend, but she thought it suited her. Shorter hair would be easier to look after in the wind and rain at Glanesfort and perhaps might make a good impression on her employer who was due back that day.

A bang on the door.

"Gilly! Are you still in there? Hurry up! Ken and I haven't got all morning and he hasn't even shaved yet."

"OK, I'm getting out now." She would have to remember to

collect the flower arrangement for Vanessa's drinks party on the way home.

As she stood up, her sister and Ken were arguing in the kitchen, their voices raised, Vanessa's full of dry sarcasm. Although she never lost her temper, she could make some cutting remarks. Poor Ken. He rarely saw this side of his fiancée and Gilly wondered what he'd done to deserve it.

She pulled a towel round her and glanced in the mirror again. She'd put on weight over Christmas and still hadn't got back to normal. Too many chocolate bars and packets of crisps. Her jeans felt tight and she was sure she could see a spot pushing its way up among the freckles on her nose. Just her luck when she wanted to look presentable. Marc Fletcher would just have to be impressed by the garden instead. She and Dean would make a serious effort to get the hedging planted before he arrived. She would call to a nursery on her way to collect the yew and box plants.

The phone rang and Vanessa shouted, "Gilly!"

By the time she opened the bathroom door, her sister had dealt with the caller. "There you are, at last. I thought you'd died in there. Listen, that was Dean. His grandmother's sick and can't give him a lift to the bus. I told him you'd pick him up in Crumlin – that's where he lives, isn't it?"

Gilly groaned. "Now I'll have to listen to him sneezing and moaning all the way down to Glanesfort. What's up with you two?"

Ken moved towards the bathroom. "My cousin..."

"Ken..." Vanessa warned.

Gilly grinned. "Oh, I get it. It's about Harry's invitation to your wedding, isn't it? Scared he'll liven things up too much?"

Gilly had met Ken's cousin a few times. He lived in London where he worked as a freelance journalist, but he often came over to Dublin for weekends and sometimes turned up on

Vanessa's doorstep, drunk and belligerent, having been thrown out of the nightclubs in Harcourt Street.

Harry had written an article a few weeks before for a magazine, something sensational about women who'd disappeared, in which he'd claimed most of them had been abducted and murdered. He specialised in gory stories, but knew how to hold the reader's attention, that was for sure, even if he made half of it up.

"I don't want him at our wedding," said Vanessa. "We all know what he's like. He's bound to cause a scene, but Ken's father..."

"He's a bit crude," Ken admitted. "But we can't not invite him. What would Dad's siblings think?"

"I'm off now," Gilly told Vanessa.

"OK, don't forget the flower arrangement, will you? The guests will arrive at half seven so don't be late." Her high heels clattered across the kitchen tiles and she appeared in the doorway to the hall. "Is the owner of Glanesfort there today?"

"That's right."

"No wonder you wanted to have your hair cut." Her eyes swept over her. "You look good, much better. I hope he's nice and, Gilly, please remember not to fall out with him. You need this job." Vanessa gave her a quick kiss on the cheek. "Good luck."

*

Sunlight picked out the dust on the windscreen of the Ford hatchback, a muddy arc where the wiper swept across. Gilly looked at the smudged glass in front of her. Would she have time to wash the car?

Dean waited opposite Our Lady's Hospital for Sick Children and wore a vivid orange raincoat, like the ones used by yachtsmen. He slouched against a lamppost, cigarette dangling in his fingers as always. She stopped to let him in and he ground the butt into the pavement with the toe of his boot.

He gave her a nod, slumped back in the seat and closed his eyes. She drove on in silence until they reached Newlands Cross where a long queue of cars forced her to brake sharply.

Dean woke up. "What the…"

"How's your cold?" Gilly asked.

"Better, but Nan's got it now," Dean frowned. "Got a temperature this morning. OK if I get the bus back early because she's on her own?"

"Fine by me," said Gilly, "as long as the hedging has been planted." Would they ever get it in before the boss arrived? Surely he couldn't expect much of an improvement when she'd only been there for a week? Fergus had said his employer was thirty-six. Young to be a widower.

As the traffic moved on, she gripped the steering wheel and accelerated past cars as soon as they reached the dual carriageway. Almost ten o'clock. She'd told the nursery she would be there at quarter past. At least Dean would be able to help her load the plants. She'd ordered bare-root yew and box from a grower who she'd known in horticultural college.

"I thought you told me you'd an older sister." Gilly glanced at Dean. "Couldn't she take care of your grandmother today?"

His pale face wrinkled up in scorn. "She's gone. She and Nan had a row yesterday. Good riddance to the…"

"Dean, take it easy, will you? What's the matter with you today?" He wasn't usually this talkative and perhaps she preferred his silences.

Dean pushed his fingers against the dashboard and drew streaks in the dust. "She and Nan never get on. She's given up her job and moved in with this man Nan hates."

"But will he look after her?"

Dean sniffed loudly. "Dunno. He's married, but his wife doesn't care. She's glad to see the back of him, I reckon."

Gilly didn't know what to say. Imagine being Dean's grandmother having to look after them. Though Dean, at least, seemed to care about her. Still, it was enough to put you off having children, or grandchildren. She didn't like to ask where his mother was.

"Where's your father?" she risked.

Dean said nothing.

"Sorry, I didn't mean to sound nosy. I just thought he might be able to help."

He glanced away. "He's gone too."

Gilly hesitated before she replied. Dean still stared out of the window, but she could see a glitter in his eyes. Tears he hoped to hide from her? Surely not.

"I don't get on with my father, either," She hoped she sounded sympathetic. "We never get on so I avoid him now, because it's easier."

He swallowed, but didn't answer. She drove on down the motorway in silence while he fiddled with his cigarette lighter, turning it round and round in his stubby fingers.

"How are you getting on with Fergus?" she ventured.

"OK."

"I noticed him talking to you yesterday. Where did he take you?" She'd guessed he was trying to get Dean to help him. Fergus was busy with his own work as the arrival of his employer drew nearer. He'd mentioned new tenants about to move in.

Dean cleared his throat loudly. "There's a leaking tap I tried to fix yesterday. It's still leaking."

"Well, you're not allowed to help Fergus today. We've a lot to get through."

His face had its usual closed, guarded expression.

"You're supposed to learn about horticulture, not plumbing.

Don't let him sweet-talk you into anything today, please."

A short, sarcastic laugh. "Sweet-talk! More like twist my... my arm."

"I suppose he thinks you owe him something because he organized this job for you?"

"Fergus didn't organize it."

"Who then?"

He shrugged. "His uncle, I guess. He's a friend..."

"Of your grandmother's?"

"Nah – my Auntie Sarah. Fergus's uncle is her boyfriend, sort of, although I reckon he's a bit old to be a boyfriend. That's what she calls him, anyway."

She turned her head to look at him, but he glanced away, as if worried he'd already said too much.

When she turned off the motorway one exit earlier than usual, he asked where they were going. She explained about having to collect plants from the nursery.

"Will we get a chance to look around it?"

She was surprised and pleased by his interest. "OK, if you want, just a quick tour. I know the guy who runs it." Had he appreciated her awkward attempt to sympathise with him about his father? Perhaps he'd decided they had something in common after all and he would make more of an effort to help her, but she wouldn't hold her breath.

When they arrived at Glanesfort, Gilly parked her car beside a dark green BMW. Large and gleaming compared to hers, with a British yellow number plate. She and Dean began to unload the bags of hedging. Probably Marc Fletcher's car, so he was already here. She looked up at the house, but saw no sign of life and decided she would have to get a move on.

"Dean, could you please go and fetch the wheelbarrow? I'll finish unloading these plants and we'll get them into the ground as soon as possible."

As soon as he'd gone, she got into her car and reversed across the gravel sweep. No way would she park her battered wreck beside that sleek machine. She drove under the arching branches of a large macrocarpa and left the Ford there, half-hidden by a curtain of greenery.

Chapter 9

"Who's that?" asked Marc from the desk, his back to Fergus who leaned against the side of the window. He tapped at the keyboard of the computer; scrolled up and down the screen.

"Gilly Townsend, the landscaper."

"Yes, of course. I'm looking forward to meeting her. How is the walled garden progressing?"

Fergus swung round to face him and smiled. "It's coming on, I guess. A lot of rain, which doesn't help. I'll introduce you to her when you've got time."

"Weather's been foul in London too. You found an assistant for her, you said. What's he like?"

"Grand."

"Experienced?"

Fergus hesitated. "Not as much as I thought, but Gilly says he's a fast learner. He's on a work experience programme."

"References?"

"Yeah, checked them out. He got a glowing report from his school principal." Fergus took out his mobile and glanced at it.

"Not a relation of yours, then?" Marc smiled.

Fergus grinned. "Nah. I felt a bit sorry for Dean, maybe,

because he's not having much luck getting a job. He lives with his nan."

"He has to start somewhere, I suppose. At least this is a short project so we can see what he's like. Do you know anything else about him?"

"Mother's dead. Father left home years ago."

Marc looked back at the computer screen. "All right. We'll give young Dean a chance. Thanks for your email about the apartments. Have you found someone to rent Number Five?"

"Not yet. There are a few people interested." Fergus handed him a file.

Marc swung the chair round and glanced down the list of names, neatly typed with phone numbers and email addresses printed out. Fergus had made an effort. "It should be easy to find someone for the apartment. We're in the commuter belt, close to two railway stations."

"This isn't London, Marc. A few years ago, we'd have had a long queue of people." Fergus shrugged. "It'll be fine... just takes a bit longer now."

"You're right. I should know. Same with my properties in Dublin. It's a shame the family in the wood cottage moved out at this time of year. Not easy to find tenants in early March for a country property." Marc leaned back in the chair and frowned.

Fergus spoke slowly. "Mrs McCarthy left because she's just had a baby and wants to be near her mother in Cork. I put an ad up on the internet – the usual website – but no takers yet."

"We'll have to find someone to take that cottage – and fast. Houses left empty at this time of the year get damp. It will only appeal to a certain type of person. Parents with young children don't like to rent a cottage beside a lake. Too dangerous." Someone interested in fishing would be ideal. Someone who would appreciate the wooden deck and space to moor a boat.

"Gilly's looking for somewhere to live," said Fergus.

"The landscaper?"

"Yeah. She asked me yesterday if I knew of anything."

"You mean for a few months, while she's working in the garden? Now, that's a good idea."

"There you are." Fergus threw him a grin. "See, Marc, things will work out for the best. I'll talk to Gilly." He left the room.

Marc stood up and walked to the nearest window. Small puffy clouds drifted across the sky and branches of bare trees stirred in the breeze. A sharp quality about the sun at this time of year, the contrast between light and dark, the vivid green of the grass.

The elation he'd felt as he drove from the suburbs of Dublin into the Kildare countryside returned. It was good to be back, away from traffic jams and constant meetings. Samuel had run towards him with open arms and greeted him with whoops of delight. He'd picked him up and swung him around before he hugged him close. A precious child, so precious. All he had left.

Later on, he would take him down to the lake and help him feed the swans.

*

Gilly raked the soil round the yew hedge, bent to pick up a large stone and tossed it into the wheelbarrow.

When she stood up, she saw three figures coming towards her from the doorway into the yard. Fergus and the small boy she met in the kitchen, accompanied by a man with brown hair. He wore a leather jacket and denim jeans. Not as tall as Fergus. Was this really the owner of Glanesfort? The wealthy Marc Fletcher?

Fergus smiled at her. "Hi there." He introduced him and Samuel, who clung to his father's leg and peeped out from behind it. Marc's eyes looked grey now that she saw them in real life. When he smiled, creases formed at the sides of his eyes and a faint scar snaked towards his right ear.

Marc gripped her hand in his for a moment. He looked around, took in the yew hedge, the mown grass, the box plants lined up in a trench ready to be planted. "I've heard a lot about your progress from Fergus. Well, it does look tidier, I have to say." His voice was deep but quiet.

"Would you like me to take you around the garden and explain my ideas?" She wiped her hands on her dungarees when she saw mud on her fingers. Had he noticed?

"I'd like to hear your ideas, but I've promised Samuel we'll feed the swans before it starts to get dark. Perhaps Monday?"

"I'll be here tomorrow, if that helps," said Gilly.

"Where's Dean?" asked Fergus.

"His grandmother's sick so he went home early."

Marc seemed to be studying her. "Do you work on Saturdays? I like your enthusiasm. You can take me through your plans tomorrow morning. Is he working out all right, this fellow, Dean?"

Fergus smiled encouragement. "He's getting on fine, isn't he, Gilly? A little inexperienced, as it turns out, but he learns fast."

Gilly nodded. Dean had improved and he'd shown more interest.

The boy's brown eyes stared at her from the safety of his father's leg, clutching his big hand in his little one.

When Marc bent to talk to his son, Fergus beckoned to her and they moved away a few steps.

He whispered, "I wouldn't say too much or we'll be late getting away from work tonight. Don't encourage him to poke around – just try to sound efficient."

"Don't you think I sound efficient?"

"I've still got the design you drew up, Gilly." Marc straightened up and gave Fergus a quick glance. "I'd like to go through it with you, if you don't mind – check out the cost of everything so I can plan ahead."

Gilly nodded.

Fergus squatted down in front of the little boy. "Hey, Sam, come and say hello to Gilly. Come on, she won't bite."

"Hi, Sam," said Gilly. "Do you remember talking to me in the kitchen?"

The boy looked up at his father and stepped backwards.

"He's a bit shy until he gets to know you," said Fergus. "Then he never stops talking – a real little chatterbox, aren't you, Sam?"

Gilly leaned towards him. "How are you?"

"Fine, thank you. This is my dad's garden," said the boy.

"Yes, I know. It will be a lovely garden one day. You'll be able to come and play here."

"Will I?" He smiled and stepped closer to her, turning his head towards his father. "Can I come and play tomorrow, Dad?"

"I don't know. That depends on..." Marc hesitated. "You don't mind if he calls you Gilly?"

"Of course I don't mind." She wasn't sure whether she should encourage the boy because children got in her way when she was trying to work.

Marc turned to go. "Right, Samuel, we've got an appointment with two swans. Charlie and Sonia will be wondering where their afternoon snack is." He nodded at Gilly. "Nice to meet you."

Fergus watched them move away. Then he laid his hand on Gilly's shoulder and squeezed gently. "Would you like to come with me to the Fiddler's Inn after work? Marc likes a pint there when he comes back from London. What do you think? You and I could walk down together and wait for him. He mightn't even turn up – it depends on his mood."

She hesitated. It was about twenty past four and Vanessa's

party started at half past seven. She would have to allow an hour and a half to get back in the Friday evening traffic. "I don't know."

"Oh, come on... only a pint or two. There'll be music tonight and you'll enjoy it. Let your hair down for once."

She gave in. "OK, just give me ten minutes to get finished up here."

Why not? He seemed unattached and she would be careful. Why shouldn't she enjoy herself? She would have one drink and could still make the florist in the town before it shut at six o'clock and there'd be plenty of time to get back to Dublin.

*

"What do you think of our boss?" Fergus flopped against the threadbare cushions on the window seat and gazed with satisfaction at a full pint of lager on the table in front of him. He raised the glass and swallowed half of it with one gulp.

"He doesn't say much." Gilly sipped her gin and tonic. The taste exploded on her tongue, the first sip of fizz. No ice available, but at least they had slices of lemon in The Fiddler's Inn.

Friday night always drew a big crowd, Fergus said, that was why they didn't have chairs, just a hard wooden bench under the smoke-blackened panes of the window. A woodburning stove belched fumes at irregular intervals and its heat filled the room. A real old-fashioned country pub, Fergus explained, unspoilt and popular with the locals.

"At least it's still open for business," he said, "in spite of the fact most people have less money to spend nowadays."

"What's Marc like?"

"Oh, he's all right, unless he's fussing about money. He always gets a bit hassled when tenants leave."

"I would fuss, too, if I lost more income." A real mixture of people, Gilly noticed as she glanced round. Old men huddled together playing cards. Some women her own age, jostling each other, laughing, and one with curly hair gesticulating wildly while her companions listened.

Fergus chatted about Glanesfort and told her he had worked there for two years. He enjoyed looking after the tenants. She laughed at his descriptions of them, the way he imitated their accents. Fergus liked an audience, that was obvious, and he often turned to talk to others at nearby tables and included them in his conversation.

He saluted a man who passed them. "Hi there, Jim, how's it going?"

Gilly waited while the two men exchanged pleasantries.

When Fergus turned to face her again, he said, "Great crowd here tonight and so far no sign of the boss. Let's hope he doesn't turn up because he's a bit intense and he expects us all to be as serious as he is."

"I can see why that would bother you."

"He's only five years older than me, but he looks more than that, doesn't he? It's his lifestyle, I suppose. Too much work and too little play." He finished his drink and rose to his feet. "Let's have another round." He pointed at her gin and tonic.

"OK, thanks, but no gin, just the tonic... my sister's having a party." She watched Fergus stroll towards the bar and hoped he'd heard her.

The ceiling hung low over the crowd, a sticky brown like treacle, and the faded wallpaper was hard to make out. Flowers of some sort. Roses, probably. Windowpanes steamed up from the heat.

"Marc looks confident and in control to me," she said when he returned with their drinks. "How big is his company?"

"He's got several big properties in Dublin and some commercial ones in London. He's a workaholic. Do you know,

I wouldn't be at all surprised if he didn't bother to show up tonight because he has to work late. People like him worry me, Gilly. He'll only live till he's fifty."

"I find work soothing most of the time. It's the only thing that makes me forget about the mess my life is in."

He pushed her glass over to her. "Don't say that because I took you to be a fun-loving person like myself. I'm very disappointed."

She shrugged and sniffed at her drink. "Fergus! I said I didn't want more gin. I have to drive home... back to my sister's house."

"Go on, live a little."

"I can't drink it. I'm sorry you wasted your money."

Fergus shrugged. "I'll drink it. Is your life in a mess? You look easy-going to me."

She hesitated. "Oh, just the usual money problems."

His eyes, those alert hazel eyes, fixed on her. "I'm going to visit my father tomorrow – I always go on Saturdays, most Saturdays, that is." He added, "He's in a nursing home near here."

"Oh. I'm sorry to hear he's in a nursing home. Is he there permanently?"

Fergus leaned back against the window. "Yeah, poor Dad, stuck in a wheelchair now, he is. He used to be so active, used to love gardening. He'd like to meet you. He'd amazing green fingers. You should have seen the little garden we had in London, crammed with flowers and bushes."

"Really? What sort of plants?"

"How would I know? I can't remember any of the names, but the neighbours were always admiring them. Geraniums, I think, and roses. That sort of stuff. But the stroke changed all that." He stared at the table. After a few seconds, he switched his gaze to her face. "Anyway, enough of this morbid talk. Tell me, a gorgeous girl like you must have a boyfriend?"

She stiffened. "No."

"No? No Mr Nice Guy hiding away in Dublin? No plans to settle down?"

"There was one." She stopped.

He nudged her elbow. "Let me guess. You dumped him because he didn't appreciate you?"

She muttered, "I don't want to talk about that two-timing..." As soon as the words came out, she regretted them.

A glint in his eyes, a sudden flash of amusement belied the sympathy in his voice. "I'd never do a thing like that."

"I don't want to talk about him."

"OK, let's talk about me instead. Do you have to go back tonight? I'm sure your sister can cope without you. A friend of mine is having a party later on, after the pub closes. Come with me."

"I can't. Vanessa's expecting me to help."

"But you'd like to, wouldn't you?"

She frowned. "Not tonight, Fergus."

"Not tonight, Josephine." He imitated her voice, made it sound prim and prudish. "Ah, well, some other time."

She changed the subject. "Do you know what happened to Marc Fletcher's wife?"

"Why do you ask?"

"I saw the photo in the kitchen. The one of them together on a beach."

"Marc had a wife but she died."

"How?"

He took a gulp of lager. "You ask a lot of questions. You're not an undercover agent of some sort, are you? The boss doesn't like questions. Maybe you've been sent by the Revenue to check up on our taxes?"

Gilly smiled. "I'm the last person the Revenue Commissioners would employ. Finance and me, we don't get along."

"Look, Gilly, I never met Marc's wife... she died before I came here, before Marc bought this place, and he never talks about her. Neither does Alice so I don't know anything." His mouth stretched into a grin. "Would you like to know more about me?"

"Maybe. Tell me about Alice. What's she like?"

"She's been working for Marc for a long time. A great cook. I reckon she's reserved, because I've been here nearly two years and I still don't know her. One of the tenants, the one with the cat, discovered that Alice used to be a nurse, looked after sick children, but she said something happened."

"What happened?"

He yawned. "Not too sure. She wouldn't give any details but I think it was something to do with a child dying. Anyway, Alice gave up nursing after that."

"Poor Alice. I met Stefans a couple of days ago."

"He's all right." Fergus turned away to talk to the man at the next table and Gilly wondered if Marc would turn up. If he didn't, she would have Fergus to herself for a little longer. If he did, she might get a chance to ask Marc if he had a place she could rent.

Fergus waved at a man at the other end of the pub. "See that guy? He's well able to strum out a few tunes on his guitar. He's got a good voice, too – sings mostly ballads."

A thin-faced woman with long, dark hair tied behind her head leaned over the counter and shouted at Fergus, "Hey, handsome, we're expecting you to sing tonight, OK? Don't let us down."

"You'll be waiting unless I'm better paid than last time!" He grinned at her and turned to Gilly. "She's the owner of this place. It's easy to get a free pint out of her when you know how."

The door to the left of the window swung open and a cold

draught rushed at their legs. Marc eased his way through the crowd, still wearing his jeans and the brown leather jacket.

Fergus sighed.

Marc lifted a hand in recognition. "I'll buy drinks. Would either of you like one?"

"Pint of lager and a gin and tonic," replied Fergus without hesitation.

She turned to Fergus. "I can't drive if I drink any more alcohol."

Marc smiled. "I won't force you. What would you prefer?"

"I'll have a bottle of sparkling water, please."

Fergus kept his eyes on his employer's back as Marc moved towards the bar counter. "It's Friday night. You can stay here and come with me to that party I mentioned. Ring your sister and say something's come up. The boss needs you... something like that."

"I can't do that."

When his employer returned with the glasses, Fergus pushed along the bench so that Marc had to sit between him and Gilly. She moved aside to allow him space.

She took the sparkling water. "Thank you." She glanced at her mobile. Half past five. She would have to leave in ten minutes.

"You're welcome." Marc took off his jacket and laid it on the bench beside her. Underneath he wore a blue cotton shirt, neatly ironed.

"Thanks a lot." Fergus raised his other half-empty glass. "Let's hope this cheers us all up."

She glanced sharply at him. Had he meant to make fun of Marc? But Fergus's eyes wandered away, travelling over the heads to the man with the guitar. He stood up.

"Where are you off to?" she whispered. Was he going to leave her alone with him?

"The gents. Back in a minute. Mind my pint for me, will you?"

She watched his tall figure move carelessly through the crowd, stopping to slap friends on the shoulder, easy to spot in his red polo neck and faded denims. He was better-looking than Ronan was and he seemed keen enough to invite her here tonight, but she would have to slow things down. Vanessa always warned her not to rush into relationships and this time she was determined to listen to her sister.

She remembered the day she'd discovered Ronan was married. He'd gone to buy coffee at the corner shop down the road from her flat and left his mobile behind. It rang and Gilly answered it. His wife introduced herself and demanded to know where he was and to whom she was speaking. After a torrent of bad language and a few details about what she liked to do to adulterous little trollops, she disconnected. Gilly locked the door, pushed his mobile out through the letterbox and ignored Ronan's yells of protest. That was the last she'd seen of him.

She waited in silence while Marc drank whiskey. Would Fergus return soon because she didn't know what to say to this man? She sensed that he glanced at her several times, but when she turned, he had looked the other way.

"Will there be music later?" His voice so soft that she had to strain to hear him above the chatter. "I expect Fergus will sing because he usually does."

Gilly grasped this chance of conversation. "Is he good?"

"Oh, yes, very."

"Do you like singing?"

His grey eyes lit up. "No, it's not one of my strong points. I can't remember the words – and I don't believe I sing in tune, either. I keep my singing for the bath, where no one hears me."

Gilly laughed encouragingly. "Me too. I wouldn't like to inflict it on anyone else."

Marc finished his whiskey. "Can I get you another?"

"No thanks. I should go soon."

"Where do you live?"

"Dublin. I'm staying with my sister." Perhaps this was an opportunity to mention accommodation.

As she reached for her glass, Gilly's knee brushed his under the table. "Sorry." She moved away, embarrassed.

He said nothing for a few minutes, then raised his eyes to hers. "If you live in Dublin, you have a long drive every day. That must be tiring."

"Yes, it is. I would like to move – will have to move soon because my sister is getting married next month. I'd like to find somewhere closer."

Another silence as he looked at her with a steady gaze.

"There's a house here." He spoke slowly. "A cottage in the woods that's just been vacated." He paused and added, "Would you like it?"

"Oh, yes, but it depends on the rent."

"We could come to an arrangement that suits us both," Marc slowly twirled his empty glass on the table. "You need somewhere to live and I don't like to leave a house empty in March. You thought the garden would take several months to finish in your estimate?"

"A few months, until July maybe." His confidence made her feel unsure of herself.

"That'll suit me fine because July is a good time to rent out a house. It's beside the lake and a bit isolated. Would you mind that?"

"I don't mind being on my own. I've lived on my own before."

"That's good."

She asked, "How much will the rent be?"

He shrugged and raised both hands, palms upwards. "Fifty euros a week. Is that all right?"

That sounded reasonable, but she couldn't afford a deposit. "I'm fairly short of cash at the moment."

"That needn't be a problem. We could take it out of the money we owe you. Would that suit?"

"Great, that's a relief. Much easier for me, thanks."

"Good. I'll show you the cottage tomorrow and you can decide then. I hope you'll enjoy working here."

"Will you need a landlord's reference?"

He smiled. "Will your sister give you a reference? No, no, I'm joking – it's fine. You'll only be here a few months. I'm sure you're reliable." His eyes lingered on her face.

"Thanks, thanks so much. I'm really grateful." She glanced at her watch. It was ten to six and the florist would shut in ten minutes. What was she thinking? Vanessa would be furious if she came home without the flowers. She jumped up, looked around for Fergus and saw him over by the bar, saw him bend to whisper in the ear of a blonde woman and drape his arm round her shoulders. Why had he bothered to ask her to come? So that she would keep Marc occupied and leave him free to flirt?

"I'm sorry but I have to go," she said. "I'd no idea it was so late – my sister's party…"

Marc drained his glass and reached for his jacket. "I'll give you a lift back to your car. It was raining when I came out."

"I'll walk, thanks."

"No, please allow me to give you a lift. I can't let you walk back in the rain."

"Thank you," she said. "Maybe it's a good idea because I'm really late."

Marc drove in silence, his gaze fixed on the road, while she stared out of the window as rain battered against the glass. The drive to Glanesfort seemed endless. Fergus was too like Ronan, too charming and amusing. Why had he suggested that she stay late and go to a party with him if he had another woman in tow?

When Marc pulled up outside the house, she almost forgot to thank him.

"You're welcome," he called after her as she strode away. "I'll show you the cottage after I've seen the garden tomorrow."

Gilly revved up the engine until the tyres spun in the gravel and drove off without a backward glance. It was now almost six o'clock and she knew she'd never make it to the florist before it shut. She would have to drive fast to get back before the first guests arrived. Vanessa expected her to be there to help with the food and she'd let her down.

She switched the wipers to full speed. Gilly accelerated as she drove. She was hungry, too, had eaten nothing since Dean's sandwiches at lunchtime and that was hours ago.

Now she was stuck in a line of cars. One tried to move out in front of her and she pounded on the horn.

She could imagine her sister's expression. I can't rely on you, she would say. Why do you never think of anyone but yourself?

But at least she'd done something about getting a place to live. Easier than she'd thought in the end. Vanessa and Ken wouldn't have to put up with her for much longer; soon they'd have their spotless love nest to themselves.

She turned right to avoid the Friday traffic on the main road. She would take the back road towards Kildangan. As she swung the car round the next bend, she regretted going with Fergus to The Fiddler's Inn. Gilly glanced at the clock on the dashboard. Perhaps she might find some flowers in a supermarket on the way. Tesco or Dunnes in Newbridge, maybe. She clenched her teeth as she put her foot down.

She saw the deer jump onto the road, its eyes bright in the headlights of the car, long legs that frantically struggled to scramble out of danger.

She stamped on the brake and spun the steering wheel to the left. The tyres skidded on a sheet of water as the deer bounded away. Gilly sat paralysed with shock while the Ford slid sideways.

As if in slow motion, it spun around once and slid into the ditch. A branch punched through the windscreen and shattered glass over her. She threw herself to one side and cried out as her head thumped against the dashboard.

Chapter 10

Gilly brushed fragments of glass from her clothes and her hands felt heavy and awkward as she touched her face. No blood. At least she hadn't cut herself. Her head throbbed and she leaned back against the seat. What now?

The car, as far as she could see in the darkness, faced down into a ditch. A hedge towered over it, so close that she could reach out and touch it. Hawthorn, with the branch of an ash through the windscreen. She almost smiled and winced with pain. Still the horticulturist in the midst of a crisis.

She tried to open the driver's door, but it was jammed tight. A wave of panic swept through her. Suppose she was trapped, suppose the car went on fire. These things happened, didn't they? She had to get out, climb out as fast as she could. The window was the only way. She wound the handle frantically and then pulled herself through the opening and crawled onto the wet grass. Her head spun and she lay on the steep slope for a few minutes. She waited until her breathing returned to normal. When she lifted her head, a high-pitched buzz in her ears forced her to lower it again. Better not to stand up. Better to drag herself up to the road.

At the edge of the tarmac, she sat up slowly. She was lucky

to be alive. The silence overwhelmed her. No cars, no lights, no moon. Just a black fog around her.

She fumbled in her pockets for her mobile. Not there. Perhaps it was on the rear seat with her jacket. She would have to get back in the window and find it, ring Vanessa. Ness would know what to do. She groaned loudly as she hauled herself through the narrow gap and onto her hands and knees to grope for the mobile phone on the floor. Dizziness returned as she dialled her sister's number.

"Vanessa Townsend." Her voice sounded distant. Gilly suddenly remembered the party.

"It's me."

"Gilly! Where are you? I told you to be early. I might have..."

"Vanessa, please listen to me. I've had an accident... crashed the car."

There was an intake of breath. "What? Are you all right?"

"Just about but the car's stuck... facing down into a ditch. I don't know what to do now. I'm the far side of Kildare town. Vanessa, I'm really sorry... the flowers, I forgot the flowers."

"Oh, Gilly! The flowers don't matter. Who cares about the flowers now? I'll have to come and get you. Can you give me directions?" She heard her sister call Ken. "There are a few friends here already. They're helping me cook."

Gilly felt a stab of guilt as she shook her head to clear the buzzing in her ears. "No, no, don't come. I'll be fine, don't leave your friends. I'll manage on my own."

"Are you sure? What will you do? Could you call someone at Glanesfort? It will take me an hour to get there but I can leave Ken with..."

"No, Vanessa please, I'm sorry I've messed things up again. You must stay with your guests and I'll ring you again later. I'm fine... only the car damaged so no need to worry."

Vanessa let out a string of objections, but the phone signal died. Gilly closed her eyes and rested her head on the seat. So tired. Tired enough go to sleep here. Another dart of pain in her head made her sit up and the panic returned. Suppose she passed out? Fainted? She couldn't stay here all night. Who else would help? What sort of impression would she make if she called Glanesfort?

Her mobile rang again and Vanessa's number flashed up on the screen. Gilly hesitated before she answered.

"Hello, Gilly? I don't know what happened, but we got cut off. I'll come to get you now. Where did you say you are?"

Nausea rose in her throat; threatened to choke her. "No... please don't worry, I'm fine... I'll ring Glanesfort like you said and get help. Go back to your guests and enjoy the party. I'm sorry about this."

"Are you sure you're all right? I can't hear very well... it's not a good signal."

"Yes, I feel fine. I'll see you tomorrow." Could Vanessa notice her voice shaking? Music swelled in the background and someone laughed.

Vanessa spoke louder. "Now promise me, promise me you will call me back later and let me know what's happening. If I don't hear from you, I'm dialing 999."

"OK, OK, don't panic! I'll ring you in about half an hour." She ended the call quickly.

Alice Rogers sprang into her mind. She would help her. She'd seemed friendly. What was her number? She would have to google Glanesfort and see if there was a number to call. The only one on her phone was Fergus's and she certainly wasn't going to call him. Probably on his way to the party with that blonde.

The light in the glove pocket still worked and she rummaged through scraps of paper, empty crisp packets and plastic plant labels. She found a biro and an old envelope. She picked up her mobile and went onto the internet. The page loaded slowly. Not much of a signal. Typical. No, wait, it was loading more quickly now. She typed the name into the search engine, her fingers trembling. What had the sign said at the main gate? Glanesfort luxury apartments. She exhaled loudly as the details appeared in front of her eyes.

*

A log fell in the grate and an orange flame shot up. Shadows danced on the pale blue wallpaper, falling and rising, as the grandfather clock in the corner struck seven. Two lamps, on matching inlaid tables, threw yellow light over the sofa in the centre of the room where Marc and Alice sat, side by side.

Marc yawned as he read down sheets of figures, computer records of rent collected by Fergus. His feet rested on an upholstered stool. He looked over at Alice, her head bowed, reading the Dickens novel *Great Expectations*.

She smiled at him. "Still working? I wish you would stop ... you've had a long day."

"I'm fine." Alice always fussed about his health. It amused him most of the time, and he liked the attention, but not when he was busy. "The new landscaper, Gilly Townsend, is interested in taking the cottage by the lake."

"That's good. She seems a nice young woman." She put her hand over her mouth, yawned and put the book down. She stood up and smoothed out the creases in her navy skirt. "I'll check on Samuel. He was so over-excited. He always is when you're back. I wish he had more children of his own age to play with."

"Could we invite some from his playschool?"

"I thought of that, but I'm worried about having to entertain the mothers as well. I haven't time, Marc. Anyway, Samuel has so much imagination... I don't know..."

Marc frowned. "You think he's lonely?"

"Sometimes." She moved away. "I hope you'll have put that work away by the time I return. Put it away and I'll bring you some cake."

He watched her leave the room. She'd wrapped his wife in her comforting blanket of care and, when Rachel died, Alice had looked after him too. He knew it wasn't ideal for Samuel to be so much on his own, without the company of other children. Perhaps when he went to primary school, he would be less demanding. He looked down at the computer printout and read down several more columns.

The door opened and Alice reappeared. "He's fine. He's sleeping like a baby." She smiled. "You look serious, Marc. Don't tell me you're still worrying about the tenants?"

"No – I was thinking about the nanny, Jane."

Alice picked up her book, ran her eyes down the page. "Ah."

"Is Samuel happy, do you think?"

"Of course he is, don't worry. It's just his age. He needs a lot of attention, but he has Stefans and me."

"No one his own age, though – and I'm away so much. It's not the ideal life for a four-year-old."

"Not your fault, Marc. And Stefans is good to him." She reached out and took the computer records. "Time to put this away."

"I give up. I'll leave it until the morning."

She glanced at him. "And forget about that nanny."

"She stole money, Alice, I'm certain of it – not just money."

Her brown eyes blinked behind her round glasses. "Well, you know what I thought of her. A brazen little madam."

"Yes, yes. The police wanted proof she'd taken things, of course. I had no proof to give them."

"A quick temper too. I never trusted her with Samuel... the poor child had to cope with losing his mother and then a nanny like that."

"But the photograph album... why would she take that?"

"Maybe you mislaid it, Marc. You weren't yourself after... after Rachel..."

"Jane took the photo album, I'm sure of it."

Alice frowned. "There's no logic to it."

It was the only photo album he had of his youth. Photographs his mother had taken. She loved her cameras. Shots of him as a boy. Boarding school photos, mostly of rugby matches; their summer holidays in France together when they were all still happy, oblivious of what was to come.

The private investigator was puzzled by this theft. Was she checking who he was? She must have been interested in his past. It was just as well that he'd never mentioned the private investigator to Alice. She had enough on her plate.

The garden designer had seemed annoyed when they left the pub. Had he said anything to upset her? Not that he could remember, but she'd been friendly until then, enthusiastic about the cottage. She seemed to get on well with Fergus, but then most women did.

When he first met her, he'd thought the boiler suit unattractive but later, in the pub, her jeans and sweatshirt revealed a slim figure. A sweet smile, and he liked her little nose and freckles. He would enjoy getting to know her better. He wondered what age she was because she looked younger than he'd expected. Fergus had checked out her references and they were good. The American businessman had emailed back a positive recommendation. She was efficient and decisive.

The telephone rang.

Marc pushed himself to his feet. "I'll get it." He walked across the room and picked up the receiver. "Good evening, Glanesfort House." He heard a woman's voice, unfamiliar at first, hesitant but urgent. It was Gilly Townsend. "Are you all right?" Marc asked. "Yes, yes, Alice is here with me. Perhaps I should come..." He glanced back at Alice. "Right, I'll come immediately. Give me directions."

*

Marc shone the torch on her face. She was leaning back against the seat, a bruise down her forehead and across one eye, her face white in the glare of light. She sat upright and blinked.

He flicked the torch beam away. "Are you able to get out?"

"Only through the window." She took the hand he offered. He helped her out and up the slope. She stood on the grass verge and shivered.

"I think I should drive you straight to hospital. That bruise looks... were you unconscious, do you think? Can you remember?"

"No, no, I don't think so. I'm OK, really... don't take me to the hospital. All I need is a lift back. I'll sleep in the cottage you were telling me about, if that's all right with you."

Marc realized he was still holding her hand and dropped it. "I'd rather you came back to the house."

Gilly got into the car without another word.

He drove slowly. "Perhaps the casualty department would really be best," he tried again.

She shook her head. "No, I'm not going to hospital. There's nothing wrong with me, honestly. Please believe me, it's only a bang on the head. All I need is a bed for the night and tomorrow I'll take the train back to Dublin... arrange for my car to be towed away." Her voice rose and, as if aware of this, she turned to him, smiled and added, "Thank you for coming. I'm sorry, it must be a nuisance."

Like a child, that sudden lop-sided smile, half-apologetic but still determined to get her own way. Hard to resist putting his arms around her to comfort her. "Don't worry. It's no trouble."

Seeming reassured, Gilly relaxed into the comfort of the passenger seat and her hands fell by her side.

Alice had waited for them in the hall and hurried off for an ice pack when she saw Gilly's face. Marc helped her up the stairs, his hand on her arm, and into the sitting room where she lowered herself onto the sofa.

"Would you like a drink?" He pointed at a whiskey bottle.

"Yes, thank you," she said. "Then you can take me to the cottage."

Alice returned and scolded him when she saw him pour whiskey into a tumbler. "Marc, really! You know alcohol is not good after a shock. She might even have delayed concussion. Sweet tea is what she should have. Here you are, dear, hold this up to your forehead." She pushed ice cubes, wrapped in a tea towel, into her hands. "I'll phone the doctor before I make the tea. Marc, you stay here with..."

"I don't want a doctor." Gilly stiffened at a sudden flash of pain when she pressed the ice cubes against her eye.

Marc smiled at Alice. "You'll find she's stubborn."

"A doctor, I must call the doctor... I'm sure you'll need an X-ray after a head injury like that."

"No," said Gilly. "I'm fine. I'll be OK in the morning."

Marc helped himself to whiskey and took a sip. "Tell you what, then, we'll get the doctor in the morning if you're not feeling better. Yes, Alice, I know you're more qualified than me, but I really don't think we can force her."

"All right, but I'll ring him first thing in the morning."

As Alice left the room, Marc sat on the arm of the sofa. "What happened?"

Gilly lowered the ice pack and closed her eyes. "It was a deer. I nearly hit a deer. Don't know where it came from."

Marc watched her in silence. Wasn't there something about not letting people with head injuries fall asleep? Should he continue to talk to her? Her face was so pale, almost grey, the bruise now a vivid purple and larger than before, creeping gradually across her face.

She opened her dark brown eyes, noticed his stare and turned her head away.

Chapter 11

Pain burned behind Gilly's eyes and her face felt stiff and swollen. What did she look like? She tried to sit up, but dropped back on the pillow when a throbbing surged through her head. There was a mirror over the chest of drawers, if she could only get to it, but perhaps it was better not to know.

She noticed that the curtains were still drawn. They didn't meet in the middle, and a shaft of sunlight fell across the navy carpet. Landscapes, all watercolours, hung on the cream walls. The mahogany bed felt comfortable, a firm mattress and cotton sheets.

Alice had lent her a nightdress covered in pink and blue flowers, with frills and a blue ribbon at the neck, long enough to reach her ankles. Something Mum might wear.

She remembered Marc Fletcher's hand holding hers as he pulled her out of the Ford. He'd held it for longer than he meant to, a frown of concern on his face, those serious grey eyes looking into hers.

A knock on the door startled her.

"Come in," she called when no one entered.

Marc walked in with a bundle of newspapers, which he dropped on the end of the bed. "How are you this morning?"

She tried to smile. "I'm much better." She would have to get out of there as soon as possible, to arrange to have the car fixed up, and go back to Dublin.

"I know someone who will tow your car to the local garage. I'll give him a call. Hopefully it will only take a few days to repair. You look very pale and your bruise is worse."

"That would be great if someone could help me with the car. Thank you. Don't bruises always look worse the next day?"

He said nothing as he walked to the window and pulled back the curtains. Sunshine flooded in and she closed her eyes.

"Is that too bright?" He'd noticed her grimace. "How's your head?"

She lay back and knew there was no use pretending. "Sore. It's worse when I sit up."

He stood near the end of the bed. "Alice has been in touch with the local doctor."

Gilly shook her head and sighed. "I wish she wouldn't... I'm such a nuisance. Thank you... for helping me last night."

"You're not a nuisance. We've got paracetemol somewhere. Would you like a couple?"

"If it's not too much bother."

Soon after the door closed behind him, it opened again and Alice came in. "Good morning, dear. How are you?" She put a tray down on the table beside the bed.

Gilly saw toast, a teapot and a glass of orange juice. "Apart from a headache, I'm not too bad."

"I've phoned the doctor. He's going to pop in at about eleven. Dr Slattery is a lovely man with such a nice bedside manner. I'm sure you'll like him."

No escaping that doctor now, but it was reassuring, in a way. A responsibility handed over. "Thank you."

"Doctors around here don't usually do house calls, but he used to be a tenant. He rented the cottage behind the yard where the American artist now lives."

Gilly sipped the orange juice. "I'm not terribly hungry, I'm afraid."

"Just eat what you feel like eating." Alice glanced at the window. "I see you've already opened the curtains."

"Marc came in. He's gone to get pills for my headache."

"Good. Are you all right now? I'll be back in about an hour. I have to get Samuel his breakfast and he makes a mess if I leave him alone in the kitchen." She closed the door behind her.

Gilly attempted to eat a slice of toast but abandoned it after a couple of bites. Her lips stung when the marmalade touched them. She put her fingers to her mouth. A swollen cut under her nose. If only she could make it over to the mirror. What must she look like?

She swung her legs to the floor and stood up. Her head swam and she clutched the table beside the bed. A few moments passed and she stepped forwards; moved along the wall to the mirror. She groaned when she saw the purple and black bruise around her eye and wished she'd stayed in bed. She stepped to the window and held onto one of the shutters. The lake lay below, dancing and sparkling. A manicured lawn swept down to it and a man on a ride-on mower drove along the water's edge.

Marc returned with a packet of tablets. She turned slowly and he came towards her. "You're up. That's an improvement."

She closed her eyes and gripped the window sash. A flash of pain behind her eyes. She felt Marc's arm go round her back and smelled lemon soap. She looked up at him, startled.

"I'll help you back to bed," he said softly. "You've gone very pale. I'm afraid you might faint."

She leaned on his arm and allowed him to help her. She lay back on the pillow. He had kind eyes that lit up when he smiled, but his face now was all concern. Tears suddenly trickled down her cheeks and she hastily raised a hand to brush them away.

She was such a pathetic fool. What was wrong with her?

She was grateful that he said nothing. He took out a cotton handkerchief and handed it to her, then lowered himself onto the wicker chair near the bed.

"I've got the paracetamol." He handed her two, which she swallowed with the orange juice. "Your sister just phoned. She was alarmed because she couldn't get an answer from your mobile. I didn't think you would be able to come downstairs to the phone to talk to her at the moment."

She nodded. No point trying to talk to Vanessa just now. She'd rung Gilly the night before, just as Alice was putting her to bed, and had sounded anxious and upset. She offered again to drive down that night to bring her back to Dublin. Gilly had to hand the mobile to Alice so that she could explain that she was being well looked after and assure her that there was no need for her to worry.

She reached out and picked up her mobile from the bedside table. Flat battery. No wonder Vanessa couldn't call her.

"I can charge that for you." Marc held out his hand. "We've got a selection of chargers in the office."

"OK, thank you."

"I told her you would ring her later, when you feel better." He took her mobile and his fingers brushed hers briefly.

Gilly turned her face towards the window. "I'm sure I'll be fine by this evening. I'll get up in an hour or two and then I'll be out of your way."

"I think you should wait to hear what the doctor says before you make any decision." He looked at the tea tray. "Would you like some tea?"

As he poured milk into the cup, she glanced at his hands. No calluses or mud under his fingernails; a gold wedding band gleamed on his left hand. She pushed herself upright and pulled the pillow behind her back for support. When he passed her the cup, she had to concentrate hard to stop it shaking.

"Feeling any better?"

"I'm OK. You said you wanted to go through the garden plan. Would now be a good time?"

"No, you're not up to it. See how you feel tomorrow."

"Tomorrow? But..."

"The doctor," he reminded her gently. He stood up and walked over the window and looked out. "Weather's better today." His mobile rang and Marc answered it immediately. "Yes, Michael. Yes. Well?" A silence before he said, "That's not what we wanted. Not what we need now. Did he give a reason? OK. Yes, yes, I'll ring you back in a few minutes."

He ended the call and came towards Gilly. "My accountant. I'll take away the tray."

"Thanks," she murmured. "Sorry I'm a ...."

He smiled. "You're not. I'll leave you to rest now. I've a few urgent calls to make."

*

In his bedroom, Marc rang Michael's home number in London. Gilly had turned very pale at the window and he was afraid she was going to faint. Lucky he had come back into the room when he did.

"Hi, it's me."

"Hi, Marc," said Michael. "Thanks for calling back. Well, what do you think? Apparently, the man's company collapsed on Friday, or the bank pulled the plug, I should say. Not quite unexpected, though. What now?"

"I'll have to call my bank and explain. I'll ask for more time. He must have known this would happen – but a bit of warning for us would have been polite."

"Nobody likes to admit to bankruptcy. Had his head in the

sand, I reckon."

Marc picked at a loose flake of paint on the window and looked out. The sun glinted on the lake and figures strolled near the boathouse, probably tenants going for walks or fishing. "Yes, I just hope it won't be us next. This makes the other sale to the Japanese vital. I shouldn't have gone near those apartments. Go on, Michael, I give you permission to say you told me so."

His accountant laughed. "I told you so. When do you ever listen to me?"

"I thought they were a bargain at the time."

"Someone will turn up to buy the Dublin apartments. You'll just have to get down on your knees and beg for a few more months when you call the bank. That all for now? I want to catch up on the England cricket match."

"Yes. Go ahead... and thanks, Michael, thanks for chasing that man down."

"You're welcome. Don't lose too much sleep over this. We'll fit in a game of tennis when you're back next week." He hung up.

Lose sleep? Another potential buyer announcing insolvency was becoming depressingly familiar.

Marc crossed the oriental rug and looked out of his bedroom door. No one around. Samuel and Alice safely in the kitchen eating breakfast. He turned the key in the lock and stepped quickly across the room. The carriage clock on the mantelpiece told him it was nearly eleven.

Another door led to what had once been a dressing room, where a safe now sat in the wall in the corner. Marc pulled heavy velvet curtains across the window and took a key from the pocket of his jacket.

He swung open the iron door of the safe, lifted out a wooden box and placed it on the oak desk in front of the window. He opened the lid and stared for a moment at the contents – the neat stack of CDs with dates labelled in permanent marker.

The amount of money hadn't seemed much in the beginning, not as bad as it might have been, but now, with his bank ringing him about the loan repayments on the London offices that hadn't sold as quickly as he'd hoped, Michael might soon start wondering where all this cash was going. He should have listened to his accountant's advice about Dublin. What had possessed him to buy those apartments? They seemed good value at the time, but a bargain wasn't a bargain if there were no buyers. If he could sell the London offices, he would then have more time to find someone for the apartments.

He took a small battery-operated compact disc player from a drawer in the desk and placed it beside the box. He drew the CD from his jacket pocket, placed it in the player, and sat to listen again to the message.

Music swelled to fill the room, introduced as usual by that strange voice – an electronic, computer-like drone that might be male or female, or perhaps neither. Frightening in the beginning, but soon he'd grown used to it. Nothing bad happened as long as he carried out the instructions.

"Good day, Mr Fletcher," said the voice on the CD, "I do hope you are enjoying Mozart's *Requiem*. We've reached the Day of Judgement. Doesn't that make you worry a little?"

The music increased in volume and a man sang in Latin. The voice remained silent until the first piece of music finished. "Shall I translate for you, Mr Fletcher? Such a pity if you miss the meaning... I'm sure you remember from your Latin lessons in that very expensive school... a school so expensive that only rich little boys like you could attend... the trumpet is summoning everyone to the throne."

How did this person – if you could call this distorted sound a person – know so much about him?

"Judgement... doesn't that frighten you? The thought of your sins read aloud in front of the whole world. All that you've managed to keep hidden for so long?"

Marc frowned and pushed his fingers down hard on the top of the desk; pressed until his knuckles grew white.

"Take note of that, Mr Fletcher… this is about others judging you and you never want that, do you? But you know the answer, don't you? All you have to do is keep paying the money and no one will find out anything about you. It's not much to ask, after all, considering what I've been put through. Don't you agree?"

He was tempted to switch off the infernal machine but he had to wait.

The voice droned on. "You wouldn't like anything… shall we say… unpleasant to come out. You wouldn't like more headlines in the newspapers."

A temptation to wrench the CD from the player and snap it in half – if only to rid himself of that voice – struck him and he closed his eyes and gripped the desk with both hands. He hated having to listen to this hateful message twice but had to force himself to keep going until he reached the part where he heard the bank's name and account read aloud because they were always different on every recording.

He picked up a biro and waited. Where would the bank be this time? The last one had been Costa Rica. It was always a tax haven where accounts could be set up easily; where employees often faced fines and even prison sentences for disclosing information about the movements of their clients' funds and assets. A country where confidentiality and secrecy reigned.

As the music continued to play, Gilly Townsend surfaced in his mind. Her pale, wan face with the blue-black bruise. No doubt she thought him respectable, a man with few worries apart from properties and tenants. What would she think of him if she heard this?

He realised that the voice on the CD had already finished reading off the bank account to which he was to send the money and he had to play it back, to listen again before he wrote the numbers down. Sounded like Belize this time by the bank code, not that it mattered where it was. He'd carried out the same routine three times over the past six months and he knew exactly what to do, what to expect. Always the same amount in sterling. Today the bank account was in the name of Wolfgang Charitable Trust. He sometimes thought the blackmailer was playing with him, amusing himself – or herself. Once the name had been The Mozart Home for Impoverished Musicians. Perhaps it was easier to set up a bank account if the name sounded like a charity.

He'd once asked Michael, very casually, how easy it would be to identify the owner of an offshore bank account. Not easy, was his reply. The holders of international bank accounts in tax havens were well concealed and often the boards of directors in offshore companies were figments of someone's imagination. He'd heard of agencies that specialised in setting up such accounts and he knew it was straightforward enough, sometimes only took a week or two and often with no need to visit the country.

Shouldn't he have gone straight to the police in London the first time a CD arrived through his letterbox? But the thought of going through it all again... of raking up the past and the dread of having it printed in the newspapers like before. No. No. The choice had been simple: he could either tell the police about the CDs so they might find a blackmailer who despised him, or he could say nothing in order to protect himself. So many years spent working long hours, building up his business from the bottom. He couldn't let down his employees who trusted him. His tenants who, when they moved on to buy their own homes, often called him for advice. Too many property developers put up with bad press these days while he strove to keep his reputation untarnished. He couldn't sacrifice that now.

What if it was the nanny? Angry at being dismissed for her inefficiency, pilfering and impatience with his son, Jane might be seeking some kind of elaborate revenge on him and she might know who he really was. But would she have the intelligence to set up something as complex as this?

Joe Milligan was positive it was she. Who else could it be? He thought it was possible that she wasn't working alone, that someone else also knew about his past. It had been so easy for Jane, a young, single woman, to disappear. She could be anywhere, but Milligan seemed confident he would be able to track her down.

Marc stood up and switched off the CD player. He would pay the money. It wasn't too much. He would pay to keep his name out of the tabloids and his mother left alone. She'd also created a new life for herself and he couldn't drag her through the mire again. Besides, Joe Milligan would soon track Jane down and put an end to it all. No one else need ever find out.

He took the CD out of the machine and put it with the others in the wooden box, turned the key and placed it back in the safe.

Chapter 12

Gilly slept in the afternoon and when she woke at four o'clock, she was able to sit up without feeling dizzy. Her headache hadn't returned and she read snippets of the newspaper Marc left on the bed. Alice brought her a salad for lunch and returned her mobile fully charged. Both Vanessa and her mother rang, in varying states of anxiety. Her sister decided she was in safe hands, but Mum needed more reassurance and Gilly had to repeat several times that the doctor had been that morning and hadn't been worried about her.

She tossed the newspaper aside and watched the sunlight dance on the walls. A clear spring day outside, cloudless sky and tips of conifers waving in the wind. Perhaps she should have a look at her garden plan and decide where to plant bulbs next autumn. They wouldn't flower until the following spring but she'd have to think ahead and leave instructions. The section on the right when she came in the door, behind the existing beech hedge where the old apple trees grew in long grass, looked ideal. Daffodils in the grass, hundreds of them gathered in cheerful clumps. Tulips wouldn't thrive in grass, but they could go in the shrub border along the wall. She would make a list of her favourites: such as 'Angelique', with pink, peonylike flowers;

'Queen of the Night', a deep purple so dark it was almost black and the beautiful 'White Triumphator', with its pure white pointed petals resembling a lily. She'd once planted a whole bed of white tulips and it looked fabulous, especially at dusk.

She heard a noise at the door, a scratching sound. She looked up and thought she saw eyes peeping at her between the door and frame.

"Hello, who's there?"

She heard a movement but no answer. She went back to thinking about the garden. An orchard with bulbs could continue into the next section, with a mown path through the middle of the long grass leading to a rose garden near the south-facing wall.

She heard a timid tap and glanced up as Samuel's face looked round the door.

"Oh hello. Come in."

He hesitated, but decided to be brave. His small hands clutched coloured plastic figures. He was wearing jeans and a Fair Isle sweater.

"Hi, Samuel, what have you got there?"

He held up the figures, black and white, with silver guns and coloured capes.

"Hey, they look dangerous," she said. "All armed to the teeth."

A grin spread across his face. "They're my space aliens. See this guy's gun?" His shyness evaporated and he climbed onto her bed.

She admired the plastic monsters in turn while he treated her to a long description of each one.

"My dad gave them to me for Christmas. They like fighting. Look!" Uttering explosive sounds, he hurled some of the aliens onto the bedspread. "Those ones are dead."

Gilly watched as the boy killed off a few more. He didn't

resemble his father with his big dark eyes and thick lashes. Perhaps he took after his mother.

Samuel, suddenly bored with his game, turned to her. "Do you mind if my dog comes in?"

"No, I don't mind."

He ran to the door and called. "Wolfie, here boy." He smiled at her as he returned and climbed back onto the bed.

Gilly looked for a dog but nothing appeared.

"He's here, by the chair," said Samuel.

She stared. No dog by the chair. Either she was blind or this child had an imaginary pet.

"He's called Wolf because he's big and black and hairy... and very fierce."

"Ah, OK."

"Are you going to stay here?" he asked.

"Not in this house. I might stay in the cottage in the woods."

"Wow! The woods! Can I come and see you?"

"Yes, of course."

"Will you tell me all about plants and things? My teacher tells me about plants sometimes."

"My mother used to tell me all about gardens, too, when I was your age."

His eyes widened. "My mummy is in heaven. I'm four. I'm going to big school in September." He had difficulty with pronouncing September.

"I'm sorry about your mother. Do you remember her?"

He shook his head. "No."

She watched him play with his space aliens. "I suppose you were too young to remember her."

"Alice is my mummy now," he said, "except I always call her Alice."

There was a knock on the door and Alice appeared. "I've brought you tea. How are you feeling?" She placed a tray with a teapot, milk jug, mug and a plate of homemade shortbread biscuits on the bedside table.

Gilly smiled at her. "I'm much better, thank you."

"Do get off the bed, Samuel," Alice scolded. "Gilly mightn't like you sprawled across her legs like that."

"I was telling her about Mummy," he replied.

"Oh... well, yes... I hope you're not tiring Gilly. She needs lots of rest, the doctor said, or else she will not be able to go home tomorrow."

The boy slid off the bed, landed with a thump on the floor and ran to the window.

He pressed his nose against the glass.

"Off you go now, Samuel, it's time for your milk and biscuits."

"I can't see Charlie and Sonia. Can we go down and feed them?"

"Not until you've had your milk." Alice sighed and glanced at Gilly.

"I can't see the white lady."

Alice frowned at him. "The white lady? Who are you talking about?"

"The white lady ghost, Alice. You know. The one my friend's dad..."

"That's just another silly local story. I do wish people wouldn't tell you stories like that to try and frighten you."

Samuel chortled and ran back to the bed, scrambling up onto it. "I'm not frightened. Me and Wolfie are gonna track down the white lady."

"She doesn't exist. There are no such things as ghosts and I'll have to have a word in your teacher's ear. No one should tell tales like that to a four-year-old. Now get down, please, get down and go to the kitchen. I'll be there in a few minutes to give you your milk and biscuits."

The little boy scowled at her. "I want to stay here. I'm not hungry, I'm not."

Alice caught hold of his hand. "I said off the bed, Samuel. Now, please, do as you're told for once. I'm very sorry, Gilly, I didn't know he was in here. He does love to chatter, poor little lamb."

"I'm not a poor little lamb," muttered Samuel, as he picked up his toy figures.

"Thanks for showing me your spacemen." Gilly felt a little sorry for the boy.

"They're aliens." He walked reluctantly to the door and looked back at her. "You will let me come and help you in the garden, won't you? You said..."

"Off you go, Samuel," repeated Alice and rolled her eyes. When he'd gone, she apologised again. "He's so inquisitive. But you mustn't take anything he says too seriously... great imagination, that child." She smiled. "Will you help yourself to tea? I must keep an eye on Samuel or he'll be out the kitchen door and down to the lake to feed the swans and I don't like him to walk down there on his own, just in case..."

Gilly nodded. "Of course. I hope you don't mind me asking, but does he have an imaginary dog?"

"Yes, I'm afraid he does, though the doctor told me it's nothing to worry about, quite common. The doctor said he once met a boy who had a whole herd of imaginary cows. Imagine that. I'm thankful Samuel only has a dog and at least it doesn't leave mud and hair everywhere like a real one would."

"I see. I know someone who had an imaginary little sister."

"Perhaps he can get a dog when he's older and able to look after one, but I don't want another responsibility just at the moment. The doctor was pleased with you, wasn't he? Not as bad as we feared. You'll be right as rain tomorrow." She smoothed the pillows behind Gilly.

"Samuel's lucky to have you to look after him."

"Oh, well, thank you. Yes, I love him dearly... he's such a pet, though headstrong, mind. His father dotes on him, too, and even when he's away, whether he's in Hong Kong or America or wherever, he phones him every night before he goes to bed." She glanced at the teapot and added, "Don't let it get cold. I'll have to dash, I'm afraid, as I've got to get Samuel his milk and... are you comfortable?"

"Yes, thanks."

"His father is away a lot and he misses him when he's away from Glanesfort. All that travelling... part and parcel of his business, unfortunately."

She was a loyal woman, no doubt about that.

Chapter 13

"I like your idea of a pool with water lilies." Marc stepped through the gap in the yew hedge. "Is it going here? How wide will it be?"

Gilly looked at the plan in her hand. "About three or four metres... big enough to be a feature." She waved a hand away from the potting shed on her left. "Surrounded by a summer garden with a seat over there opposite the shed door. You can see four entrances in the yew where people walk into this section. The garden's made up of four large areas – each with its own theme. It's quite a formal layout, you see."

He held out a hand and took the plan, glancing at it. "I see what you mean. You mean plants that flower all summer, like roses?"

"The rose garden will be over there." She pointed to the top right hand corner of the walled garden. "That's the sunniest spot and roses thrive in sunshine. By summer plants, I mean the late spring ones like aquilegias and alliums; then Campanula lactiflora and catmint, day lilies and herbaceous geraniums. Maybe we could try lupins to see if they like the soil. I find them hard to grow in limey soil. When I tested this soil, it had quite a high pH so they mightn't survive."

He nodded and handed back the plan. "And the perennial section further up... what would you plant there?" He smiled at her and shrugged, lifting his hands with palms upwards.

"At this time of year we'd have hellebores and *Pulmonaria officinalis* flowering. Have you ever lived in France?"

"Why do you ask?"

"The way you shrug like that..."

"My mother is French and lives there. Maybe I picked it up from her." He gave her a long look. "And you?"

"I've always lived here in Ireland." She turned away from his gaze and wished she hadn't asked that question because now he probably thought she was nosy. Sometimes she just opened her mouth and questions popped out, as if they had a life of their own. "Anyway, the perennial garden... yes, lots of plants that come back every year. I don't think annuals would suit you because they require a lot of maintenance and you need to keep replacing them. I thought I might limit the colours to pink, purple, white, blue and pale yellow. There are so many... Sedum superbum, Thalictrum 'Hewitts Double', Phlox, Alchemilla mollis for the front of the border – it self-seeds in gravel - some of the bigger campanulas... Monk's Hood or Aconitum has dark blue hooded flowers but it's poisonous so maybe not safe if there are children around."

"I wouldn't put it past Sam to try to eat the flowers or to feed them to the swans."

His son, who was running past on his third lap of the garden, stopped and muttered breathlessly, "What?"

"Maybe give that plant a miss then," suggested Gilly. "So, what do you think of my plan?"

His mobile rang and he took it out of his jacket pocket and glanced at it before switching it off. "Interesting. I'm inspired by your enthusiasm." He put his head to one side and the lines at the side of his eyes creased when he smiled. "And you sound like you know what you're doing, which is reassuring. How about having a look at the cottage? Do you feel up to it?"

"Oh yes, headache's all gone today."

She followed him to the wooden door, noting his energetic walk. He kept fit, obviously. She imagined him going for an early morning jog around a large park in London before he turned up at his office, while Fergus was lighting up his first cigarette of the day over a mug of black coffee. Marc wasn't as laid back as Fergus, but he listened to what people said. He weighed and balanced every comment with such precision that it made her slightly nervous. She would have to remember to choose her words carefully.

They turned left out of the door and followed a gravel path through tall laurels as the boy skipped and hummed behind them. The shrubs opened onto a lawn with clumps of birch trees, under which daffodils swayed in the breeze. Samuel grabbed her arm and pointed up at a bird box.

"Fergus told me a goblin lives in there."

Gilly laughed. "Fergus might have told you a fairy story."

"Do you know the story about the goblin?"

"No, but I'm sure you will tell me."

He shook his curls. "Nope. I forget."

Marc swung round, hoisted him up and placed him on his shoulders. The boy shrieked with delight.

"Run, Daddy, run!"

Gilly walked faster to keep up as they entered a wood where tall beech and oak trees cast shadows over the gravel path. No leaves yet but their heavy branches already filtered out most of the sunlight.

She glimpsed a clearing ahead and a sparkle of water as Marc groaned and lifted down his son.

"You're heavy, Sam. I need a rest."

Gilly reached the lake and stood beside him. A wooden

deck ran along the grassy bank and water danced and glittered, lapping against the posts.

"It's beautiful," she breathed.

"Thank you. They certainly knew how to landscape properties in the late nineteenth century, didn't they?"

Further back stood a stone cottage with a red door and window frames, bathed in sunlight.

"Can I go in?" Samuel pushed past her.

"Move aside, Sam, don't block the way." Marc gave him a gentle push. "Have a look around, Gilly. I'll keep this little chatterbox downstairs with me so that you can concentrate."

A circle of lawn separated the back of the cottage from the wood and a large lime tree stood on the edge of this, bare branches stretching over a patchwork carpet of purple, yellow and white crocus.

Marc unlocked the door and they went inside. The kitchen had a terracotta tiled floor and pine harvest table, with chairs painted red. Padded cotton cushions lay on each one.

"My dad had a dog," said Samuel.

"Not my dog." Marc looked up. "She belonged to an old man down the road and when I was about eight or nine he let me take her for walks."

"A Jock Russell."

"Jack Russell. Yes, she was, and very fond of chasing cats." He glanced back at his son and held up a warning finger to silence him. "Gilly, go upstairs and have a look at the bedrooms."

"I'm coming too." Samuel ran towards the stairs.

His father shrugged. "As long as Gilly doesn't mind."

"No, no, it's all right, don't worry." She followed the boy up to a landing. The furniture all matched in the main bedroom, still new and clean because the previous tenants hadn't stayed long. "I like the white painted floorboards and the striped curtains," she said to Samuel.

"There's another bed in this room." He pushed the door open. "I can sleep here when I come to stay with you."

Not if she had anything to do with it. He was far too lively for her to keep an eye on. She might only turn her back and he'd be in the lake. This was definitely not a suitable home for small children.

The other room was half the size with the same matching pine, a single bed under the window and a red rug. She left Samuel gazing out of the window and returned to the kitchen.

"It's perfect." She smiled at Marc, who had just finished a phone call.

"Good. That's what I hoped you would say."

"Can I move in tomorrow evening? I haven't got many belongings so it shouldn't take long." She remembered that she wouldn't have her car back until Wednesday. "No, wait; I've no transport tomorrow – unless I can persuade my sister to drive me down. Maybe I should wait a few days."

"Move in whenever you like. I'll give you the keys now. When I spoke to the man at the garage, he said your car might be ready tomorrow, but I wouldn't bank on it. I can give you a lift to the railway station tonight."

"Oh, thanks. Thanks a lot."

Samuel clattered down the stairs, calling his imaginary dog and disappearing out of the kitchen door.

"What else is there to show you? There's a telephone – that's in the hall – I'll ask Fergus to get it reconnected." Marc hurried after the boy. "Need to keep an eye on this young man."

She followed him outside and he locked the door and handed her the keys.

"It's yours now. I hope you'll be happy here," he said.

Tulip leaves under the kitchen window were already pushing their pointed leaves through the soil and would soon flower. A wooden bench stood against the wall.

Samuel picked up a stick and hurled it into the shrubs. "Fetch, boy! Good dog." He ran laughing towards the trees. He bent to pull up grass and hurried towards the deck by the lake. "Charlie, Charlie, Sonia..."

Gilly plucked a daffodil from the grass verge and held it to her nose. "This one has a fantastic scent. Do you know what we found in the old orchard?"

Marc turned to face her.

"Pheasant Eye Narcissus," she continued. "They won't flower for a while but they're in the long grass under the apple trees. They've got this circle of orangey red in the centre of single white petals and a lovely scent."

"You really love your work, don't you? I feel I should learn more about gardening because in my line of business people expect properties to be landscaped these days."

"Hey, Dad, Charlie and Sonia are coming."

Two swans glided towards them, one in front of the other. Samuel threw grass into the water and they bent long necks to inspect it.

"The swans he likes to feed," Marc explained.

"Have you got the oats and peas, Dad?"

His father handed over a paper bag from his pocket and turned to Gilly. "Alice won't allow him to feed them bread. It's bad for them, apparently."

Samuel's dark eyes fixed on hers. "Do you know that swans fall in love and stay together forever and ever? Alice said."

Gilly glanced at Marc. What expression was in his eyes? Could it really be amusement, appreciation? She swallowed and returned his smile. An attractive man like him, with polished charm, wouldn't be interested in her.

Across the lake, stone jetties jutted into the water, with a backdrop of more beech and oak. The wood ran close to the bank along the far side.

"Fishing platforms for the tenants and the local anglers' club," said Marc, as if reading her mind. "There's a path through the trees. You can walk all the way around the lake."

"It's huge," Gilly murmured.

"We have a boat, if you want to borrow it. Can you row?"

She shook her head. "Never tried."

Marc put his hand on Samuel's shoulder. "Not too close to the water."

The boy shrugged him off and scampered back along the gravel path.

"It's really lovely," Gilly said. "Thank you for letting me rent this house."

He moved closer to her, looked into her eyes and her pulse quickened. "You're welcome. I hope you won't be too lonely down here."

"No... no, I'll be fine."

"It's isolated. The woods behind, not everyone's idea of..."

"I don't mind. I'm happy to have somewhere of my own to live."

"I'm glad you like it. The lake covers about fifteen acres. Maybe you'd like to come with me for a walk..." His mobile pinged with a text message and he turned away to read it. "Better go back. Where did Sam go?"

The boy leapt from behind a tree and shouted, making Gilly jump.

*

"I hope I'm not taking you out of your way." Gilly leaned against the soft cream leather of the passenger seat.

Marc turned the key in the ignition and the engine of the BMW growled to life. "It's not a problem. The railway station is only a short drive from the main road."

"Thanks. I'm really grateful for all you've done for me."

He drove down the avenue, the trees on either side fading into darkness. Daffodils on the verge tossed in front of the headlights. The earlier sunshine had given way to heavy clouds and wind. The weather forecast warned of a storm, but Gilly intended to be back in Vanessa's house before it started.

Marc said nothing and she decided not to talk, as she didn't want him to think her a brainless chatterbox. Alice had told her he was on his way to meet an architect for dinner. He obviously had something on his mind. His expression was more serious and it was impossible for her to tell what he was thinking.

As the car swung out of the gate, Marc turned and his eyes lit up. "You look worried. Forgive me, Gilly, I'm not being very sociable."

"It's OK. Don't feel you have to talk just because I'm here."

"I'm used to being on my own, that's the trouble," he said. "Most of the people I meet in London are connected with work – clients, estate agents, my employees in the office. I suppose that's why I like it here. I like the silence. I can appreciate it more than you, maybe."

Did this mean he thought she talked too much? "I like being on my own, too, you know. I like walking."

There was another silence while he concentrated on a bend in the road.

She turned away and stared out of the window. She felt tired and a niggling headache had surfaced.

"I enjoy walking." He glanced at her. "I often go for walks around the lake. Would you like to come with me? I also wonder would you be interested in looking at a property with me sometime?" he asked. Was that a gleam of interest back in his eyes as they swept from her face to the road in front? Hard to tell in the dark. "It's an old mill near Monasterevin. The owner is thinking of doing it up to start a business there."

"Oh, I'd love to." She added quickly, "I mean, yes, of course I'll look at it. Do you want me to look at it from a landscaping point of view?"

"Yes." He glanced away and she feared it was to hide his amusement at her enthusiasm.

They said nothing for the rest of the journey. Ten minutes later the car drew up outside the station. She felt strangely depressed at the thought of returning to Dublin. The wind had risen and dead leaves chased across the gravel while a clock swung on chains above the entrance.

She thanked him again and stepped out of the car. He switched off the engine and followed.

"Don't come in," she said. "I'm a bit early so I'll go to the waiting room. I'll be fine."

He put a hand on her arm to stop her moving away and she could feel the light grip of his fingers through the sleeve of her jacket. He stood close to her and looked into her eyes.

"You've got a lovely smile." His voice was so low that she wondered if she imagined this. So have you, she could have answered. So have you. She swallowed, but the words stuck in her throat, refusing to come out and the moment passed.

He let go of her arm and walked back to the car, turning to raise a hand before he got in. Gilly watched the tail lights of the BMW fade away as apprehension mingled with excitement spun inside her, like the leaves at her feet that whirled and scattered into the darkness.

*

Marc slowed down the car when he turned off the main road. Perhaps he shouldn't have mentioned her smile. She'd seemed surprised, taken aback and, for once, lost for words. It wasn't like him to say that to someone he hardly knew. What had come over him? But she was a breath of fresh air and on the same wavelength as him. She seemed to know immediately what he was thinking. Or perhaps he was imagining this.

He changed gear as a lorry thundered towards him, a high, dark shape that loomed out of the night. If he was honest with himself, what he really wanted was to hold her small face with its swollen, purple bruise in his hands and kiss her, but that was the last thing he should do.

His fingers tightened on the steering wheel. He glanced at his watch. Eight o'clock. Time to make the transfer. He indicated to the left, drove off the road onto a wide grass verge and noted the dark wood that ran along both sides. The wind moaned among the branches. He glanced in the mirror. No other headlights in sight. If that poor girl saw what he was about to do – she really looked no more than a girl – she would be horrified. No, he would have to keep his distance from her. He could be friendly, but he couldn't risk getting involved with her. There was too much at stake and it wouldn't be fair on her.

He took his mobile phone from his jacket pocket and opened up his internet bank account.

He held the mobile beside the envelope on which he'd scrawled the international bank account details and, using the glare from its screen as a torch, began to key in the numbers. Modern technology made it quick and simple; the money would soar into cyberspace and wing its way from his account in London to land in the account of Wolfgang Charitable Trust in Belize. Once, when Michael queried what these regular payments were, he'd told him they were donations to different charities around the world. He would have to call this one a charity that helped underprivileged children develop their musical talents. The accountant had trusted him so far and accepted his lie with only a slightly raised eyebrow and the tiniest hint of sarcasm. Very generous, he said, very commendable.

Marc logged out of his bank account. His father was a coward, a coward and a liar, and he was growing like him.

He pushed open the car door and stood on the damp verge of the road for a few minutes, wind numbing his face, fists clenched. Anger was a waste of time and energy. No, he couldn't get involved with that innocent girl, or any woman. He would have to sort this out first and put a stop to the blackmail. That was what Joe Milligan recommended. Keep things quiet for the moment. Pay the money and let Joe get on with tracking down the missing nanny. Soon he would find her. Soon all this would be over.

He got back into his BMW and dialled Milligan's number.

"Hello." The older man answered promptly. "Hello, Marc. How are you, my friend?"

"Are you alone? Can you talk?"

"Yes, yes. I'm in my flat."

Marc explained about the CD. "I've just sent the money. The usual amount."

Joe was silent. Marc could hear him breathing heavily; he was slightly asthmatic and carried an inhaler in one of the many pockets of his coat.

"Ah," he said, eventually. "Ah."

Marc drummed his fingers on the dashboard. "So, what progress did you make in the last week? Did you find out anything useful in Leeds?"

Another silence.

Nobody could ever accuse Joe of being impulsive. "Yes, I did. Yes, quite interesting actually. I'll take the train back again on Tuesday to pursue that particular line of enquiry and it's promising, my friend, very promising. Yes indeed, I don't like to speak too soon but this time I really think we might be getting somewhere. The university... but I won't go into details now. When are you back in London?"

"End of next week. We could meet on Thursday. We need to get to the bottom of this, Joe. I don't like the way things are heading and what if..."

"Of course, of course," interrupted Joe sympathetically. "No one will hurt your son, Marc. That hasn't been mentioned, has it? If this really is the nanny – and I'm sure it is – she's not likely to hurt him. Why would she risk that? We've discussed this before and I'm sure she knows who you are. It must be that. These people play at blackmail and take your money, but when it comes to the crunch, when they're finally run to ground and threatened with legal action, you can't see them for dust. They're not so brave then. They're cowards underneath it all, Marc. All bullies are cowards underneath it all."

"How many blackmailers have you run to ground?" Marc noticed a sharp, sarcastic tone in his own voice. "It's taking far too long, Joe."

"When I was a detective in the police, we had many cases like this. Many, many cases, my friend. And rest assured, if circumstances change... if things get a little... shall we say rough, then of course you must go straight to the police. I would be a fool to advise you against doing that. But give me another few weeks, maybe even a month, because I believe I'm getting close."

Marc glanced at his watch. The architect would be at the pub in Newbridge in half an hour with his plans for the Dublin apartments.

"Got to go, Joe," he said. "I'll ring you before Thursday and you find out all you can in Leeds."

Joe assured him he would and murmured a goodbye. The car engine started with its reassuring purr and Marc drove off.

Chapter 14

"I'd like to meet this guy Marc Fletcher – check him out. I'm sure he's got something to hide." Vanessa frowned as she scrolled down her computer screen. "Oh no, here's an email for Ken from his cousin Harry." She clicked to open it.

Behind her, Gilly tossed another shirt into a cardboard box. "Do you always read Ken's emails? Doesn't he object?"

"Ken and I share everything. Harry says he's looking forward to the wedding and he encloses a link to his latest article. What's this about? Something the tabloids would like, no doubt." She clicked again. "Yes, it's up to his usual standard. Gilly, listen to this headline: Missing Woman Found in Prostitution Ring. I would hate to be the family of that poor girl. Tragic. And having that insensitive oaf sniffing around and writing about their horror would make it even worse."

Vanessa turned away from the computer to watch her sister packing. "Marc sounds a bit too good to be true, if you ask me. He obviously has a shady past that's going to catch up with him one of these days. How do you think he made all that money?"

"He buys and sells property, Ness." Gilly sighed. "Now you're beginning to sound like Harry. I thought you said you would help me pack."

Vanessa leaned forward to pick up a crumpled shirt. She folded it and laid it back in the box. "Does anybody know what really happened to his wife?"

"Harry has definitely succeeded in getting you on his wavelength. She died – both Alice and Fergus told me that. Marc Fletcher is a discreet sort of guy. He doesn't blurt out his misfortunes to everyone he meets, and the same goes for Alice."

"You mentioned that Alice said it was an accident?"

"I don't see what all this has got to do with you and me."

"I'm worried about you, that's all. I think you should keep your distance from this man. I can tell you find him attractive... just be careful. If you get involved with this guy, who you know nothing about, and it doesn't work out... well, that's your job – yet another job – down the drain."

A brown leather boot, its lace missing, flew through the air and landed with a thump on the shirt. Gilly turned back to the cupboard and searched for its partner.

"Gilly! What's the point of me folding your clothes if you're going to throw... all right, all right – I'm sorry if you think I'm interfering but really, just think for a minute, will you? I think it would be better if you concentrated on the project. What's Fergus like?"

Gilly swung round, her voice rising. "Fergus! Give me some credit for once. Fergus may be able to turn on the charm, but he'd be nothing but trouble – drinking and running after women in all directions."

"I thought you liked him."

"Sometimes I do – but you should see the way he treats Dean like a slave, sending him off to do his dirty work all the time, cleaning out drains and stuff. And what do I know about Fergus? Nothing, apart from the fact that his father is in a nursing home near Glanesfort." She slammed the cupboard door. "Where is that other boot? Would you have a look under the bed?"

Vanessa looked and then straightened up. "No sign of it."

Gilly emptied a drawer into the cardboard box. "That's everything. There's no need for you to panic because Marc won't want to get involved with someone like me. I'm just not in his league. He probably has some chic, glamorous girlfriend back in London, anyway. He was kind to me, and so was Alice, that's all. But this job means a lot to me and I promise I'll be careful, OK?"

Vanessa frowned. "He could have a girlfriend in London and still..."

"I like his grey eyes, though, because when he smiles they sort of light up," Gilly added.

"That's the worst excuse you've come up with yet. Now you sound like a lovesick teenager."

"I just fancy him a bit, that's all."

"We all know where that usually leads, especially when you've a tendency to go around with your heart on your sleeve. Is that all you're bringing?" Vanessa stared at the cardboard box. "I suppose they're all the clothes you've got? What about those botanical prints?"

Gilly glanced at the wall. "You keep those for a while, if you like, until I've got somewhere more permanent to go."

"Thanks. Would you like to borrow a suitcase? That box looks desperate. They'll think you're a bag lady if they see you arrive with that."

"Nobody will see."

Vanessa shrugged. "OK, suit yourself. Did you ring the bank back today? Your account manager sounded anxious to talk to you."

"Yes, yes, I spoke to him. Good news, he's leaving and they're assigning me a new one – a Russian woman."

"Was he happy to hear about your new job?"

"Happy enough, but not keen on extending my overdraft any further. I told him I would be paid again soon."

"I don't know how you cope with being overdrawn all the time. I wouldn't be able to sleep at night. I suppose a Russian might keep you in order." Vanessa strolled over to look at herself in the mirror which hung behind the door and pulled back her hair, twisting it on top of her head. She wanted to try out different styles for her wedding, now only about five weeks away.

Gilly glanced round. "Did you see my socks? I don't seem to have many. Have you got some I could borrow? Or I could buy them on the way down if we leave now before the shops shut."

"I can lend you a couple of pairs for the time being. I saw a lovely suit in Brown Thomas for Mum to wear to my wedding. It's dove grey."

"Sounds nice. Did you find a suit for me? Not high heels, Ness, you know I can't wear them without falling over."

Her sister laughed. "I'm going to miss you, you know."

"I doubt you will."

"I will — so will Ken. It's going to be so quiet without you here. I'll ring you often, just to check you're OK, and maybe you'll invite us down for Sunday lunch in your country cottage."

"In five weeks you'll be a married woman and far too grown-up to fuss about your little sister and worry about her future."

"I would like to see you make a success of your life. You know a lot about plants, a lot more than many landscapers, I'm sure. You were top of your year in college, remember."

"Why, thank you, that's the nicest thing you've said to me in ages. I want to make the walled garden a success. This job is a big opportunity and, if I can pull it off, who knows what other projects might come my way. Banish your fears, dear sister, and rest assured that I'm not quite stupid enough to risk throwing it away by getting involved with the boss."

Vanessa raised an eyebrow and tilted her head to one side. They looked at each other and smiled. She turned back to the mirror to apply lipstick. "Maybe you'd like to bring someone to the wedding," she suggested, sounding more magnanimous.

"You mean a man?"

"Of course I mean a man. Someone respectable, mind. Not just any hairy creature you find wandering along the road."

Chapter 15

A cold, pale mist shrouded the lake as the dawn sun painted silhouettes of trees pink on the far bank. Gilly locked the door of the cottage. Frost glistened on blades of grass that crunched under her walking boots as she zipped up her jacket and wrapped her scarf around her neck. She breathed in deeply and drew the scent of pine needles and damp leaves into her lungs.

As she turned to make her way along the gravel path into the trees, she glimpsed a white shape on one of the stone jetties. She screwed up her eyes and held a hand up to block out the sun. Yes, definitely someone across the lake. Perhaps one of the fishing enthusiasts Marc had mentioned, but Gilly couldn't see a fishing rod and, as she stared, the figure appeared to swing around to face the cottage. It was impossible to see her face but her hair, so blonde that it was almost white, was long enough to reach her waist. Gilly raised a hand to wave, but there was no answering greeting from the other woman, who stepped backwards along the jetty into the darkness of the wood and disappeared from view.

"Weird," said Gilly aloud. She strolled along the path towards the walled garden and out onto the lawn. Hadn't Sam mentioned something about a white lady? Alice had been quick to dismiss the ghost story about a woman who haunted the lake. There was no such thing as a ghost, so what had she seen?

It was too early to go into the garden. Dean wouldn't be there for another hour at least and Gilly wanted to explore more of the land around Glanesfort. Fergus had mentioned a walk up a hill with a view across the plain. She would try to find that.

As she passed in front of the stone steps that led to the front door of the house, she spotted Fergus walking towards her, his hands in his pockets and shoulders hunched against the cold.

"Hey there." His breath hung on the icy air. "You're up early."

"I could say the same about you."

He shrugged. "Yeah, well, I've got some business to attend to. One of the apartments needs my loving care."

"I'm off to find the hill walk you mentioned. How do I get there?"

He pointed across the lawn to an ornate gate into the wood. "That's the quickest way. Follow the path to the right until you come to a lane that runs along a big field. The lane will take you up to the next field and then out onto the hill." He glanced at his watch and moved away.

"Fergus?"

"Yeah?"

"I... did you ever see..." she hesitated.

"What? Did I see what?"

"A woman by the lake... dressed in white." The words sounded ridiculous as they stumbled out and she began to wonder if she'd imagined the figure. The sunlight in her eyes, the mist on the lake... she couldn't be certain what she'd seen.

He stared at her, obviously not understanding what she was saying.

"A figure across the lake dressed in white," she added. "Sam told me a story about a ghost and that he was going to track her down with his imaginary dog."

Fergus's mouth stretched into a wide grin. "Oh that. That's just a local legend, Gilly, and some other child mentioned it to him in playschool, I guess."

"Ah."

A teasing light danced in his eyes. "You saw our lady of the lake? What did she look like?"

"I must have imagined her. The sun was shining in my eyes."

"Did she have long blonde hair?"

"Well, yes, but..."

"That's her all right." He laughed and turned away. "Better keep an eye out for her. She's a bit vindictive, I hear."

Gilly followed him, grasped his arm. "Fergus, what do you mean?"

"Don't worry, I'm only winding you up. Of course it's all nonsense. You imagined her, like you said. The locals say she was a daughter of the family who lived here a century or more ago who went off the rails after a tragic love affair. She threw herself into the lake and drowned. It's all garbage. And now, if you'll excuse me, I have an appointment with a blocked washing machine and its owner is in a hurry to get to work. See you later."

Gilly let go of his sleeve and frowned as he walked away. Was it possible that the dawn sunlight and the fog on the lake conjured up the illusion of a woman with long white hair? Without binoculars, it was impossible to tell what she'd seen. Perhaps it was an angler and what looked like hair had been a scarf of some sort. She would forget about it.

She made her way across the neatly mown lawn. She opened the gate and followed Fergus's directions until she came to a large field where green shoots of corn swept across the brow of a hill. Halfway up the slope another gate opened into a boggy swamp with clumps of reeds. She noticed a track trodden down by cattle, with a small wood on the right. Mud squelched underfoot. She should have worn wellington boots. She followed the track around a corner with a clump of birch trees on her left.

Walking cleared her head and helped her to relax. Strange that it was hard to sleep in the country with no traffic or sirens to wake her, but perhaps it was the new surroundings. She would have to get used to the silence, broken only by birdsong at dawn. They were so noisy, those cheerful birds. A magpie must have built a nest in the trees behind the cottage because, even though she'd only been living there for two days, its rattling call had woken her up both mornings.

Around the corner ran a stream, choked with briars, mud banks pockmarked by hooves. She sprang across, resting a foot lightly on a flat stone in the water. Not good land compared to that behind the house where fertile grass surrounded parkland trees of oak and beech. She liked the contrast, the unruly wildness of this hill.

A herd of Aberdeen Angus watched with large, dark eyes from their shelter under the overgrown hedge; some were lying down, a sign of rain her mother said.

At the top of the hill stretched a hedge of blackthorn, ash and hawthorn. She turned to face the way she'd come. The house stood below, protected from the wind by the south-west woodland; it looked smaller and less intimidating somehow, with its chimneystacks and elegant Georgian windows. A furl of wood smoke rose from the nearest chimney. Alice would have lit the fire and was probably trying to persuade Samuel to get dressed for playschool.

The lake lay beyond the walled garden, twinkling and innocent in the sunshine. A glassy eye surrounded by trees.

Gilly sat on a tree stump and felt the damp seep into her jeans. She smelled it too: the sweet, warm moisture from the ground. A blackbird sounded an alarm call behind her on the branch of an ash. *Tic tic tic tic tic.* Like the birds in the walled garden whenever the ginger cat appeared.

How old was the house? Who had built it? She tried to picture the families who had lived in it down the generations, the old and the young, people who worked the land: a thriving community in those days. Even now, the property still seemed to exist in a world of its own.

A rattle behind startled her. She jumped to her feet, swung round and something birdlike in her chest fluttered against her ribs.

"Are you admiring the view?" Marc asked.

"Yes." She hadn't expected this. Would he mind her exploring his land?

He came towards her, dressed for the outdoors in a green waxed jacket and jeans, and stood beside her, looking down at Glanesfort. "How are you feeling? Your bruise looks a bit better."

Gilly put a hand up to her face and touched the swelling. "It's not so sore now, thanks. I was trying to imagine all the people who have lived in your house over the decades before you bought it."

"Five families have lived here. The father of the man who sold it to me rescued it in the late seventies when its previous owners ran out of money."

"How old is the house?"

"Built in 1793."

"Oh, very old – and when did you buy it?"

"Two years ago, that's all. I'm only a blow-in compared to those who have gone before."

She noticed his half-smile. He didn't seem to mind being an outsider.

He glanced at her. "How's the cottage?"

"Great. It's comfortable and warm."

"Quiet? Very quiet, I should imagine, compared to Dublin. I hope you're not too lonely. If you are, I'll lend you Samuel." He looked at his watch. "Time I headed back. Are you staying here or would you like to walk back with me?"

"I'll come with you."

He led the way down the hill, talking about the house and its history. The previous owners had moved away, emigrated to Canada when the recession came. They'd been reluctant to leave their home, but relieved to sell it to someone who would look after it and restore it.

"I was grateful for their trust," he said. "There are many who would be wary of someone like me."

"Why?" She remembered what her sister had said. How had Marc made his money? Was it just a result of hard work? There'd been several scandals and allegations of corruption involving property developers in recent years. Along with bankers, people viewed them with suspicion and made them the butt of numerous jokes.

He didn't answer.

"What was the last owner like?" she asked.

"In his fifties – a nice man. He lost his job so he and his wife decided to leave. They have relations living in Canada."

"It must have been a wrench, if his family had been here for so long."

Marc turned to look at her. "Yes, I'm sure it was. They left behind most of their furniture." He explained about a new roof and gutters on the house; the apartments in the yard converted from farm buildings and stables. "It was a mess when I moved in. There was even a pigeon nesting in the attic. I had to make many changes."

"Do you enjoy renovating houses?"

He stretched out a hand to help her over the stream. She thanked him and took it. The house was obviously one of his pet subjects.

He stood still and looked down into her eyes, as if trying to read her mind. "I love old properties. Their link with the people from the past, their place in history. I think we share this creative urge, don't you? We both like to take something historic and beautiful and save it from decay." He released her fingers. "As you know, the walled garden was completely let go. They couldn't manage all that work. I think they felt guilty about how run-down the place had become. The last owner asked me to keep him updated on improvements. He's still interested in his old home."

"You sound like you're already very attached to Glanesfort."

"I am. I'm fond of it... a home for my son... and for me because it's so... so peaceful." He stepped on ahead and fell silent.

He was elusive, if that was the correct word: one minute she had his full attention, the next his mind was elsewhere. Who would have thought he'd feel they had something in common? The creative urge to save beautiful things from decay. The way he said it sounded quite romantic. And yes, he was right. She often felt driven to rescue gardens that had been abandoned. The potential of a neglected garden excited her.

She wondered if she should mention the white figure at the lake. What would he think? He might decide she was over-imaginative and gullible so it would be better not to risk it. She could mention what the boy had said.

"The lake is lovely, Marc. It must have taken a lot of men to create it years ago."

"Yes, it's amazing what they were able to achieve without excavating machines."

"And thank you for providing the men to rebuild the wall in the garden. It's nearly finished now. I wonder which came first, the walls or the lake.' She glanced at the stretch of silver water, watched it glitter in the sun. "Sam told me the story about the ghost."

"What ghost?" He turned to look at her. "Oh, you mean the white lady?"

"He wants to track her down. Was there... did a woman really drown there?"

"A local legend – stories like that often come with a house as old as this. I've never found any evidence that she actually existed."

Gilly frowned. It must have been an angler. She wouldn't mention what she'd seen. She realized he'd asked her a question and was standing at the corner of the wood, waiting for a reply. "Sorry? What did you say?"

"I asked how you're getting on with the pool."

"Oh, I didn't hear you, sorry. Dean and I dug out a lot of soil yesterday. Tomorrow I hope to get started on the concrete base. We'll need to buy lining material for it. What should I do about paying for that?"

"Fergus will tell you where to go. We have an account with a local hardware store. If you need to go somewhere else, Fergus can give you cash – just keep the receipts for him."

"OK thanks, I'll do that."

"How's Dean getting on?"

"He's doing well. I think he might have found his vocation."

Marc turned to smile at her. "Perhaps you're inspiring him. I know you inspire me."

Was this a compliment? She wasn't used to compliments and felt awkward. To change the subject, she pointed at trees in front of her, a circle of hawthorn mingled with gorse on a bank by the edge of the wood. "There's a clearing underneath these."

"It's an old ring fort," he replied. "It's marked on the Ordnance Survey map."

"Oh, that's interesting. I've seen them before, but not as close up as this one. How old is it?"

"Possibly early medieval. There are many of them in Ireland because people used to build their homes inside them."

"You know a lot about history."

"My best subject in school. I studied history in Cambridge until..." he hesitated and looked away. "Well, until I had to drop out to earn a living."

"I liked history, too, but I was better at biology. Not cutting up frogs and worms but the botany part of it."

"I can't imagine you being squeamish about dissection."

"I suppose you think I'm unladylike. No, no, don't apologize, I'm used to it."

"I didn't mean that... you shouldn't jump to conclusions. I would never call you unladylike. That would be... impolite. It would also be untrue." His eyebrows met in a frown of concern.

She shrugged and flashed him a grin. "It doesn't matter. Tell me more about ring forts."

"There's a lot of superstition about them. Our postman likes to tell me I can't touch this one or remove any of the trees because misery and pestilence will befall me. My wells will dry up and my cattle will die – if I had any, that is. Those Aberdeen Angus we passed on the hill belong to the farmer who rents the land."

They both laughed and moved on, back towards the gate and the long lane through the fields that led to the house.

"My mother's superstitious," Gilly said. "Single magpies, peacock feathers in the house, walking under ladders and breaking mirrors... there's no end of ways to bring bad luck down upon ourselves."

"My mother always told me we made our own luck. Though I think she changed her mind later."

Later? What did he mean by that? "Does your mother visit you in London?"

"Not any more. She prefers Paris."

"Do you see her often?"

"No, but I talk to her on the phone."

"Does your father enjoy living in Paris?"

He hesitated. "My father's dead." He glanced at his watch and walked faster, as if to escape any more questions. He held the gate open for her and she thanked him.

"I enjoyed our stroll and chat, Gilly," he said. "We must visit the mill I mentioned because I need your expert advice."

"Yes, of course – whenever it suits you." It was gratifying that he called her an expert.

"I have to fly to London tonight, but I'll be back again soon. We'll go next week." He reached out and took her hand, gave it a quick squeeze. "Until we meet again. I look forward to that. I think we're on the same wavelength, you and I."

She stared at her hand, held firmly in his strong one, and wondered how to reply.

He laughed and moved away. "Don't look so alarmed. I'll see you soon."

"Yes, I'll see you soon," she echoed and remained beside the gate until he had walked up the steps and into the house.

Chapter 16

Joe Milligan was sitting at a round table in the far corner of the Dog and Bone pub when Marc arrived. His raincoat lay on a chair beside him and he leaned over a newspaper, his long fingers clasping a half-empty glass of ale. His train from Leeds must have been on time. He'd suggested meeting there because it was close to King's Cross station, near to Pentonville Road.

Marc raised a hand in salute and went to the bar where he ordered another ale for Joe and a bottle of lager. A few stragglers remained after lunch hour, as if reluctant to return to their offices, and a large woman with a tight black leather skirt looked him up and down.

"Hello, love," she said. "Like to buy me a brandy?"

Marc glanced at the barman, who looked about twenty.

"Up to you," said the young man, as he topped up the glass and pushed it across the counter towards him.

Marc shrugged and handed over the money for the brandy. The woman thanked him and said he was a kind man who would get his reward in heaven.

"Well, well." Joe eagerly took the ale from him. "Thank you, my friend. That looks very good and I feel I deserve it after my long and arduous trip." He shifted his chair over to make room for Marc, folded up the newspaper and sighed with satisfaction.

Black and white photographs hung on the walls above panels of dark wood and a gas fire glowed cheerfully in an open grate under a pine mantlepiece. The photos were mostly of dogs, some old faded ones of greyhounds and a few of terriers and gun dogs.

The woman at the bar knocked back her brandy, rose to her feet and buttoned up her jacket, while an old man on her left bent to feed a black hairy spaniel chips from his plate.

Joe waved at the woman and raised bushy eyebrows. "She's always here, God love her. Drink can be a cruel master."

"You must know this place well." Marc took off his coat and lowered himself onto a hard wooden chair.

"I used to live nearby before I moved into the flat in Shepherd's Bush. I've a friend who plays cards so I meet him here sometimes. Do you want to get anything to eat? The food's all right."

"I had an early lunch."

Joe nodded and fixed him with his twinkling blue eyes. "Food's good all the same."

"I'm not hungry. Would you like something?"

"Now that you're offering, I'll have the steak and kidney pie."

Marc beckoned to the young man who strolled over. He ordered the pie for Joe.

"A direct train from Leeds," said Joe, "and it only took just over two hours. Amazing, isn't it, how fast public transport is these days? Imagine how long it would take me to drive there."

"I thought you didn't drive."

"I don't – no point owning a car in London and, anyway, too many lunatics on the roads these days. So, how was Ireland? Still raining there?"

"Not all the time." Marc smiled. "It was a bright, cold day when I left last night."

"Yes, it was the same here. It's cold for March. And how's the little lad?"

"He's well. He was glad to see me. He's a bit lonely, I think, when he's not in playschool. He's sociable, unlike his father."

Joe finished the first drink and lifted the second one. "Cheers, my friend." He glanced around and lowered his voice. "I suppose you have to be careful, in your line of work."

Marc wondered what he meant. Joe had a habit of issuing sweeping statements and Marc suspected that he used them to draw people out, to lure them into a false sense of security. He sipped his lager and said nothing.

"I'd have loved a son,' said Joe. 'Only I could never find a woman patient enough to take me on. Women can be difficult at times. They're very fond of timetables and routine and regular meals and the like." He laughed and nodded at his pint. "Not too keen on the beer, if you know what I mean."

"I suppose not. Any chance you can get to the point, Joe?"

The older man sighed, but didn't look offended. "I've got a client at the moment who's doing my head in. Do you remember the one who gave me a reference when you asked for one? Between the two of us, she's convinced her husband is having an affair. He's too old to be carrying on, if you ask me. All he does is sneak off to the pub for a quiet drink."

Definitely time to get Joe to focus. "Tell me how you got on in Leeds. You said you've some information for me."

"Ah, yes, I do." He shot a quick glance at the old man with the spaniel and lowered his voice. "I've got these. I took one on the university campus and the other in Beckett Park." He fumbled in a pocket of his coat on the chair and produced two rather crumpled photographs, which he placed on the table and slid towards Marc.

One was of two women sitting on a park bench in the distance; the other a group of students outside a doorway, heads close together as they pored over a mobile. Marc picked them up and studied the photo in the park. One of the women had long dark hair and sunglasses; slim with long legs and wearing what looked like navy trousers.

"Well?" Joe raised his ragged eyebrows encouragingly. "What do you think? Is it her?"

Marc examined the second photograph. The same dark-haired woman, this time with a red beret, was pointing at the mobile. Could it be her? The long dark hair, high cheekbones, her rather pouting lips. Definitely a resemblance, but hard to tell from so far away. "Did you take any close up?"

"No, it wasn't possible."

"It's like her but... it's hard to be certain. What is this woman doing in Leeds?"

Joe shifted his weight on the chair and rubbed his hip as if suddenly in pain. "She's a post-grad student. Her name is Jane, Jane Aldridge, and she's doing a Masters in some area of History of Art. I tracked down her landlady and she gave me a bit of information about her – a very helpful woman. Jane shares an apartment with two of the girls in that photo."

"Jane Aldridge? The nanny was called Jane Smith."

Jim smiled and shook his head. "Smith, Jones, what does that matter? She would have made up the name."

"She gave me references."

"So? She probably got her friends to write them and to answer the phone when you rang up to check."

"Perhaps."

"I'll have to go back to Leeds and stay a few days, keep an eye on her. You mentioned she stole things. If I could get into her apartment when she's not there, I could have a look."

"I told you she took an old photo album that belonged to my mother. Also a photograph of me in a silver frame."

Joe swallowed the rest of his ale. "She had to prove it was you, I'm sure of it."

"Before she began sending me the blackmail CDs? I want you

to talk to her, Joe. Don't mention my name, but try to arrange to meet her somewhere private and I will join you. I want to ask her about the blackmail."

The private investigator considered this. He drew in a breath and let it out slowly, rubbed a hand against his chin.

"You think it's a bad idea?" Marc asked. "I need to talk to her, Joe. I can't let this go on indefinitely. If she's to blame, I need to tackle her about it."

Joe sighed and pushed up his shirtsleeve to look at his watch. "We have to be careful not to... not to threaten... she could go to the police, claim we mistreated her... so many harassment claims these days. You know what I mean?"

"I just need to talk to her." Marc lowered his voice. "There won't be any threats."

"All right, I'll do it. I'll try to persuade her to meet me... not sure how I'll manage that, but I'll think of something, don't worry."

"Thank you."

"It's half past two. Have we time for another drink? You getting the tube back to your office?" Without waiting for him to reply, Joe slipped an envelope out of his jacket and pushed it across the table. "My latest bill."

Marc opened it and glanced down the handwritten list. The total at the bottom was underlined twice. He raised his eyes to Joe's lined, weather-beaten face. "This is expensive."

The older man grinned. "Hotels, train tickets, photography, hours of surveillance work... it mounts up, you know... can't do all this for nothing." He sighed. "I'm getting closer to her. Of course, if you'd rather go to the police..." He leaned across the table and dropped his voice to a whisper. "You told me what it was like before... the journalists, the headlines in the newspapers. Is that really what you want?"

"No, no, of course not."

"A little more time, that's all we need." Joe rose to his feet slowly and grimaced. "My hip hurts like hell today – must be the cold. Now, how about that drink? It's my turn to treat you, my friend."

Chapter 17

Gilly locked her car, wondering why she bothered when it was likely she would have to pay someone to steal it, as the front door of Glanesfort opened. Marc came down the steps, briefcase in hand, wearing a navy pinstripe suit, pale blue shirt and check tie.

He stopped, shot her a quick smile and glanced at his watch. "Hello, Gilly. I see you have your car back. I'm running late, I'm afraid... got to go... a meeting in Dublin." He came towards her and gave her a quick kiss on both cheeks.

"You've been away." A week in London, Alice had told her. "Lovely day, isn't it? The weather's really improved now that we're halfway through March."

"Yes." He moved away across the gravel, searching his jacket for his car keys. "I'll see you tomorrow. We must talk about the garden – I've been neglecting it, I'm afraid." He opened the car door and looked at her. "And I haven't forgotten about our visit to the mill."

"I'm free later on."

"Sorry, Gilly, not today. This meeting might go on all afternoon." He threw his briefcase onto the back seat of the BMW. "What about Monday afternoon? At the moment, I've got an hour or two free in the afternoon."

"Great. What time?"

"Say half past two? I'll meet you here, at the front steps. See you then." He shot her an apologetic smile, got into the car and started the engine. The gravel spun under the wheels as he drove off.

She walked towards the path that ran along the wall of the garden. Had he thought of her and the garden when he was away in London? She'd found it difficult to keep him out of her mind. He was so busy and was probably preoccupied with other concerns. Maybe he really did have a girlfriend and spent the week with her. Alice never mentioned another woman, but she was loyal and chose her words carefully.

Fergus had been more attentive in his boss's absence and had dropped in one evening with a bottle of wine. They'd watched a film on television together before he left to go to The Fiddler's Inn where he was meeting friends. She still considered asking him to Vanessa's wedding, which was now just over one month away. As long as he wouldn't think she was encouraging him. He would be an amusing companion, or she could go alone. Who needed a man tagging along anyway?

She tapped the packet of tree ties against her leg as she walked and hummed a song she'd heard on the radio that morning. By the time she reached the door into the walled garden, she was glad she hadn't asked Fergus now that Marc was back. She imagined the look on her boss's face if she mentioned it. He might be too polite to refuse. No, no, what was she thinking? How mortifying if he said no and why would he want to go with her to a family wedding – especially her family? Besides, a very very bad idea to get involved with her employer, although it wouldn't really mean getting involved, would it? It would only be a fun night out. She could explain that her invitation was just a friendly gesture because he'd been kind to her after the car crash.

No sign of Dean in the garden. Gilly frowned when she saw the abandoned pool liner still lying beside the heap of soil. She'd told him to start fitting it first thing. Where had he gone?

Samuel walked in the wooden door by the potting shed with Alice in tow. He ran towards her, waving his arms like propellers and skipping. "Hey, Gilly, hey, Gilly. My dad's home!"

"Yes, I just met him."

Alice smiled at her. "Would you like to come for a coffee? We haven't seen much of you this week."

"Thanks, I'll come about four o'clock, if that's all right with you. I've got to finish something here first."

Alice nodded, took hold of Samuel's hand. "I'm going to give this young man a bath."

Samuel wailed. "Can I stay here with Gilly?"

"Gilly's busy, pet. Come with me now and there'll be a special slice of cake for you at four o'clock." She glanced back over her shoulder. "You'll find Dean with Fergus in Apartment Five. New tenants will move in next week so they are painting."

Gilly rolled her eyes and followed them into the yard. Apartment Five had a navy blue door that stood wide open and, waving goodbye to Samuel, she marched over to it. Raised voices came from inside.

"Dean! Watch it, will you? I said be careful. The old lady who's going to rent this place will complain to the boss if the floor's covered in paint." Fergus came out into the hallway and walked to the door where he chucked his half-smoked cigarette onto the gravel.

Gilly noted his expression of mild alarm when he saw her. "Fergus, I need Dean."

"We're busy. Come back in an hour."

"Now, Fergus. I can't wait an hour."

Fergus ignored her and strode back into the apartment with Gilly following. "Here, give me that roller, will you?" he said to

Dean. "Watch how I do it."

Dean's narrow dark eyes glanced at Gilly before he handed over the roller and stepped back.

Fergus climbed up the ladder and rolled paint up the wall. "We need to get the place looking smart because I hear this tenant is fussy and I don't want complaints, especially as she'll be living next to me. What's the matter with you this afternoon, Deano?"

"Nothing."

"Can't you say something? It's boring enough without having to talk to myself all the time. Put the sheet underneath, will you? That's what that is, in case you're wondering. It's for stopping the paint going on the floor."

"I know that."

"Then why don't you use it? The boss will be along to check our progress later today and you know what he'll say if it isn't finished."

Dean pulled the sheet under the stepladder. "Where does he go when he's away?"

"London, checking up on his properties over there."

"He must be loaded."

"He's made a few quid all right. Here, Dean, roll this in the paint again. Pass it back to... be careful.' He climbed down the ladder and stared at Gilly. "Are you going to stand there all day? You can help, if you like."

"I'm going to ask Marc about this, Fergus. You can't just take Dean away to do your work whenever you feel like it."

"Can't I? Don't forget I'm the one who got this job for Dean."

"He's employed to help me in the garden," Gilly replied. Fergus was exasperating, exasperating and stubborn.

"He's staying here for the next hour."

"Well, maybe I better..." Dean shifted from one foot to the other, eyes cast down. "Gilly said it was urgent."

Fergus moved closer to Gilly, looked down into her eyes and grinned. "No point us falling out over this, sweetie pie. Why don't you go back to the garden and I'll send young Deano along when we've finished this wall? Another hour – that's all it will take."

Gilly didn't return his smile. "We need to discuss this with Marc, Fergus. I can't rely on Dean to get work done if you keep snatching him away."

"All right, all right. Keep your hair on, Gilly. Sorry I can't oblige, but I'm under pressure, too, you know. I've a heap of things to do for Marc. You're not the only one with a deadline, sweetheart." He picked up another roller and pushed it into the tray of magnolia paint.

Dean frowned. "I'd better do as he says."

"No you won't, not if I have anything to do with it." Gilly said. "You're employed to help me and he's always trying to make use of you."

He didn't reply.

"I'm going to tell Marc about this – I'm not going to let you push me aside, Fergus." She swung away and moved off across the yard.

Footsteps hurried behind her and Fergus called out, "Come on, Gilly. Be reasonable. Look, I'll make it up to you, OK. Wait, please." He followed her into the garden and closed the door, leaning against it as if to prevent her escape. "I don't want us to fall out and there's no point involving the boss, can't you see that? What's the problem? All we have to do is come to an agreement between ourselves. If I need Dean urgently, then you agree and if you need him urgently, then..." He opened his hands and spread them wide for emphasis. "Fair enough?"

"What happens if we both need him urgently – like this morning? What happens then?"

"We toss for him."

"What?"

Fergus laughed and fished a euro coin out of his pocket. "I'll let you make the call. Do you want the one euro side or the harp side?"

Gilly hesitated. "Do you seriously mean if I win this toss, you will give Dean back immediately?"

"Sure. I'm a man of my word. You know that." An innocent gleam in his hazel eyes made her wonder if he was joking. Hard to tell with Fergus. "Go on. Choose."

"OK... well, I suppose... I'll have the harp. And don't try to fix the result – I'm watching you like a hawk."

He spun the coin into the air and let it drop on the grass. They both dived for it but Gilly grabbed the euro and held it up, triumphant.

"I win, Fergus."

Fergus shrugged. "All right, I give in. I'll tell Dean to get back to the garden straight away." He smiled down at her. "Friends again? Hey, why don't you come with me to see my father tonight? It's Friday night and I'm going to drop in and see him before I go out. He'd love to meet you. I told him all about the work you're doing in the garden."

"How far away is the place?"

"Only about a half hour drive. Green Glades Nursing Home. Will you come?"

She considered his invitation. To be fair, he was the one who suggested a compromise about Dean. Perhaps she owed him something and she'd mentioned before that she would like to meet his father.

She nodded. "OK, I'll come. You'll have to wait until after five o'clock and we can give Dean a lift to the bus on the way."

"You're a darling." Fergus pressed the euro coin into her palm. "Here, take this and buy yourself some sweets."

*

Fergus's father, his legs wrapped in a tartan rug, lay back in the wheelchair which his son had parked in a window of the day room. Outside a vast cedar sheltered a circle of wooden benches, surrounded by a striped lawn dotted with evergreen shrubs.

Fergus chatted about the sun, the blue sky, told him what a lovely evening it was and that spring had finally arrived.

"The damn weather," he muttered to Gilly. "That's all I can talk about these days – so difficult to know what to say to him."

She found it hard to make conversation also. What could you say to someone who rarely replied? He just stared at his hands, lying limp on the cheerful squares of the blanket across his knees. Pale, freckled hands, with purple veins.

"He's thinner – even in the last week he's got thinner," said Fergus. "Dad, this is Gilly. Remember I told you about her? She's renovating the garden at Glanesfort."

The pale blue eyes slowly moved to her face and Fergus's father stared at her.

"That's right." She tried to sound cheerful. "It's fun – a big challenge. We're making a pool at the moment."

Fergus fell silent and gazed across the vast lawn.

"I'm going to plant water lilies in the pool." Gilly decided to keep talking. "And it'll have goldfish. The owner of Glanesfort has a little son who loves the thought of goldfish swimming in the pool."

The old man nodded again. His cheekbones protruded and when he smiled his mouth twisted to one side. Fergus had explained about his stroke on the drive over to the nursing home.

"She's been working hard," Fergus said.

His father beckoned with a scrawny finger and Fergus leaned close to his face. "What's that, Dad?"

Perhaps talking about plants caught his attention, rekindled his love of gardening.

Fergus sounded a little desperate when he continued, "Yes, she's the one I was telling you about. It's a fine place, Dad, Glanesfort is a fine house. You'll have to see it one day... maybe in the summer when you're feeling stronger. Gilly might have finished the garden by then. I could wheel you around it."

His father looked up, a flicker of interest in his eyes, but his head fell forward again as if the effort of holding it up was too much for him.

A care assistant with *Joan* printed on the badge pinned to her white tunic approached them.

"Time for bed, Frank." She bent to look the old man in the eye and pat his arm.

Fergus shot her an angry look and squeezed his father's thin hand. "I have to go, Dad. I'll come again soon. You look after yourself, won't you? Don't let Joan bully you too much."

The care assistant giggled. "He's a naughty son, isn't he, Frank? Bully you, indeed. As if..."

The room felt suffocatingly hot and Gilly glanced around at the residents seated in armchairs, reading or staring into space. The heat drained her energy and she yawned.

"We'll go," said Fergus, standing up. "I'll be back on Sunday, Dad. Mind yourself."

"He's fine with me, aren't you, Frank?" The woman leaned to straighten his father's rug. "Oh, Fergus, by the way, Hope is looking for you. If you wait on the terrace outside, I'll ask her to come out to you."

As they walked down the corridor towards the front door, Fergus told Gilly how long years of coping with an invalid had taken their toll on his mother. So had the job she'd taken to pay the fees of the nursing home when his father became too much for her to handle. She hated having to make that decision.

"Packing in a canning factory was exhausting for someone of her age," he said. "She would come home worn out, often too tired to eat. The fight went out of her. Dad spent ten years in and out of hospital before we decided to put him in a home."

"It's very sad, Fergus – must be terrible when he was such a keen gardener. Is it seriously expensive to keep him here?"

"It's cheaper than the ones in Dublin. Green Glades was once a private house, which is why we liked it. It has several acres of garden. Come with me and I'll show you the terrace around the corner."

As they stepped up onto the flagstones, Fergus pointed at a plastic table and chairs. They sat down. The evening sun felt warm and Gilly breathed fresh air into her lungs. It was good to get out of the stuffy room.

"It amuses me that the manager's name is Hope." Fergus took out his cigarettes and lit one. "They hate me smoking here, but they can't stop me outside. Yeah, Hope and I get on well and at least she's amusing."

"Probably essential if you work here."

"Yeah, I guess so." He frowned and lapsed into silence, inhaled another drag from his cigarette and leaned back to blow smoke rings into the rapidly cooling air. The sun slipped behind a copse of tall conifers.

Gilly shivered. A woman in a navy blue uniform made her way up the steps towards them. She had bright red lipstick and blonde hair swept back into a tight bun at the nape of her neck. She smiled at Fergus, who introduced them, and held out her hand.

"I'll leave you alone." Gilly stood up to walk away.

Fergus frowned. "It's all right, don't go." He turned to the manager. "How's my father?"

Hope's smile faded. "Not well, I'm afraid. He has gone down a lot since Christmas."

"Yeah, he's wasting away."

Gilly strolled down the steps to give him some privacy. Poor Fergus. He obviously loved his father very much. She moved away quickly towards the Land Rover; she had no wish to hear any more.

He joined her five minutes later and unlocked the doors. He drove in silence down the avenue and out onto the road.

"I'm sorry," Gilly murmured.

He kept his eyes firmly fixed on the road ahead.

"It must be very hard for you to see him like that – to see him deteriorate."

Still Fergus said nothing.

She sighed and fell silent.

When they reached the outskirts of Kildare town, he suddenly turned to her and grinned. "Hey, how about we get something to eat? I know just the place – cheap and cheerful."

He took her to a wine bar. It looked like it had once been a cellar, with arched walls painted white and tiny windows framed with muslin.

Fergus ordered a bottle of wine and the waitress poured them both a glass. They ate steak and chips while Gilly told Fergus about her plans for the garden. He listened half-heartedly.

Candles glowed above red and white check tablecloths, sending shadows dancing across the ceiling.

"My father seemed a bit tired today," he said. "Hope is quite pessimistic. Hey, that sounds a bit weird, doesn't it? Hope being pessimistic."

"How horrible for your father to be stuck in a wheelchair. What does he do all day?"

"Waits for his next meal, I suppose. Hope says the new nurse has been reading to him and he loves it. A book she found about gardening. Doing up an old garden or something. I forget what it's called."

"Maybe it's the one about the old Irish gardens that were restored. If it is, it's a good one. It must be a strain for you, seeing him like that, not being able to do anything for him."

"I do my best. I go and talk to him. I bring chocolates, he likes them, and I read to him."

She smiled. Fergus must really love his dad. She knew several people who had put parents into a nursing home and then almost forgotten about them. Left the staff to take over their care.

"It must be terrible for your mother, too," said Gilly. "Does she still have to work?"

"Sure does. Between us, we just about manage to scrape enough together to pay for Dad, though it's not easy." He looked around the room, which had filled up since their arrival.

A woman sat at the next table, wearing a short black dress and lace-up boots to her knees, and he cast an appreciative glance at her. "Will we get another bottle of wine?" he asked.

"OK, but we might need to order a taxi home. Have you always lived in Ireland? Your accent sounds... well, more English sometimes."

He pushed his hair out of his eyes. "We lived in London."

"How did you end up here?"

He shrugged. "My mother wanted to come back. She didn't like it over there, so when Dad had his stroke, we sold the house in London and moved here. It's cheaper to live here. Do you want a dessert? There's this amazing chocolate and ice-cream stuff."

He changed the subject and turned his attention to Gilly, asking her questions about her family. The work she'd done before the job at Glanesfort.

She plunged a spoon into the tall mound of ice cream. Should she mention Vanessa's wedding? Perhaps he would find something like that boring.

He yawned and helped himself to the rest of the wine. He'd

drunk most of the second bottle and his words were slightly slurred. "I'm tired. Sorry, it's nearly my bedtime. All that painting is wearing me out. Don't forget I get Dean tomorrow – all day."

It was half past eleven. "That's fine. I don't intend to work in the garden tomorrow. Alice has asked me to go with her to an antique fair. She doesn't get much time off and I thought it would be fun. Stefans will keep an eye on Sam."

"Poor Stefans. The boy's a handful."

"How long have you been employed by Marc?"

"A couple of years."

"But how did you end up working for him?"

"How do you end up working for anyone? Just happened to be him, that's all. I saw the ad on the agency website and applied for it."

"Did you enjoy living in London?"

"Yeah, when I was in my teens, I had all sorts of crazy dreams – you know the way we were at that age. I used to sing in a band with a friend down the road. We sometimes played at other guys' parties."

"I imagine you enjoyed that. What happened to the band?"

"When Dad became ill, my mother had to sell our house. We moved to a smaller house on the other side of London so I lost touch with the guys. We weren't that good – never going to be serious stars." He finished the coffee, pushed away the mug and stood up. "Yeah, London before then was great." He pulled out his wallet. "I'll pay for dinner."

She phoned for a taxi while he strolled up to the cash desk and produced his wallet. When they sat together on the back seat of the cab, he told her more about his band; how he'd played guitar and sung; how they'd composed their own songs.

"We had a following of teenage girls – maybe they were about fifteen. It was funny because we sounded so terrible... don't know what they saw in us."

Fergus chatted on about his friends in the band while the taxi swept them along the dark country road. He turned to grin at her as it swung in the gates, "You like Glanesfort, don't you? You're glad you came?"

"I was lucky to get this job."

The taxi driver stopped the car at the front of the house. She glanced up at it. The curtains were drawn and shutters closed; the only light was a glow from a window at the side of the house, which was Samuel's bedroom.

When they stepped out onto the gravel, the outside security light flicked on and caught them in a spotlight.

"It's like Fort Knox here," said Fergus, blinking, "with all the security Marc has."

"Let me pay for the taxi." Gilly handed over the cash and they stood together on the gravel. The cool night air embraced her. "Thanks, Fergus, I enjoyed the evening."

He placed his arm round her shoulders. "It was my pleasure. How about a nightcap? I've got a bottle of whiskey..."

"No, I'd better not." She moved away. "Thanks all the same, but I should get some sleep."

He followed her, put his hands on her shoulders and turned her round to face him. "What's the matter? Just a quick drink – I thought you would like that and then..." He bent to kiss her.

Gilly stepped back. "Look, I've really enjoyed myself but I can't... I need my sleep tonight, honest. I'm tired."

"Anything wrong? I thought we were getting on well."

"We were... are. I mean, I'm tired, Fergus, I..."

"OK, no problem. I just thought... another time, maybe?" He reached out and brushed the tip of a finger along her cheek. "Sleep well, sweetie pie. I'll see you tomorrow."

He moved away without offering to walk her back to her cottage, but perhaps it was just as well that he didn't. She headed off towards the dark copse of trees. If she decided to invite him to Vanessa's wedding, she would have to make it clear that he was just a companion, nothing else. She'd have to be careful about that. She still had a month to make up her mind so would say nothing for the time being.

The path through the wood lay in shadow ahead of her. She took out her mobile and switched on the flashlight app, directing it at her feet. The last thing she wanted was to trip over a branch or a briar now and injure herself when there was no one about. She remembered Marc asking if she was lonely in the cottage. No, not lonely, but she felt a tingle run up the back of her neck as this was the first time she'd walked back so late at night. Branches overhead obscured most of the pale light from a crescent moon.

She reached the clearing with a wave of relief and stood on the bank to look out over the lake.

The water sucked and slapped at the wooden posts of the deck and the moon hung over the tree tops on the opposite shore, where silver trunks of birch shimmered among the beech trees.

Her eyes slid down to the fishing platform and her heart leapt inside her, pounding furiously.

A white figure stood on the end of the stone jetty.

Gilly ran towards the front door, her shaking fingers fumbling with the key. She pushed the door open and slammed it behind her. Her pulse racing, she flicked on the light and leaned against the wall.

What was the matter with her? Had too much wine brought on this surge of panic? Surely, she must be imagining that pale form?

She crept to the window and peeped out. The black lake gleamed and clouds surrounding the moon glowed with a translucent light. The calmness of the night mocked her thumping heart.

She forced herself to look towards the stone jetty and saw nothing but the shaded empty pier. The figure had vanished.

Chapter 18

"The fox ate Anna's duck," said Samuel, raising worried brown eyes to Gilly's face.

"That's terrible," she replied. "Who's Anna?" The name sounded vaguely familiar.

She and the boy were on their hands and knees, red bricks piled around them on the dark, crumbly earth. Samuel dug holes with a hand trowel nearby while she firmed the surface of a trench mixed with sand and gravel before placing a brick along the length of string that marked the edge of the path.

He slowed her down, delayed progress, but she was learning patience. He enjoyed helping her and she had given him his own little patch of ground beside the potting shed. His eyes lit up with excitement when she suggested it and showed him how to draw a line in the earth to sow seeds. Already some of his radish seedlings had appeared. She appreciated the fact that he seemed to like her and that he wanted to learn how to grow plants.

"Anna lives in a cottage with a cat. Fergus said he saw the fox running away." Samuel smudged soil across his face as he scratched his forehead.

Dean had lifted all the original bricks along the existing paths the previous week and had left them ready for re-laying.

She sat up, wondering where he was, and spotted him by the east-facing wall, preparing a bed for the soft fruit bushes.

Gilly closed her eyes and felt the warmth of the sun on her face. So good after the long, wet winter. The sky was pale blue, cloudless. She could see a glint of silver high above, a jet, white lines trailing behind it.

Dean walked towards them, one sleeve of his denim shirt rolled up, the other buttoned down at his wrist. The tattoo on his left arm, the one with the sleeve rolled up, was a spider's web, which looked horribly realistic.

Samuel's eyes filled with interest when he saw it and, when Dean stood beside them, he asked where the spider was. Dean lifted his sleeve to reveal a black widow near his armpit and the boy jumped back in alarm.

Dean grinned. "Don't be scared, it's not real, though it is the correct size."

Samuel moved closer and reached out to touch the spider with his fingers.

"I like black widows," said Dean. "They're not as terrifying as people think. I watched this documentary on the television and they only bite when attacked."

"I thought they were deadly," Gilly said.

"Not always – only to small kids and old people. So don't ever sit on one, Sam."

"What's on the other arm?" Gilly asked.

"Nothing." Dean glanced away.

"Then why don't you roll up both your sleeves?"

A dark, sulky expression came over his face. "Don't want to, that's why."

At least his language had improved. He made an effort in front of Samuel, who he seemed to like.

"Is there another spider?" asked the boy. "Can I see, Dean? Please, please, let me see."

"No."

Samuel didn't give up easily. "I'll give you a sweet if you show me."

"You haven't got any sweets." Dean pulled a face at him, rolled his eyes and stuck out his tongue.

The boy laughed. "Fergus is bringing me sweets. I'll give you the black jelly ones I hate."

While they bargained, Gilly looked at the time on her mobile phone. Almost one o'clock. Another hour before meeting Marc to go to the mill. Her pulse quickened at the thought of seeing him again.

When she looked around, Dean was pushing up his other sleeve. She watched, as enthralled as Samuel as he exposed a long, snakelike scar, paler than his white skin, with small even marks where the stitches had once been.

"Dean!" she cried out. "What is that?"

Samuel's brown eyes widened. "It's not a spider."

"Satisfied?" Dean quickly rolled the sleeve down again and fastened the button. He nodded at the boy. "You owe me two sweets, Sam. Don't forget."

"How did you get that?" asked Gilly.

He frowned, eyebrows meeting at the top of his thin nose. "An accident. What'll I do next?"

She recognised that look, the stubborn tilt of his chin. Something he didn't want to talk about.

"The fruit bushes have to go in next. I'll help you, but I have to go in fifteen minutes." She and the boy followed him along the path, where the soil had dried out in the sun. She held the plants upright while he shovelled the earth into the trench. "How's your sister, Dean?"

"Back in rehab."

"Oh, I didn't realize... sorry."

"I never said." He pressed his lips together, rolled his eyes.

"And now her married boyfriend's wife wants him back because they have three kids. She has a savage temper. I reckon my sister better stay in rehab or the wife will kill her – that's if Nan doesn't kill her first."

Samuel stared at him and turned worried eyes to Gilly, who laughed, put her arm round his shoulders and gave him a quick hug.

"Don't listen to him, Sam," she said. "He's only joking, aren't you, Dean?" Better to tell a lie than frighten the boy.

Dean nodded and looked away.

*

Gilly sat on the steps at the front of the house, drinking the coffee Alice had made her. She'd changed into a clean pair of jeans and a cream cotton jumper embroidered with pink and blue flowers. It had a small hole in the back, which Marc mightn't notice. Her freckles had multiplied in the sun and she wondered if she should put on some make-up to cover them up but decided against it.

A book lay beside her on the limestone slabs. Of course he was probably still in Dublin and might have forgotten about her and the mill.

She need not have worried because the BMW swept up the drive five minutes later and he stepped out of the car. He glanced at his watch.

"I stayed in Dublin last night," he said. "I've only just got back because the traffic coming out of the city was terrible. I think there was a crash on the M7."

She stood up. "It's OK – I've only been here for a few minutes."

Where had he stayed the night? In a hotel? Or perhaps he had stayed with friends? She knew so little about him and the world in which he lived and worked.

She held out the book. "Would you like to borrow this? It's the one about a family renovating a Victorian flower garden."

He smiled. "Thank you. I suppose you hope I might learn something." He held the car door open for her and she got in. "I like reading," he said as he sat beside her.

"Good. Where is the mill, Marc?"

He started the engine. "About fifteen minutes the other side of Monasterevin, near the river."

"Did your meeting on Friday go well?"

"Quite well, I suppose. I met someone who might buy a house I own in Raglan Road. He turned out to be someone I was in school with – a strange coincidence."

She looked out of the window. A light breeze fluttered through the hedgerows and yellow patches of primroses peeped from grassy banks. Seed heads of clematis moulted among the briars. Old Man's Beard, a good name for it.

Ten minutes later, they reached the town and Marc drove down the main street and across the metal suspension bridge over the canal. He nodded to the right. "Have you noticed the aqueduct? They built that in 1826 to take the canal over the Barrow River."

Gilly stared at it. "That would have been a huge undertaking in those days."

He swung right at a T-junction. "The mill we're going to see was built a bit earlier, around the turn of the century."

"You seem to know a lot about the area," she said.

"Not as much as I should." He glanced at her. "You're looking well. You've got a suntan since I last saw you."

To her embarrassment, she felt herself blush. "Thanks. The weather improved while you were in London." Damn! Now she was back onto the weather again. "Are we nearly there?"

He looked at her again, a glimmer of amusement in his eyes. "Don't you like compliments? Another few minutes, that's all.

Are you finding it easier to sleep in the cottage?"

She assured him that it was fine, just what she wanted. "It's a change from Dublin – very quiet. I no longer get woken up by the sound of traffic and sirens in the streets."

"So you're getting used to being on your own?"

"Alice has been to see me a few times and Fergus has dropped in."

"Are you and Fergus getting on all right? No rows, I hope."

He made them sound like children, like squabbling children. "No, he's been... been helpful."

"Good."

"Marc..." She hesitated. She'd kept it to herself for three days. She had to tell someone and it might as well be him. Perhaps he would have a more rational solution than Fergus.

"Yes?"

"There's a woman... a woman down at the lake."

He shot her a quick look. "Someone fishing?"

"Maybe... I don't know but I saw her at strange times. Do people fish at dawn and after dark?"

He said nothing for a few minutes and she wondered whether she should repeat the question. She opened her mouth and he glanced at her again. "What did she look like, this woman?"

She tried to sound casual. "Oh, it's quite a long way across so it's hard to tell, but she looked... well, she looked pale."

"Pale? You mean pale as in ill?"

"No, no. Pale, white... dressed all in white."

Another silence while he negotiated a narrow road along the side of the river.

"Long white hair... unless it was a scarf... I don't know for sure," Gilly added.

"Anyone else see this woman?"

"No, I was on my own. Do you think I imagined her? She was standing on the jetty, on the fishing platform opposite the cottage."

"Standing there early in the morning and after dark?"

"And she disappeared minutes later. I mean, she went into the wood behind the lake. Have you ever heard anyone else mention her?"

He frowned. "We've already talked about the local story of the woman who drowned in the lake, but I don't believe that's what you saw. I can see this has worried you."

"Not really. I'm not afraid of ghosts."

"I don't believe in ghosts, Gilly. You saw a shadow, perhaps – a trick of the light."

She should never have mentioned it because he obviously thought she'd imagined it. She clasped her hands together, twisting her fingers in her lap.

"Or perhaps someone fishing, wearing light clothes," he said.

"I thought that too – the first time."

He drove down a lane and, after a few more minutes, he stopped the car. "If you're nervous about the cottage and the fact that it's so isolated – and it is isolated – maybe you'd like to stay in the house with us. We've several spare bedrooms and..."

"You think I'm making it up."

"No, but I can tell you've been frightened by something."

"I'm not frightened. I knew I shouldn't have mentioned it to you. I thought you might come up with a sensible solution, that's all."

"I'm sorry I don't have a sensible solution. Tell you what, though, next time you see this woman, you call me. I'll give you my mobile number. Give me a call and, if I'm at home, I'll come and have a look."

"OK. Thank you." Time to change the subject. "Are we here?"

He pointed in front of them. "There's a lane that leads to the mill. You can see it over by those trees. I know it's a bit far from the town, but I'm sure people would come to visit a business out here if it was attractive enough. The owner would like to turn it into a small hotel."

Gilly squinted in the sunshine and saw a three-storey stone building rising above a hedge, more like a warehouse than a mill, iron bars in the top windows. Gaps yawned in the slate roof.

They walked down the lane together. Marc stopped when they came to a wooden stile, overgrown with brambles, covered in lichen, and turned to her. "Be careful here. I nearly fell the last time... it's slippery." He climbed over. "This side is worse. Mind that rotten plank."

She took the hand he offered and jumped down beside him. "Thanks."

He stood for a moment, looking into her eyes, then let go of her hand and walked on. Ivy crept up trunks of trees that surrounded the mill and a low wall had tumbled down in a few places, with piles of stones covered in moss. Marc opened a gate and they went in.

"I'll show you the mill first and then you can take a look at the landscaping side of things."

She followed him, going into the shadow of the enormous building. It was colder out of the sun. A solid oak door, studded with metal, stood before them and she reached out to lift the latch.

"It'll be locked," said Marc. "It always is. The owner gave me a key as he has gone abroad for a few months." As he spoke, she pushed the door open. "That's odd. It's always been locked before."

A chill hung on the air inside where no heat from the sun penetrated the thick walls. Windows threw small patches of light across the flagstones, like patchwork.

"Imagine having to work in this place nearly two centuries ago. It must have been terrible, so dark and spooky," Gilly said.

"Yes, not a pleasant place to work. Shall we go up the stairs?"

The stone steps wound up to the right and disappeared into darkness. Gilly saw vast cobwebs laden with dust and imagined rats scuttling across rotten floorboards; she hesitated but didn't want him to think she was afraid. She followed him up the stairs, keeping one hand on the wall.

A long corridor at the top stretched down the centre of the mill, with wooden doors on either side. Marc rattled several handles.

He turned to her. "All locked. What do you think of it?"

"It's... well, it's kind of creepy, isn't it? I don't know. I suppose you'd have to knock down the interior and start again."

He raised his eyebrows, amused. "You don't like it?"

"Not really. I find it hard to imagine it as a hotel but you would know more about its potential than me."

As they descended, she noticed a few of the steps were crumbling at the edges, worn to a shine by the feet of workers long ago.

Outside again, she saw no sign of any previous garden, just a field grazed by sheep. Gilly paced out the area, making mental notes, imagining pathways and groups of shrubs and trees. Marc listened to her comments, seeming interested, asking questions, his alert brain ticking over. She suggested a water garden because of it being close to the river.

"Maybe you could have a path lined with lavender on the way to the water garden, if you wanted to keep it simple. Or how about a walk of pleached limes?"

He nodded.

"I'll draw something for you, if you like."

"Thank you." He moved towards the gate. "That would be helpful."

Gorse bushes sheltered one corner of the field, with their almond-scented flowers a blaze of yellow.

"Let's sit down here for a minute," he suggested. "Have you got time?"

"Yes." She glanced at her mobile. She'd left instructions with Dean to finish planting the fruit bushes. That would keep him busy for the rest of the afternoon. No text messages from him so he must be getting on all right.

She sat beside him, leaning against the wall. He removed his jacket and tie, which he folded beside him on the grass.

Gilly closed her eyes as the heat from the stones warmed her back. A thrush trilled from the branches of a beech tree on their left, pure notes floating on the air. The sun was calming, soothing and she yawned.

She was aware of his presence even with her eyes shut, could visualize him with his shirt sleeves rolled up to the elbow, the light hair on his arms. After a long silence, she opened her eyes and saw that he lay back on the grass, relaxed, almost as if asleep.

A kestrel hung in the sky high above them, motionless except for its quivering wings. Hunting something, it had a victim in its sights. A field mouse or a vole, perhaps.

Gilly yawned again. The heat diminished her shyness with him. She picked a blade of grass and, on impulse, tickled his mouth with it.

Marc flicked at his face with a hand and sat up.

"I was just trying to make you smile," she said.

He laughed. "You must think me very serious."

"Not now that I know you better." She looked up at him as he leaned over her. The faint scar stretched from his right eyebrow towards his ear and she wanted to run her finger along it and ask him how he'd got it. Such expressive eyes, the way they lit up when he smiled. Eyes that, when they focused on her, made her feel special somehow.

"Ah, so you used to think so." He took her face in his hands.

An annoying blush rushed to her cheeks. She didn't reply.

Very slowly, he bent to kiss her. His lips briefly brushed hers before he lay back on the grass. "That's for making me smile. I think you're a breath of fresh air at Glanesfort. Sam told me all about the little patch of garden you gave him. He's very excited about it. So thank you also for that. It's kind of you to make friends with my lively son."

She swallowed hard. "He's a sweet boy – I thought it would keep him busy."

"He has taken to you. He often talks about you. Are you happy at Glanesfort, Gilly? Do you like the place?"

"Yes, of course. It's a beautiful house and the garden is interesting... a challenge."

He turned his head to look at her. "I would like you to tell me if there are any problems. I don't just mean about the figure you saw at the lake."

"What other problems are you expecting?"

"Perhaps I'm imagining things, but I sometimes worry that my charming manager – although very good at handling the tenants – can be a..." He hesitated and shrugged. "Perhaps you get on well with Fergus?"

"We get on fine."

"Good. It's relaxing here, isn't it? It's not often I get a chance to..." He let out a deep breath. "I have so little time. I expect you think I'm rich and have everything I want in life. Most people do."

Was he teasing her?

"Well?" he asked. "What do you think? I'd like your opinion." He raised himself up on one elbow and gazed intently at her.

"People don't always know what it's like to run a business," she said carefully. "I don't find it easy, especially these days when the banks are so reluctant to lend money. I'm sure you find it more difficult than others believe."

"You're right. You understand me, Gilly. Not many people do. I can imagine how hard it has been for you too. I've heard of several landscapers in Dublin who have gone out of business, the ones who over-stretched themselves and had nothing to fall back on when the property developers went bankrupt and couldn't pay them."

She nodded. "Yes, I was nearly one of them. I couldn't pay my rent, but my sister helped me out. She doesn't understand my business, but at least she gave me a bed. She has a good job and is getting married on the seventeenth of April. She asked me if I'd like to bring someone." The words were out of her mouth before she could stop them.

He glanced at her. "Have you got someone to bring?" He added, "I hope you don't think that's a rude question."

"No, I haven't – and no, I don't."

He glanced at his watch and rose to his feet. "I'd better go. There's a marketing conference... I told Alice I would be back in time for the afternoon break." He held out a hand and helped her up, touching her shoulder for a moment.

She could feel the weight of his hand even after he removed it, the pressure of his fingers.

"I want us to be friends," he said.

She found it difficult to calm that fluttering birdlike creature inside her rib cage. "OK, I'd like to be friends."

They were silent as they walked back to the stile. Gilly watched the sunlight on the back of his head, a few silver streaks in his brown hair.

He stopped and turned round. "I'll come, if you like."

"What?"

"To your sister's wedding. Only if you'd like me to, of course."

She hesitated, checked his expression to see if he was joking. Would he really want to come to a wedding with her? Her family wedding when he had no idea what her relatives were like?

"What do you think?" he asked. "It would be a chance for us to get to know each other. I'd like that."

She reached out and gripped his arm. "Oh yes, that would be great. Thank you. I hope you know what you're letting yourself in for. My family is... well, a bit weird."

He laughed, put his arm round her waist and helped her climb the style. "All families are a bit weird. I hope I don't have anything else on, but I'll check that date and let you know." He glanced again at his watch. "Look at the time! Alice will have something to say to me."

*

The dining room hummed with conversation. The air was stuffy, filled with loud laughter, the smell of food and clatter of forks on plates.

Marc found Alice laying out teacups on a table beside the kitchen door.

"Marc, there you are. Where have you been?" She brushed grass from his back with her hand. "Just look at your jacket. What have you been doing?"

"I went for a walk and I sat down for a rest in the sunshine."

She gave him a sharp look. "The managing director is looking for you." Alice nodded towards an overweight man with a flushed face. "He's over there. By the way, Michael rang from the office. He couldn't get you on your mobile and I told him the signal is appalling here. He said to tell you that Mr Fukuda sent an email and it's good news. He's coming to London. Have I got his name right?"

"Yes, yes, Mr Fukuda. That is more than good news, Alice." This meant that their office building was still in the running, a great relief. He could trust his accountant to help him with this as Michael knew his way around places like Japan, Hong Kong and

Shanghai; Marc would ask him to help entertain the Japanese team.

He made his way through the crowd and introduced himself to the managing director. He listened to his comments, the compliments mixed with complaints; the food was great but a pity about the slide projector, which had broken down halfway through the morning. A young man had obligingly fixed it.

That must have been Fergus. Gilly might not have understood what he meant when he mentioned Fergus, but he hoped she had the sense to be careful. It bothered him to think of Gilly with Fergus. Marc thought of her lying on the grass, her bright smile, the small, determined mouth. Even the hole in the back of her jumper was somehow endearing.

The man beside him chatted on about marketing, the successful strategy the company adopted. Spreading the word, he said, that was what was important.

It had taken months to fall in love with Rachel when they were students together in Cambridge and she was keener on teasing him than thinking about romance. She'd make a beautiful bride, his mother assured him, with her wavy blonde hair and dark eyes. Like pools of chocolate, he used to tell her and that always made her laugh. She mocked him and called him a French romantic.

Rachel hadn't been in a hurry to get married, in spite of his mother. Nine years together before they became man and wife in that registry office in her home city of Bristol. She focused on her career, of course, and Rachel's career had meant a lot to her. Competitive, she was always competitive. I'll race you to the top, she used to say, let's see who gets there first. She liked high-flying clients who achieved wealth and success. She might still be alive if she'd adopted a less ambitious approach.

"Mr Fletcher?"

Marc looked up and saw the managing director frowning at him. "I'm sorry?"

"Are you booked up in May? We might consider holding another conference."

"I'll have to check and let you know." He moved back towards Alice. He still missed Rachel. Her confidence had inspired him. Gilly didn't have the same confidence, but she was brave. He knew that already. Why else would she take on the garden? Why else would she agree to live alone in the cottage by the lake, in spite of whatever it was she'd seen or imagined?

Recently he'd noticed that his memories of Rachel were fading. Harder to remember the way she spoke, the exact shade of her hair, the touch of her skin against his.

Yes, Gilly fascinated him with her quick sense of fun and her mixture of determination and vulnerability. She might be the one he'd been waiting for. The woman who would finally help him move on. Gilly wasn't impressed by his wealth, he knew and liked that. In that field, near the mill, with the sun on her face and the scent of gorse around them, he'd felt a strong desire to take her in his arms and assure her that he would love and protect her if she would allow him. She was a kindred spirit and, although at very different levels, their businesses were similar. He sensed in her the same creative spark, the same urge to transform an old building, or in her case a garden, to design something that would complement and enrich the past. There was a physical attraction, of course, but he felt more than that. Much more.

But he would have to tread carefully. There was still that other matter. He couldn't begin to explain about his past just yet. He couldn't drag her into that. She liked him, though, and was drawn to him, too, of that he was certain.

"Why are you smiling like that?" Alice patted his arm. "You look... what's the word... absorbed."

"Do I? Let's have a cup of coffee, Alice – you need a break."

"Don't worry about me. I'm as strong as an ox. The principal from Samuel's playschool phoned five minutes ago. I would have told you earlier, but you were talking to the managing director."

"What did she want?"

"She didn't say, but she wants you to call her. Quite urgent, she said." Alice frowned. "I hope Samuel's been behaving and is not in trouble. Do you remember when he hit that girl on the..."

"I'll ring her immediately." Marc moved through the crowd and out into the hall. He pulled back the oak door and walked onto the steps. He sat on a wooden seat to the left of the macrocarpa and selected the principal's number.

She answered immediately and he introduced himself.

"Marc, thank you for calling me so promptly. A little problem."

His heart sank. What had the boy been doing now? "Problem?"

"Yes, but I hope it's nothing – just had to check with you, let you know. It happened at eleven o'clock break when the children were out in the playground."

Samuel had punched some child, that was what she was going to say. Only last week he'd been reprimanded for pushing another boy out of his way.

"Mary and I were helping a girl – little Jennifer had fallen over and grazed both knees and was distraught, poor child. We didn't see the woman until after we had coped with Jennifer, I'm afraid."

"The woman?" he repeated slowly. "What woman?"

"She was standing by the railings on the road and talking to him. Must have been for only a few minutes because Jennifer was soon up and running about again... yes, only perhaps for five minutes... or ten at the most."

"What woman?" Alarm rose inside him and he gripped the mobile tightly in his hand. "Who was she?"

"We don't know because she moved off as soon as we approached and Samuel said he had never seen her before. She had long blonde hair and a red knitted hat. A long coat and boots... yes, I think boots. Quite the hippy, Mary said. I'd never seen her before either. Does she sound familiar to you?"

"Long blonde hair? I can't think of anyone like that who would know Samuel."

"Yes, very long and... well, yes, very blonde, almost white, in fact." She cleared her throat. "We thought perhaps a friend of yours? Of course, she may not have known him. Perhaps he was telling the truth after all..."

Long white hair? The woman Gilly mentioned, the mysterious figure at the lake...

"Samuel said she asked him about the school and what time he went home. She had a little boy of her own, she told him, and she wanted to send the boy to the school, but Marc, if that was really the case, why didn't she wait to talk to me about it? We need to take this sort of... um... event very seriously these days. I never encourage the children to talk to strangers. We strictly forbid it, in fact."

His mind clicked into action. "Right, thank you for telling me this. I think, if you don't mind, I will come to collect Samuel right away. I'd like to question him before he forgets about this woman. Thank you again for letting me know."

Chapter 19

Gilly and Dean sat side by side as they ate their sandwiches, leaning against the broken frame of the old greenhouse. They'd removed the glass and were waiting for a carpenter before any more progress could be made.

Marc always rose unbidden in her thoughts these days. She would be thinking of something else: the hostas or the plants in the pool – whether they looked like they were settling in – and Marc would appear in her mind. Sometimes serious, sometimes smiling and other times leaning over her and kissing her. Almost a week had passed and, although he'd been around the garden with her, checking her progress and listening to suggestions, he hadn't mentioned the wedding. Perhaps he'd discovered a more important engagement in his diary and didn't know how to explain that to her. She would have to pluck up the courage and ask him.

Dean yawned and stared up at the sky.

If he was free to go, what then? She considered this option with alternate waves of pleasure and panic. Of course she shouldn't encourage him too much, should avoid getting involved with her boss and putting her job at risk. She would have to emphasize that it was just a bit of fun.

"What do you want to do next?" Dean asked.

"I don't know, the rest of the hostas, I suppose. We should plant them today in the pool garden. We also need to plant more of the *Iris sibirica* at the edge of the water. I think they'll look good there, with their grassy foliage and purple-blue flowers. I've promised Sam he can help me choose the goldfish when the time comes."

She pushed at the soil with a stick.

Dean took a mobile phone out of his pocket and stared at the screen.

"Where did you get that? Is it new?" she asked.

"Yeah. Bought it with my wages."

"I hope you're not squandering all your money on fancy phones." Listen to her talking. As if she knew how to save money. Poor Dean was entitled to buy himself something nice.

"No." His face looked red, sunburnt. The country air was doing him good, making him less defensive and tense.

She glanced at him. Both sleeves of his shirt were down, covering his arms. "Where did you get that scar, Dean? Can't you tell me?"

He twirled the Marlboro packet in his fingers. "I was knifed."

"Oh my God! Who by?"

Silence.

"I won't tell anyone, Dean. I'm just curious, that's all."

He hesitated. "My father..." Another long pause. "He gets drunk... violent."

"Your father did that to you? I hope you reported him."

"He's... he's been inside... but not for this." He looked down and poked the soil with his cigarette packet.

"Do you mean he's in prison? Is that it?"

"Yeah, he was... out now, worst luck. Nan keeps him away from us... he's afraid of her. If he comes near the house, she bolts the doors and threatens to call the cops."

162

"I can't imagine... Does Fergus know?"

He nodded.

"What did your father do?"

"Drugs."

She stared at him.

"He's an addict, like my sister. I don't want him coming down here causing trouble. He's like a crazy man sometimes. He was put away for... he robbed a corner shop one night and beat up the owner. Gilly, if you tell the boss..." His voice rose in panic.

"Dean, calm down. I've no intention of telling him – why would I?" She stared at him. "You should have told me before."

"Nah... you'd have thrown me out."

She said nothing. Perhaps he was right. If he'd mentioned it in the beginning, she would have used it as an excuse to get rid of him. Now... well, now she felt sorry for him and, she had to admit, she also liked him. She leaned against him, reached out and touched his hand, squeezed his stubby fingers for a second and turned away. "You can tell Fergus that I know about it, that it doesn't make any difference."

"Yeah?"

"We're not responsible for what our fathers do."

He smiled and watched her for a few minutes, as if considering something. "Do you like Fergus?"

"He's all right, he's amusing but he can be a bit ... a bit irritating."

He spoke slowly. "I... Gilly, I think you should be careful... that is, if you like him. He's got lots of other women."

She opened her mouth to speak, but the words lodged in her throat.

"I'm telling the truth, I swear," Dean muttered, as if afraid she didn't believe him.

"Lots of other women?"

"Yeah, that red-haired one for starters. Anna, who lives here. I've seen him... seen them."

"You said lots."

"Yeah, he's always boasting about how... how women fall for him. His... whatever you want to call it." He shrugged, glanced again at his phone. "Yeah, I swear to God I'm telling the truth. You needn't believe me if you don't want to."

"You mean while he's asking me out and flirting with me and..." She closed her eyes. He'd wanted her to stay the night on Friday. She imagined him laughing, his head thrown back and the smirk on his broad face. "I thought he liked me. Does he think I'm a complete fool?"

"Sorry," said Dean. "Maybe I shouldn't..."

"I might have known that he'd be like this."

He tapped the phone screen. "Yeah, well, that's Fergus. That's what he's like and I don't know what you're into, but I just thought I'd warn you."

"I'm glad you told me – and I do believe you. I definitely believe you." At least she hadn't encouraged Fergus; for that she was thankful. For once in her life, she'd had some sense that night and hadn't allowed herself to become yet another notch on his deeply scarred bedpost.

She glanced at Dean. "Thanks for telling me."

He smiled and the gate from the yard in the wall on their right swung open.

"Gilly, Gilly!" Samuel ran towards them, wearing a bright orange buoyancy aid.

"Hello, Sam."

He swung around. "Look at me! Daddy's gonna take me out in the boat."

His father approached, his feet crunching on the new gravel path. She glanced at Dean, who stared at his employer, a sulky look on his face.

Samuel caught his father's hand. "Can Gilly come, Dad? Can she come with us? You said..."

Marc's eyes held hers. "I'm going to teach him how to row and I was wondering if... Are you on your lunch break? Maybe you'd like to come with us? There's a small boat on the lake." He nodded at Dean. "Of course, if you're busy..."

Did she look busy? She jumped up. "Yes, I'd love to come, thank you. Dean, can you keep planting hostas, please. I'll be back in..."

"An hour," said Marc. "An hour will be enough. I'm sure you don't want me to distract you for too long."

Samuel skipped towards the gate, towing his father behind him, his voice high-pitched and excited. Dean remained seated on the ground and pushed his phone into his pocket.

"What's wrong?" she asked.

"Nothing."

"There is. You look... grumpy."

He got to his feet. "He fancies you, the boss."

"Don't be ridiculous."

"He does. I can tell by his eyes. He's always looking at you."

Heat rose to her cheeks and she turned away. "I'm not in his league."

Dean sighed. "Why would that matter to someone like him? I'll see you later. Don't fall in the lake and drown."

Samuel shouted at her from the gate, "Come on, come on, let's go."

Gilly caught up with Marc and the boy in the yard and walked with them to a door in a high wall that brought them out on the vast lawn at the back of the house. The grass felt springy under her feet, neatly mown by the local man on his ride-on. It swept down to the edge of the lake, which lay dark blue and dancing in the afternoon light. On the left, a small boathouse built of cut stone sheltered under branches, hidden from the house.

Marc pulled open the door and Gilly saw a red wooden dinghy bobbing on the water inside.

He turned to Samuel. "I forgot the picnic. Can you run back to the house and ask Alice for the sandwiches? And lemonade."

"Aw, Dad..."

"Go on, it won't take you long. Gilly and I will get the boat out."

The boy scampered back up the lawn and Marc sat on a wooden bench by the pier and patted it. "Come and sit beside me for a few minutes."

She sat down, leaving a space between them. He put his arm along the back of the bench, behind her shoulders.

"First of all, I apologize for taking so long to get back to you about your sister's wedding party."

She held her breath and glanced quickly at him.

"I've changed a few meetings around so now I am free to come... if you still want me to, that is."

"Of course. That's great, thank you so much." She heard the relief in her voice and hoped that he hadn't.

He looked at her, more serious now, and raised his eyebrows enquiringly. When she smiled at him, he inched closer on the seat, took her hand in his. "Now, about your white lady... the figure you saw at the lake."

"Oh that, forget about it... maybe you're right, maybe I imagined her. She hasn't been there this week."

He glanced away, out across the lake and, several minutes later, murmured, "I'd like you to let me know immediately if you see her again."

"Yes, of course – I said I would." She gave his fingers what she hoped was a reassuring squeeze.

They sat there holding hands for another five minutes while Gilly rested her head on his shoulder. The lapping water lulled her, made her feel almost drowsy and sitting there with him felt so natural, as if she had known him for years. Patches of the lake darkened where a slight breeze rippled the surface.

After a while, he let go of her hand and stood up. "Now let's get this boat ready before Samuel comes back."

He had to duck his head under the lintel of the boathouse and she followed him in. The door creaked shut behind them.

There wasn't much room on the stone platform and it was quite dark inside, their reflections glowing eerily white in the green water. Two figures close, almost touching. She turned her head and again he regarded her with a serious expression in his eyes.

"If I'm going to escort you to a wedding party, don't you think we should...?" His voice was no more than a whisper.

She smiled. It seemed completely natural when Marc gently took her face in his hands, leaned forward and put his lips to hers. She lifted her arms round his neck and held him close, their mouths joined in a soft, exploring kiss while her heart thumped against his. Any reservations she might have had vanished into the darkness.

Several minutes later, or perhaps longer, a voice called. It was Samuel. Marc moved away and knelt to undo a rope attached to a rusty iron ring set into the stone at their feet. Another call rang out, louder this time. He stood up.

"Tomorrow night," he murmured into her hair, "I'd love to take you out to dinner. Would you like that? I have to go to London early the next morning, but I've got some free time tomorrow."

She nodded. "But I just need to ask you something."

"What do you want to ask?"

"You haven't got any chic, sophisticated girlfriends in London, have you?"

"Chic and sophisticated? I can't think of any."

"Or maybe even poor, untidy ones? Or girlfriends of any sort?"

"None at all, last time I checked."

They both laughed and he put his hands on her shoulders, turned her round and guided her out the door where she almost collided with Samuel.

The boy stood on the lawn and frowned, his hands on his hips. A small basket of food and a bottle of Alice's homemade lemonade lay on the grass.

"What's so funny, Dad?"

Chapter 20

"Ready, darling?" asked their father and squeezed Vanessa's arm.

She pulled away. "Dad, not so hard, please! That hurts." She smoothed the ivory silk sleeve with a trembling hand.

Gilly sighed, glanced at the rows of backs waiting in the church and shot a sympathetic look at her sister. Outside the door an elderly couple, who'd arrived late, panted up the hill.

"So sorry, so sorry, dear," they muttered as they passed.

Helen, her sister's matron of honour, beamed encouragingly. "You OK, Ness?"

She nodded and forced a strained smile. Gilly examined Helen's navy silk suit. Everything in place, flowers in her short blonde hair, immaculate shoes.

Her sister faced the aisle again and said, "The distance to the altar rail seems to have doubled since the rehearsal two days ago. I can see Ken and his best man waiting, without even a backward glance to see if I've arrived. Aren't they laid back?"

"I'm sure they know you're here," Gilly said.

"Such a fuss about nothing," said their father, looking his watch. "The bride is supposed to be late, but really, Vanessa, it's now ten minutes... almost eleven, in fact."

"Did you check the flower arrangements, Helen? Nothing

drooping? I don't want anything to wilt in this heat. Mum said she'd go round and see before the service but she was so late."

"The flowers look fab." Gilly bit her bottom lip and warned herself not to jump to her mother's defence. This was Vanessa's big day; she should be excused a little stage fright.

"Thanks, they're just green and white – an expensive florist but worth it." Vanessa inhaled a few deep breaths as if to steady herself.

Hats bobbed along the seats as the guests chatted among themselves.

"Doesn't Dad look distinguished," said Vanessa, "in the grey morning coat he had made for the occasion?"

"Yes," said Gilly and hoped she sounded enthusiastic. He'd combed his short grey hair back from his face and trimmed his neat moustache.

"Come on." He was getting impatient. He was only four inches taller than Vanessa. He placed his arm through hers. "Let's get going."

He'd been irritable all morning and hadn't eaten much at lunch; grumbled about how long it took women to get dressed; snapped at Mum when she spent too long chatting to their aunt on the phone. Perhaps he was nervous, like the bride. Only their mother appeared calm.

Vanessa cast a final glance up the church. "Where did my boss end up? I hope she's got a good seat and can see how carefully and tastefully everything has been organized."

"I think I saw Ken seat her beside his cousin Harry," replied Gilly.

"What? Are you serious?"

"Joke."

"Not funny." Vanessa gave her a push. "Go on, go and sit down. I can't have you traipsing after me if you're not part of the bridal party. Where is Marc Fletcher? You said he was coming."

"Not till the party afterwards. He's got a meeting in Ballsbridge – about to sell an expensive three-storey house."

"I'm looking forward to being introduced to him. I just hope he won't get drunk and unruly."

Gilly suppressed a laugh because he was the last man on earth she could imagine behaving like that. She reached out and gave Vanessa a quick kiss on the cheek, breathed "good luck" into her ear and made her way up the aisle to find their mother.

She glanced back and heard her father say, "Let's go, Vanessa. Let's get this show on the road." He waved at a man near the altar who raised his hand as a signal to the organist. Music swelled to fill the church and they set off, her father nodding formally at people he knew while the bride stared resolutely in front, a fixed smile on her face.

Gilly slid into the pew beside her mother and kissed her powdered cheek. "Hi there, they're on their way." She admired aloud her mother's new suit and matching hat. Dove grey with a pink blouse and ribbon on the hat, matched with grey gloves. Her hair was pinned up on her head. "You look very stylish, Mum."

"Vanessa chose everything." Her mother looked down at her hands. "I don't know... do you think so? I feel a bit silly, really. Are you sure I look all right?"

Gilly edged closer to her. "You look great. Vanessa bought my navy suit, too. What would we do without her?" She stifled a laugh.

The air was heavy in the church, weighed down with the scent of lilies and a cloud of different perfumes. Humid weather had returned that morning, a leaden grey sky and no wind to dispel the heat.

Her mother's pale blue eyes seemed distant, as if her mind was miles away. Pink lipstick gleamed on her small mouth and she looked uncomfortable; perhaps her new clothes didn't quite fit.

"Vanessa's a bit nervous," she said. "Won't admit it, of course, but I know she's on edge. We've missed you, darling. Why don't you come home more often? We've hardly seen you since Christmas."

"I know – I'm sorry. I've been so busy. It's my job... takes up so much time."

"Oh, how is it going?"

"It's a big challenge, but I'm getting there."

The organist pounded on the keys and some of the congregation turned to catch a glimpse as Vanessa made her way up the aisle on their father's arm. Gilly had been to the hairdresser that morning. The wide-brimmed navy and cream hat hid most of her new hairstyle, but she would soon get rid of that. She looked forward to changing out of her rather tight cream jacket and navy skirt.

The bride and her father moved past their pew, Vanessa's slim figure in her ivory silk suit, a long straight skirt. She looked as stylish and elegant as always.

Gilly watched her sister link hands with Ken, noticed the intimate smiles that flashed between them. Tears sprang into her eyes and she looked at the floorboards; swallowed hard. Mum pulled out a tatty tissue, dabbed at her face and sniffed, as her father stepped into the pew beside her with a brief smile.

Her mother leaned over. "Doesn't she look lovely?" she murmured, pushing the tissue back into a pocket.

Gilly agreed.

"Ssh." Her father frowned at them and Gilly felt a familiar stab of irritation.

Her mind wandered off as the marriage ceremony began. Would Marc find the hotel? She hadn't seen him since they'd gone out to dinner seventeen days before. He'd flown back to London the next day, something to do with a Japanese company and his office block.

After dinner in a local Italian restaurant, they'd got a taxi back to Glanesfort and he'd walked with her to the cottage. She asked him in for coffee but he declined. He had a five o'clock start next morning with meetings all day in London so he had to get some sleep. He kissed her goodnight and, after she'd watched him stride off into the trees, she cast a quick glance towards the fishing platform on the other side of the lake. No one there.

He'd phoned her yesterday when his flight arrived back in Dublin, but he hadn't time to say much.

A little knot twisted in her stomach at the thought of seeing him again.

Her father stared ahead of him as Vanessa and Ken began their marriage vows. What was running through his mind? She hoped that he would keep his sharp tongue under control and make an effort today, this special day, with so many members of the family present. He never liked scenes in public, after all.

"Don't you think they make the most perfect couple?" she said softly to her mother.

Her father answered for her. "I couldn't have asked for a more suitable son-in-law."

*

Gilly sank into the cushions of a sofa in the hotel foyer. Nearly six o'clock. Would he be on time? What would she do if he didn't turn up? Of course he would turn up because she'd received a text only an hour before to say he was on his way. She had to get a grip and stop thinking like a giddy teenager. She fought back waves of panic and looked down at her black dress; one she'd found in a charity shop but it had a designer label and fitted perfectly. So much more comfortable than the suit. It cost her fifteen euro. A bargain. Thin straps stretched across her shoulders and a long row of tiny buttons ran down her back. She bought it because she thought it made her look thinner and more sophisticated.

She sipped her glass of champagne slowly and enjoyed the feeling of calm that crept over her.

The hands of the huge brass clock above the receptionist's desk crawled towards six. Ten to. Five to. Her nervousness returned when she glanced at the entrance to see him walking towards her, wearing a dark grey suit, a white shirt and a navy striped tie.

She pushed herself off the sofa.

"I like your dress, Gilly. You look great." His eyes swept over her and he gave her a quick kiss before handing her a bunch of white freesias.

"Oh, thanks, thanks a lot – they're my favourite flowers. How did you guess?"

"They smelled nice. What are they called?"

She laughed. "Freesias, Marc, they're called freesias. I'll give them to the receptionist to put in water. "He followed her over to the desk as she added, "I'm so glad that you're here. I was afraid you wouldn't come."

"I said I wouldn't let you down, didn't I?" Amusement lingered on his face. "You don't seem to have much faith in me."

"It's not you – it's just men in general." She handed over the flowers. "I hope you enjoy this party."

The champagne had helped her confidence, but she would have to be careful not to drink too much.

They moved towards the ballroom where damp air hit her, mixed with the powerful scent of lilies. The room was crowded, hot and airless.

Poor Vanessa didn't have a sunny day for her wedding, but at least it wasn't raining – although rain might relieve this oppressive heat. Who would have imagined they'd get a heat wave in the middle of April?

"How did you get on with your offices in London last week?" she asked.

"I don't know yet. The Japanese team has to go back to Tokyo with a report. It's a waiting game, but I can't help feeling impatient. I've had good news about the house in Raglan Road. Nigel and Bernice loved it. All they have to do now is sign on the dotted line and it's off my hands."

"Congratulations."

He leaned forward and put his arm round her shoulders. "Thank you. I think we'll celebrate tonight."

A young man bearing a tray of champagne glasses stopped to offer them each one. Gilly and Marc made their way over to the French doors at one end of the ballroom, which opened onto wide limestone steps and a view of Dublin bay. Dalkey Island lay in the foreground with a misty expanse of Irish Sea beyond.

They stood on the top step and looked at the water, lying motionless and grey below them. A lawn ran down to a fuchsia-covered wall where the cliff beyond dropped sheer to jagged rocks. Dark clouds were gathering ominously on the horizon.

Above their heads, two gannets wheeled and then dived, one after the other, into the deep.

Gilly pointed at the seabirds resurfacing. "Did you know that a gannet keeps diving until the day it makes an error and breaks its neck? Or so my mum told me."

"That sounds like the property world – one risk too many and the whole business goes down."

She stared at him. What did he mean?

He shrugged. "We live in uncertain times."

"This heat is unbearable, isn't it?" she said. "It's almost as airless out here as it is in the room."

Behind them, the room buzzed with two hundred guests, their raised voices and shrieks of laughter piercing the suffocating air.

Marc didn't have a chance to reply before Vanessa swept

onto the step, kissed her sister and glanced sideways at him.

"Hello, so you're Marc Fletcher." She smiled and held out a hand. "I've heard all about you from Gilly."

"Hardly all..." Gilly muttered.

"Congratulations," said Marc as Vanessa pecked the air on either side of his face.

"Thank you," she said. "Gilly, you look great, but you've been avoiding your family as usual. We haven't seen you for hours. Where have you been?"

The matron of honour appeared and whispered something in Vanessa's ear.

"Not already! I'll be there in a minute, Helen. You go and find Ken, will you? He'll know what to do." She turned to face them again. "Harry, my husband's cousin, is making a nuisance of himself so I'll have to sort this out." She aimed another smile at Marc. "Nice to meet you – maybe we could have a dance later." She added over her shoulder as she walked away, "Gilly, I wish you would make an effort to talk to Daddy."

Gilly grinned. "She's already calling him her husband, did you notice?"

"Perhaps you should go and talk to your family. I'll be all right – don't worry about me. I'm used to being on my own."

"OK, I'd better get this over with." She left him at the bar where she heard him order a Jameson with ice. She saw her father near the door and pushed her way through the crowd.

He glanced at her with a quick twitch of his mouth that passed for a smile. "Ah, Gillian, there you are. Doesn't your sister look gorgeous?"

"Yes."

His eyes glanced over her, sharp brown eyes that missed nothing. "You're looking well, Gillian. I like your dress. Did Vanessa choose it?"

"No, I did." She felt tempted to tell him where she'd bought it.

"Well done. Vanessa has wonderful taste. She bought your mother's outfit, you know. It's always hard to get her to dress up, isn't it, so difficult to get her out of her gardening clothes." His smile came and went so fast that she wasn't sure whether it was a joke. He didn't make many. "Yes, I have to admit, Gillian, you're looking better than I've seen you look for some time – not that we see you very often. How's the new job going?"

"Quite well, so far." She could see him waiting for her to continue. "It'll last about another two and a half months. The recent good weather has kept us going – made it easier than I thought."

"And this man who owns the place, he's here tonight?"

"Yes."

"Quite a lot older than you, I hear – and married, too." Again the brief movement of his lips, as if he found this amusing.

"Widowed," said Gilly. Vanessa had obviously been filling him in. "Only eight years older than me – that's not much. You're ten years older than Mum, aren't you?"

"He's a property developer, I hear. Well, I just hope he's a solvent one – there are not many of them around these days." He laughed. "I'd like to meet him, Gillian, point him out to me."

Vanessa appeared at his elbow. "He seems nice and he's good-looking. He's over there by the bar. I'll introduce you, Dad."

Gilly took this opportunity to escape and slid away, leaving them together. It would be polite, of course, to go with them, but Marc would be well able to cope with her father. She circled the room, shaking hands with Vanessa's colleagues, kissing aunts and uncles she hadn't seen for years. Some of them even claimed she'd grown and probably thought she was still a teenager. Meeting them like this made her feel like she was caught in a time warp; it could just as easily have been Vanessa's twenty-first birthday party or another cousin's wedding because they never seemed to change. She rarely saw them without their party clothes, unless it was a funeral, of course, but that usually finished much the same way with food, drink and family gossip.

Ken smiled and waved across the heads. "Hi, Gilly, you've met Harry, haven't you? He's my seriously embarrassing cousin from across the water."

Harry the journalist pounced on her like an enormous bear and wrapped her in his hairy arms. He'd taken off his tie and half unbuttoned his white shirt, already stained with beer, and his sleeves were rolled up to his elbows.

Gilly laughed as she pushed him off. "Go away! You're such a monster, Harry – control yourself!"

His bloodshot eyes gleamed under bushy eyebrows. "Bit of a dull do so far, don't you think, but I reckon you'll liven things up a bit." Black hair sprouted on his massive chest and his stomach bulged over a thin leather belt.

Ken raised his eyes to the ceiling. "Don't let Vanessa hear you say that. My darling bride is on the warpath. She's already caught this imbecile throwing ice down some poor girl's front."

"And the girl loved every minute of it." Harry put a paw on Gilly's arm. "Every minute of it, I assure you. So, tell me, how's the sex life, Gilly? You've got a rampant reputation, haven't you?" He thrust his face close to hers and she could smell beer and cigarettes on his breath.

"You're obviously mistaking me for someone else." She removed his hand. He was already drunk with a mischievous leer. Hoping to cause trouble and looking out for it, to liven things up, as he put it.

Ken led him away. "I'm taking this crazy man out for some fresh air."

"There's not much fresh air out there." Gilly looked around for Marc.

Vanessa had decided not to seat everyone for dinner.

Instead, waiters circulated with trays of canapés, tiny mouthfuls of smoked salmon and cream cheese. Puffs of pastry filled with mushrooms and various dips for chicken pieces on trays. Gilly didn't recognize some of the food; by the time it had been rolled, squashed and garnished, it could have been anything.

Marc leaned against the bar counter and he looked relaxed, a glass of whiskey in one hand while he chatted to a red-haired man. When she joined them, they were discussing the death of the tiger economy in Ireland.

Marc smiled at her. "Finished?"

"Finished what?"

"Your family tour. I'm an only child so I don't know what it's like to have a large family."

His companion grinned. "I do. My wife and I have one hundred and one relations between us. Weddings are hell. Are you this man's better half?"

"Oh – no, no. I'm the bride's sister."

"Gilly Townsend," said Marc. "And this is..."

The man smiled again, pushed his glasses back onto his thin nose. "Brian O'Neill. I'm an estate agent – that's why I was glad to bump into your... your friend. I'm Ken's second cousin once removed, or something like that. My wife's the one who loves weddings, not me."

Across the room, members of the band assembled on a low stage, fiddling with equipment. Six of them, Gilly noticed, and not one of them looked under fifty. She hoped they would be capable of producing the lively music Vanessa had promised.

"Well, I'll leave you both to it." The estate agent shook Marc's hand. "It was a pleasure to meet you. Good luck with those apartments in Grand Canal. I'll be in touch if I hear of anyone interested. I hope you enjoy the wedding, in spite of your misgivings."

"What misgivings?" asked Gilly when he'd gone.

"He's joking. I wouldn't dare say anything like that." He looked amused. "You'd better have a drink, Gilly, you seem on edge. What would you like? Gin and tonic? Or maybe we'll have champagne? Yes, let's have champagne to celebrate the sale of Raglan Road.' He ordered a bottle. 'I met your father... your sister introduced us."

"What did he say?"

"He asked me a few questions about my business – checking up, I suppose. Making sure I'm good enough for his precious daughter."

"He only has one precious daughter," Gilly muttered, then thought that sounded churlish so she smiled and put her hand on his arm. "My sister is like him, more organised and successful than I am."

"You shouldn't run yourself down."

"Will you dance with me later?"

"Only if it's a slow one because I'm not much of a dancer."

"Dare I ask if you're enjoying yourself?"

"I am now that you're back." He caught her hand and pulled her towards him. "Are you enjoying yourself?"

"Not particularly. I've been interrogated by my father, patronised by my elderly relatives and molested by the bridegroom's cousin – not much fun."

He laughed. "That's what I like about you – you have a good sense of humour."

As they sipped champagne and talked, the band struck up and played vigorous rock and roll hits from the sixties. Vanessa and Ken danced past and her sister raised her eyebrows mockingly at Gilly. Other family members came up to them, hoping for an introduction to her latest boyfriend.

"He's so handsome," Vanessa's best friend Helen whispered in her ear. "Where did you find him?"

"They're all admiring you," Gilly told him, when Helen

moved away.

"I can't imagine why." He poured her more champagne.

"I think it's because you're... um... a little different to my previous..."

"Your previous young men? They probably think I'm far too old for you."

"Only eight years older than me." She shouldn't have said that because now he would know that she'd worked out their ages.

"You look younger, if you don't mind me saying so. I'd have thought you were about eighteen."

"You couldn't think that, Marc! I'm twenty-eight, for goodness sake. How could you think I'm still a teenager?" She turned to stare at him and a flush rose to her cheeks, but she laughed when she saw his expression. "You're winding me up, aren't you? Because I told you what my aunts and uncles said earlier."

His amused eyes held hers and a wave of happiness swept over her. She reached out and touched his face, told him how lucky she felt that he'd agreed to come with her, that she also thought him good-looking.

Later he danced with her, when she reminded him about it. He'd a much better sense of rhythm than he'd led her to believe and held her close to him, his hands warm on her back. She could feel the heat coming from his body, the damp patch of sweat on the back of his shirt and the steady thump of his heart.

"Marc?"

"Mmn?" He hummed softly to the music.

"Are you going to stay in Dublin tonight?"

"I'm seriously considering it because I can't drive the car home when I've been drinking. I suppose I could check into a hotel and get a taxi or I could call Stefans if I really want to go back. What are your plans?"

"I haven't any as yet."

"Oh good. I've just noticed all the buttons down the back of your lovely dress. It must take ages to..."

Gilly shrieked as a large hand landed on her shoulder and dragged her away.

Marc fell backwards against another couple and struggled to keep his balance. A woman screamed.

When Gilly swung around, she saw Harry elbowing Ken out of the way and shouting. He hurled loud, slurred obscenities at the crowd.

"Stop it, Harry!" Ken grabbed his arm, but his cousin immediately pushed him off.

Harry stood swaying and pointed a vibrating finger at Gilly. "You watch yourself, do you hear?" His bloodshot eyes fixed on Marc. "I know who you are – I know you now. I've spent the last ten minutes watching you and it's come to me at last."

"Harry, please," pleaded Ken, looking too nervous to attempt another tackle.

"That London property developer... the one whose wife was killed in the car crash."

Silence fell around them as people turned to stare.

"You're the one whose photo was all over the papers. I remember now, the driver was killed instantly and was a celebrity of some sort – an actor, yes, an alcoholic celebrity." Harry's voice rose.

Colour drained from Marc's face.

"I know," Harry said, "because I covered the story for the local rag." He paused dramatically and, seeing he had everyone's attention, he continued loudly, "Tough on you and your little boy, wasn't it? Especially when you found out that they'd been at it." His black hair flopped over his forehead as he squinted at Marc who remained stiff and silent.

"The poor stupid... poor stupid, beautiful – oh, yes, she was beautiful, wasn't she? I can remember that. Those big, sexy eyes...tell me something, Fletcher, why didn't you admit she was having an affair? You could have made life much easier for yourself – but I suppose it was too big a blow for your manly ego."

Still Marc said nothing but his lips turned white.

Fury hit Gilly like a wave of heat. She sprang forward and snatched a pint of lager from a man beside her. "You're a liar, you're a liar!" she screamed at Harry as she hurled the contents of the glass into his scarlet, bloated face.

Chapter 21

Harry froze, beer dripping from his hair and beard. Ken and three other men seized their chance and grabbed him, two on each arm. A silence grew around them, conversation ceased, a circle of eyes watched. Her father and Vanessa pushed through the crowd towards her and she swung away.

Marc touched her arm. "I think you should come with me." He took her hand and Gilly followed him as they pushed their way through the crowd towards the door.

She glanced over her shoulder and saw Harry lurch forward and struggle in an effort to shake off hands that restrained him. He bellowed like an enraged bull, dragged the men with him and cursed loudly.

Gilly's limbs shook, her palms sticky with sweat. Just in time, they'd stopped him just in time before he hit her.

The humidity had given way to torrential rain, which lashed down, hissing and spitting on the tarmacadam. A taxi waited at the bottom of the steps. Marc let go of her hand and tapped on the window.

"Can you take us to a hotel in the city centre?" he asked when the driver wound it down.

Rain soaked his shirt and it dawned on her that his jacket,

her coat and the freesias were still in the hotel.

"No problem," said the driver.

They got into the back and the taxi pulled away. They sat back, each in a corner, a wide seat between them.

Gilly stopped shaking and tried to laugh. "That was close."

His forehead creased into a frown. "I appreciate your coming to my rescue, but what you did was very dangerous."

"What else could I do? You didn't do anything – you were just standing there letting him rant on... all that stuff about..."

"It would have been better to ignore him."

Why did he look so stern? She muttered, "But he's drunk – I know what he's like, he would have hit you."

"He might have hit you if we hadn't left."

"I'm sorry, I thought I was helping you. He's so ignorant."

"I know that. I've met him before. You should have just ignored him and let the others take him away."

"I had no idea he'd come out with something like that in front of everyone," she said. "I've seen him make a scene before, but I never imagined he'd know you, of all people."

"He doesn't know me." His voice sounded weary. "He wrote about the car crash, that's all."

"But he said..."

"He tried to make a big story out of a tragedy because the driver was a celebrity." He closed his eyes and swallowed.

Rain pelted against the windows of the taxi and ran in rivers down the gutters outside, spears of water hurled from the darkness above. Nausea welled in her stomach and moved up into her throat. Her anger ebbed away and a wave of remorse struck her.

"I'm sorry, Marc, I'm so sorry about what he said. Your wife... I never knew." She looked out at the lamplit streets. "Marc, I'm really sorry. I don't think before I do things sometimes and I didn't mean to upset you." Tears stung her eyes and she hastily brushed them away with a hand.

He shook his head. "You're not the one who upset me, Gilly. You don't need to apologize."

She lay back against the seat and remained silent until the taxi pulled up outside the door of the hotel.

Marc paid the driver and they ran to the shelter of the foyer. Rainwater ran down the back of her neck and she shivered. She followed him to the reception desk where a woman recognized him and smiled.

"Mr Fletcher, good to see you. Would you like a room?"

"Yes, please. My usual room, if it's available." He glanced at Gilly. "Is that OK with you? You don't mind staying here tonight?"

"No, that's fine, thanks." She was supposed to be staying in the hotel in Dalkey with Vanessa and her family, but it was too late to think about that now.

He signed the appropriate forms and Marc led her to the bar. "Would you like a drink?"

"I'd prefer coffee, please." She sank onto a sofa as he ordered this and a glass of whiskey for himself. When he eventually looked at her, his exhausted expression shocked her, his eyes bloodshot in his white face.

What had Alice told her about him? He wasn't a man that liked talking about his past.

No wonder, with a shocking event like that, no wonder he preferred to blot it out.

Gilly sat on the edge of the seat and sipped the hot liquid. She struggled to think of something to say.

Marc finished the whiskey and ordered another one. He spoke slowly. "I remember that journalist well. A few of them kept coming back, looking for more... I remember him because he was the most arrogant and persistent – never thought I'd meet him here in Dublin." At least his voice was back to normal. "Rachel was an architect. She had just finished a project for the actor... a kitchen and garden room extension, something like that."

"Did she know him well?"

"Not really... only while she was working for him. He was married to an Australian model and there was no way they... Rachel, she wouldn't, I know she..." He leaned forward and put his face in his hands.

"It must have been terrible... for you... for the Australian, his wife."

"Yes. She and I got the same treatment. Hounded by journalists, phone ringing nonstop, photographers camped outside the door. It was only because he was a celebrity. They didn't care about Rachel or me. I'd never heard of him, but he was well known in one of those TV soaps."

"Heartless. I suppose Harry and the others thought it would make a better story if they made up an affair. What you must have gone through... what the actor's wife must have suffered."

"She wrote to me afterwards." Marc sipped the whiskey. "She told me it was all a pack of lies, of course. She said she liked Rachel and saw quite a lot of her when they were working on the house."

"You don't have to say anymore, Marc. I can see it's painful. You don't need to tell me."

"Perhaps it's better if you know."

"You must have loved her very much."

"Yes, I did." He eyed the whiskey glass but didn't move.

They fell silent. The rain still poured down outside. Gilly saw it through the window, hurtling onto the deserted street.

"She was in a coma for three days," he said. "She would have been in a wheelchair if she'd lived because of the brain damage."

"I'm so sorry."

"I would have been with her if I hadn't had to go to New York on business. The actor asked us both out to dinner to celebrate the end of the project. I so nearly postponed the business trip because she wanted me to go with them."

"You might not be here today. Did his wife go?"

"Yes, but she was lucky. She was in the back and thrown clear. Only cuts, bruises and shock. Only... how can I say lucky when she had to witness the whole thing."

He lapsed into silence again and Gilly noticed her reflection in a large mirror behind the bar. Dark smudges under her eyes and a face almost as white as his. So tired. Exhaustion numbed her brain. She glanced at the sofa and saw that Marc was lying back against the cushions.

Over cups of coffee at the antique fair, Alice had divulged a little, told her that he worked so hard because he tried to keep focused on the present. He was one of those men who erected a wall against painful events in an attempt to block them out. All very well until someone like Harry arrived with a sledgehammer to batter down the bricks and leave his pain exposed for all to witness. Gilly suspected that men like Harry seemed to take pleasure in exposing what others struggled to keep private. How dare he do that to Marc in front of all those people he didn't know, in front of her family!

Where did this leave her? She stirred her coffee with a teaspoon. She could never measure up to Rachel, a successful architect and the love of Marc's life. But she was being selfish, thinking of herself at a time like this. He was the one who needed sympathy.

"You're taking a long time to drink that coffee," he said suddenly. He put his arm round her shoulder and pulled her close. "Talk to me, please. Tell me all about yourself so that I don't have to think anymore."

"Oh... um...what would you like to hear?"

"Anything. Tell me anything."

Gilly took a deep breath and rested her head on his shoulder.

What to say? Nothing too serious. Perhaps she could tell him a light-hearted version of what it had been like to grow up with Vanessa as a sister. She explained how they'd shared a bedroom and, because of squabbling, their mother felt compelled to divide it in half. The set of house rules Vanessa had set out in her neat ten year old's handwriting, pinned on the back of their door: *Vanessa's bedtime nine o'clock. Gilly's eight o'clock. Half an hour extra on Fridays and Saturdays. Take turns to have the first shower.* Vanessa was always very fair about washing.

Gradually he relaxed until he began to laugh. "She sounds like a perfectionist," he said. His smile was tired, sad. "She's very different to you, isn't she? I'm sorry, I should have told you how Rachel died before now so that it wouldn't be such a shock for you but I didn't expect... and it's just that I find it so difficult... such a hard thing to talk about."

"Then don't say anymore." She stroked his cheek with a finger. "How did you get this scar?"

"It wasn't from anything heroic or romantic, I'm afraid. It happened during a rugby match in school. Would you like another coffee?"

"No, thanks, I should go to bed. I'll go to reception and ask for another room."

He glanced at his watch and nodded. He turned towards her and cupped her face in his hands, stared into her eyes. "You're full of energy and enthusiasm," he said, slowly. "It's what I find so attractive about you – I hope you won't lose that, whatever happens." After a silence, he added, "This evening hasn't turned out the way we hoped... the way I hoped, I mean... is it possible to start again, do you think? To go back to where we were before that arrogant oaf interrupted us?"

She smiled and put her arms round his neck. "You mean like this? When we were dancing and you were saying something about the buttons on my dress?"

He nodded, an amused light in his eyes. "That's exactly what I was thinking. Let's go upstairs and take it from there."

*

She must have fallen asleep. She looked around in the darkness and saw only a glimmer from the street lamp through the curtains. She turned, reached out and felt the warmth of his body. He lay on his back, his head towards the wall.

"Are you awake?" Gilly whispered.

He moved. "Mmn... yes, I am now."

"I can't see you. Will I open the curtains?"

"No, don't. No – it's nice like this."

"Are you afraid someone might look in?"

"I prefer it this way." He raised himself up on an elbow and leaned over to push her hair back from her face. "How are you? Are you all right?"

"I'm fine – must have fallen asleep. It was lovely, wasn't it? You made me feel... I don't know... appreciated."

"I thought that was the whole point of it, really. Isn't that how you're supposed to feel?"

"Maybe... but not in my experience."

He didn't reply. The tips of his fingers traced along her chin, down the side of her neck.

"Marc, do you mind if I ask you something?"

"Depends what it is."

"Since Rachel, since she died, how many women..."

"Gilly! What sort of a question is that?"

"I'm just curious, that's all."

"I haven't asked you about your boyfriends, have I?"

"There's not a lot to tell you. The few I've had have been serious mistakes." She waited but he didn't say anything. She stretched and yawned.

His hand moved slowly down to her stomach. "You've got nice skin, so soft and smooth."

"Tell me, Marc, what do you think about, when you're not thinking about work?"

"I don't know, I suppose I think a lot about Samuel, wonder where he is, what he's doing. I talk to him every night on the phone if I'm away."

"Yes, I know, Alice told me."

"And I thought about you when I was in London."

"What did you think about me?"

"I remember thinking about the walled garden – yes, definitely, the garden and whether that fellow Dean is any good and... ow! Don't pinch – that hurt!" He laughed and placed his hand behind her head, pulled her closer. "All right, I'll admit I thought about this too – being with you like this – quite a lot of the time." He leaned over her, his mouth close to her ear.

She turned her face to kiss him. "You're feeling better now."

"Am I? I suppose this is what comes of thinking about you. Now, Gilly, please, no more questions. I know of only one way to keep you quiet."

Chapter 22

"Hey, Daddy, look! There's a mermaid in the river. Look, down there, I can see her long green hair."

Marc put his arm round Samuel's waist as he sat on top of the narrow stone bridge and leaned over one of the recesses. He watched the Barrow River idle underneath. Shallow water for late April, strands of green weed – the mermaid's hair – caressing rocks on its bed.

"I can't see the mermaid, Samuel, but there are some minnows over there. See?" When he'd first bought Glanesfort, he'd read that the Pass Bridge was the oldest in Monasterevin, marched over by the Earl of Essex and his army on their way to Munster in 1599, and there were rumours that Cromwell had also used it on his destructive journey.

He told his son this and touched the limestone. "Just imagine the soldiers, Sam, their shiny swords, their boots clumping on the stones, the plumes on their helmets waving in the breeze."

The boy's eyes gleamed. "Tell me more."

Marc hugged him close. "I don't know any more. It was a long time ago – four centuries ago. Do you know what a century is?"

He shook his head.

"A hundred years. A long, long time." Men who fought and

died four hundred years ago, but who were still alive today in people's minds. Still in his mind when he stood against this bridge. Everything around him linked to the past – everything, in its own way, affected by it. No matter how hard people tried to get rid of the memories, no matter how desperately he tried to exorcise his, they shaped and changed him.

"I can see the ducks down there. Fergus and I feed them. Can I go down to the river?" Samuel jumped onto the road. "I won't fall in, I won't, Daddy. Can I, please?"

"All right, but be careful."

"Thanks, Dad. I love you."

"I love you, too, young man."

He watched his son run along the grass verge and scramble over the wall into the field that sloped towards the water. A little charmer. Heaven help the girls when he grew up. He was like his mother's brother, Pierre. Same dark curly hair and recklessness. Pierre lived in America now and had married three times.

Two swallows skimmed low over the river and shot up into the air with the agility of fighter jets. The birds had been back for three weeks now and had already patched up their nests in the old barn behind the apartments at Glanesfort. Marc liked to see them chattering on the telephone wires, with the sun gleaming on sleek blue-black feathers and chestnut bibs. Brave little warriors that flew all the way from Africa to hatch and bring up their young in cooler climates; the harbingers of summer.

Since the evening with Gilly, after her sister's wedding, he'd forced himself to think about Rachel. She belonged to his past, packed into a box in the attic of his memory, but still in his mind and in the mind of that journalist. Rachel would never be forgotten because, even though she was dead, she was part of his life, part of the person he'd become.

He realized how little Gilly knew about him. His carefully hidden secrets and, worse still, the shame kindled by that memory he'd attempted to pack away forever. How could he ever tell her about his father's suicide? Or the reason for the suicide? No point digging up the past. Far better to keep it where it belonged, packed away in boxes where it couldn't hurt anyone else.

He remembered the sunlight on her hair the following morning as she lay beside him. She'd put behind her the drama of the previous day and moved on. Laughed and chatted with him about Glanesfort, his work in London and her beloved plants. Since then, he'd found himself drawn to the walled garden and spent time listening to her talk about her plans. She'd taken him to a public park with renovated woodland, a lake and shrub borders bursting with late spring flowers and scents. To inspire him, she said. He helped her buy plants and young trees at a nursery and learned their Latin names. Nomenclature. Latin names were international, she explained, while common names for plants often differed from country to country and were more confusing. They went out to dinner twice and he put off going back to London until the following week.

Marc gazed towards the town on the left bank of the river. He'd left his car in the main street because a walk in the morning was good for Samuel. It used up some of his energy and calmed him down.

His mobile pinged and he fished it out of a pocket. A text from Fergus thanking him for his sympathy. Fergus's father had suffered another stroke the night of the wedding; about the same time that Gilly had hurled lager at that obnoxious journalist. The nursing home staff had found him slumped on the floor in his bedroom. Fergus was grateful for a week off work to spend time with his father and mother.

Samuel waved at him from below and he raised a hand and beckoned. The principal from the playschool had called earlier to assure him that there'd been no further sign of the blonde woman. She believed it was a one-off incident.

Joe Milligan had sounded concerned when he told him what had happened. The private investigator reported that he'd been back to Leeds, but had discovered that Jane and her flat mates had gone away on holiday after Easter and wouldn't be back until the end of the month. The landlady told him students had a wonderful life and mentioned Madrid.

Marc spotted the post van driving along the road towards him.

"Samuel, be careful, you're too close to the edge. Come here, please, we have to walk back to the town."

Michael's report had been good when he phoned from the London office. Miss Hirome, PA to Mr Fukuda, had sent an email. The Japanese team wanted them to fly out to Tokyo to make a presentation. His London offices had made the final list of three and that sounded promising.

A sale would keep Marc's bank manager at bay for another few months, until he found a buyer for the Dublin apartments. If he found a buyer. His business often felt like it swung on a thread; one wrong negotiation and the line would snap and the whole lot would tumble down. Michael, always pining for Asia, would be the one to take with him to Tokyo.

"Samuel! Come back up here, please. We have to go home now."

The post van stopped beside him and the driver, a cheerful man with red hair and freckles, grinned at him. "Hello, Marc. Going fishing?"

"No, I wouldn't have the patience." How friendly these local people were. He asked, "Would you like me to take the post for Glanesfort? It'll save you driving out there."

"OK, there's not much, only a few letters and a small package." He handed over the bundle and revved up the van. "Be seeing you, then, take care."

Marc flicked through the mail. Bills addressed to him, more interesting letters for some of the other tenants. A rather suggestive postcard for Fergus from Amsterdam with a cucumber cartoon on the front and *Remember Andrea* written on the back. He wondered if Fergus had remembered Andrea. Probably not, if she felt compelled to send that sort of communication. He noticed the brown package with the North London postmark. The familiar capital letters and the hard shape inside made his stomach churn. More torment. As if he would ever be able to forget when he received these constant disturbing reminders. Marc tore open the cardboard and looked at the CD with the word *Recordare* written on it in black marker.

"Hey, Dad, look, it's Gilly!" Samuel ran towards him.

He turned to see her Ford hatchback drawing up, heard the rattle of its exhaust pipe.

She switched off the engine and wound down the window. "Hi there, you two. Out for a walk?"

He pushed the CD into his jacket pocket and glanced up. "Yes. We left the car in the town and strolled along the river."

"Looks like it might rain any minute," she said.

He noticed the darkening sky. "I hope we make it back in time."

"Want a lift back to your car? I don't mind a detour. I've been at the nursery where I've been spending more of your money, Marc." She stretched over to push open the passenger door.

He opened the back door for Samuel and got in beside her, holding the letters on his knee.

"Anything for me?" she asked. "A reprimand from Vanessa on her honeymoon, perhaps? I haven't received a postcard from her yet, though I did eventually get a phone call from my father telling me off for aggravating Harry's public display at my sister's wedding."

Her vitality filled the car as she chattered on.

He smiled. "You deserve a telling-off, I suppose, as any woman who throws beer does."

"Your car is very old and noisy," Samuel shouted from the back. "Isn't it, Dad? My dad's car is much faster than yours."

"Your dad's car was much more expensive than mine."

"I apologize for my son's rudeness," he replied. She was wearing her navy boiler suit, the rip in the knee now larger. He could see the pale skin underneath and had to turn away to resist the temptation to touch it, to feel its warmth and softness.

"Do you remember the red squirrel we saw in the garden two days ago?" Her dark eyes sparkled with enthusiasm. "Near the fig tree? Dean knows all about them. He's really keen on wildlife and apparently pine martens are reappearing in the wild and they kill grey squirrels and that allows the red ones to survive."

"I want a pet squirrel," said Samuel. "I'm going to call him Rusty."

She had a special smile for Dean, too, a rather teasing and slightly bossy one. Poor Dean, the young man was besotted with her and she didn't even notice. So unaware of her own attractions. It was refreshing, compared to some women.

"That's a good name, Sam," she said. "Marc, are you listening to me? You look like you're on another planet."

What was on the CD? More about how the past would be exposed if he didn't pay up? Accompanied by Mozart, of course. Mozart had been terrified when he was composing parts of *Requiem* – had feared he was writing about his own death. What sort of crazy lunatic created these CDs? He would listen to it after lunch when Stefans drove Alice and Samuel to the supermarket.

"I hear you," he replied. "Squirrels making a comeback."

She shot him an amused glance and then looked suddenly serious. "By the way, Marc, did Fergus tell you that his father doesn't seem to be improving?"

"Yes, I heard that."

"Poor Fergus, he's very upset because he loves his dad. I was wondering if you would like to come for dinner tonight?" she asked. "I could make something simple, like spaghetti bolognese. I'm not a great cook."

"Thank you. I would like that and I can console myself with the thought that I'm doing you a favour because you'll have a chance to practise your cooking." He enjoyed teasing her.

She laughed. "I'm not that bad."

"I hope not. I can't afford to take time off work with food poisoning." The BMW was beside them now as she pulled in.

She gave him a little push. "Get out, rude man."

"Can I come tonight?" asked Samuel.

"No, young man, you'll be in bed," said Marc.

The boy sighed. "It's not fair. I'm never allowed to go anywhere."

*

The most annoying thing about cooking was the way onions burned so quickly. Gilly turned away for a few minutes and they changed into little black crisps when she glanced in the saucepan. Still, she had another half an hour before Marc arrived so she could start again. She opened the cupboard beside the sink to find another onion.

A knock on the door. She looked up at the clock. Even he wouldn't be this early. Another knock, a sequence of taps.

She walked over and swung open the door. Samuel stood on the gravel path, wearing pyjamas and black furry slippers with plastic eyes and some sort of teeth at the toes.

"Hi, Gilly." He pushed past her.

"What are you doing out of bed at this time?"

He shrugged and smiled. "Alice said I could come."

"Alice most certainly did not – and definitely not on your own. Where is she?"

"Talking on the phone."

"So you made a quick getaway?" She closed the door and sighed. What should she do now? She would have to ring Alice who would be frantic as soon as she noticed he'd gone. She smelled smoke and ran back to the cooker to pull off the saucepan.

Samuel went to the kitchen table and climbed onto a chair. "Me and Wolf wanted to come and see you. He's here beside me."

"Stay there for a few minutes while I chop more onion. Then I'm ringing Alice."

"Daddy's in Dublin."

"No, he's not. He's coming here."

"He went to Dublin." Samuel laid his curls on the table and yawned.

Gilly scraped the blackened onions into the bin and scrubbed out the saucepan. She put it back on the cooker and poured in olive oil. "Maybe you'd like to watch the television in the next room while I do the cooking," she suggested.

"No thanks, I'm tired."

She tossed in the chopped onion. "You should have stayed in bed. You should try not to upset Alice, you know."

He frowned and rubbed his eyes.

"I'm going to call her now," she said.

Another knock thumped on the door, more urgent this time.

Gilly opened it again and Alice said, her face lined with anxiety, "Oh, Gilly, have you seen Samuel? He kept talking about you and supper so I thought... I can't think how I didn't notice... the door was open so maybe Marc..."

"Yes, don't worry, he's here with me. He's been here for about five minutes. I was just about to phone you. Come in."

Alice let out a squawk like a macaw when she saw the boy, from either relief or rage, Gilly couldn't tell. She went over to him and grabbed his arm. He started to wail and struggle.

"Come with me now this instant! Why are you so naughty? You know you're not to go out in the dark on your own." Alice pulled him again as he clung to the table, tears in his eyes.

There was another knock at the door as Gilly peered into the saucepan. Now the onions weren't cooking at all. What was wrong? She saw that she'd turned off the electric ring. Damn, damn, damn. She couldn't concentrate with all these distractions.

The door opened and Marc came in, a frown on his brow that deepened when he saw Alice and Samuel. "Is something wrong?"

"Yes. This young man disappeared out the front door – which you left open when you came back from Dublin, by the way – and ran over here," said Alice.

Samuel pushed her out of his way and ran to throw his arms round his father. Marc put a bottle of red wine on the counter and picked up his son who was now crying hysterically. A bit too hysterically. He was a gifted little actor. Gilly winced as his lamentations echoed around the small kitchen.

Marc carried him over to the table and sat down with the boy on his knee.

"He has to go back to bed," said Alice.

"Yes, yes. Let's all just calm down, shall we?" Marc looked at Gilly and rolled his eyes. "Sorry about this. I'll take him back to the house in a minute."

"You spoil him." Alice's face creased and she pushed her glasses back on her nose. "He won't do a thing for me if you spoil him like that."

Marc was a patient man at the best of times, but Gilly saw exasperation in his eyes.

"Alice, dear Alice, I have been away all afternoon," he said slowly. "I drove to Dublin at short notice because I was informed by the new owners that the Raglan Road house had been burgled. We found graffiti on the front door and a broken windowpane. They were not impressed. I had to arrange to get the window fixed and find a man to scrub off the graffiti. I've only been back for half an hour so I might have had a momentary lapse of concentration."

"So that's why you left the door open. Honestly, no wonder you forget things when you work so late." Alice pulled the curtains and tidied a few cookery books into a neat pile. She glanced around to see how else to occupy her hands.

"I'm sorry." He took off his leather jacket and hung it on the back of a chair. "It's warm tonight, isn't it?" He got up, grasped Samuel's hand and said in a firm voice, "I'll come back with you, Alice, and we'll put him to bed together. I hope you don't mind, Gilly. I'll be back as soon as possible."

"No problem," she replied. "I'm still cooking." It was a relief to see them all leave the kitchen so she could get a grip on dinner.

She diced a red pepper and added it to the onion with minced steak. Then she opened a can of tomatoes; tipped in the contents with some red wine and a handful of mixed herbs from a jar in the cupboard. She turned down the heat and set the timer for twenty-five minutes, beginning to feel she had the meal under control at last. Now she could cook spaghetti and steam the sugar snap peas.

She lit the fire in the little sitting room. She'd found some logs in the wood, still damp after the afternoon's rain; they hissed and spat from behind the grate, oozing resin. A smell of the woodland rose from the flames, fresh and sharp.

She went back into the kitchen to check on the bolognese. Marc's jacket had fallen on the floor, at the foot of the chair on which he'd hung it, and she moved over to pick it up, admiring the leather, the soft suede collar. As she lifted it, a CD fell with a clatter onto the tiles.

Looking at the name, she scooped it up. *Recordare* in handwriting, whatever that meant. Curious now, she walked over to the dresser and popped it into her stereo. Violins filled the room, followed by the singing of a church choir. Maybe Marc liked classical music.

Gilly didn't know much about it, but she liked this as it had a haunting, pleading air and she turned up the volume a little as she stirred the mince and tomato sauce.

The music died away and a voice began to speak. A weird voice that didn't sound human, neither male nor female, more like an electronic computer voice:

"Good day, Mr Fletcher. Yes, welcome back to Mozart's *Requiem*. *Recordare* is one of my favourite pieces. Guilt is a terrible thing, isn't it? It eats away at you and destroys any relationship." Gilly's grip tightened on the spoon. "Did your poor dead wife know what your family did? Someone like you doesn't deserve to be happy..."

This wasn't a CD of music after all. It was some sort of threatening message.

"And as for your little boy, does he know what sort of family he has been born into? Will he grow up to find out just how deceitful his father really is?" Gilly's hands trembled as she put the wooden spoon down on the counter and turned up the volume again.

More music played and then faded away. "I would keep a very close eye on your son, Mr Fletcher. A very close eye indeed. We don't want anything to happen to him, do we? Now, all you have to do is send..."

The door thumped against the wall as Marc burst in. "Turn that off! Where did you find it?"

She pressed the button and silenced the voice.

He held out his hand. "Give it to me, please."

He almost snatched it from her as she stammered, "It... it was in your jacket pocket. I thought it was your music, otherwise I wouldn't... I would never have put it on. Oh Marc, what is it? Who sent you this?"

He said nothing.

"Is it a joke? It must be a joke, surely?"

"It's not a joke – I only wish it was."

"But why? Why would someone send you a thing like that... like blackmail? Is it blackmail?"

Another silence while they stared at each other.

"You have to tell me. Please tell me," she said.

His eyes held hers for a moment longer before glancing away. "I don't want you to mention this to anyone. It would be dangerous. No one must know about it."

"I won't say anything. Please tell me what it is. You sound so angry."

His voice softened. "I'm not angry with you, Gilly. Not with you... and I'm sorry if it seemed like that. I never meant you to hear this – I thought I'd left it in my room when I changed my clothes."

"Are you going to tell me what it is?"

He wouldn't meet her eyes as she stood gazing up at him.

"Have you told the Gardaí?" she asked.

"No, I only heard it this afternoon."

"You must! This man is threatening to hurt Samuel."

He frowned. "How do you know it's a man? I can't tell."

"I don't know. I suppose it could be a woman. Have you had one of these before?"

He turned away and closed his eyes as if to shut out her question.

"Have you, Marc?"

"Yes but this is the first time Samuel has been threatened."

"I don't understand. Why? What have you done?"

"I can't tell you, Gilly. I'm sorry, but it's too risky."

"You are going to tell the Gardaí?" She clutched at his arm, her fingers holding onto his shirtsleeve.

"Of course."

"Will you come into the sitting room?"

Did he hesitate for a few seconds before he followed her? In the other room, she threw a couple of logs onto the fire and they sat on the sofa. As she placed the kitchen timer on the pine coffee table, a wave of unreality hit her as if, any minute, she would wake up and discover it was only a nightmare. A glance at the grim expression on Marc's face, his visible inward struggle to hold back the words, told her otherwise.

"Please tell me what you can."

He sighed. "If you know about this... if I tell you, perhaps it might put you in danger too."

She frowned. "Me? Why me?"

"We are not dealing with a normal person. This man... or woman is twisted – has a twisted mind."

"A woman? Do you suspect a woman?"

He stared at the sizzling fire. "It started when Samuel's nanny Jane went, or about six months afterwards. I think Alice might have mentioned her to you. I had to fire her... I thought she was behaving badly towards Samuel... smacking him, though he was too young to say anything. The first CD arrived in the post at my house in London."

"So you think this comes from a nanny? What does this person want?"

"Money, of course. That's what he or she always wants."

A log spat out a spark and Gilly jumped with fright.

Marc continued. "The CDs are always posted from different areas in London. I've had six altogether over the past eighteen months and always with music from Mozart's *Requiem*."

Mozart, so that's what it was. "I hope you told the police in London about the nanny."

"I did, yes, but they couldn't do anything about her without evidence."

"But the CDs, surely they are evidence?"

Silence.

"You told the police about the CDs?"

"No, no, I couldn't."

"Why not? Wouldn't the police know best how to track down a blackmailer?"

He took a breath. "I can afford the money, it's not too much." His mouth formed a straight, firm line. "This CD is different, though. This time it mentions Samuel and it warns me not to get involved with you, so it's much more serious. It mentions your name later on."

She raised her hands to her face. "Me? How does he, or she, know about me?" The tips of her fingers felt icy cold. Had someone been watching her? In the garden? The white figure at the lakeside? At Vanessa's wedding?

An idea struck her and she turned to face Marc. "What about that journalist, Harry? He writes such melodramatic stuff – could it be him? You said he caused trouble before, when your wife died."

"Why would he do that? For the money? Then why not ask for a larger amount?"

"I don't understand... what's the point? Why does the blackmailer want money spread out over the year?"

"He means to frighten me, to threaten my son, to stop me from having a relationship." He turned to her and shrugged. "Why, you ask, but isn't it obvious, Gilly? This person hates me, truly hates me." His breath came out in shudders and he closed his eyes, as if struck by a sudden sharp pain in his head.

"Marc? Are you all right?"

He put a hand to his forehead, pressed hard, his eyes still shut.

"I must go," he said quietly. "I'll go back to the house now and I'll ring the Gardaí immediately. I can't risk putting Samuel or you in danger."

Three minutes left on the timer but she'd lost all interest in dinner. "I don't understand why you didn't tell the police in London about the CDs if you told them about the nanny. What stopped you?" She stared at him. "What have you done that you can't tell the police? Oh my God, Marc, what have you done?" Tears stung her eyes.

He put his arm round her. "Don't cry, Gilly, I haven't done... look, it's very complicated."

"But to just ignore it..."

He took his arm away and took both of her hands in his. "I didn't just ignore it. I hired a private investigator to track down Jane and I hired Stefans as a bodyguard for Samuel, just in case. I bought Glanesfort too. I know it was also a business investment and seemed like a bargain at the time, but I thought it would be safer for Samuel to leave London, just in case this madman, this maniac ever threatened him."

"Stefans is a bodyguard?"

"Yes, recommended by the local Garda sergeant here. He was in the Lithuanian army and he's very well trained. I don't tell people he's a bodyguard, of course, or the tenants might be alarmed. They like the idea of a security guard around the place, though. The Garda sergeant was very helpful and asked no questions. I suppose he thought that people like me – people with money – are always paranoid."

"And Alice, does she know?" One minute left on the timer. A sharp pain twisted in her stomach and she swallowed quickly.

"She knows about Stefans and she knows I worry about a threat to Samuel. That's why she agreed to come here because she thought it wasn't easy to keep him safe in London." He hesitated. "She doesn't know about the blackmail and I don't want to frighten her." He stood up.

She looked down at the rug, saw where the spark from the fire had made a small, black mark, while hot tears brimmed in her eyes. "But if... as you say... if I'm mentioned this means, doesn't it... that I can't... that we can't..."

He nodded. "Yes, I'm afraid it does. It's safer to stay away from me. At least for the time being, until I get this sorted out. So promise me you'll say nothing. The less others know about it the better. I can't put Samuel or you at risk. As I said, I only heard the CD this afternoon on the way to Dublin in the car and I was going to tell you tonight, but I hadn't quite worked out what to say. And there's that attack on the house in Dublin, an act of meaningless vandalism unless..."

"Unless you think it's connected to this crazy person on the CD?"

"Exactly. Someone is out to make life difficult for me, Gilly, to prevent me being happy, so please help me by trying to understand. I don't want you to think that I don't care about you. It's because I care about my son, and you, that we can't be involved with each other. You must see that."

She murmured, "You do care about me, don't you?"

"Of course, my love, of course. I care very much about you, but I don't want to... please try to understand."

"What have you done?"

"I can't tell you. There's too much at stake. I would if I could. Please don't cry, sweetheart. You must try to see the situation I'm in, that I can't... that we can't put the ones I care about in danger. I can't risk it."

The timer went off, shrill ringing pierced her ears and she slammed her hand down to switch it off.

She turned away, burying her face in the cushions behind

her. "You could do something if you really wanted to."

"Like what? What do you suggest I do?"

"Face up to whoever is doing this. Face up to whatever you have done. Surely it's not that bad... whatever it is. I can't imagine you doing... You're a kind man, Marc, you're not..."

"You don't know what happened. You might change your mind, if you knew."

"But even so, if you continue to hide it away, it only gives the blackmailer power over you."

He shook his head, refusing to listen. "I'm going to tell the Gardaí now and I'm going to warn Alice and Stefans that we must keep Samuel under constant supervision."

"And will you tell the Gardaí about what you've done, what's behind this blackmail?" She got up and wiped her eyes with a tissue. The bolognese was ready by now but she didn't care. The thought of food made her feel nauseous.

"Yes, of course I'll tell them. I have to tell them now. I hoped... thought it might not go this far."

They walked to the door and she opened it. The lake glimmered in the evening light, bronze reeds puncturing its smooth silver surface. Swans and some ducks further out; one of the swans with its head under the water, tail feathers sticking up, wiggling its rear end. She looked at Marc and realized that they had both glanced towards the empty fishing platform.

"Could it be her?" she murmured.

"I was wondering the same thing. Samuel's teacher told me a white-haired woman came to the school railings and was talking to him. I didn't tell you earlier because I didn't want to frighten you."

She shivered. "That's worrying. I haven't seen her since. Perhaps she was watching me and spying on me."

"It's possible. Anything is possible. Make sure you lock your door."

Chapter 23

A dark sky and the Irish Sea merged in a grey line off the Wicklow coast. The wind threw the scent of salt and seaweed into Gilly's face as she stood on the footpath. Waves crashed over large boulders along the bottom of the pier, sending spray into the air, while seagulls circled overhead.

"I'm longing to show you the wedding and honeymoon photos." Vanessa laid a hand on her arm. "Let's sit down over there."

Gilly nodded and thought how well she looked, rested and even slightly suntanned, although Vanessa had a horror of sunburn. They both wore winter jackets on this cold May afternoon and Gilly put up her hood to keep out the breeze.

Vanessa linked her arm and guided her to a bench. "It's good to see you. I thought you sounded quite down on the phone."

Greystones lay behind them, its mix of grey and brighter painted houses gazing out to sea. Old buildings nestled together and in front, protecting them from the waves, stretched the vast, modern pier made of honey-hued concrete.

"I'm all right," said Gilly.

Two brave women sat on a rug on the stony beach, watching children run to and from the water. A girl threw a tennis ball and a black dog dived into the sea to retrieve it. On their left lay the unfinished development of the North Beach. An older and a newer Ireland, a town where two eras overlapped.

She managed to smile at her sister. "You look great, by the way."

"Thanks. We had a fab time in Sardinia. I kept my best photos on my mobile."

Vanessa tapped the screen and a close-up of the smiling bride and groom appeared, gazing into each other's eyes. "Here, you flick through them. No, wait, there's one I want to show you of Marc... there, see. Doesn't he look handsome in that photo? And see the way he's looking at you when he doesn't realize the camera is on him."

Gilly glanced at the photo and then out to sea. In this shot, his smile creased lines at the corners of his eyes. She hadn't seen that smile for at least a week. Only met him once and he'd looked distant and serious.

Vanessa's eyes swept over her sister's face. "So, tell me all about Marc. What's he really like? I thought he seemed nice at the wedding, polite with a sense of fun."

Gilly looked at the ground. "Yes."

"What do you mean by that? Are you all right?"

"Yes."

"Sure? Daddy was as annoyed as I was at the way Harry treated Marc," Vanessa said. "Of course he was furious with that stupid oaf and poor Ken was mortified – totally mortified. Ken's parents told me they'll never invite him anywhere again. They thought it served Harry right when you fired that beer over the rude, obnoxious pig, but... Gilly, listen to me, Daddy said... he told me something."

"What?"

"He wanted to find out for himself about Marc so he made a few enquiries in London." Vanessa glanced at her. "Do you want to hear what he found out?"

Gilly rolled her eyes. What had her father been doing now? Ringing around his business friends and snooping?

"Do you?"

Gilly sighed. "All right, tell me."

The wind blew Vanessa's hair across her face and she raised a hand to push it behind her ear. "Well, for starters, unfortunately Harry was right about Marc's wife. She was killed in a car crash with a celebrity. The actor was driving and his car went out of control and hit a lamp post."

"I know. Marc told me. He was an alcoholic and his poor wife was in the back seat."

"Daddy got in touch with a friend in the UK who knows a lot about the property scene. His friend says Marc runs a careful business, which is unusual enough these days, isn't it, with so many property developers up to their necks in debt and in all sorts of trouble. They all have debts, of course, but his aren't too bad although..."

"Although what?"

"Well, one of Dad's friends heard a story that there's a big negotiation going on with a company in Japan over a block of offices. This friend said Marc needs to sell the building and that his bank is putting him under pressure, but I don't know how true that is. You know how people talk."

Gilly glanced at her mobile. No message from him, nor did she expect there to be one.

Her sister continued. "Anyway, he said he only discovered one strange fact about Marc."

"Yes?" Gilly put a fingernail in her mouth and bit it. "And what was that?"

"That there is no record of anything about him more than sixteen years ago. Everything throughout the last sixteen years, I mean, has been transparent but..."

"But what... what exactly are you saying?"

"Not too sure, really. It seems that Marc Fletcher just appeared in London sixteen years ago and before that, there's nothing – like, nothing at all. No sign of him attending school or university in the UK or even that he arrived from another country. There's nothing."

"His mother lives in France and his father died. I know that much."

"Is that so? Dad couldn't find anything about a mother or a father."

Gilly stared at her. The voice on the CD stated that Marc didn't deserve to be happy because of his family, because of his father. She couldn't tell her sister about the threatening message. A knot of worry twisted inside her. What had they done? Something so bad that nobody could ever know? It had to be something serious enough to force him to pay out thousands to a blackmailer.

"Where are the honeymoon photos?" She decided to change the subject.

Vanessa frowned. "Is there something wrong, Gilly? You seem... well, you seem depressed."

"I'm fine."

"Has anything happened to upset you?"

Gilly tried to smile. "You know me, Ness, I'm easily upset."

"No, but seriously, you can tell me, can't you? What's happened?"

How to answer this question? Her sister always noticed her moods. Gilly turned again to face the grey sea. The wind had died but huge waves still rolled towards the rocks beneath, churning foam. Churning like the anxiety in her stomach. What could she say? That she missed him. That the days were dull without his company. And in another couple of months, she would finish the garden and move on to another job and would never see him again. Her time in Glanesfort and with Marc Fletcher would be over. She rubbed her sleeve across her eyes. The last thing she wanted was to cry in front of Vanessa.

Gilly's mobile bleeped and she glanced hopefully at the screen. But no, just a text from Fergus. She turned to her sister, took a deep breath. "Marc is very busy at the moment so I haven't seen much of him since the wedding. Japan, the London offices, whatever... you know how it is for people like him." She opened up the text message. "Fergus says he's lonely and he wants me to join him for a drink in The Fiddler's Inn tonight at eight."

Vanessa shot her a sharp look, but said no more about Marc. She took out her mobile, opened up her honeymoon photos and handed it to Gilly, who flicked through them.

"Sardinia looks amazing, Ness. Was it warm?"

"Yes, lovely during the day."

Gilly dutifully admired the blue sea, the dazzling sky and the shots of the happy couple, embracing each other. She handed back the phone with a smile. "You're very lucky, aren't you? To find someone like Ken, I mean, someone who you can share everything with."

Her sister nodded. "You will too, one day, Gilly."

"Mmn, maybe. It's not looking so good at the moment."

"Have you had a row with Marc?"

"No, no, not a row but... I don't really want to talk about it now. Anyway, remember what we said about me not getting involved with the boss. It's not a good idea." She turned to face Vanessa. "Promise not to tell." It was like being a teenager again. Promise not to tell...

"Promise."

"I've been offered a new job." Gilly tried to inject enthusiasm into the words. Four months ago, she would have been thrilled; would have jumped at the opportunity. Now she would have to put it off until she'd finished at Glanesfort.

"That's great. Where?"

"I got a call yesterday about it. It's in County Galway... a new country house hotel with a big golf course. They're looking for someone to landscape the grounds."

*

"Not too many here," said Fergus as he glanced around. He nodded at a couple sitting on the left of the stove in The Fiddler's Inn. "I suppose it's often quiet during the week." He yawned and picked up his pint of stout. "Thanks for coming, Gilly."

She smiled and raised her glass of lager in salute. "No problem. How's your father?" She liked the pub without the noise and bustle. It looked more faded than before, in need of a lick of paint, some of the seats torn with foam sprouting out of holes in the plastic covers.

Fergus's hazel eyes were slightly bloodshot and he hadn't shaved; a reddish tinge of stubble roughened his jaw. "Not good."

"Sorry to hear that."

He put down his glass and pushed a beer mat around with a finger. "He's very weak, I guess. Sometimes it takes a while for him to understand what I'm saying. Sometimes I'm not sure if he understands at all."

"It must be horrible to see him like that."

"Yeah, it is." He took another gulp of stout and frowned. "Not sure if he knows who I am some of the time. He didn't recognize my mother the other night."

Gilly glanced towards the door when it opened and another couple came in. Whom did she expect? Fergus had hardly invited Marc to join them.

"Alice is in overdrive," said Fergus. "Apparently the boss has invited his clients to dinner tomorrow night and she's only just heard they're coming. She has to cook for the four of them. I thought he'd be in better form."

Gilly stared at him. "Better form?"

"Yeah, you know, don't you? He's just sold a five-bedroom house in Raglan Road for €1.4 million and he's going around like the world is about to end. I don't understand him sometimes."

"He mentioned something about that house."

"Some rich bloke from England bought it. He's married to an Irish woman. Wouldn't you be deliriously happy if you'd just made €1.4 million? I know I would." Fergus took out his cigarette packet, realized he couldn't smoke without going outside and put them back in his pocket with a groan. "Something happened at the house in Dublin last week, though. Something that brought Marc back to Glanesfort in a very bad mood."

The broken window and the graffiti. She didn't reply; waited for Fergus to say more. He pushed his long, fair hair out of his eyes and yawned again. "Did he tell you? He showed Stefans the photos."

"What photos?"

"Ones he took with his mobile of the damage done. Someone broke a window and sprayed something on the door. The new English owner was furious about it."

Gilly shrugged. "Isn't there always a risk of that if a house is left empty?"

"Stefans said it was a bit weird, though, because there was only one word sprayed on the door."

"Something obscene, probably."

"No." Fergus leaned forward and looked into her eyes, more alert. "Not obscene at all but insinuating, I suppose you could say."

"Aren't you going to tell me what it was?"

"Yeah, of course; just thought the boss might have already told you."

"I've only seen him once this week."

Fergus regarded her intently for a few seconds before his attention went back to the beer mat. He picked it up and began to tap on the table in a drumlike rhythm. "I thought you and the boss were... special friends."

"No."

He tossed the beer mat aside. "No? Well, then, I'll let you in on the secret. Stefans told me... *Thief.* That's what was sprayed on the door. *Thief.* What do you make of that?"

"Why would someone write that?" Gilly shrugged. "Some boys with nothing better to do, I suppose."

"Do you think they were writing about our boss or the new owner or someone else? Anyway, Marc came back to Glanesfort like an anti-Christ breathing fire and fury. He'd had to find someone to clean it off and also to mend the broken window."

Gilly couldn't imagine Marc in a temper and thought him more likely to go tense and quiet if he was angry. Fergus wouldn't know about the blackmail CD, would he? Unlikely that Marc would tell him, as he only felt compelled to tell her about it because she'd listened to the music and the threats.

"So," said Fergus, when she didn't answer. "What do you think?"

"Don't know... maybe vandals?"

She'd only seen Sam a few times since he appeared in the cottage. He met her on the way to playschool with Stefans one morning and asked if he could come to see her in the garden later but the bodyguard hurried him into the Land Rover and shut the door. "Mustn't come," Stefans told her. "Boss wants him to stay in the house or school. Not outside." Poor Sam, a prisoner now in his own home. How would a lively four-year-old boy cope with that?

Fergus ran a hand through his hair. "It's nearly half past nine. I'd better go soon to check on the old man. Gilly, it's depressing, seeing him like that. Sometimes I wish he'd died suddenly, you know, like a heart attack or something, and it would all be over."

"It's hard on you and your mother." In her mind, she saw a red brick house with three storeys, an elegant door with the word *Thief* sprayed across it in paint. What had he done? Or perhaps the graffiti meant nothing. Just a random word chosen by random vandals.

"Marc is going to Tokyo soon. He's got a meeting over there. Another big deal worth millions, I suppose." He put his hand in his pocket and took out the cigarettes again. "I've got to go out for a smoke. Want to come with me? I think it's stopped raining."

Gilly followed him out into the damp evening air. He lit one, took a long drag and closed his eyes, his face pale in the dull light.

"Are you OK, Fergus? You look awful."

"What?" A sudden irritable edge to his voice.

"I think you look terrible. Are you sure you're feeling OK?"

"Yeah, yeah, I'm all right. I'm tired, that's all... haven't had much sleep this week." He stood looking across the road into the forestry. Midges clouded around their heads and he waved a hand to disperse them. He didn't say any more and they stood in silence while he finished his cigarette. His hand shook as he stubbed it out on a windowsill.

"I better go now, Gilly, I need to get to the nursing home. Hope doesn't like me to arrive too late." His mobile rang and he fished it out of his jacket pocket. "Yeah?"

She watched in alarm as his face turned even paler. "Fergus, what is it? What's wrong?"

"That was Hope," he said, as he lowered his mobile. "My father's dead."

Chapter 24

The black Mercedes rolled up the avenue and glided to a halt on the gravel as Gilly and Dean unloaded plants from the back of her Ford. She gave it a quick glance and continued with her work, placing containers of *Cosmos* and *Penstemon* 'Garnet' in the wheelbarrow, which would flower pale pink and deep wine. She studied their labels with deliberation so she didn't have to look up when two people climbed out of the car. Dean headed off towards the walled garden pushing the barrow.

Marc came down the front steps to greet them and shake their hands. He noticed Gilly and walked over, bringing his friends with him, and introduced her to Nigel and Bernice. Nigel, he said, was a schoolfriend from England who now lived in Dublin.

Gilly remembered that he'd mentioned Nigel before, the time they'd gone to see the mill. That day seemed a long time ago, the time he'd first kissed her. Today his eyes held hers for an instant and then glanced away.

Nigel was tall and heavy with receding fair hair. He had small blue eyes, a double chin and a figure that suggested too many expensive dinners.

His wife looked like Vanessa and her office colleagues, with a neat, well-dressed figure. She wore a pale pink suit with gold buttons and Gilly felt reluctant to hold out her own rather grubby hand. She shook the other woman's quickly and put hers behind her back.

"Marc and I met up again when he sold me a house in Ballsbridge," said Nigel. "I hadn't seen him for years, but he hasn't changed much. Gone a bit greyer, perhaps, and is considerably richer, but there you are." He smiled at her with large, uneven teeth. "So you're the gardener? Makes a difference to a property like this, doesn't it? A good garden, I mean."

Bernice smiled politely, without much interest.

"I'm the garden designer," said Gilly, quietly. She watched Marc, who stared at the gravel and pushed the pebbles about with the toe of his shoe.

"We're here for dinner," volunteered Nigel. "Marc has given us a tour of the estate, which is a fine place, I must say. Isn't it, Bernice? I've always fancied a place in the country. We live in suburbia, don't we, darling, although on the outskirts of Foxrock – a rather upmarket suburbia, I must admit – but nothing like this." He waved his large hand around him.

Marc directed his polite smile at him. "Then start saving, Nigel, and I'll sell it to you." He looked at Gilly. "I'm sure you want to talk to me about the garden benches." He took hold of her elbow and moved her further away, out of earshot.

"How are you?" He spoke in a low voice.

"OK."

"I haven't seen you for several days. I've been very busy."

"So have I." He smelled of lemon soap and his hair was damp, as if he'd just had a shower.

Marc looked into her eyes. What expression could she see in his? Pity? Concern? So hard to tell and her stupid, annoying heart thumped loudly now that he stood so close. All her resolve, all those hours spent wide awake at night telling herself to forget him, evaporated in an instant.

"We'll still be friends, won't we, Gilly? I would like us to be friends," he said.

"Yes."

He glanced at the couple who waited for him, then back at her face. "You look tired."

"I haven't been sleeping well."

"I know the feeling. I must go. Nigel and Bernice are staying the night and we're going back to Dublin tomorrow evening."

"You're not serious about selling this place, are you?"

"I don't want to have to part with Glanesfort unless it's really necessary." He glanced again at the couple. "I'm flying to Tokyo early on Sunday to meet a colleague from the office. We have a meeting with Mr Fukuda and the consortium on Monday so... Gilly, will you promise me that if anything happens to worry you, or frighten you while I'm away - anything at all – that you'll contact Stefans? His number is in a book in the drawer near the phone."

She nodded. "Of course I will. Did you talk to the Gardaí?"

"Yes, yes." He moved away. "They're looking into this, don't worry. Stefans will keep a close eye on Sam. He'll check your cottage too. If you feel safer in the main house..."

"I'm fine, don't worry."

"Soon this will be over, Gilly. Then I..."

"It will never be over if you don't face up to this blackmailer. Why can't you see that?"

Alice appeared at the top of the steps. She waved and called, "Marc, telephone, Marc, telephone!"

He raised a hand. "I'm coming." He shrugged and half-smiled at Gilly. "I'd better go in."

"Fergus's father's funeral is on Monday, Marc."

"I know, but unfortunately I'll miss it. I've explained why to Fergus and he's taking a week off to be with his mother." He looked back at her as he walked towards the steps up to the front door, "Remember what I said about Stefans."

Nigel moved over to stand beside her. "He showed us the

walled garden – we think you've done a terrific job, don't we, darling?" He waited for Bernice to nod before continuing. "Even Marc has to admit that and he's fussy, very fussy indeed. I imagine that's why he's successful. Attention to detail and all that. Isn't that supposed to sort out the men from the goats?"

"The sheep from the goats," said Gilly. "I don't think he really intends to sell this place." Nigel might be making plans, fancying himself as the master of Glanesfort. She pictured him striding around the grounds, with two enormous mastiffs at his heels, while Bernice sat in the shade of a tree, sipping Pimms with her expensively dressed friends.

"Hadn't we better go in?" Bernice glanced at a slim gold watch.

"In a minute – you go on, if you like," replied her husband. "Marc and I were in school together. He was a terrific cricketer and played on the first eleven for years – a brilliant batsman who scored many centuries for us. Do you like cricket?"

"I know nothing about it." Gilly wished they would go because she wanted to get on with planting the border. She was going to take Dean with her to choose a metal seat for under the rose arch as he could help her lift it into the car. She spotted him as he strolled back with the wheelbarrow for another load, cigarette between his lips.

Bernice smiled briefly at her and headed off towards the steps.

"Those were the days," said Nigel. "Yes, indeed, there was no one as good as Marc Hillington with a bat."

"Hillington?" She stared at him. "You mean Fletcher, don't you?"

The broad smile slipped from his thick lips. "Fletcher?" Then he laughed. "Why yes, how stupid of me! I'm getting confused in my old age – a senior moment. Of course I mean Fletcher. Hillington was... let me see, yes, Hillington was the captain of the cricket team. I always used to confuse the two of them. Well, goodbye then – nice to have met you."

Gilly watched his large, lumbering shape crunch away across the gravel and wondered. Not an intelligent man, Nigel. He could easily have made a genuine mistake, but had he corrected himself just a little too quickly to be convincing?

Chapter 25

Rain rattled on the cluster of umbrellas, resembling large toadstools in the long, wet grass, a few bright ones among the black. Underneath them, people stood in silence as the undertaker's men lowered the pine coffin into the grave.

Gilly shared her purple umbrella with Dean, who was wearing his black leather jacket, his hands pushed into its pockets.

The priest read the prayers.

When Gilly looked across the grave, she saw Fergus opposite with his pale, thin mother clutching his arm. Fergus stared into the deep hole, his face set in an expression she'd never seen before. More like anger than grief. Poor Fergus. His shoulders were hunched against the wind.

She recognized a few faces in the crowd. The owner of The Fiddler's Inn shared an umbrella with one of the barmen; a couple of the tenants from Glanesfort, including the old lady who had moved into Apartment Five beside Fergus. It was thoughtful of her to attend the funeral. A younger woman with long red hair stood near her. Gilly knew who she was: the striking American artist called Anna, whom Dean had mentioned as one of Fergus's girlfriends.

Alice and Stefans hadn't come. Alice had a bad cold and

didn't want to get one of her chest infections from standing out in the rain and Stefans was collecting Samuel from playschool. Marc, of course, had arrived in Tokyo that morning. He'd flown from Dublin to London on Sunday morning and then on to Japan.

The priest finished speaking and moved towards Fergus to shake his hand. She watched them exchange a few words.

She whispered, "Come on – let's go over to him."

Fergus shrugged when she asked him how he was. "Numb," he said. "I feel kind of numb."

Dean frowned and shifted his weight from one foot to another.

Fergus stared at him for a few minutes before reaching out to pat his shoulder. "Thanks for coming."

A tall man dressed in black, with a long coat and Russianlike fur hat, squelched across the grass towards them. The ends of his grey hair were wet and straggly, while his face, with its large nose, looked purple in the gloom. He helped himself to his hip flask as he walked and held it out to Fergus.

"Here, my boy, you need a shot of this."

"Thanks." Fergus took a sip and made a face. He turned to Gilly and Dean. "This is my uncle, Matthew Browne."

"Pleased to meet you," said Matthew. He put the hip flask back in his overcoat pocket and nodded at Fergus's mother, who looked quickly away. "Pity it's such a dismal day to send off poor old Frank. Talk about pathetic fallacy."

Fergus muttered, "What are you on about? I suppose you've been drinking most of the morning?"

Matthew drew back purple lips and smiled. "Just my way of coping with grief, dear boy."

Fergus turned his face away.

The older man grinned at Dean. "Hello, hello. Aren't you Sarah's nephew? I don't think I've seen you since you were fifteen years old. Didn't I recommend you to Fergie for a job somewhere?"

Dean nodded. "Yeah."

"A gardening job, I seem to remember. And how are you getting on, young man?"

Dean shifted awkwardly from one foot to the other. "All right, thanks, Mr Browne."

"Working for Fergie's rich boss, eh? That's a nice cushy number for you."

Dean shot a look at Gilly.

She came to his rescue. "We've got to go now, Dean." She said goodbye to Fergus and his family.

"Fergus, I'd like a word," said his uncle.

"Not now."

"Just a quick word." He'd a deep voice, a slight Irish accent.

There was something theatrical about him. He spoke in a melodramatic way and his clothes were unusually old-fashioned. The black overcoat with large cape looked like something Sherlock Holmes might have worn.

She tapped Dean's arm. "Let's go, Dean."

As they walked away, Gilly turned to look back. Fergus was close to his uncle, his face almost touching his, a furious look in his eyes.

"Look, I think they're having a row."

Dean swung around as Fergus strode away. His uncle gazed after him.

"What was that about, I wonder?" asked Gilly.

He rolled his eyes. "Who knows? Maybe they don't get on. That's the uncle I told you about, my Auntie Sarah's friend, and he's a bit weird. He used to be a barrister so he knows all sorts."

As they watched, a woman in a brown coat came across the wet grass towards Fergus. Gilly couldn't see her face as she held a black umbrella low over her head and her high-heeled shoes sank with each step. Fergus put his arms around her and kissed her. Probably yet another one of his many girlfriends.

Dean appeared not to notice. "Let's get out of here," he said, "I could do with a drink."

Chapter 26

"I am very sorry, sir, but your room is not ready. Check-in is two o'clock." The receptionist at the front desk spoke perfect English and bowed in an apologetic manner.

All Marc wanted was to lie down for an hour or two to get some sleep or, if not sleep, at least a rest. To lie flat and close his eyes. It had taken several hours to get through immigration and collect their luggage, pass through customs and then get a taxi from Narita airport to take them to the hotel in Chiyoda.

"Tell you what," suggested his accountant, "we'll get some coffee first and then have lunch because you have a one and a half hour wait for your bedroom. Or would you prefer to have a rest in mine?"

"No thanks, it's all right. I'll survive."

Michael bought coffee for the two of them.

His colleague had been irritatingly relaxed on the flight. Soon after they were in the air, the stewards produced lunch and, when cleared away, they lowered the blinds and, within minutes, off to sleep went Michael, head to the side and breathing softly, while Marc flicked through the movie channels. He eventually decided to watch a French film about the Resistance during the Second World War; well made but ultimately depressing when the heroine was shot and died in the arms of her grandfather. Sleep still eluded him so he turned in desperation to his notes. By the time breakfast arrived two hours out of Tokyo, his appetite had vanished.

Michael stirred sugar into his coffee, yawned and stretched. "We can have a look at the lunch menu in one of the restaurants if you like. I'm exhausted. I'd forgotten how long that flight is."

"How can you be exhausted when you slept the whole way?"

"It's not the same as being at home in your own bed, though, is it? You should have taken a sleeping tablet, Marc."

"It would make me feel worse because, when I wake up, my brain feels like someone has stuffed it with heavy cotton wool."

Michael's attempt at a sympathetic smile looked more mocking than caring. "It's good to be back in Tokyo again. I haven't been here since my days with Mr Azuma."

"Ah, Mr Azuma – wasn't he your favourite boss?" asked Marc.

"He was one of the wealthiest men in the world at that time." Michael ignored his attempt at sarcasm. "He was responsible for developing many of the major office and retailing complexes in Hong Kong, Taipei and Shanghai – as well as Tokyo."

"Remind me again why you were so indispensable to him. Something to do with a project here in Tokyo, wasn't it?"

"If I'd been indispensable, I wouldn't be working for your modest outfit. No, not a project in Toyko, I lived here but I was on contract to assist with a Hong Kong project."

"A wonder you ever came home."

"Believe me, I didn't want to. One of the worst days of my life was the day I was told my contract would not be renewed and it dawned on me that I would have to return to England."

"Is London really that bad?"

"How can you say that? The rain, the suffocating atmosphere, the sheer loneliness of London… I don't know how you can bear it. I can't wait to get back to Tokyo or Hong Kong. Living in London is like a death sentence."

"That sounds a bit extreme."

"You've never lived in Asia, Marc, you should try it. Once I got used to the culture shock of life in Tokyo, I found the reverse culture shock of London was far, far worse. It's so... damp and depressing – as well as boring and lonely." He added quickly, "No offence meant. I'm grateful to you for giving me a job when I couldn't get anything in Asia."

"No offence taken. I'll miss you when you leave." Boring and lonely? His colleague had a point.

They finished their coffee and Michael stood up. "I think we should find my room and leave our luggage there. Then perhaps some lunch?"

Immaculately dressed in their uniforms, the hotel staff offered unceasing courtesy. The bellboy, who turned out to be a tiny girl wearing white gloves, welcomed them graciously to the lift and did her utmost to wrestle the suitcases away from Michael. He had his reputation as an English gentleman to defend and refused to relinquish them. She smiled and bowed, but looked ill at ease and a little embarrassed when he insisted on carrying both his and Marc's cases into the lift. They made an incongruous pair, the dark-haired Japanese girl and his tall, fair-haired colleague, struggling in the doorway until Michael finally claimed victory.

Michael's room on the twelfth floor was larger than Marc had expected, spotlessly clean with a view over the garden and city. Suitcases dealt with, they went to find lunch. Shops lined the downstairs corridors of the hotel, arched windows displaying fashion and other expensive designer items. There was even a florist near the front desk where a bunch of sweet-scented white flowers reminded him of Gilly.

The hotel was vast, a main building with an additional tower, and long, long corridors. Over thirty restaurants, offering menu choices from Japanese to French, to Italian to Chinese, and more.

Michael chose a restaurant on one of the top floors with a panoramic vista of the city from which they could see, almost hidden in the mist, the foothills of Mount Fuji. They looked down on the garden, immaculate Japanese style with waterfall and clipped hedges, traditional red footbridge and stepping stones over pools of water. He pointed out the skyscrapers of Shinjuku in the distance.

Once seated, he glanced down the menu. "What about sushi? You should be able to manage that, although I know you're a steak man. How hungry are you?"

"Not very hungry."

"You never are. I often think you live on fresh air, Marc. Fresh air and Irish whiskey, of course."

Marc laughed. "You order something for me. You're the Asian expert, after all."

"How about a cocktail to start?"

"Not for me, thanks. I need to concentrate on our office building and the meeting with the chairman this afternoon."

His colleague reluctantly agreed and selected miso soup, salad and sushi for two.

"I hope you enjoy your first visit to Japan," said Michael. "You see what I mean about their manners, don't you? All Japanese hotel staff are extremely well trained. They're very efficient and never expect a tip. In fact, don't attempt to give them tips because you will only insult them."

"I'll try to remember that. Mr Fukuda said he would be at this meeting later today when we'll get a chance to meet the chairman before tomorrow's presentation. I'm still impressed by his perfect English."

"I agree. I lived here for five years and I never managed to learn Japanese. I decided to soak up a bit of the culture instead."

"I'm anxious about our presentation," Marc said. "You and I both know that our offices are not of the same calibre as the other two selected by Mr Fukuda and his team. Not in such a prestigious area, for starters."

"But your building has other attributes that may appeal to the Japanese. Remember what the architects said? A little modification and it will be just what they are looking for – and not as expensive as the other two. Mind you, it will take the corporation weeks to consider all the pros and cons of three separate pitches – more than weeks, perhaps."

Michael knew the Japanese business mindset, one of the main reasons Marc had asked him to come along. So much depended on the outcome of their presentation: the refurbishment of his apartment building in Dublin and the purchase of the three-storey red brick house in London. And, more worrying still, the future of Glanesfort. He needed cash in the bank now, not months away. There were also the demands for cash from the blackmailer. But he couldn't think about that at the moment.

"I hope I have the patience to see this to the end," he said, "because I dread the thought of selling my home in Ireland."

"You wouldn't let Glanesfort go, would you? I thought it was your favourite, your refuge from the stress of living in London – the jewel in your portfolio's crown."

"I won't part with it unless I'm desperate. I really need to sell this office building as soon as possible."

"I often compare the Japanese way of doing business to an ocean liner." His colleague smiled. "It takes an age to get the thing going but, once in motion, it's almost impossible to stop. Bear with the corporation and all will be well in the end."

Their food arrived with a flourish of courtesy.

"We'll have to take a stroll in the hotel garden while we're here," said Michael. "Pools of Koi carp and a waterfall. You're into gardens these days, aren't you?"

"They improve a property. You see how the garden here makes a difference in a city of tower blocks. A green area with water is..." What was it? "Peaceful and restful, I suppose."

"How's the walled garden coming along at Glanesfort? It must be nearly finished by now."

Marc looked him in the eye. "Not finished, no. There's still at least a month to go."

"I rang Fergus this week to commiserate with him after his father died and he said it's almost complete. He told me a bit about the young landscaper, Jenny."

"Gilly."

"Yes, Gilly. Somehow, I get the impression that your charming Irish lad did not succeed in luring her to..."

"What did Fergus say about her?"

"She's amusing and almost pretty, but she's stubborn and likes to get her own way."

Marc frowned. "I think she's pretty."

Michael watched him fiddle with his food. "I'm sorry if I said something wrong."

"You didn't. I'm tired, that's all." Would Gilly listen to what he'd said? She could be obstinate, but Stefans knew to keep an eye on her and the cottage. If he saw anything unusual, he would phone the Garda station. Not a good time to have to travel so far away, but this meeting was important. He'd paid the latest blackmail demand and perhaps all would be well. That was how it had been in the past and there was no reason to suspect anything different.

Half a plate of sushi and a salad later, Marc returned to the front desk and the receptionist told him, with another gracious bow, that his room was ready. Another uniformed girl appeared to escort him to the twelfth floor. Efficient Sally had managed to get two bedrooms with a garden view on the same corridor by sending an email after making the online booking, but it was just his luck that the previous occupants of his room had overstayed their allotted time. No time for a sleep now before the car came to pick them up.

*

Marc and Michael arrived fifteen minutes early for the courtesy meeting with the corporation's chairman and were shown into the room where it was to take place. A low table, about a foot high, stood in the middle with three armchairs along each side and another at the head. The two men were invited to sit with their backs to the wall, facing the door, an old Samurai custom.

"So no one can sneak up on us from behind," whispered Michael.

The Japanese businessmen filtered in. Most of them had been on the London trip, including Mr Fukuda. They exchanged business cards – called name cards here – in a dramatic ritual with those they had not already met, each man shouting out his name and company as cards were presented with both hands and a bow. As instructed by his colleague, Marc received every card with both hands and studied it earnestly to show respect, before putting it on the table in front of him, opposite its owner.

Mr Fukuda looked the same as he had in London, lean and fit with glasses. This time he wore a pink shirt and discreetly striped tie with his grey suit. All Japanese businessmen seemed partial to grey suits.

The door opened and the men jumped to their feet. The chairman entered. He made his way to his place at the top and sat down, immediately picking up the phone on a small side table to order green tea. He could have ordered anything because he spoke in Japanese, but this was what arrived a few minutes later. Marc loathed green tea, but would have to make an effort to get it down.

The chairman looked at his visitors and smiled. He was a big, heavy man and elderly, with a very short haircut and grey hair. He wore the obligatory grey suit with a white shirt and dark tie.

The chairman didn't speak English so his comments and questions were addressed to Mr Fukuda, who translated and redirected them to Marc and Michael. When Marc asked him something, Mr. Fukuda put his head to one side before answering, as if considering his options carefully. He said he would join them for dinner later, accompanied by three more members of the team that had visited London. The formal discussions about the office building would take place at ten o'clock the following morning in the boardroom.

Dropped back to the hotel after the meeting, they had showers, changed and helped themselves to a quick drink from the mini-bar in Marc's room. Beer for Michael and a whiskey for Marc.

Michael, in livelier form after several beers, confessed that he hoped to catch up with an ex-girlfriend the following night, when their more formal pitch to the board of directors was completed.

"This evening we're being taken to an authentic Japanese restaurant in Roppongi. It's a very popular and expensive area with shops, boutiques, embassies, bars and, of course, night clubs," said Michael. "You'll have to remove your shoes before you go into the dining room and sit cross-legged on the floor."

"Are you joking?"

"No, I'm perfectly serious. The corporation will take us to a private room, which will only be big enough to hold the very low table. I've tried for years to sit as motionless as the Japanese when eating, but it's extremely difficult for a Westerner. Believe me, it's almost impossible."

While Marc sat in the bedroom armchair and gazed out of

the window at the garden below, Michael explained that he'd met the alluring Aiko Yamashiro in an advertising agency.

"She also speaks English because her father was born in America and brought up in Hawaii. The family moved back to Japan in the 1960s, when her dad was a boy, because Aiko's grandfather wanted to die here."

"I suppose you have a taste for exotic women," Marc replied. Foreign yet familiar because of her US association, he could well imagine her appealing to Michael.

"She improved her English working with international companies in the ad agency. She's interesting because she defies traditional Japanese convention with relish and is perfectly comfortable hanging out with a *gaijin*, that's a foreigner like me. She told me once she feels like an outsider in her own country because of the family's American connections – and because the more conservative Japanese women often view her with suspicion."

Belonging and yet not belonging. Marc knew that feeling well. He'd been the hero of his school rugby team one week and an outcast the next. Nigel always liked to remind him of his French blood and had shouted, "Stupid frog, you can't even convert a try" in the changing rooms after a league final and had meant it. Two successful conversions that day counted for nothing because a draw wasn't good enough.

Not good enough for his father either, who had watched from the sideline and turned away in disgust when the ball missed the posts. His mother was never there to defend him because she hated rugby and believed it a rough game. Louise made a fuss of him when he came home with cuts and bruises, but nothing could persuade her to cheer him on in the wind, rain and mud on the sideline of a rugby pitch at an expensive English boarding school.

"Perhaps Aiko should go to Ireland," Marc said. "Everyone would welcome her there."

"You're beginning to sound like you're quite smitten with Ireland – or maybe smitten with a young lady who lives there."

Marc smiled and didn't reply.

Michael grinned and rolled his eyes.

The corporation car arrived to take them to dinner. Roppongi thronged with people and brightly lit streets throbbed with the sound of car engines in traffic jams. The air was surprisingly clear and everywhere Japanese salarymen headed out for drinks with their bosses.

No sign of Mr Fukuda, who missed the first dishes. This didn't bother the others, who started to drink Japanese saki and eat with undisguised relish.

"Do you think he's going to turn up?" Marc asked Michael.

"Oh yes, at some stage. This is normal for Japan, don't worry." He muttered this under his breath so that the others would not hear.

Michael, swallowing down chilled saki, kept nodding encouragingly at his weary boss. They had miso soup, more sushi and all manner of vegetables, chicken and rice, moving onto burgundy after the saki.

He was right. Mr Fukuda appeared half an hour late, just in time for the burgundy. Marc liked the wine and agreed to a refill.

Mr Fukuda made an effort to entertain his visitors. He asked Marc about his son and appeared interested to hear about his house in Ireland. He explained how much he enjoyed French wine. He had been to Beaune, the capital of burgundy wines, once on a holiday. He listened attentively when Marc told him his mother lived in Paris and asked polite questions about the city.

Mr Fukuda only mentioned the London property once and, as soon as he spoke, his colleagues around the table fell silent. "Our chairman is a little concerned about the reconstruction costs and wonders if you would make an allowance for these in your figures."

"We haven't included those costs, but we will take a look at this matter before tomorrow's meeting," replied Marc. This was an irritating development as it meant he and Michael would have to spend more time going through the presentation and have these figures ready before ten o'clock. It was a pity they hadn't mentioned this earlier. He glanced at his company secretary, who raised his eyebrows very slightly and then turned to smile at Mr Fukuda.

Later, they visited a bar off a backstreet nearby. He remembered going up in a lift, a bit queasy now when he noticed that his stomach left the ground floor seconds after he did. One of their Japanese companions proudly told them Tokyo's better-off businessmen and local celebrities frequented it. Artwork decorated the walls and the room glowed with soft lighting; a buzz of chatter and music surrounded them. Michael began telling stories about his time in Asia.

Marc tried to concentrate on the conversation. Light-headed, he longed to close his eyes as long hours without sleep threatened to overwhelm him. Michael looked happy, laughing and enjoying himself. He persuaded Marc to try Yamazaki Japanese whiskey, but Marc put his hand over the glass when Michael tried to refill it. He had to stop drinking so that he would be able to work out the revised figures before the meeting in the morning.

By the time the car dropped them both back to the hotel at eleven o'clock, he already regretted the whiskey. The walk from the lift to his bedroom felt as long as the one to their boarding gate at Heathrow, but a good deal more unsteady. He parted company with Michael outside his door and they exchanged cheerful goodnights.

He climbed into bed and fell straight to sleep.

At three o'clock in the morning, he woke with a start and took several seconds to recall where he was. For another hour, he tossed from side to side under the covers but no comforting cloud of sleep descended. Eventually, he got up and stood staring out of the window.

Dark areas among bright lights marked where the trees and garden were in a city much greener than he'd imagined. Out in the darkness, he could just make out the tower blocks of Shinjuku rising to meet the sky, red lights flashing on top as a warning to aircraft. Such a vast, busy city where he was only one among thirteen million people.

As he gazed out on Tokyo with a mixture of awe and frustration, Michael's words about his ex-girlfriend resurfaced in his mind. She felt like an outsider. Among thirteen million others, he was also an outsider. He pressed his forehead against the cool glass of the window, shut his eyes and longed to be back at Glanesfort. A sense of isolation flooded him as he looked down at the streets below.

The seed sown in his mind in Ireland began to germinate. What had Gilly said to him?

Face up to whoever is doing this. It will never be over if you don't face up to this blackmailer. Why can't you see that?

Easy for her to say, of course, because she didn't know what had happened; had no comprehension of the devastation it had caused his family all those years ago. What else had she said? By keeping this hidden, he was giving the blackmailer power over him. She had a point there. He knew that his silence and determination to keep the past locked away was enabling the person who sent the CDs of Mozart's music and the threats. And now, it wasn't just him who would suffer if he failed to pay the money. His son and Gilly, both innocents, might also be at risk because of him.

Joe Milligan had tried to brush this off, as usual. Blackmailers were cowards, he'd said, they issued threats because they were faceless; no one knew who they were. People were afraid of them. Just bullies.

Nigel had been a bully in school, but eventually Marc had decided to go to the housemaster to tell him what was going on. Not to save himself but to save the younger boy Nigel had moved on to torment. A boy two years younger who was Asian, lonely and alone among foreigners. Strange how being here in Tokyo had brought that memory back.

Joe Milligan had failed him. Marc knew that now. He'd wasted too much time waiting for the tall, cheerful private investigator to find the nanny. Perhaps his patience with Joe had been a form of subconscious procrastination, another attempt to block out the past. He would phone him when he returned to London to tell him that he could no longer continue to employ him. That he was putting this matter in the hands of the police. He would tell them everything, just as he had told the Gardaí in Ireland.

Could it really be that simple? Suppose he chose to tell Gilly what his father had done? Perhaps, deep down inside him, he'd wanted to for weeks and only realised now that his happiness might really lie in his own hands; that it was time to take a risk. He resolved to take the first step straight away, before this sudden, lucid sense of purpose left him. In the morning, he might blame it on the wine and the Japanese whiskey, but now, in the middle of the night, he felt compelled to act.

Marc glanced at his watch. First he would have to ring his mother, warn her about what he intended to do, which was only fair because she too might suffer from the repercussions.

He walked over to the telephone and dialled the Parisian number.

Seven hours behind Tokyo so she and François would be finishing their evening meal and, although an affable man, his stepfather disliked interruptions when eating. Marc hoped

Louise would pick up the phone and he intended to appease her by making an effort to speak French.

He heard the ringing tone. It continued for several seconds and then ceased. A voice answered and he said, *"Maman? Allo. Oui, c'est moi."*

Chapter 27

Marc spotted Joe Milligan near a park bench and watched him toss bread to the ducks from a crumpled brown paper bag. He made his way towards him, sidestepping pushchairs and small children on tricycles. The ducks quacked and squabbled, churning up the pond water to a thick green soup as he reached out to shake Joe's hand. He took his sunglasses out of his shirt pocket and put them on. The heatwave was stretching towards the weekend and people sprawled on lawns, eating sandwiches, reading and sunbathing. The temperature in Tokyo had been twenty-three degrees and here it was twenty-seven, unusually hot for London in May.

Joe squinted at him under bushy eyebrows. "Ah, Mr Fletcher, you made it back from Japan in one piece. How did your meeting go?"

"I'm waiting to find out. Japanese corporations don't make quick decisions."

"And how was your flight?"

"The flight back was even longer than the one out. I didn't get into Heathrow until after eight o'clock last night."

A red football landed with a splash among the ducks and sent them paddling off, protesting indignantly. A boy ran to the edge of the water, shouting for his mother. He looked about Samuel's age.

"Let's sit down," suggested Joe. "My old legs aren't as young as yours." He waved a hand towards the bench.

Marc joined him on the wooden seat. "I've got your money here." He took the fat envelope of cash out of his suit trousers. "I have to say, Joe, your last bill was a lot more than I expected. Do you have receipts?"

"Of course, of course, don't worry. I can send on anything you want." He took the envelope and ripped it open, flicked through the notes and put them into the breast pocket of his jacket. "Thank you, you're a gentleman. I'm afraid investigating is expensive but, if you ask around, you'll find I'm really very reasonable compared to some of the bigger outfits."

Marc didn't reply.

"So," continued Joe, "no sign of a sale in Japan?"

"No, not yet, but there's another company interested now. Before I left the office to meet you here, I had a Mr Kiu Fat on the phone. He owns a Chinese investment company."

"An interesting development."

"Perhaps. A friend mentioned that Chinese speculators were looking for property investments in London." Perhaps Kiu Fat had heard that a Japanese corporation was sniffing around. He would call him back later when he'd heard from Michael.

He watched a young couple on the lawn to the right of the bench. Students with folders spread out around them. They lay close, arms around each other and moved nearer to share a lengthy kiss.

Where was Gilly? He'd tried to phone her several times from the hotel in Tokyo. He'd tried in the afternoons because of the time difference, hoping to catch her before she went to work and had let the mobile ring for several minutes. She hadn't answered. Alice hadn't seen her either when he called her the previous night from his apartment in London. Maybe she was with her sister. Or perhaps something had happened to her mobile; she often forgot to charge it or left it lying in the garden. Still no answer that morning when he tried at seven-thirty.

"I understand your decision to go to the police. I only wish I'd managed to get more information for you," Joe muttered. "I feel your frustration but it's not been easy... not as easy as I hoped. There's still no sign of the lass returning to Leeds and now I have to go away myself."

"You're going away?"

"Yes, that's right. I'm off to Australia."

"Australia?"

"Yes, yes." He looked down, seeming interested in the lace of one shoe, which he leaned forward to tie. "I just thought I would like to see the country before I get too old for the long flight out. I've a few friends there who will put me up." Joe had abandoned his usual relaxed attitude. What expression was in his eyes? Wariness?

"You've spent six months searching for the nanny and all you've come up with is this postgraduate student in Leeds. A postgraduate who seems to have left the country."

"Yes, that's true, unfortunately."

Marc frowned. "Joe, I mentioned on the phone... on the phone when I called you, about the Gardaí in Ireland. I had to tell them about this... can't put it off any longer. The last CD threatened my son."

Joe fiddled with his shoelace. "You must do what you feel to be right and I don't blame you, my friend. That's a most unpleasant development, most unpleasant indeed." He sat upright and got up slowly and stiffly. He glanced back towards the pond where the boy's mother poked at the ball with a long stick, trying to push it towards the bank. "To be honest, I feel bad. I've charged enough and I know the outcome isn't exactly satisfactory. Here, let me give you back a couple of hundred quid as a goodwill gesture." He reached into his pocket.

"No, it's all right." Marc stood up, took off his sunglasses to grip his hand and thought his blue eyes lacked their usual sparkle, that he looked tired, his face more lined than before. "You might need that money now you're going away. I hope you have a good time in Australia." He'd noticed the threadbare jacket, the frayed end on the lace, shoes worn at the heel. Perhaps Joe hadn't much money to spend on himself.

"Thank you." The older man squeezed his hand longer than was necessary.

"Who knows, maybe we will meet again someday."

Joe laughed. "I hope we won't, my friend. I hope you get all this... er... unpleasantness sorted out long before I return to England. You've been through the mill. Goodbye then and look after yourself, won't you? And that little boy of yours. Take good care of him." He didn't meet Marc's eye and, even though his voice sounded calm, something was bothering him. Not his usual expansive, cheerful self.

Marc thanked him again before he walked away. When he reached the gate out onto the street, he turned and saw that the private investigator still stood in the same position, watching him and that he raised one of his large hands to wave. Marc waved back and moved into the bustle of the road outside the park, as the sunseekers and picnickers headed back to their offices and their colleges.

He did not doubt that he'd done the right thing, but a slight sense of loss hit him. He would miss that big hulk of a man, would miss his self-assured manner, but he couldn't help thinking that today something had changed. It was hard to put his finger on it. Joe had seemed reluctant to chat in his usual way and, when he'd said goodbye, something akin to regret lingered in his eyes.

*

"It's weird, Marc." Amanda took a key out of her black shoulder bag and opened the navy blue door, her hand resting on the brass knob for a few seconds. She spoke in a low voice. "When Mrs Wilkie rang, she said Joe Milligan left in a hurry. He gave her the key to his apartment to give to his landlord and she couldn't resist taking a peep. The flat was completely cleared out."

Marc glanced up at the yellowish brick, the white plasterwork around the bay window to the left of the door. He hadn't been to Shepherd's Bush for a long time, as he preferred to leave the day-to-day management of tenants in Amanda's capable hands.

It was a tall house with three storeys; two more bays on the next floor above. The glass of smaller windows on the third floor glinted in the sunlight. He remembered the day he'd bought these apartments; he owned three, one in the basement and two on the third floor. Another landlord, whom he'd met a couple of times, had purchased the other four several years before.

"Mrs Wilkie lives in the basement flat. She's the one who's got the black bin bags I told you about." Amanda's short, dark spiky hair framed her angular face with its cherry-red lipstick.

The hall had a high ceiling with walls painted magnolia. Cheap and easy to slap on when one tenant moved out and before another appeared. The previous owner had already converted the house into flats. Marc had even inherited two of the tenants.

She closed the door behind them and her silver bracelets clunked against each other. "I remember telling you he was a private investigator. He mentioned what he did for a living when he moved in and he'd already made friends with Mrs Wilkie I think he told me the day her fridge broke down. Anyway, I remember that's why I gave you his business card back then.

Did you ever need his services?" Her lips twitched in a half-smile, as if expecting him to deny this, as if someone like him would never need to employ a private investigator.

"Actually yes, I did. We always met somewhere else – usually in a pub or a park." He added, "I asked him to check out something for me."

She led the way up the stairs.

"He had this second-floor flat." She unlocked the cream door and pushed it open. "I asked his landlord for the key – the landlord is a nice guy and obliging when things go wrong with these apartments."

Amanda stepped across the sparsely furnished room and flung open one of the three sashes in the bay, screwed up her face and complained about the stale smell of cigarettes. A square mahogany table stood in front of the windows, covered by a white cotton tablecloth stained with coffee rings. A comfortable-looking red sofa faced the tiled fireplace.

Marc glanced up at a damp mark on the ceiling. It ran like a finger pointing towards the bay window.

"I'll get the plumber to check out our flat overhead. Perhaps there's a small leak somewhere." Amanda pulled her mobile out of her bag and tapped in a message.

"He's left it tidy," Marc said.

"Yeah, but I think the old lady downstairs helped. She's the one I'd like you to meet. She says she knew Joe well and she's... well, she'll explain about it. I'll take you to meet her now."

A beige carpet led them down to the basement and to another cream door. Amanda knocked and a woman with startling red hennaed hair and heavily applied make-up opened it. Dark orange pencil lines replaced her eyebrows and she wore a navy smock and white trousers. She waved them towards the sofa and two big armchairs, both covered in faded floral chintz. She smiled and nodded when Amanda introduced them.

She shook hands with Marc. "Yes, I'm Margie Wilkie. So you're the owner of this flat? It's lovely to meet you. I've only ever meet Amanda, you see, but she often mentions your name. I'm sure you're a very busy man."

She'd obviously been expecting them and carried a tray with tea and custard creams from her kitchen. Amanda helped her with the cups and reminded her about why they had come.

"Oh, yes, Amanda, I was great friends with Mr Milligan – Joe. He was a good neighbour, Mr Fletcher. Very kind to me... kind to Charlie too. I'll miss him now he's gone."

She moved with an agility that belied her eighty-three years over to where a blue budgie peeped at them from his cage near the bay window. He hopped closer to the bars and tilted his head to one side. She bent to look at the little bird, then chuckled and whistled.

"You told Amanda you had found something, Mrs Wilkie?" Marc prompted.

"Oh, Margie please – do call me Margie. Mrs Wilkie reminds me of my mother-in-law and she was a frightful battleaxe."

Amanda caught Marc's eye and raised her eyebrows.

He tried again. "You found something in Mr Milligan's belongings?"

"Yes, yes, I did. Joe left a scrapbook in one of the bags and when I opened it up, well I... poor man, he was quite incapable of cleaning out that flat on his own, so I gave him a hand and... well, he left a box and several bags with me, and his stereo. He's not throwing out the stereo, you understand, said he'll come back some time and collect that, but the bin bags are to go into the rubbish."

Amanda tapped Margie's arm. "Could you show us the scrapbook you mentioned, please? Mr Fletcher would be interested to see it."

"Of course, of course, I'm sorry to waste your time nattering,

Mr Fletcher, you must be a busy man... do have another custard cream. I shouldn't really have looked in his rubbish, I know, but the bag felt so heavy and I phoned Amanda as soon as I found it. It's in this box here with the stereo and his music." She gestured towards a large cardboard box in the corner of her sitting room.

Marc followed her over, bent down and flicked through the CDs in the box. "Did he like music, Mrs Wilkie?"

"Oh yes, he loved it. He often played music. He used to invite me in for a cup of Earl Grey tea and explain about the composers. Classical music, all of it. Joe had no time for modern pop music."

Somewhere, deep inside him, Marc felt his intestines tighten.

"Opera was his favourite, of course," she said.

He pulled out a CD and gripped it tightly, staring at her. *The Magic Flute* by Wolfgang Amadeus Mozart. "Did you and Joe listen to Mozart, Mrs Wilkie...Margie?"

Her wrinkles deepened in a frown of concentration. "Mozart. Let me see, he also liked Wagner and Linst, or should that be Liszt? But yes, I believe we did. There was one he often played."

"*Requiem?*" Marc fixed his eyes on her face. The word stuck in his throat and he had to force it out.

"Yes, that was it. Joe loved that one – so sad and haunting at times. Isn't it in the box?"

"No. Perhaps he took it with him." Marc noticed that his voice sounded shaky, as if he was having trouble breathing.

Joe Milligan loved Mozart's *Requiem.*

Margie reached into a plastic bag and lifted out an A4 sized book. She handed it to Amanda. "Here it is, dear, the scrapbook I mentioned – and the photo album is in another bag. I presumed it was Joe's family, although he never mentioned a family apart from the young lady who used to visit him occasionally. Funny he should want to throw it out, though." She turned to Marc. "That's what made me wonder... I thought it was a bit odd to want to get rid of it and I had a look and then I saw... well, I noticed that the cuttings are... well, all about you."

Amanda opened the scrapbook, held it out to Marc, pointed. "See here."

He hadn't seen those words for two years, but the headline in the newspaper still sent a current coursing through him like an electric shock: *Celebrity Actor Dies in Car Crash.* Two photos: one of a bald man and the other of a woman with curly, blonde hair.

Margie was the first to speak. "Your wife, Mr Fletcher, isn't she? I remember when that happened... so horrible for you. I lived here then, you see. I couldn't believe it when I saw these cuttings. There are more about you and your business. I don't understand why Joe kept these."

Marc looked at another photo, one of Rachel and himself at a charity ball. The tightness in his intestines crawled up to his abdomen.

"Here's the photo album." Margie opened the heavy book. "I showed it to Amanda because I thought it was strange to leave it behind when it was his family, but it's not his family, is it? I couldn't believe it when I saw your name written inside the cover. Why, goodness me, Mr Fletcher, that's you, isn't it? The very image of you – and is that your little boy? Ah, bless the little angel."

Marc flicked through the pages and his heart thudded against his ribs. "I haven't seen this for a couple of years. Samuel is only a baby."

Amanda tapped at a photo. "Is that you when you were a teenager? Your parents?"

There he was, dressed in rugby gear, his mother wearing a long coat with a fur collar and looking cold, hunched against the chill. He held a silver cup in his hands, a broad grin on his face and knees smeared with mud. She must have come to watch that day. Marc closed the book with a snap. "Yes. My mother and father at my school. Margie, there are a few questions I'd like to ask you about Joe Milligan. You mentioned a young lady who visited him. Who was that?"

Margie gave him a detailed description of Joe Milligan's niece. A beautiful girl, she said, had been an actor or a model or something. Long dark hair and a wide smile with the whitest teeth she'd ever seen, like in one of those ads on television.

"Did you talk to her?" Marc asked.

"Oh, yes, I used to be invited down to meet her sometimes. She told me she acted on the stage," Margie said. "A lovely girl and her uncle was so fond of her. I think she travelled all over England with her plays. I often thought Joe would have made a good actor... such a strong voice for a man of his age."

Marc waved away the plate of custard creams. "No, thank you. Do you know her name?"

"Yes, of course. He told me her name was Ruby, Ruby Milligan."

The room seemed to grow smaller, dimmer as Marc reached into his jacket pocket and pulled out his wallet. He opened it and took out a photo, handing it to Margie.

She studied it. "Yes, that's her, that's Ruby. Goodness, do you know her too? Isn't she beautiful? So proud of her, he was. Poor Joe, I hope he enjoys Australia. It's a long, long way from friends and family."

Marc walked over to the window, stepped round the table with the budgie's cage, and looked out; the chatter of the two women faded behind him. He heard cups rattle on saucers and held up a hand to shade his eyes from the sunlight that streamed down into the area outside. Up on the street, dogs trotted along on leads, attached to invisible hands that belonged to legs and shoes and boots. Wheels spun beside the pavement, silver hubcaps glinting in the sun.

He gripped the top of an antique window seat and the mahogany wood pressed into his palms. His mind raced, thoughts whirling like the wheels outside. Who was this man Joe Milligan? Who the hell was he? Almost definitely using a false name and working in tandem with the nanny. If the two of them had laid this trap for him, he had been stupid enough to walk right into it.

"More tea, Mr Fletcher?" Margie's voice filtered through.

"No, thank you. I must go." He turned back to nod at Amanda. "We need to go."

He thanked Margie for her information and walked out with the scrapbook and the photo album wedged under his arm.

"Want a lift back, Marc?" Amanda gestured towards her black Mini Cooper parked nearby. "Save you getting a taxi or the tube."

"Thanks. It's only twenty minutes in the car, isn't it?"

She gave him a sharp look as he sat in the passenger seat, but said nothing. Amanda, like his personal assistant, Sally, knew when he didn't want to discuss something.

"Are you going back to the office?" she asked after a few minutes.

"No. I think I'll go home," Marc said. "I've got something I need to do."

How had Joe found him when he'd been so careful to conceal his real identity? Was Joe one of the many enemies his father had made? Joe had kept the photo album taken by the nanny and was obviously related to her, Jane or Ruby or whatever her name really was. He'd been told so many lies and didn't know what to believe, their elaborate smokescreen swirling and shifting like a fog on the Thames.

Amanda turned right onto Shepherd's Bush Green and slammed her foot on the brake. She swore softly. "Hey, I never saw that biker!" A black leather clad figure flashed past them and revved into the distance.

Marc grabbed at the dashboard to prevent him falling forwards. The scrapbook and the photo album on the back seat of the convertible Mini fell on the floor. He glanced at Amanda and quickly looked away, imagining the private investigator sitting in that sparse flat, playing Mozart's *Requiem*; carefully recording the messages sent to torment him.

They approached Hammersmith Bridge Road.

She was not a postgraduate student in Leeds University. The role of the private investigator had been a ruse, another way to extract money from him while keeping him close, encouraging him to confide in him. Joe knew what he was doing and who Marc was. Keep your enemies close. If it wasn't so serious, he would laugh at the irony of it all. No wonder Joe had put him off going to the police for so long.

Amanda drove on while the Thames idled beside them. Low tide joined Chiswick Eyot to the mainland, a pathway of stones and grey mud where birds hopped and zigzagged, beaks probing.

The scrapbook, meticulously compiled, showed the lengths to which these two had gone to be certain he was their target, the man they'd determined to hunt down: his father's son. Marc watched an oystercatcher run in short, jerky steps towards the water's edge. Rachel's death two years before had been the catalyst. Their photographs in the newspapers had given him away because it was he, not Rachel or the celebrity actor, they had wanted to track down. They must have recognised his face in the photographs and planted the niece as a nanny in his house, to check out the minor details of his life, steal the photo album. All part of the plan to prove his identity. He'd been stupid to advertise for a nanny, should have gone to an agency, but he could blame his grief at his wife's death for that. He hadn't been thinking straight.

Joe Milligan was probably boarding a plane by now, suitcase in hand, heading off to Australia or, more likely, one of those tax havens where Marc sent the money. Countries where Joe must have set up bank accounts under the names of dubious charities: Belize, Burmuda, the Cayman Islands and several others. It was all very complex and all very clever. Joe had completely taken him in with his easy-going, scruffy manner.

Amanda dropped him at the door, drove off down Chiswick Mall and held up her left hand to wave. Marc watched the Mini grow smaller and gazed at the river. A young couple, who looked no more than teenagers, strolled hand in hand. A grey-haired man passed with a fluffy white dog that attempted to sniff at his ankles but was yanked away.

Joe certainly believed in keeping his enemies close. So close that the enemy thought of him as a friend, a friend who sympathized and pitied him. He'd been foolish to fall for this. Back in the park, Joe had seemed unusually evasive, but had looked sorry to see Marc go. He'd watched him leave with concern in his eyes and raised a hand to wave.

Marc turned away from the river and shivered. Hard to believe this was happening to him, that he'd been duped. This tall, shabbily dressed man with the kind blue eyes was not a private investigator or an ex-detective sergeant in the police. Marc knew those credentials would soon prove false and would belong to some other accomplice or friend. He would have to come to terms with the fact that Joe Milligan was a fraud, a devious blackmailer, who might even have set other plans in motion before he disappeared.

Marc unlocked the familiar door and closed it behind him. He would go upstairs and phone the police.

Chapter 28

Gilly watched the late night news. All bad news, as usual: murder; a bank robbery; a hit and run incident somewhere in Dublin. One of the reporters reminded her of Marc, the same height and brown hair, but lacking his sudden bright smile; his Gallic shrug. Odd that he hadn't tried to phone her from London since he'd arrived back from Japan, but perhaps he'd been busy. Perhaps this was what it would be like now that he'd decided it was safer to keep his distance.

She couldn't find her phone and thought that maybe she'd left it in her car. Perhaps he didn't want to phone her and was determined to carry out his resolve to keep her at arm's length. What harm could a quick call do?

In the kitchen, she made herself a mug of coffee.

No sign of Alice these days, who kept Samuel locked up in the house in the evenings.

Fergus was in terrible form and had barely said a word when she dropped in to see him earlier. An overflowing ashtray and empty bottles of beer stood on the kitchen counter. She left after ten minutes because he pointed out that he was too tired to make conversation and lay on the sofa with his eyes shut, unshaven and yawning. Still coming to terms with his father's death and recovering from those long sleepless nights at his bedside.

She decided she had three choices: she could go to bed or she could open up the envelope beside her on the sofa and begin to draw a plan for the Galway hotel garden or she could watch television. She flicked through the channels again and found a documentary about canal trips. She should really start on the planting plan because she had to call them on Monday and arrange to see the golf course. She still couldn't believe that they would pick her for the project. She pulled her feet up under her in the armchair, while the mug of coffee steamed below her on the carpet.

Where was Marc? Marc Fletcher. Marc Hillington. Who was he? Not who he claimed to be, that was certain. He'd seemed so honest, so kind, but perhaps all along he'd been fooling her. She felt a tingle up the back of her neck when she remembered the chilling computerlike voice on the CD with its haunting message.

Did your poor dead wife know what your family did? Someone like you doesn't deserve to be happy.

What had his family done? She would try to search his name online and see what she could dredge up about the name Hillington. She would have to borrow Vanessa's computer because she'd reversed over her mobile with her car and cracked the screen. She could only use it for phone calls now. Noises outside made her sit up. A thump. A splash. She listened for several seconds, but there was only silence.

Could she trust a man who might have lied about his real identity? The Galway project would mean more money and would get her away from Marc. If she wished to get away... She closed her eyes tight and pressed her fingertips together. Did she want to get away?

Another noise, this time closer. Twigs snapped on the lawn outside. A crunch on the gravel path. She got to her feet and moved to the window where she parted the curtains and looked out into semi-darkness. All was quiet except the murmur of the television behind her. The water gleamed in the dusk, grey and glinting as the moon floated over the woodland on the far shore. She waited a few minutes, holding her breath, straining her ears as her heart began a painful drum roll in her chest. Still silence. She must have imagined those sounds. This was what came from living alone and watching violent reports of crime on the TV news.

She let the curtains fall back together and turned away.

Another sound came from the window, a low tap, tap, tap. Gilly picked up the remote and turned down the television. There it was again, louder this time: tap tap, tap tap. She crept towards the window, reached out with her hand to part the curtain.

A white face stared in at her. White face framed with white blonde hair. Black holes for eyes.

Gilly screamed and dropped the remote with a clatter.

The face, so pale that it glowed in the half-light, stared at her for several seconds before breaking into a leer.

Gilly screamed again and yanked the curtains across. Her legs felt weak, shaky as she ran to the kitchen.

What had Marc said? Ring Stefans, she must ring Stefans.

She pulled open drawers and rifled through them to find his number. A drawer in the kitchen. She couldn't remember which one. She stopped and listened, her heart pounding. Should she go out and tackle that white figure? No, no, her stomach churned at the thought.

An engine started up. She ran back into the sitting room and over to the window, swung the fabric aside and stared out. There on the water – something moved quickly across the flat mirrorlike surface. A rubber dingy with an outboard motor, wash spreading behind it and steered by the white-haired shape crouched low in the stern.

Gilly stumbled into the dark hall, groping for the torch. She found it on the table and, flicking it on, flung open the door and shone the beam of light across the grass towards the deck. The engine throbbed more softly now as the boat disappeared into the darkness. By the time she reached the bank, the boat nosed against the fishing platform on the other side and only a faint hum remained that, seconds later, cut out. Gilly strained her eyes and saw the figure climb out and walk briskly towards the trees.

Gilly drew long breaths of air into her lungs in an attempt to calm herself as her eyes grew accustomed to the dark. She flicked off the torch and walked slowly back towards the cottage. She was two strides away when she noticed them: large, black letters sprayed across the wooden door, an uneven scrawl like graffiti. She directed the beam of the torch and read the word: *Thief.* Her heart raced again as she stumbled inside, turned the key in the lock and shot across the bolt.

Stefans. She had to ring Stefans.

"Where did Marc say the number was?" she shouted aloud, searching through the drawers again in the kitchen.

Her mobile rang in the sitting room. So it wasn't in the car. Where was it? The ringing stopped and immediately started again. She followed the sound, bent down on her knees, saw the phone on the floor under the sofa and grabbed at it. Panic threw her mind into confusion. Who was this? The figure in the boat? Someone else to terrify her? A long number she didn't recognise. She hesitated, tapped the broken screen with a trembling finger and answered.

"Gilly? It's Marc."

"Oh, oh... it's you." Her voice choked.

"Gilly? What's wrong?"

She held the phone away and took a few deep breaths. She could hear him call her name. She put it back to her ear. "Marc,

I... something's happened and I'm trying to find Stefans's number."

"What's happened?" His voice sounded louder, more alarmed. "Try to calm down. Are you crying?"

"It's... no, Marc, I think I'm going to be sick. I feel sick..."

A silence. Then, "Are you ill?"

"No, no, not that. It's... I've seen... I've seen it."

"What have you seen?"

She swallowed hard, aware that she wasn't making sense. "No, you don't understand. A face at the window."

Another short silence while he considered this. "A face at the window? What face, Gilly?"

"That white one, you know, the white-haired woman," she burst out. "Oh, it was horrible, Marc... she stared in at me and she sort of smiled. I think she smiled."

"I'll ring Stefans immediately."

"I can't find the number."

"Gilly, listen to me now. Calm down and listen to me. I want you to lock the doors and windows and wait for Stefans. I'll give you his number again in case I can't get through to him. Have you got a biro?"

"Where are you?" she asked after she'd written it down.

"I'm in London, in my apartment. I wish I was there with you. Tell Alice to... no, I'll tell her myself."

"When are you coming back to Glanesfort?"

"I'm booked on a flight to Dublin the day after tomorrow, but now I'll have to decide what to do. I'll ask Stefans to call the Gardaí tonight and I want you to stay where you are until he arrives. Do you hear me? Don't leave the cottage unless you're with him. When Stefans comes, go back with him to the house. You must sleep in the main house with Alice. Gilly, listen to me for once, please."

Her nausea was subsiding. "OK." She remembered the graffiti.

"She wrote on the door, Marc."

"What?"

"The word *Thief* on the door."

He said nothing but his breathing grew louder. After a few seconds he murmured, "I've... look, Gilly, I understand this has frightened you, but it might be just vandals – local boys who've been drinking and think it's funny to dress up and scare you."

Someone had scrawled the same word on the door of the house in Raglan Road in Dublin. Fergus told her Stefans had seen a photograph of it. *Thief.* She couldn't find the words to ask him what she longed to know.

"Dressed up in white clothes? I don't think so," she said. "It's the same figure I saw before but this time... this time she was close up and her face sort of glowed in the dark."

He hesitated again before he asked, "Has your mobile been off? I tried ringing many times this week."

"The battery was flat for a day and I lost the charger. I had to drive to Dublin to get another one from my sister's house – then I couldn't find the mobile."

"No wonder. I thought something like that might have happened. Gilly, sweetheart, I'd like you to come over to London. I'll book a flight for you tomorrow. I did a lot of thinking in Tokyo."

"How did your business presentation go?" He sounded worried, his voice urgent, but should she go? Part of her longed to escape from this, to run back to the safety of Vanessa's house.

"All right, I suppose, but I won't know for weeks. The Japanese have got two other properties to consider." His voice softened. "Gilly, please come to London."

"The hotel in Galway," she muttered. "I have to ring them on Monday."

"What hotel?"

"It's a new job – a big one."

"No, please, let's talk about this. Don't do anything rash."

She closed her eyes, squeezed the mobile. "I'm a bit... um... confused, Marc."

"I know, I know, but I'll explain everything, I promise."

"I'll think about it."

"I really need to see you." He spoke calmly, slowly. "In Tokyo I had time to think about things and I came to a decision."

She blinked away tears, wiping them with the back of her hand. "What sort of decision?"

"A lot has happened since I last saw you and I want to try to explain when I see you. I'll call Stefans now and I'll ring you back in about half an hour. Be careful, please be careful."

Chapter 29

Gilly sat in business class on the Aer Lingus flight to Heathrow. People with briefcases open on their laps made notes about who to call on their mobile phones when the plane landed. The woman on her left checked her watch and adjusted her make-up with the aid of a tiny mirror she unfolded from her handbag. As soon as they were in the air, she took out her mobile and plugged in her earphones, as if to make it clear there would be no conversation.

Gilly had put on her cleanest pair of trousers for the occasion, red jeans with navy trim on the pockets, and a white cotton shirt. She checked to make sure her handbag was still under the seat in front, glad she'd remembered to throw in her sunglasses before she left the cottage. Sunglasses helped confidence, concealed her eyes and signs of emotion.

The man on her right was a suave, olive-skinned Italian called Roberto. He handed her his business card and said his job was marketing Italian shoes and, although his smile seemed friendly, Gilly spotted uneasily that he kept looking at her feet. She pushed her sandals further under the seat in front.

Gilly listened half-heartedly and stared at puffs of white cloud below. The wings of the plane glinted in the sunlight.

Anxiety welled inside her as a knot tightened in her stomach. What would Marc tell her? Now that she was close to finding out, did she really want to know? She'd brought only a small bag so that she wouldn't have to wait at the carousel for luggage.

The steward came with coffee and a croissant for Roberto while Gilly sipped her tea and remembered how Sergeant Dunne had thought the white face at her window to be a deliberate trick to scare her. The person who sprayed the word *Thief* on the door might be the same one as in Raglan Road. Was it definitely a woman? Or could she have seen a man wearing a wig? Impossible to say because of the dark but the figure had looked slight.

She frowned and picked at the rim of the cardboard cup with her fingernail. Sergeant Dunne must already know about the blackmail CDs but perhaps he didn't want to mention them in front of her. How much had Marc told him?

The plane landed on time and, as she walked into the Arrivals Hall, she could feel a traitorous tremble in her legs in spite of her resolution. Crowds jostled at the rail as couples embraced and small children ran to greet their families.

"Hello, Gilly." His voice made her turn and, with a cautious smile, he put his arms around her and held her. His cheek touched hers and he said as he let her go, "It's good to see you."

He looked tired, his eyes streaked with tiny red veins, as if he hadn't had much sleep. "I've got a little surprise for you." Marc took her hand luggage. "Are you hungry? Have you had any lunch?"

"No – I didn't feel like eating anything on the plane."

When they reached the car park, he pointed at a red hatchback and opened the car door for her, holding it while she got in. She wound down the window. The stifling heat of London overwhelmed her and she saw it was twenty-nine degrees on the digital gauge.

He drove in silence until they reached the M25 and then

glanced at her. "This is my PA Sally's car. I had to borrow it because mine is still parked at Dublin airport – been there for a week."

"Oh."

"You're very quiet."

"I'm still recovering from the shock of having to sit in business class."

"I'm afraid it was the only seat left."

She didn't reply.

"Now, here's my surprise." He glanced at her. "It's a garden – one in an old Victorian house I'm trying to buy. Would you like to see that?"

"OK, I don't mind."

"All right, we'll go there. I've bought something to eat and a bottle of white wine. It's so warm today I thought we could have a picnic."

"That's nice." She nodded and glanced at him as he concentrated on driving. He wore black jeans with a pale blue shirt.

She watched his hands move on the steering wheel, with their neatly cut nails, and she had to turn away and stare out of the window.

"How are you feeling?" he asked.

"I'm all right."

"I've thought a lot about what you said." He glanced in the mirror and accelerated to overtake a lorry. "In Tokyo, I came to a decision to tell you something, but I'm afraid that you..." He looked at her, as if waiting for her to say something.

Gilly avoided his gaze. "That I what?"

"That you won't like what I want to tell you. In Tokyo, I... well, I suppose I had time to think."

"About what?"

"About what you said, that I'd have to face up," again he

stopped speaking to look at her and added, "to the blackmail."

She said nothing.

"And I realized that you were right. I would never face up to it, unless I really had to or really wanted to."

She wondered if he could hear her heart thumping, that irritating treacherous organ determined to betray her. She looked out of the window at the cloudless sky, the brilliant sun that shimmered on the pavements and twisted her fingers together in her lap.

After about twenty-five minutes, he stopped the car engine outside a red brick, semi-detached house. He took a brown paper bag from the back seat and asked her to follow him. Together they walked along the side of the house to a wooden gate that sagged on its hinges, where he unlocked the padlock and stood aside for her to go ahead of him.

She saw a narrow garden with a brick wall along each side. An old apple tree, limbs coated with moss, bowed against the right wall, and a broken wooden swing hung from ropes tied to a branch.

"Would you like to sit under the tree?" asked Marc. "The grass is long but it's dry."

They sat down and he placed the paper shopping bag between them. Leggy floribunda roses straggled against the walls. An air of neglect hung in the sultry heat. Another unloved garden waiting for someone to rescue it. She glanced up at a blaze of blue sky through green leaves and could hear the hum of traffic in the distance.

Marc put his hand on hers and left it there for several seconds before she gently withdrew hers. She didn't feel ready for that sort of gesture. Let him come out with whatever it was he wanted to tell her; it would be better to know what that was first. She watched as he took off his jacket.

She remembered the day he'd shown her the mill and how

they'd sat in the grass, the bird song and the sunshine – the excitement she'd felt when he leaned over her, the amusement in his grey eyes. But here the heat sapped her energy and made her perspire. Her shirt was sticking to her back. She waved at a fly that buzzed in front of her face.

"This house," he said, "reminds me of one we lived in when I was a child, when I'd just started school. I suppose that's one reason why I want to buy it, because it reminds me of a time... a time before everything went wrong." He took ham and salad rolls out of the bag and two wine glasses.

She stared at her roll and any hunger vanished. Marc pulled the cork out of a bottle, poured wine into a glass and handed it to her. He tipped a little into his.

He plucked a few strands of long grass, began to wind them around his fingers and said, "There's so much I haven't told you and I'm tired of hiding the truth." He sipped his wine. "I'm going to tell you something but it's not easy, Gilly, it's not easy, believe me."

"Maybe it would be better... better not to say anything. Do I really need to know?" She felt an urge to stand up, walk across the long grass, out the gate and away from him, away from this awkward, embarrassing situation, this uncertainty.

He seemed determined to make her listen, but his voice remained calm. "Yes, you do. You have to know. It's the only way that you... that I..."

"Marc, your friend Nigel said something, called you a different name. Are you going to tell me that you... that... are you trying to tell that your name is Hillington?"

His voice was barely audible. "Yes, my real name is Hillington."

She waited as several long minutes of silence passed, watching him as he twisted the blades of grass while he kept his face averted.

"But it's worse than that," he said.

"Leave it, Marc, don't tell me. I'd rather not know if it's so painful for you." She squeezed the wine glass with both hands and spilled some of the liquid.

"And yet I dread telling you because it's something I've lived with for sixteen years – and I'm afraid you'll despise me when you know."

"Sixteen years? Marc, I... Listen, I have to tell you... my sister told me that my father has been checking up on you."

He stopped winding the grass around his fingers and stared at her.

"He's like that, my father. He can't resist meddling. He asked this friend of his, someone involved in property here in London, to find out anything he could about you."

"Go on."

She shrugged. "He didn't find anything bad, apparently, about your business over the last sixteen years. The strange thing – what he thought odd – was that nobody seemed to know anything about you more than sixteen years ago."

He tossed away the grass and plucked a few more strands. "He would have found plenty if he'd looked under Hillington."

"He's not that good a detective." She smiled suddenly at the thought.

She reached for his hand as the grass tightened around his fingers. "Stop, Marc, you'll cut off the circulation. Tell me why you asked me to come over, please."

He shut his eyes for a couple of seconds, took a breath and said, "When I was twenty, my father committed suicide."

"Oh my God, no!"

He continued, slowly and deliberately, forced out the words, linking his fingers with hers. "He sealed up our garage and he started up the car."

She closed her eyes, but said nothing.

"He'd been caught embezzling, you see. He was an asset manager, a financial advisor who helped people with investments, that sort of thing."

"Embezzling?"

"Yes. It had been going on for years, apparently. I don't know how people found out, but it made the papers – the front pages because his was a high profile company. He wasn't able to live with the disgrace – the shame and the guilt – my mother knowing..."

"Embezzling." Why did she have to repeat everything like some stupid parrot?

He raised his eyes to hers. "So now you know. My father stole money, embezzled money that didn't belong to him – paid for most of my education with it. It was money that belonged to innocent people who were saving up for their old age."

"What happened to you and your mother?"

"We were both left without a penny – like his clients were. Can you imagine having to come to terms with that? The shame of that? How could I try to earn a living with people knowing that about me? I wouldn't have had a chance of getting a job."

"So you changed your name?"

"Yes. I was young enough and people knew nothing about me. I was halfway through college, so I left and went to work on building sites where it was easy to be anonymous. My mother was very upset by our... our disgrace and the media attention. She refused to live in England and moved back to France, wanted me to go with her, but I couldn't. I just wanted to get away from my family, even from her – start a new life, I suppose. Does that sound harsh?"

"No, I can understand that. You wanted to be normal, to be treated the same as everyone else." She noticed the warmth of the sun on her arms. It wasn't so bad, was it? He wasn't the one who had committed the crime.

"Yes, I couldn't bear the thought of people looking at me and thinking that I was the one whose father..."

Pity for him swept over her. "But why, Marc? It's not as if it was your fault, is it? You had nothing to do with it."

"I am his son."

"That doesn't mean you're like him."

"I rang my mother from Tokyo because I wanted her to know that I planned to tell you. It seemed only fair to warn her because it affects her too. I hadn't spoken to her about it for sixteen years. We never talk about it, Gilly."

"What did she say when you rang her?" She imagined his mother as a small, elegant woman, dignified and perhaps a little arrogant.

"I never told her about the blackmail because I didn't want to worry her." He lifted up one hand, shrugged. "I just told her that I'd met someone – that I wanted to tell you. I was surprised by her reaction. She didn't mind as much... well, as much as I thought she would. I thought she'd object, forbid me to say anything... but no, she said to go ahead if it would make me feel better." Marc's hand still lay in hers and his fingers relaxed as he found it easier to talk.

"She's obviously a sensible woman. Whoever is behind this wants to ruin your life. You should have told the police in the beginning. You should never have paid the money."

"I realize that now, but I was afraid... you don't understand what other people think. My father ruined innocent people, stole their savings. I tried to forget, dropped out of college, changed my name and I was doing OK, getting on all right, making money. I started my own company and everything was fine until the CDs starting coming."

"But it's not your fault, Marc. It's not your fault and you shouldn't have to pay."

"Very easy for you to say that, but it seemed a small price to pay someone who claimed to have lost everything because of my father. The blackmailer always claims to have suffered because of my father – that I'm responsible and have to pay the money back."

"This person, whoever it is, is using you and the fact that you feel so ashamed. You should have refused to have anything to do with it."

"I know, but I didn't because it seemed simpler to pay. It wasn't even a huge amount of money in the beginning." He looked up. "If something were to happen to Samuel... I can't risk my son being harmed... or you." He released her hand, plucked at the grass and threw small clumps of it up into the air. "It became harder to talk about it as the years went by and there was also my mother to consider. We came to a decision to try to forget and pretend it never happened. She's all right now because she's got François and she's happy. Maybe she doesn't care about it anymore."

"You made it hard for yourself."

"You don't understand, do you? It's because you're different... different to me. If it was you, you'd shout it out – tell the world about your father, I suppose, and not care about the consequences?"

She frowned. "I suppose I'd blame my father and not myself."

"Yes, you would, wouldn't you? As the years passed – and I made money, it became impossible to tell anyone about my past. Suppose people thought I'd built up my business on stolen money?" He stared at the ground, the tension back. "And who could blame them? Nobody would ever trust me or do business with me."

"They would understand that it wasn't your fault."

He laughed bitterly. "You don't know what my mother and I went through. The journalists camped outside our door, the cameras and horrible things in the papers. If my father hadn't killed himself it would have been... he didn't bother to leave a note so the police had to treat his death as suspicious. He didn't care about us... cared only about himself. We were left to deal with the consequences and it took the police a while to decide it was definitely suicide."

She spoke softly. "He was a thoughtless, selfish man, Marc, but you're not like him. You're kind and good. I would have trusted you. You gave me a job, remember, when I was desperate, with the bank hassling me and nowhere to live."

"But your father's not a criminal, Gilly."

"No, but he's never done much to help me and I don't care because I'm not going to let him try to run my life."

Marc looked at her, reached out to touch her arm. "So now you know. Don't you feel let down? Don't you think you can never trust me again?"

"Of course I don't. Why should I? I'm just glad that you've told me." Gilly leaned over and kissed his forehead. "At least I know now. I thought it would be worse, somehow – don't ask me what, I don't know – but definitely worse than this because I was scared it was you. I thought... I was afraid you might have done something terrible."

"I dread to think what was going through your mind." He put his arms around her, held her tightly against him. "I don't want you to go back today." He kissed her quickly on her lips, stood up and held out his hand to help her to her feet. "You haven't touched your food. It's too hot to stay here. Let's go back to my apartment for a shower and you can decide what you'd like to do. I'll do anything except drive you to the airport."

"In that case, the first thing you're going to do," said Gilly, "is phone the police. It's time to tell them about the blackmail."

"Yes, you're right and I have already done that." He took her hand, led her towards the gate. "There's been a development: something strange happened this week, concerning the private investigator I hired. I'll tell you all about it in the car."

*

A typical single man's apartment, Gilly thought as she looked around at the white walls and the chairs, two sofas lined up at right angles to the fireplace. Spotlessly clean wooden flooring, with black and white photographs on the walls of old and modern buildings: views of London, Paris, Prague and Lisbon.

He waved a hand at a white sofa. "Have a seat. Would you like more wine?"

She noticed a photo of Samuel and his mother on the mantelpiece, the same one she'd seen in the kitchen at Glanesfort.

"Yes, please."

He opened a glazed cabinet, took out two glasses and filled them. "I've got something here." He put down his glass, moved over to a chest of drawers and returned with a gift-wrapped package. "For you - I bought it in Tokyo."

"Oh, thank you." She pulled off the scarlet tissue paper. "Wow! A silk shirt. What a gorgeous colour." She held up the turquoise garment and twirled around, laughing. "So soft and beautiful – you are kind, you're really kind."

"The hotel where Michael and I stayed was like a shopping mall. Now you've something to wear that has never belonged to your sister." He smiled as she danced in front of him. "I'd like to see you try it on. I'm going to have a shower."

He explained that there was a shower in the main bathroom and a bath in the ensuite off his bedroom. "You choose which you want."

Gilly chose the bath and, as it was filling, she searched the gleaming bathroom and found a bottle of bubble bath in a basket under the basin.

The sun flitted through a skylight window in the ceiling and the wooden boards felt warm under her feet.

She climbed in, lay back in the warm water and pushed the bubbles with her toes.

After about ten minutes, Marc knocked on the door and carried in her wine, handing it to her. His hair was wet from the shower and she smelled lemon soap. He wore jeans and a white T-shirt and his feet were bare.

"Thanks," she raised the glass. "Here's to you."

He smiled. "Here's to us, you mean – and to the difference."

"Difference?"

"The difference between us – imagine how hopeless it would be if we were both like me." He sat in a wicker chair and put his bare feet on the edge of the bath. "What do you think about the private investigator?"

"I don't really know what to think. It must have been a shock – to find out so suddenly like that."

"When I saw the scrapbook, I couldn't believe it. I trusted him, Gilly, I told him things. I always thought he liked me... felt sorry for me, in a way. He actually seemed like a nice man."

"What will the police do?"

Marc frowned, little vertical furrows between his eyebrows. "They'll check to see if he really did go to Australia. I don't think they'll find him. I bet he left the country on Friday or yesterday morning and he might have flown to some other country. He'll be long gone by now – and we don't even know his real name."

"What about his niece?"

"She could be anywhere. In Ireland, perhaps?"

The white face at the window? Was that her? The woman talking to Sam at the playschool fence?

"Don't look so worried, Gilly."

"I think we've already seen her, haven't we? At least, I have and so has Sam. Is he all right, do you think? Will Stefans and Alice..." Her voice trailed off.

"Of course he is. I trust Alice and Stefans to keep him safe.

They're used to keeping an eye on him. The police here in London and the Gardaí in Ireland know what they're doing. They'll track that woman down if she hasn't already gone away with her uncle." He put down his glass and reached out to touch her shoulder. "I feel more optimistic now that I've told you everything, Gilly. I think they will leave me alone because I've been to the police. I won't send them any more money."

She twisted her head to kiss his hand. "Good, that's a relief."

"Have you thought about what you'd like to do? We could go out for something to eat, maybe."

"I haven't brought anything suitable to wear." Anticipation stirred inside her. "Though there is that very beautiful turquoise silk shirt – but what can I wear with it?"

"You needn't wear anything with it."

She laughed.

"We could have some food delivered," he suggested. "There's a place near here that does very good Thai takeaways – better than some restaurants." He saw her lean forward to catch the sponge, as it bobbed among the bubbles. "Here, let me get that."

Marc snatched it away when she reached for it. He squeezed water over her head and she shrieked when it ran down her face. Dabbing at her with it, he murmured, "I wouldn't like to rub off your freckles – that would be a shame."

Gilly wrenched the sponge away and threw it to the end of the bath. She turned to grin at him and he grasped her face in his hands, suddenly serious.

"I love you," he said, softly. "I'm sorry that I was such a..."

She threw her arms round his neck and leaned against him, soaking the front of his T-shirt, her mouth brushing his ear. "Don't apologize, please. I love you, too, Marc. I missed you so much."

He got to his feet and pulled her upright. She stepped out of the bath and he wrapped her in a large towel. They stood in the sunlight, arms round each other as their lips met. Marc picked her up and carried her into his bedroom. He dropped her gently on the crisp white sheet.

He lay beside her and took her in his arms. "You see," he said, "I had no intention of taking you back to the airport. I'm going to kidnap you and keep you here until those people in Galway give your job to somebody else."

*

Later they lay together, his arm across her waist, on the warm, crumpled bed. Sunshine danced through the window and threw dappled shapes across the wooden floor.

Marc was asleep and she felt his breath rise and fall against her cheek. His face looked calm, the faint lines relaxed. If only she could hold this moment, freeze it in her memory like a photograph.

Far away in the distance, she heard a telephone ring.

He opened his eyes. "Is that the phone?"

The ringing grew louder, persistent.

"Don't answer it."

He sat up. "It might be something urgent, the office."

"You've an unrelenting sense of duty."

He kissed her forehead before he lowered his feet to the ground and wrapped a towel around his waist. "I hope it's Michael to tell me that the Japanese have made up their minds. I told him to call as soon as he heard anything. Don't go anywhere, darling, I'll be back in a minute."

She lay down and looked up at the ceiling, listening to his voice in the living room, but unable to decipher the words. Perhaps he might show her around London later. So many places she'd like to see. She'd love to go to Harrods. The London Eye might be fun. She'd never been on that.

She heard him put down the phone, his footsteps hurrying back to the bedroom, his voice urgent. "Gilly, get up please! We've got to go."

"What? Who was it?"

"Alice, it was Alice. Samuel has disappeared."

Chapter 30

"Sam might be home by the time we get back. Remember the night he came over to the cottage?" Gilly tried to inject optimism into her words as she sipped her coffee in the bar at Heathrow airport. Still another hour to wait because the first flight back to Dublin with seats available was at ten o'clock. Another hour before boarding. She'd eaten all of the chicken salad Marc bought for her, but he hadn't touched his. He'd been silent most of the journey to the airport and now sat upright in his seat, drumming his fingers on the table and glancing at his watch about every ten minutes.

"That's possible, I suppose. He's a little devil for wandering off." His mobile rang and he answered. "Yes, Alice, any news?"

Gilly drew in her breath and her fingers tightened on the coffee cup.

A young woman collecting glasses wiped their table and smiled at them both. "Everything all right?"

"Yes, thanks," replied Gilly. No point telling her that everything was far from all right.

Marc's eyebrows came together in a frown as he listened to what Alice was saying. "Yes, that's what I think. The lake, that's the first place... ask Stefans to walk around it. Ask him to mention that to Sergeant Dunne." He ended the call and stared into space, his lips compressed into a firm, straight line.

"He isn't back yet?" Gilly said.

He shook his head.

"But Sam knows how dangerous the lake is, Marc, he wouldn't go down there on his own."

"Your cottage is beside the lake and he went there on his own."

"Would he try to feed the swans? Alice is always telling him not to go near it."

Glanesfort was just over an hour from Dublin airport and most of the drive would be in the dark. Poor Samuel, lost and alone in the night or worse, not alone.

His fingers gripped hers. "He's four years old and headstrong. Where has he gone? I'm glad you're with me, Gilly. Alice said that he was only alone on the front steps for a few minutes. She heard the phone ring and went inside to answer it."

"Poor Alice. She must have got such a shock to find him gone."

"Who would he go with? I told him not to accept sweets or lifts from strangers. Do you think that someone picked him up? Joe Milligan? His niece?"

"Would he get into a car with a complete stranger?"

"I don't know."

"Would he remember the nanny?" Gilly returned the pressure of his fingers. "Maybe not, if it was two years since he saw her."

"I don't know that either. If someone offered him sweets, he might go with a stranger," Marc said. "Like drugs, aren't they, sweets to children? Perhaps if Alice gave him more, he wouldn't demand them so often." He turned his face away. "And yet I think Samuel has some sense. We can only hope that he would be too afraid to go with someone he doesn't know. His playschool teacher gave all the kids a lecture about that recently, after...

well, after she spotted him talking to that woman."

Gilly watched the light fade outside the plate glass window, clouds tinged with yellow and pink as another plane headed up into the sky. Mozart's music and the sinister computer voice floated into her mind. The voice had threatened to harm the boy. Or harm her? A four-year-old would be an easier target.

"Mrs Wilkins seemed to like Joe Milligan, didn't she? She said he would have made a good actor. Do you think that he is an actor, Marc?"

"He's certainly good at playing a role."

"Using music in a blackmail message was weird, though – very elaborate."

He shot another look at his watch. "Eccentric, I'd call it. I suppose I thought him a bit eccentric even as a private investigator, but I'd never hired one before and he played the part well. Adding in Mozart's *Requiem* probably amused him, gave the whole thing emphasis – like a film with a soundtrack."

"I think it's horrible," she said. "Amusing himself while causing you such... such torment."

"He probably thought I deserved it, don't you think?"

She pushed a beer mat around the table, shook her head and said nothing.

"I think I'll have a drink," he said. "We still have another forty minutes before we need to head down to the boarding gate."

The waitress reappeared and Marc ordered a whiskey.

*

A chill hung in the drawing room, a hint of dampness in the gathering darkness in spite of the earlier heat of the day. Gilly asked Alice if she should light a fire. The room wasn't used often, only on special occasions for entertaining and business bookings.

Ornate plasterwork decorated the high ceiling and dark

portraits glowered from the walls, bought at auctions like the ones in the hall – gloomy faces of Victorians long dead. There was an elderly matron over the mantelpiece, dressed in black with a white lace collar, and she stared at Gilly with disdain, as if thinking how foolish they were to lose a child. A boy in her day, her expression seemed to imply, would have been properly looked after by his nanny; would never have been allowed to stroll out onto the front steps in the evening when he should have been eating his supper in the nursery.

Alice brought them tea, scones and toast, making an effort to remain calm. Her training as a nurse probably helped; used to dealing with a crisis, but she found it difficult to sit still and constantly jumped up out of her armchair to fetch more tea, to answer the phone, to keep her anxious fears at bay.

The Gardaí had sent out a missing person alert. In the morning, divers from the Garda Water Unit would search the lake and the river. They were in the woods now and Marc was with them. Stefans was going back over the CCTV footage yet again, checking to see if he had missed anything.

"What exactly did Stefans show you on the replay?" Gilly asked.

Alice picked up a spoon and stirred her tea more vigorously than usual, the hot liquid spinning in circles. "The CCTV footage showed Samuel on the front steps of the house. Fergus made him a pretence fishing rod out of a bamboo and a length of string a few weeks ago. He was standing on the steps with the thing... you know, fishing, tossing the string and pulling it in."

"What time was this?"

"I can't remember. Perhaps about four o'clock. I ran to answer the phone."

"And did you see him running off on the CCTV?"

"He stayed on the steps with the bamboo for about five minutes or so and then he looked up... looked towards the avenue, where the trees are, and walked off that way."

"And no one else was there? What was he looking at?"

"No one – at least we couldn't see anyone, but there might have been someone in the trees. He never got as far as the second camera, which is further along."

"So he disappeared somewhere after the first camera and before the second camera?"

"Yes, that seems the only explanation, according to Stefans. Samuel could have gone in two directions. He might have walked to the left through the wood towards the lake or to the right towards the river that runs along the road."

"I don't believe he has drowned." Gilly knelt in front of the fire and coaxed the wood into flames with a poker. "He's not that stupid." She wouldn't mention to Alice that she feared Samuel could be miles away by now. Marc should be the one to tell her about Joe Milligan and his niece.

The grandfather clock in the drawing room struck midnight with loud, resonant tolls that made them both jump.

"And where was Fergus?"

Alice held out a plate. "Have another scone, dear. No, I can't eat any more, I feel a bit sick, to be honest. What did you say? Oh, yes, Fergus... Fergus was away at his mother's house. The poor woman has taken her husband's death very hard, you know. I went to see her a few days ago and she looks so thin and frail. I can understand why Fergus is worried about her."

Marc returned about half an hour later from the search in the woods, but had no good news. He said very little and politely declined Alice's offer of tea and food. He sat on the sofa beside Gilly and stared into the fire.

Fergus wandered in soon afterwards and shook hands with his boss.

"Hey, I'm really sorry about our little man, Marc. When Alice rang me, I felt I had to come back to see if there's anything I can do... feel bad I didn't keep an eye on him. Let's just pray he's hiding somewhere and maybe playing a trick on all of us."

"I should have kept a better eye on him myself over the past months." Marc stood up to pour whiskey and handed Fergus a glass. "If he was playing a trick, he would be back home by now. I can't see him wanting to stay out in the dark."

Alice stifled a sob and groped in her pocket for a tissue.

"I'll help you look tomorrow... crack of dawn," Fergus said.

"Thank you."

Fergus took a seat on the other side of Gilly, reached out and squeezed her hand for a few seconds. She glanced at him, but said nothing. He drank the whiskey quickly, too quickly, and stood up to get himself a refill.

After a long silence, Marc said, "I'm going down to the river again. I'll walk down and have a ..."

"You've already been down there," said Gilly.

"I would prefer to do something constructive than just sit here."

"All right – let me come with you. We'll bring a torch. Has anyone got a torch?"

"Don't go!" Alice cried, all self-control suddenly abandoning her. "Don't leave me here on my own! Please, don't go."

Gilly caught her hands, stared into her face and said calmly, "Alice, let Marc go and search. I'll stay here with you."

Fergus knocked back his whiskey. "I'll stay with her. You go, Gilly."

*

Gilly shook the torch as the beam faded. She switched it off and on again, but the light died in the darkness. "Battery's flat," she said. "Perhaps we should go back to the house. It's nearly half past one."

Marc leaned over the bridge, looking down into the dark water. He didn't reply.

"We should be able to see our way," she said. "It's amazing how much light there is from the moon – or maybe our eyes become accustomed to the dark. I can see as far as the willows on the far bank."

Why did she always talk too much when she was anxious?

The black river glistened in the moonlight and, overhead, a shape glided past on silent wings.

Marc looked up. "What was that?"

"A barn owl. I often see them near the cottage. Their wings make no sound – it's what makes them good hunters. Shall we go back?"

"Back?"

"To the house. Maybe you should try to get some sleep."

"No, I don't want to sleep. I must stay awake in case..."

She could see the outline of his face, the shadows under his eyes.

"Suppose they hurt him, Marc? Suppose they threaten to hurt him?"

He swung towards her. "We have to stay calm, take this one step at a time. It doesn't do any good to think the worst, not yet. He might have wandered off and not be able to find his way back. Or perhaps someone will find him and bring him back. I have to try to think positively or I will... I will go insane. Perhaps I shouldn't have left the house. Let's walk back – suppose there's been a call while we've been away?"

She kept her voice steady, blinked back the stubborn tears. "If he's been kidnapped, they mightn't... they mightn't make contact tonight. They do that sometimes, don't they? Kidnappers make you wait, make you suffer."

"Gilly, sweetheart, please don't keep thinking too far ahead." He turned to her, put his arms around her and held her tightly against him so that she could feel his heart beating. "At first light tomorrow, divers from the Garda Water Unit will search the lake. If there's no... if they don't find him, we'll have to assume that he's been abducted by someone."

"Perhaps the house to house check tonight will help. Someone might have... might have... seen... seen him." Tears welled in her eyes and trickled down her cheeks.

He squeezed her tighter. "Listen to me, I want you to stay in the house tonight – don't go back to the cottage. Stay with me tonight. You don't know... we don't know who might be hanging around. I don't want you to be on your own."

"Oh, Marc, you needn't worry, I've no intention of going back to the cottage alone." How could she bear to risk seeing that white face at the window, darkness behind it, the hollow black eyes and the haunting leer?

His voice remained low. "This is my fault... and my father's. If he hadn't done... if I hadn't kept it secret then this maniac, Joe Milligan or whoever he really is, wouldn't have control over me."

"He is a maniac, but we have to hope they'll catch him, Marc. Catch him before..."

"If only I had brought Samuel to London with me. He wanted to come." He stared down into the water and sighed. "Did my father realize what he was doing, I wonder, when he decided to kill himself? Did he even stop to think what it would do to his family?"

"How can you ever know the answer to that?" She sniffed and wiped her eyes with the sleeve of her jumper.

An engine throbbed in the darkness. A sudden beam of headlights flashed round the corner and caught them in a spotlight. Gilly's thoughts scrambled over each other. Fergus at the wheel of the Land Rover. He'd found Samuel and was coming to tell them. Or the Gardaí had found him in the house to house search. Or maybe they'd found him wandering along the road. A surge of optimism swept through her. He'd been found and was safe.

The Land Rover slowed and stopped beside them. Fergus stretched across the passenger seat to push open the door. "Hey there, I came to look for you."

"Has he come back? Has anything happened?" Marc asked.

Fergus glanced at him.

"What is it?"

"No sign of Samuel, but your mother wants to talk to you, Marc. She sounded very worried – said you'd left a message earlier." He jumped down from the Land Rover. "Here, you take this and drive back to the house. Gilly and I can walk."

Gilly tried to follow him, but Fergus pulled her jumper. "Let him go, let him have some time on his own."

Marc started the engine and glanced down at the two of them.

"Is there someone you've fallen out with? Someone who might take Sam as a way to get back at you?" Fergus asked, holding the door open.

Marc said nothing for a few seconds, as if considering whether to trust him. He turned away. "You tell him, Gilly."

"Are you sure?"

"Go on, tell him about my father, and tell him about the CDs and the blackmail and the music – the whole bloody lot. What difference does it make now? Tell him."

Marc shut the door and drove off, accelerating into the night. Fergus turned to Gilly, his expression serious in the moonlight, and laid his hand on her shoulder. "CDs? Blackmail? Tell me, tell me all about it."

Gilly looked down at the river. Where was Samuel now? What horror was he going through? "Oh, Fergus! He must be so frightened."

"We have to get him back," Fergus said, his words slightly slurred. "Tell me everything."

She leaned back against the bridge and stared into the woods around her. She drew in a deep breath and told him what she knew. He listened without speaking, then placed a cigarette between his lips as his lighter illuminated his face, his hand shaking.

"That's terrible, Gilly... terrible, I can't believe it. To think that Marc has been going through all this and I never even knew. It's unbelievable." He inhaled and blew out smoke rings, lifted his chin and closed his eyes.

"Well?" she asked. "Any ideas where he might be?"

Fergus regarded the glowing end of his cigarette and shook his head. "Nope, I'm afraid I've no idea."

They stood together in silence until he tossed the butt into the river. Gilly shivered and tapped him on the arm.

"Let's walk back to the house. It's cold here. I'm freezing."

Fergus followed her up the avenue. After a few minutes, he said, "I have thought of something."

She spun round to stare at him. "What?"

"I might be wrong but... and I don't like to lay the blame at someone's door without evidence so..."

"What, Fergus? Tell me."

He hunched up his shoulders, shoved his hands deep into the pockets of his jacket and yawned. "Dean's father. Did you hear about him?"

"Yes, Dean mentioned some trouble with him. In prison, I think, or maybe he's out now. Yes, I remember he said he was out."

"Yeah, a bit of a jailbird all right. Well, I think he might dream up something like this. Dean's always worried about his father coming down here and he did have something to do with an armed robbery."

A breeze whispered through the beech trees on their left, like voices gossiping, murmuring agreement. Dean's father. Could Samuel have fallen into the hands of such a man? Could he be connected in some way to the private investigator and his niece in London? Surely not.

Fergus put a hand on the small of her back, pushed her forward. "Come on, Gilly, let's go back. It's getting late and we need to get some sleep before tomorrow. I'll have a word with Dean in the morning."

So would she. She would definitely have a word with Dean.

Fergus left her at the front steps and headed off around the house towards his apartment. She met Alice in the front hall, pale but with her emotions reined back under control. She accompanied Gilly up the staircase to the guest bedroom on the second floor where she'd stayed the first night after her car crash. Had she seen Marc? No, Alice replied, she had no idea where Marc was because he had gone out after speaking to his mother.

*

Gilly spent most of the night wide awake, tossing from one side of the bed to the other, sitting upright with her heart pounding at every unexpected sound. Sometime after four o'clock, when she got up and looked out into the moonlit garden, she saw shadows move in the shrubbery near the trees. She clutched the chest of drawers near the window and attempted to focus her blurred vision. No, it was nothing, just her imagination running wild. She eventually drifted off to sleep and woke at nine o'clock.

When she opened the kitchen door, Marc and Alice sat on stools at the counter drinking coffee and eating croissants. Alice poured another cup and smiled wanly as she handed it to her.

"No sign of him," she said, her eyes red-rimmed. She yawned

and rubbed a hand over her face. She'd aged in the last twenty-four hours, her face pale and lined.

"The Gardaí are searching the lake and more houses and gardens this morning, door to door searches." Marc stood up and felt in his pockets for his car keys. "I'm going to the station now. They want to go through everything again. Did you manage to get any sleep?"

"Not a lot. Where did you spend the night?"

"I couldn't sleep. I checked the garden again, round the back of the apartments. I'm sorry to be in such a hurry, but I have to go now."

"That's okay. Please tell me if there's anything I can do to help."

"No, there's nothing you can do at the moment and I think you should stay here, Gilly. Promise me you won't go outside the gates today."

"I'd like to help with the search."

"Stay here, please. It's safer. I would prefer if you stayed here with Alice, Stefans and Fergus."

"But I could drive..."

"No, Gilly."

Alice murmured, "I'd like you to stay here, Gilly. Stay with me while Marc is away. The divers are still searching the lake. We can go out and see..." Her voice trembled.

"All right, but first I have to find Dean and tell him what's happening. It's only fair because he'll be in the garden by now."

She followed Marc to the door.

"Did you hear what I said?" he asked. "You must not go anywhere on your own. Stay with Alice, Fergus or Dean and I'll be back as soon as possible." He bent forward and gave her a quick kiss on her lips. "Please be careful, Gilly."

"Poor Marc," said Alice softly when the door shut behind him. "This is so hard for him, so terrifying for all of us."

Gilly's mobile rang. The sympathy in her sister's voice brought tears to her eyes.

"It was on the news," Vanessa said. "A missing boy in Kildare and a photo of him. Only when I saw his name... I've never met him, you see."

"Oh Ness, it's terrible."

"Can you believe that I got a call from Harry to ask questions? What the hell is he like? I didn't mention that you were at Glanesfort because I was afraid he would drive straight down there."

"Oh my God, he's the last person Marc needs right now. If he rings this house, I'll..." Harry could hardly have anything to do with Samuel's disappearance, could he? No. No. Just a journalist looking for a story. Dean's father sounded a more likely suspect. Harry was a boorish lout but not a criminal.

"I have to go, Gilly. I'm in work, but be careful, won't you? Don't do anything rash. I'll call you later. I'll come down if you need me."

She rang off and Gilly turned to Alice and asked, "Would you like to come with me to the garden?"

"I think I would prefer to stay in the house, in case... if anyone rings or... I will come to find you straight away if there is... if I hear anything. I pray we will hear soon that he is safe and sound." Alice picked up the empty mugs and carried them to the sink.

"What about the lake. I thought you wanted to see..."

"No, I've changed my mind. I don't think I can... can bear the thought of that. I can't cope with this waiting – not knowing where he is, or how he is. Poor little Samuel, do you think he is still alive? I pray he is still alive."

"We have to hope he is, Alice. I'll be back as soon as possible so please don't worry. I won't be long."

"All right." Alice rinsed the mugs and stared out of the

window towards the wrought-iron gate that led from the lawn into the wood.

Gilly walked out the front door, down the steps and followed the path to the back of the house. She stood on the top terrace and looked down at the lake. Grey water today, reflecting the clouds above. A light drizzle wet her face. Two Garda cars and a van stood on the bank near the stone jetty while black figures waded in the water.

She hesitated before she walked towards them. Did she really want to witness this procedure up close? What if they found Samuel's body? She couldn't cope with that. She forced herself to set off down the lawn and a hard lump of fear in her throat prevented her greeting Sergeant Dunne, who was sitting in the patrol car. He acknowledged her when she drew closer, his usual genial features grave.

"Morning. How are things up at the house?"

"Only Alice there at the moment." Gilly swallowed and added, "Anything happening down here?" If they found his body in the water, all hope would be gone. At least while he was missing, they could cling to the belief that he was still alive.

The sergeant shook his head, reached for his cap. "Nothing. I'm on my way to meet Mr Fletcher." He started the car. He lowered the window. "If you hear something, a phone call or if some sort of communication arrives, you will let us know immediately, won't you?"

"Of course." She watched him reverse and swing the car round to drive off. For several minutes, she stood in the drizzle while figures in the distance rose to the surface of the water. Arms waved and a voice called out. She held her breath, her stomach lurched, but the diver shook his head. Thank God, nothing. She remembered Dean and turned away.

When she reached the garden wall, she stopped a few strides short of the red door. Raised voices came from inside; a man cursed loudly. She moved forward, peered around the door and saw Fergus standing over Dean, bent forward with his face very close to his. She couldn't see his expression, but his words resonated with anger. Why were they quarrelling? Was Fergus questioning Dean about his father's whereabouts? She slipped behind the wall and waited as the two men walked towards the door.

Dean shouted something, his voice raised, but she couldn't catch what he said. Fergus stepped closer now; his hand reached for the latch and she said, "Hi, Fergus, did you tell Dean about Samuel?"

He looked at her, startled. A reddish stubble darkened his jaw. "Gilly, you gave me a hell of a fright! Yeah, yeah, of course I told him."

Dean didn't look up and stared at the toes of his boots.

Fergus continued. "Marc told me not to do anything, to let the Gardaí do the searching, but I have to do something. I can't just hang around and let whoever has poor little Sam...I feel so helpless."

"Be careful, Fergus, don't do anything without asking Marc."

"Don't want to upset him anymore, I suppose, the poor guy's worn out. See you later." He wandered off towards the house and stopped halfway up the path to light another cigarette from the butt of his previous one, which he chucked into the laurels.

They watched him, Dean with a scowl.

"So what was that all about?" she asked.

"What?"

"The row I heard between you and Fergus. Why was he talking to you like that?"

"Oh, that? Nothing." A silence fell between them until he lifted his eyes to glance at her. "Poor Sam, he's a great little man. If anything happens to him..." He frowned, opened his mouth and shut it again.

"Dean, why were you arguing with Fergus?"

His scowl deepened.

Gilly forced a smile. "You would help us, wouldn't you? If you know anything we don't know? You would help the boss find his son?"

Still silent, Dean put one of his grimy fingernails in his mouth and bit it, a stubborn look on his face.

She sighed. "I don't know what to tell you to do in the garden because I can't think straight. What did you do yesterday? Were you spreading gravel? Just keep going with that."

She would have to mention his father, but how should she phrase the question?

He cleared his throat. "Gilly..."

"Yes?"

He twisted his mouth to one side but said no more.

She waited while her heart began to thud against her ribs. "Go on."

"Fergus was asking me about my father. He says he's to blame for... for this, but I don't see how..."

"I was going to ask you too. You told me before that he's crazy. Could he have taken Sam?"

Dean's dark eyes shot her a frightened glance before he cast them down to the ground. "I dunno... I know he's crazy but... he's not crazy enough to take... to kidnap a kid. Fergus said his uncle is suspicious, thinks my dad has something to do with this. His uncle is the old guy who got me this job. I told you about him before, remember? My Auntie Sarah's boyfriend, right?"

"Yes, you did."

"Yeah, well, he's a weird guy, the uncle. Been involved with all sorts of... a lawyer or barrister or something for... for criminals. He helps people in trouble, people like my dad... knows my dad well."

She took a deep breath to calm herself. "Did he represent

your dad? You know, at his trial?"

"Yeah, I guess, I didn't want to know so I... like I said, he's a bit weird."

"I met Fergus's uncle with you at the funeral, remember? Martin? Martin Browne, is that his name?"

"No, it's Matthew, Matthew Browne. I'm not supposed to mention him. He doesn't like people to know what he's up to, see. Fergus would..."

"He won't find out," she replied impatiently. "So, what do you know about his uncle?"

"He got me this job, right? Warned me to be straight with everyone, or else he wouldn't help me again... wouldn't help Nan." Dean threw her a desperate look. "I like it here and I don't want to lose my job."

She grabbed his shoulders. "What do you mean? Do you really think your father has something to do with Sam's disappearance? We are talking about a four-year-old boy here, a four-year-old boy's life. Marc is going crazy with worry. What are you trying to say?" She dug her fingers into his leather jacket.

Dean wriggled out of her grasp and backed away, reversing against the garden wall. "I dunno, I'm guessing, that's all."

"And you think Fergus's uncle might know something? About your dad? Talk sense, Dean, I don't know what you're trying to say."

"I dunno if my dad is involved. It's not his style."

"Where is he now?"

"No idea. Nan and me, we never see him."

"Where does Matthew Browne live?"

"London."

"Got his phone number?"

"No."

"Come on, Dean. You can do better than that."

"My Auntie Sarah has."

"Where does she live?"

"In London, near Islington. I'll have to ring Nan for her number."

Gilly nodded. "Right, you get it from her, please. Here's my mobile. Ring her now and get it." She waited while he called his grandmother.

Not much to go on. Just a suspicion of Dean's. What if she could get Matthew Browne on the phone and ask him about Dean's father?

She wouldn't mention this to Fergus because he wouldn't want Marc to know that his uncle had worked as a barrister for criminals. He wouldn't want Marc to know his uncle had sent him Dean, the son of a convicted criminal. Yet Fergus obviously suspected Dean's father.

All so complicated and hard to know what to do for the best. She would have to ring Matthew Browne herself and ask him some direct questions. She might catch him off guard, as he wouldn't be expecting her to call, wouldn't know who she was.

Dean had a brief conversation with his grandmother, got her sister's phone number and rang her. Gilly listened and pulled a biro out of the pocket of her jeans.

"Hi Auntie Sarah. Yeah, it's me. How's things? Yeah?"

Gilly held up the biro. "I'll write down Matthew Browne's number."

Dean nodded at her. "Yeah, that's right. No, it's a good job, yeah. Hey, do you have Matthew Browne's number? Can I have it?"

Gilly paced over to the garden door, picked off a sliver of peeling paint with her fingernail. She could hear Dean's voice rise in surprise.

"Not seen him? Since when? Yeah, well he's a bit... What's his number? Thanks." He called out Matthew Browne's number and Gilly wrote it down on her arm.

Dean said goodbye to his aunt and ended the call. He handed back her mobile, hunched his shoulders.

"What's up?" she asked.

"Auntie Sarah said she hasn't seen him for a few days and he's not answering his phone. Did you get the number?"

"Yes, thanks. Maybe Matthew Browne's away, or something. Don't look so worried, Dean. Marc won't fire you because of your father. He isn't like that." She turned to go. "I'll let you know what happens. Please keep spreading gravel and I'll be back in half an hour to help out."

He agreed, anxiety lingering in his close-set eyes.

Chapter 31

"Hey, can I have a word?" Fergus came down the path as Gilly closed the garden door behind her.

She looked up at him as he towered over her. He glanced at her arm where she'd written the phone number.

She covered it with her other hand. "It's the number of Marc's office in London."

"I think we're friends, aren't we, Gilly? Can I trust you with something?"

"Yes, of course."

"It's Dean," he said. "I think he knows more about Sam's disappearance than he's letting on."

She kept her eyes on his face. "Why do you think that?" She could smell alcohol on his breath, a mixture of beer and nicotine.

"Look, Gilly, let me tell you what he said." Fergus hesitated and glanced over his shoulder, as if to check Dean wasn't watching them. "That's why you heard us arguing back there."

Her heart beat faster. "But Dean doesn't seem to know..."

"Doesn't he? Well, I doubt he told you all about his father. The man is a gangster, Gilly, he's violent. I felt sorry for Dean and that's why I suggested him for the job here. Now I'm not sure that I did the right thing."

"But Dean said… he said your uncle persuaded you to get Dean a job."

"That's right. You met my uncle at my father's funeral, didn't you? Yeah, he suggested Dean to me. My Uncle Matthew's like Robin Hood and likes to think he's helping the poor and needy. I suppose it makes him feel good." He ran a hand through his hair, pushing it back from his face. "Well, I think Dean's father might be mixed up with Sam's disappearance."

"Are you sure?"

"No, I'm not sure, but I think I know how to find out. There's a place near here that I had a look at earlier this morning. It would make an ideal hiding place."

Gilly digested this information, turning it around in her mind to try to make sense of Fergus's suggestions. Maybe Dean hadn't told her the whole truth, maybe he knew where his father was. But he'd seemed sincere only a few minutes before, concerned about Samuel. Perhaps he hadn't wanted to admit how far his father would go, or had gone.

Fergus put his arm round her shoulders and gave her a quick squeeze. "I know you like Dean, Gilly, but you've got to try to believe me. These people come from a different world to you and me. You don't know what they're like. I wouldn't tell you this if I didn't think it was true – I wouldn't let my uncle down. We all thought Dean deserved a chance – that he would make an effort to get on when he was given this job."

"But surely you don't think he's helping his father? He hates his father. His grandmother won't let him near her house. His father attacked him with a knife, Fergus. He'd never help him – and he's very fond of Sam."

"All right, maybe I'm being a bit hard on him. Dean mightn't know the truth. His granny always tries to shelter him. My uncle says his father is out on probation." Fergus turned away. "That's what the argument was about in the garden when you walked in. I was trying to get him to tell me where his father is. As I said, I went somewhere this morning and, from what I saw, I think I know where he has hidden Samuel."

"If you know that, you should tell Marc first."

"OK, we'll tell Marc now."

"He's in the Garda Station at the moment. I don't know how long he'll be, but he only left about half an hour ago."

"Why don't we drive into the town and see if we can find him? We can bring him with us."

"Marc told me to stay here. He doesn't want me to leave the grounds." Why was Fergus so convinced he knew where Samuel was?

A flicker of excitement flooded through her. Suppose they found the boy. Marc would be overjoyed. Could it do any harm for her to go with Fergus? Hadn't Marc said to stay with Alice or Stefans or Fergus?

"All right, I'll come with you and we can drop in at the Garda Station and pick Marc up on the way."

"Yeah, good idea," he replied.

"What about Alice? She's expecting me back. I'll just go into the house and tell her what I'm doing."

Fergus handed her a set of keys. "Here, take these and fetch the Land Rover. I left it outside my apartment. I'll go and tell Alice what we're doing and I'll see if she's got any biscuits. I'll meet you at the front steps."

He strode off in the direction of the main door.

Baking would be the last thing on poor Alice's mind, Gilly thought.

She found the Land Rover parked near the apartments and climbed in. Easy enough to drive because she'd borrowed it before on a number of occasions to collect larger plants. The engine started immediately. She reversed slowly and drove under the arch, out of the yard and round to the front.

Fergus was waiting by the portico, leaning against a pillar. He came to the driver's door and asked her to move over. He slid onto the seat and drove off down the avenue, a cloud of dust swirling behind them.

Hunched at the wheel, he turned to grin at her. "Thanks for coming with me, Gilly. I just hope I'm right."

"How was Alice?"

"She looks exhausted. Poor Alice is in a bad way. No biscuits made today."

They bumped over the cattle grid and out the gate. "I think I'll ring Marc on his mobile," Gilly said, "and tell him what we're doing."

"No, don't waste your phone credit. We'll be at the Garda Station in a few minutes and you can tell him then."

She attempted to question him about his uncle as they drove along the narrow road where chestnut and lime trees stretched their boughs across as if to embrace each other.

"Dean said your uncle is a barrister."

"Dean doesn't know him well."

"He told me he represented criminals."

"You make him sound like a criminal himself. He used to be a barrister and, yeah, he used to represent poorer people who couldn't afford the top barristers. He believed in justice, you see."

"Justice for criminals?"

"They weren't all criminals, Gilly. Some of them were innocent. Or some were accused of worse than they'd actually done."

She remembered the tall man with a large nose and black fur hat. Fond of alcohol because he carried a hip flask. "Would your uncle know anything about Samuel's disappearance?"

Fergus glanced at her. "What's Dean been telling you? My uncle lives in England, Gilly. He knows nothing about this."

"But he suggested Dean for the work here at Glanesfort."

"Uncle Matthew has a long list of dependents of clients who have been inside. He likes to look after the innocent ones, that's all. He's like Robin Hood, I told you. If he can save another young person from turning to crime, he thinks he's doing well."

That sounded sensible. Young men like Dean needed all the help they could get and Robin Hood was a hero to many and a villain to some; it all depended on which side you were.

Fergus put his foot on the accelerator, swung the Land Rover round the corners and she had to grip the dashboard to stay upright. He glanced in the rear-view mirror as they reached the outskirts of Monasterevin, drove over the Pass Bridge and turned right for the town with the Barrow River flowing beside them.

"Tell you what, Gilly, I'll give Marc a call myself and explain." He brought the Land Rover to a halt.

She waited while he glanced at his mobile, selected a number and held the phone to his ear. She heard it ring.

"Hey, Marc, it's me, Fergus. Yeah, yeah, I'm fine. Listen, I've got Gilly with me." He grinned at her. "Don't worry, no, she's fine. I've had an idea about Sam, right. I think I might know where he could be. Yeah, Marc... well, if you can't come now, Gilly and I can go on. No, I won't do anything stupid, trust me. Gilly and I are going to have a look at this place and I'll call you back if we find him. No, we won't go too close, we'll keep a safe distance. Yeah, yeah... bye." He put the mobile back in his pocket.

"Well?"

"It's OK, we have the boss's approval so no need for you to feel guilty. He said he's still in the Garda station and we're to go on without him."

Fergus rammed the Land Rover into gear and took off. He turned right at the junction and drove out into the countryside for another fifteen minutes. After a crossroads, he braked, shot another glance into the rear-view mirror and turned left down a side road.

Grass grew in the middle of a lane with tall hedges on either side. It looked familiar, though. Had she been here? She noticed a shed with a rusty red roof and remembered. A few months back, Marc had taken her along this road on the day he showed her the old mill.

Fergus parked the Land Rover in the gateway of a field and they got out. Gilly followed him down the grass path towards the mill. Today an overcast sky threatened rain, but last time it had been cloudless and blue. It seemed obvious now that it would make a suitable hiding place for a child. No one used this building; no one came near it. The hawthorn hedge and the tall trees by the road hid it from view. Why hadn't she suggested looking here before?

Fergus slowed his steps as they approached the front of the building, held up his hand to silence her. "Let's be careful, Gilly. We don't know what to expect."

She looked up at the grim façade, the dark windows with their iron bars, some with broken panes.

She put a hand on Fergus's arm. "Stop! We shouldn't go in here. What did Marc say? Let's wait in the Land Rover and see if anyone comes out. Fergus, stop! Let's go back. It might be dangerous."

He took her arm. "We can go inside and listen... make a run for it if anyone appears."

She pushed him away. "No, Fergus, are you crazy? Wait... what's that noise?"

She held her breath, her muscles rigid.

"It sounds like crying, doesn't it? From inside the mill." She stared at him. "Fergus, I bet you're right about this. That sounds like Sam crying."

He pulled open the heavy door and looked in. No one there as they climbed the stone steps towards the shadowy passage above; now all was silent except for the cawing of crows outside. Inside a chill gripped her, the gloom lit only by squares of light through the windows. Fergus picked his way slowly up the damp, slippery steps and disappeared into the darkness of the second floor.

Loud wails of distress started up again, echoing throughout the empty rooms.

Fergus broke into a run and Gilly followed, panting behind him, her legs heavy and reluctant to move. He pushed open the door at the end of the passage. She hung back, but he reached out to her and gripped her arm.

*

Marc plumped a red cushion behind him on the window seat in the kitchen and leaned back. He glanced at his mobile. A text from Michael who'd flown to Paris to meet Kiu Fat and his colleagues from the Chinese investment company. Michael wondered if there was any news about Samuel. His PA, Sally, was fielding calls in the London office, keeping tenants and colleagues at bay.

Alice came in with a basket of clean clothes. "I'm going to do some ironing, Marc. It'll pass the time and take my mind off this horrible..."

"Good idea."

"I suppose he can be trusted, can he?" Alice put the basket on the table and plugged in the iron.

"Who?"

"Sorry, I was just thinking... that fellow Dean... is he trust-worthy? If he thinks Gilly might have gone with Fergus... But Fergus wouldn't be involved in this, would he? It seems most unlikely as he's so fond of Samuel."

"I don't trust anyone," Marc replied, "except you, Gilly and Stefans." If Gilly didn't come back soon, he would ask Stefans to search the CCTV recorder. It was easy to become paranoid, to panic. He'd asked Stefans to keep an eye on everyone who went in and out of the front and back gates. He was probably playing through all the CCTV videos and checking every car registration.

"I can't believe Fergus would..." Alice's voice faltered as she set up the ironing board.

"I don't want to believe that he's involved but we have to keep an open mind. He isn't answering his mobile. Neither is Gilly. I can't get a reply from her, although that's not unusual. Anything even slightly suspicious needs to be checked out."

Alice stared miserably at the pillowcase. "Would you like coffee? It was bad of Gilly to go off without... she shouldn't have gone off without letting me know. She said she was coming back to the house."

"I went into the walled garden and spoke to Dean. He last saw her walk off to talk to Fergus and said she wanted to ask Fergus about his uncle. I couldn't get much out of Dean about the uncle, but I gather Gilly met him at Fergus's father's funeral."

"Fergus never mentioned an uncle to me. Coffee, Marc? I'll make it."

He stood up. "I'll make it." He walked over to the counter and switched on the machine. He opened the cupboard above and scanned the packets. "It made me wonder why Gilly would be interested in an uncle of Fergus. Latte, cappuchino?"

"Americano, please. There's a box with Americano pods in it. Yes, that's the one." Alice folded the cotton rectangle, gave it a quick press and put it on the table. She picked up another creased one. "I don't understand why anyone would want to take a poor defenceless boy and..." Tears welled in her eyes and she gripped the handle of the iron and stabbed at the pillowcase.

Marc slipped the pod into the coffee machine and placed a mug underneath. "Suppose Gilly has put herself in danger? Why doesn't she listen to me? I told her to stay here with you."

He pressed the button as his mobile bleeped. A text from Stefans. He read it out to Alice. "*Land Rover left after you. Talk now.*" Marc returned to the window seat and rang Stefans. "Yes? Got your text."

Stefans sounded reassuringly calm. "Mr Fletcher, I checked CCTV again and the cars. The Land Rover left after you went to the police."

"Who was in the Land Rover?"

"Two people, Fergus and Gilly."

Marc glanced at Alice, but she obviously couldn't hear what Stefans was saying and continued with her ironing, one eye on the coffee machine. "Are you sure?"

"Fergus drove the Land Rover out of the gate and Gilly beside him. You can look at the recording."

"Thank you, Stefans. Keep going through the videos. Have a look at the ones from yesterday again. Are you sure you can't see Samuel in any of them?"

"No. Samuel was not there. Not in any car. I will check again. Maybe he was lying down?"

Marc took the mug of coffee from Alice, his pulse quickening. Lying down in a car? Perhaps someone had forced him to lie down so that the cameras wouldn't pick up the boy at either of the gates. If that was the case, his abductor knew the cameras were there. But plenty of houses had CCTV these days and a kidnapper would be aware of this. If Samuel had left the premises on his own, Stefans would have found him on the CCTV recordings. The Gardaí had been the first to point this out when they'd discussed it yesterday.

"Stefans?"

"Yes, Mr Fletcher?"

"Please have a look at the copy of the video of Samuel at the front door again. Yes, the one we gave the police. He walks away from the steps with a stick in his hand. He walks towards the front avenue." The last sighting of Samuel. Annoying there was no camera between the house and the first bend in the avenue but perhaps the kidnapper – and it looked like a kidnapping now – had lured him into the woods and taken him out over the wall by the road. Again, it would have to have been someone who knew the positions of the CCTV cameras.

Stefans said he would check and disconnected.

Marc stared into his coffee. He had to stop his mind racing ahead, thinking the worst. He had to stick to the facts.

"Tell me, please." Alice's voice quivered. "What did Stefans see?"

"He said that Gilly left in the Land Rover with Fergus, just as Dean suspected."

"Why didn't she tell me she was going out? I don't understand. She's usually reliable."

"She drove the Land Rover to the front steps and Fergus got in. It's odd she didn't come inside to tell you and she promised me she'd stay here. I don't like this, Alice. I think something made her leave like that."

"You mean Fergus made her leave?"

"I'm going to have a look at the recording now – check if it looks like she went willingly." He would go to the control room and watch the video. There had to be a reason why she'd calmly left the property with Fergus without telling Alice and without phoning him, in spite of his insistence that she stay put. Stubborn and headstrong as she was, surely she wouldn't do that unless she had been duped in some way. She wouldn't have ignored his instructions and not contacted him. Nor would Gilly have abandoned Alice when she knew how frightened she was.

Fergus must have persuaded her to go with him. Fergus,

with his silver tongue. Fergus, who wasn't answering his mobile. But could he really be involved? He liked Samuel, got on well with him. Would he do this to the boy? He would have had no problem getting Sam to go with him because Sam trusted him.

Marc tightened his grip on the mug. The identity of the uncle Dean mentioned might be crucial. Who was he? Dean's reluctant description worried him. Tall and about seventy, with blue eyes. Could Fergus's uncle be Joe Milligan? Fergus had been working at Glanesfort before he'd hired Milligan but was it possible the two were related? Milligan had never sounded Irish; he claimed to be Scottish and certainly had a slight Scots accent, but that could also have been put on, all part of the act. Dread rose up from his stomach and crept into his throat. The blackmailer who sent Mozart's *Requiem* had sounded obsessed, insane. Was it possible that this lunatic, assisted by Fergus, had abducted both Samuel and Gilly?

Alice folded the last pillowcase and laid it on the pile. Her eyes filled with doubt and she opened her mouth to speak.

"I'm going out to see Dean again," Marc said quickly. "He's too afraid to talk to me. I think I'll take him to the Garda station and see if they can get any useful information out of him."

Chapter 32

Samuel lay on an iron bed, his face pale and smudged with dirt and tears. A woman with long dark hair sat beside him, wrapping his hand in a length of torn sheet. Blood dripped onto the wooden floor as the howling continued.

"For God's sake, do something!" snapped the woman. "I can't get him to shut up. He put his arm through the window and broke the glass." She nodded in Gilly's direction. "Why did you bring her here?" Her accent sounded English.

Gilly swung round to stare at Fergus, who still gripped her arm. He kicked the door shut behind them and locked it; pocketed the key.

Her heart thumped wildly. "Fergus? I don't understand. What's going on?"

Samuel sat upright and shouted, "Daddy, Daddy... is he with you? I want Daddy!"

Fergus let go of Gilly and walked over to the boy. He bent down and stroked his head. "There now, Sam, don't make such a fuss. We'll help you."

The woman had tied a knot in the makeshift bandage and rose to her feet. Her hair swung back and when Gilly saw her high cheekbones and dark brown eyes, her stomach leapt and tightened into a painful spasm. The woman in the photograph that Marc had shown her. The missing nanny. It had to be her.

Fergus frowned at her. "I brought my little gardening friend here because she was getting too close to the truth. It was easy to fool her and now we have double leverage." He turned to Gilly and pointed at the bed. "Sit down there."

Her mind spinning, she did as he ordered. Stupid, stupid! How could she have been such a fool? How could she have believed him? Of course Dean and his father had nothing to do with this.

Fergus grinned at her, as if it was all a joke. "Allow me to introduce my sister, Jane."

The woman ignored her and walked over to the window.

"Your sister? I don't believe... she can't be. No, no... Fergus, please," Gilly said. "You've got to take us back to Glanesfort. Marc will..."

"Sorry, sweetie pie, I can't do that."

She remembered Vanessa's mobile in her pocket and fished it out. "Then I'll call him now, tell him Samuel is safe. Marc will sort this out."

Fergus snatched the phone from her hand. He tossed it to Jane. "Here, catch!"

She switched it off and pushed it into her jacket pocket.

Gilly leapt to her feet. "Fergus, what the hell do you think you're doing? What are you going to do with us?"

He pushed her back onto the bed. "I said stay there! It's quite simple, Gilly, I am going to leave you here in the mill where you will be able to keep an eye on Sam." Amusement faded from his eyes. "Then we're gonna take Sam away and leave you here. I'm sure your darling Marc will come to rescue you at some stage, if he really cares about you."

Tears brimmed up in the boy's eyes. "No, no! I want to stay with Gilly. I want my dad."

"Oh, shut up, Sam! Stop that whining. I'm not going to hurt you."

Samuel's sobs prevented him from answering.

"Fergus, you can't do this," Gilly pleaded. "I can't believe this is happening – that you'd do this."

"I can and I will."

"Where are you going to take him?"

"As if I'd tell you that. You think you're so clever, don't you? You think the sun, moon and stars shine out of Marc Hillington. Do you even know his real name is Hillington? He's not the paragon of virtue you think he is, Gilly."

He bent down, lowered his face to stare into her eyes. She shrank back, but he seized her shoulders with both hands and shook her hard, sending a shooting pain down her neck.

"If you knew what he's like – what his father was like – you mightn't be so madly in love with him." He pushed her away in disgust. "If you'd seen what my own father went through, the misery my poor mother had to put up with, you might see sense."

"Your father?"

"My father, yes. He would have died in poverty if Marc had his way. I bet you don't even know what his father did."

Her heart pounded. "I do know, Fergus. He told me. It wasn't Marc's fault."

"His father stole my father's savings and he didn't even have the courage to admit it because he chose the easy way out and gassed himself. He was a filthy, thieving coward."

Gilly gripped the edge of the bed. "It was nothing to do with Marc. He didn't know what his father was doing because he was only a student at the time, so how can you blame him?"

The woman at the window still remained silent. She stared at Gilly, her expression blank and emotionless, as if she was deaf and couldn't hear a word.

"How can you do this to a child?" Gilly yelled at her. "You can't take him away from his father. He loves his father."

Jane's cold dark eyes swept over her. "I have nothing to say to you."

Samuel's sobs dwindled to whimpers as he hid his face in the blankets.

"We've no sympathy for his sort," said Fergus. "It was easy for him, with all that money that didn't belong to him, to start again with a different name, wasn't it? People like my dad paid for his posh education while the rest of us were left to grovel about in the gutter." His voice rose as he swung his foot at a toy army tank and kicked it across the floor.

It smashed against the wall and broke in two.

Samuel let out a wail of horror and leaned against Gilly. She put her arm round his waist.

She longed to argue with Fergus, to denounce his insane words, but she pressed her lips together. Dangerous to get Fergus worked up like that because she didn't know what he might do. Safer for her and for Samuel to keep him calm. She didn't recognize Fergus in this mood, his face contorted, like a demon lashing out.

Fergus pulled a wooden chair towards him and sat down. He took out his cigarettes, his hands shaking, and put one in his mouth. He tossed another to his sister. "You see, Gilly, my uncle was clever enough to track him down, though it took a long time because he'd changed his name. Then we thought up a plan between the three of us." He flicked his lighter, drew on his cigarette and threw the lighter to Jane. "Marc had to pay for what his father did – he had to fork out for an expensive nursing home and more."

The woman lit her cigarette and stared at Gilly.

Did she look like Fergus? No, nothing like him with her slim build, thin shoulders and arched eyebrows.

Jane switched her gaze to Samuel and said, "But now our father is dead and you know what? We don't feel like letting Marc Hillington get away without suffering. Maybe Uncle Matthew thinks it's time to call a halt, but Fergus and I don't."

Fergus added, "After six months Uncle Matthew started to go a bit soft, began to feel sorry for Marc. He wanted to stop when Dad died so that's why we went our separate ways."

"Your uncle is involved in this? The one who Dean…"

Fergus blew smoke rings into the air. "It's really very simple, Gilly. My family was all in this together. We made sure that Dad had the best care possible for his last days."

"Your uncle that I met at the funeral?" The cramp in her stomach returned and she bent over, wrapping her arms around herself.

Fergus smirked. "Yeah, yeah. The same one. He really loves amateur dramatics. He made an excellent private investigator."

"I don't understand."

"He kept an eye on Marc in London and he managed to extract more money from him. Marc deserves this, Gilly, and if you'd kept away from him, you wouldn't be here."

The boy lay motionless and moaned.

"You'd better resign yourself to the fact that he might not want you back," Fergus said. "He mightn't think you're worth paying a ransom for. Then you'll have to stay here in the cold and dark on your own."

Poor Sam, to have to listen to this insanity. She reached out and took his little hand in hers. Tears blurred her vision and she wiped them away, swallowing hard.

"The Gardaí will find me." A confident reply, but fear touched her all the same with its cold, sweaty fingers.

"I wouldn't be so sure." He nodded at Jane. "Come on, sis, let's go and get some food. We'll bring you back something, Gilly, if you behave yourself. I don't want you to starve just yet."

They left, locking the door behind them.

Gilly heard their footsteps on the stone steps growing fainter. She ran over and pulled the handle, rattled it and kicked at the door. She pounded with her fists and screamed. Next, she tried the window, but there was no way past the iron bars. She shouted again as Fergus and Jane walked out into the daylight below. The woman didn't look up, but he turned his head and grinned. He lifted a hand to wave mockingly.

"Come back here! Come back and let us out," she yelled, her voice shaking. Panic rose in her throat, choking her. She buried her face in her hands and wept.

Then she remembered the boy. He sat pale and upright, watching with terror in his eyes. Poor Samuel. She would have to calm down; no need to frighten him even more. She had to behave like a responsible adult.

Gilly moved towards the bed and hugged him.

"My hand hurts," he said quietly. "I'm really, really scared and I want to go home. I want my dad."

"So do I, sweetie," she said. "So do I."

Gilly had no way of telling the time. It dragged past, second after second, minute after minute, while the damp and cold seeped into her. The tips of her fingers felt numb. Samuel shivered and she rubbed her hands together and wrapped the blankets around the two of them. He pressed against her and closed his eyes. She hoped that the heat from both their bodies would keep away the chill.

The huge room had only a few wooden chairs and the metal bed on which they lay. Vast black cobwebs clung to wooden beams and wind whistled through the broken windowpane.

An hour had passed since Fergus and his sister left, or maybe only half an hour. So hard to tell without her mobile phone. Would Dean be wondering where she was? Had Marc returned to Glanesfort? He'd told her not to leave the grounds.

Fergus had fooled her so easily by his call to Marc in the Land Rover. Obviously no one at the other end. Or else he'd rung his sister instead. What an idiot she'd been to trust him and go with him like an innocent child, as innocently as Samuel had done. So gullible to be taken in by his manipulation and lies.

Surely Marc and Alice would have missed her by now? Alice knew she had gone off with Fergus. Or did she know? Perhaps that too had been a lie and Fergus had never actually gone into the house to talk to her. He could have waited for the Land Rover on the steps by the portico and not bothered to tell her. The CCTV camera trained on the front door area would record her leaving with Fergus but Stefans might not find that suspicious.

The only hope would be for the Gardaí to search the area and find them, but they would have to hurry. Soon Fergus and Jane would be back to take Samuel away. What could she do to stop them? If she put up a fight, she would come off worse because Fergus was too strong. She closed her eyes and tried to think logically, but her mind felt heavy and confused.

She must have dropped off briefly, because when she opened her eyes again, the light had faded outside, or perhaps it was because of rain clouds that hung low in the sky. Her mouth was dry, her tongue stiff. She could hear the patter of rain on the roof.

Samuel opened his eyes and stared at the ceiling.

"Hi, Sam, how are you, pet?"

"OK, but my hand hurts."

"I'm sure it does." She touched it gently. There were bloodstains on the cloth, but the cut didn't look too deep. Would it become infected without treatment? "Tell me how you got here. What did you do when you left home?"

"Me and Wolf were fishing."

"Where?"

"On the steps."

"And you met someone?"

"Fergus waved at me. He was in the wood."

Gilly stroked his hair. Fergus hiding in the trees. So that was how he lured the boy away. "Where did Fergus take you?"

"To the road... to the scary woman."

"Did you recognize her? She used to be your nanny, but you haven't seen her for two years. You mightn't remember her."

He shook his curly head.

She smiled. She would have to try to make light of this trauma for his sake. "But you haven't been completely alone, have you? Wolf is with you and he will look after you."

"No, he's not! That's just stupid."

"It's not, Sam. He's over there by the window. I can see him. Look, his tongue is hanging out and he's wagging his tail."

"Stupid!" shouted Samuel. "He's not here. He's not real... he's not real because I made him up." He burst into loud sobs.

She drew him to her. Did Fergus realize what he was doing to a small boy? Selfish, crazy man. How she hated him for destroying Sam's imaginary dog.

The sound of the Land Rover's engine made her sit up.

"They're coming back," she breathed into his ear.

He buried his face under the blankets. They clung to each other as footsteps grew louder on the stairs. The door swung open and Fergus entered.

"I've got some bread and cheese," he said, waving a plastic bag.

"What time is it?" Gilly asked.

"About one. We took longer than we meant to, but we'd plenty to do and shopping to get. Jane will be back in a minute – she's down below organizing things." He held a hand up to his ear and imitated someone on the phone.

"What things?"

He laughed, his good mood back. "The journey, of course.

Don't ask me where. Ah, that would be telling! Somewhere a long way from here, that's for sure."

"I suppose you plan to join your uncle in Australia."

"Yeah, maybe someday, but we'll go our own way for the moment. Matthew chickened out when Dad died so he won't share our latest little windfall. He's a bit of a liability with his wild ideas."

"I suppose he dreamed up the idea to use Mozart's *Requiem*." She stared at the dusty floor, attempting to keep her voice neutral, to repress the anger simmering inside her.

"Yeah, yeah, that was him. I have to give him credit for originality." He handed her a loaf of bread, tub of margarine and a packet of cheese slices. "Make Sam a sandwich, will you? I don't want him wailing with hunger before we get to our destination."

"I don't want it," said Samuel.

Fergus grinned at him. "Hey, come on, Sam, cheer up. You'll love where we're going. It's a big surprise and will be so much more fun than Glanesfort."

"How am I supposed to make a sandwich without a knife?" Gilly asked.

"Do you think I'm stupid? I'm not giving a girl with a temper like yours a knife. Make it with your fingers. Use your initiative."

She glared at him. How had she ever thought him attractive? A sneering bully of a man who relished making fun of those weaker than himself. But she had a choice. She could remain angry and stubborn or she could play Fergus at his own game. Tackling him physically was out of the question. That was a no-brainer. She would try to outwit him psychologically, although it would be difficult because even now he was regarding her with a smirk, as if he could read her mind.

"You should be on the stage," she said. "You and your nanny sister and your private investigator uncle. You're all excellent actors, Fergus. You certainly fooled Marc and me. You must be delighted with how your family vendetta is playing out."

He laughed. "Yeah, well, you're easy to fool, sweetie pie."

"And Marc."

"He's not as easy to deceive as you because he's naturally suspicious. So bloody reserved and cautious." He sneezed into his sleeve. "The dust up here is giving me an allergy. I'd bring you a brush to tidy the place up only you might try to be brave and hit me over the head with it." He put his head to one side and grinned at her. "Look at you! So self-righteous and indignant." He pointed at a bucket and toilet roll on the far side of the room. "That's there in case you feel the urge. Never say I don't look after you."

She glanced at it and shuddered. How long was she going to have to stay here in this filthy place? What would happen if no one found her?

"Will you leave me food to eat when you take Sam?" she asked.

Fergus moved towards the door. "I'll be back when it gets dark."

"Fergus, please, what have we ever done to you? Sam is only a boy. Let him go and take me instead."

Samuel looked up at her with pleading eyes.

Fergus shook his head. "Nah, we're holding onto him because he's our ticket to a better life. Marc might not pay out for you, but he'll definitely want his son back."

A flush burnt her cheeks and she turned her head away.

As he reached the door and unlocked it, he added, "But don't worry, sweetie pie, we've changed our minds. Jane and I will take you with us. You'll come in useful to look after Sam and stop him moaning. See you later." He slammed the door behind him and turned the key.

Gilly forced a smile. "Did you hear that? It's not so bad, Sam.

At least I'm going with you."

He nodded without much enthusiasm. "Yeah, I don't wanna be on my own."

*

Gilly rubbed at the grime on the window and glanced at Samuel. "I hear an engine. It must be Fergus coming back." She bent to peer through the dust. "Yes, look, there's a car coming, but it's not the Land Rover. A black van, I think it's a small black van, but it's hard to tell in the dark."

"Will Fergus bring us more food?" Samuel ran over to join her. "I'm so hungry, Gilly."

"So am I – hours since we ate all the bread and cheese."

She watched Fergus climb out of the van and strained her eyes to see the registration plate. D 864… or was it 354? If she could memorize the numbers before he took them away from here. Perhaps she could scratch them into the plaster on the wall. Or in the dirt on the windowpane. But Fergus would see that, wouldn't he? Far too obvious and he would be furious. Might change his mind and leave her behind. She looked down at the bare wooden floorboards. If only she had a knife, she could carve the numbers into the floor. What time was it? After midnight because it was dark outside.

Footsteps clattered on the steps up to the door. The key turned in the lock and Fergus walked over to them.

"How are the captives?" He laughed, more like his old self. "I bet you're looking forward to your dinner?"

"Where is it? I don't see any dinner," Gilly said. "We're starving here. You left us for hours."

Fergus grinned again. "Sorry, sweetie pie, Jane and I have been very busy."

As he came closer, she could smell alcohol. That explained

his improved mood. She bit her bottom lip and kept her voice steady and polite. "Are you going to give us food to eat now, Fergus, please? At least give Sam something. I can hear his stomach gurgling. It's not fair to leave a boy so long without food."

"Oh don't worry, you'll both be fed before too long. If you're good, you'll get fed." He moved over to one of the wooden chairs and sat down. Watching her with amusement dancing in his eyes, he stretched out his long legs. He lit a cigarette and inhaled deeply. "We're going on a holiday."

"A holiday," Samuel said. "Is Dad coming too?"

"He might come later," said Fergus. "It'll be a surprise for him. He doesn't know where we're going."

A knot in Gilly's stomach tightened. "Where are you taking us?"

"Somewhere nice, you'll see. I can't tell you now or it will spoil the surprise."

"You're bloody crazy!" Gilly muttered. "Let us go now and maybe Marc will forget all about this..."

"He won't forget about this. I do not intend to let him forget about this. He's had it coming to him for a long time and I'm going to make sure he remembers it." His voice was still soft but a hard note had crept into it.

Gilly walked back to the window and bent down. She would have to leave some sort of clue that they'd been here. Could she leave something that might be found by someone searching the mill?

She peered again at the registration plate on the van and said, "It's very dark, Fergus. What time is it?" She couldn't let him see what she was planning. Any attempt to thwart him would mean no food for either of them, or worse.

"About half twelve, I reckon." He pulled out his mobile and pressed a button. "Yeah, near enough. Twenty-five past. Why?"

"Just wondering." Was it 53... or 65...312? Impossible to see the numbers clearly and she had no idea what type of van it was. If only she knew more about cars. It was definitely black with a door that opened at the back like those ones on the continent. Maybe it was French.

Fergus finished his cigarette, threw the butt on the floor and trod on it. "Right, you two, it's time to go, so here's the deal. You will both come quietly with me, making no fuss. You won't do anything stupid like trying to escape. You will climb obediently into the back of the van and stay quiet. Any shouting, crying or other noise and you won't get food until tomorrow. Do you understand? You behave well and you get something to eat."

Samuel nodded immediately. Food mattered more to him than indignation at this stage.

Gilly frowned but decided to comply. "All right," she said. "But how long do we have to wait until you feed us?"

Fergus stood up and yawned. "An hour or two, maybe. Not too long if you behave. I will add on another couple of hours for every noise you make." He smiled again, obviously relishing the control he had over them. His mobile pinged and he glanced at it. "That's a message from Jane. We're ready to go."

His sister came into the room a few minutes later. Gilly tried to catch her eye, but Jane remained expressionless and ignored her. A shame she was so sullen because she would be beautiful if she bothered to smile.

Jane took hold of Samuel's arm and pulled him towards her.

"Come with me," she said. "Be a good boy and I won't get cross with you."

"Do as she says," Gilly told him. "We want our dinner."

Fergus gripped her left elbow and steered her towards the door, while Jane followed with the boy.

Gilly's mind raced. She couldn't leave a clue up here for others now and she was certain that Fergus would clear the mill later of any evidence they had left behind. As they walked slowly down the stone steps with only the light from Jane's mobile to guide them, she wondered what she could leave outside without them seeing. What had they done with her mobile? Probably dumped in the canal or the river by now.

Outside damp grass soaked her shoes, although the night felt warmer than inside the mill. A crescent moon slid from behind the clouds and threw a wan light on them while the mill towered behind them, dark and sinister, the bars of its windows bared like teeth.

An idea came to her. They were behind the van and Gilly could make out the registration clearly. That year's model, probably hired for the purpose. Fergus pulled open the door and light flooded the interior. The floor was metal and bare, with only a length of rope coiled in a circle. What was the rope for? Was Fergus going to tie them up? A metal panel sealed off the front of the van. No windows.

Jane helped Samuel to climb in. He sat on the cold floor and stared at Gilly.

"You get in." Fergus squeezed her arm. "Go on, move! You're a big girl and you don't need my help."

She pulled her arm away from him and bumped against the door. Without making a sound, she slid to the ground.

Fergus grabbed her arm again. "What do you think you're doing? I said no fuss, remember?"

Gilly got to her knees. "Sorry, I lost my balance, that's all." She clutched the back of the van and began to pull herself upright, sliding one leg underneath the vehicle. As she stood up, she slipped off the shoe on the foot under the van and quickly heaved herself into the back, landing with a bump beside Samuel as a stab of pain shot through her left shoulder. She winced but hurried into a sitting position, pulling her foot without the shoe underneath her out of sight.

Fergus slammed the door and darkness engulfed them. She reached for Samuel and put her arm around him.

Fergus shouted to Jane and she heard footsteps going back to the mill. The front door of the van banged on the driver's side. The woman, probably. Another ten or fifteen minutes passed. Gilly rested her head against the side of the van. What was he doing? Probably tidying away any sign that they'd been there. She could imagine him trying to scrub the bloodstain off the floorboards by the window where the boy cut his hand.

The footsteps came back towards the van. Would he notice her shoe underneath? She hardly dared to breathe until she heard the passenger door shut and the engine start up. They moved off slowly along the uneven lane, Gilly and Samuel clinging to each other to keep their balance when the wheels bumped down into potholes.

If a search party came to the mill, they would find her shoe. They might also see the wheel tracks but they would have no idea where she and Samuel had gone.

"Do you think Fergus is going to kill us?" Samuel's question made her jump in the darkness.

"No, I'm sure he won't."

The boy rested his head on her shoulder and yawned. "I don't like Fergus. He's horrible. And that woman is scary. She's like a witch, Gilly. Do you think she is a witch?"

"I don't think she's a witch, Sam. I can think of another name for her but it would be too rude to tell you." Gilly stroked his hair in what she hoped was a soothing gesture.

How little she knew about children and yet here she was, sharing this nightmare with one. Only three months ago, she'd complained about her client's children and it had cost her the job.

"Your dad didn't like her when she was your nanny." Gilly stroked Samuel's hair again and planted a quick kiss on the top of his head. "That's why he sent her away."

"Did Daddy think she was a witch?"

"I think your dad will have plenty to say to her when he rescues us."

"Will Dad rescue us?"

"Of course he will," she whispered in Samuel's ear. Where was Marc now? He would be frantic with worry, wondering what had happened, where they were. She hadn't dared ask Fergus if he'd demanded a ransom for them yet. Perhaps he and his sister would be sensible and not ask for too much money. Marc would be able to pay a reasonable amount but if they asked for more than he could afford, what then? Goose pimples rose on her arms and she pushed that thought away. Better not to think too far ahead.

"I think we should try to be very nice to Fergus and Jane," she said. "If we're nice to them, they might be kinder to us."

"They might give us food."

"Yes. If we're nice to them, they might not be so mean to us. Do you understand? If we're really good..."

If Fergus and his sister dropped their guard at all, she would be ready to take advantage. She could be manipulative, too, if she put her mind to it.

Samuel didn't reply and she wondered if he had fallen asleep. He moved against her and sighed.

A few minutes later the boy was asleep, his head in her lap. Gilly's shoulder ached and she cried out in pain when the van swung round a corner and threw her against the metal side. Samuel murmured a few words, but slept on as she lay down and closed her eyes. She was tired, so tired.

She woke when the van stopped and swerved suddenly to the side of the road. The back door opened and she blinked as the light came on.

Fergus stared at them. "What are you two doing?"

"Resting," she replied.

He handed her a paper bag. "Here's the food. It's cold by now, but it's better than nothing."

She peered into it. Battered cod and chips, greasy and soggy. She remembered her resolution and murmured, "Thank you, Fergus. Are we nearly there yet?"

"Halfway." Fergus turned away and reached for the door.

Gilly couldn't see much behind him. The moon had disappeared and there was only a black shape like a hedge with a deep ditch in front of it. No lights, so they were still out in the country. No one nearby to help. Which direction were they heading? North or south? East or west? They'd been travelling for an hour or two. Difficult to tell how long when she'd fallen asleep.

"Can you leave the light on, please?" she asked and saw him hesitate. "Sam is afraid of the dark."

"I'm n..." protested the boy but he fell silent when she poked him gently in the ribs.

Fergus shrugged. "Yeah, why not? Any noise, though, and I'll turn it off again." He slammed the door.

Chapter 33

Samuel's brown eyes gleamed as he ran from one narrow window slit to another. He placed his hands flat against the thick grey stone and peered out.

"Look, Gilly, look! There's a river down here. A river and horses." He pressed his face on the glass pane and closed one eye to focus.

Gilly smiled at his enthusiasm. She lay back on the four-poster bed and took in their new surroundings. An improvement on the previous cell. No comparison. Early morning sunshine shone through the window and threw a strip of light across gleaming dark floorboards. No dust on the heavy old chest of drawers with brass handles. A long mirror on the matching wardrobe. She hardly recognized her reflection, her pale face and tousled hair. The sheets on the bed beneath her were crumpled after their three hours' sleep, white linen sheets with a heavy cream bedspread, embroidered with red poppies. Roses, maybe. She peered at them. No, definitely poppies.

"We even have running water." She pointed at the door in the corner. "We've got an ensuite bathroom. It's luxury."

The boy walked back to the bed and pulled himself up beside her, resting his dark curls on her shoulder.

She touched his hand. "How's the cut?"

He uncurled his fingers, pointed at the scar. "OK now. Do you think soldiers live in this castle?"

"No, not now. They might have centuries ago. I think this is what people call a Tower House. I think the first ones were called Norman Keeps."

"Keeps?"

"Yes, it's a tower. A tower built by the Normans. They came from France in the ... I don't know, the middle ages maybe. Your dad would know. He's good at history."

"From France like Grand-maman?"

Gilly tickled him. "Your grandmother is not as old as that."

Samuel shrieked with laughter, jumped up and ran to the oak door leading to the spiral stairway. He rattled the handle and pulled.

"It's locked," Gilly said. "Fergus locked us in. Do you remember? He carried you up the winding stairs."

He shook his head.

"You were asleep. It was just starting to get light... dawn." She moved across to the window and knelt down. Five horses grazed on the far side of the river, one chestnut and four greys. The grass rolled away, treeless and vivid green, towards a strip of sea on the left. A single strand of barbed wire straggled along the edge of the field. Probably a drop down to rocks or perhaps a stony beach below. The water danced and glittered in the sunlight.

Where were they? What direction had Fergus taken them? Four hours in the back of the van from Kildare. Where would that journey take them? Not Waterford or Wexford. They'd driven further than that. West coast of Ireland? Clumps of scarlet fuchsia below meant an acid soil. An old weathered gate pillar in the grass where the horses stood in a group, nose to tail, flicking flies away. A dry stone wall ran along two sides of the field. Maybe this was

Connemara or how long would it take to drive from Kildare to
Donegal?

Samuel found a book about Norman tower houses on the
shelf beside the four-poster bed and sank onto the floor cross-
legged to flick through pages of photographs. The curtains that
draped the bed looked new, embroidered gold brocade. Whoever
had furnished the room had money. An elaborate holiday house
that didn't belong to Fergus and Jane. Marc never mentioned a
tower house so it probably wasn't his.

She closed her eyes. Fergus's breath had smelled of whiskey
when they'd arrived at the tower. He shouted over the wind and
ordered her out of the van, then leaned in to pick up the sleeping
boy. Gilly stepped outside, her face stung by the salt-scented air.

Jane had looked exhausted, with dark smudges under her
eyes, and she yawned as she unlocked the huge front door and
stood aside, wrapping her thin cardigan around her. She hunched
her bony shoulders and shivered. Fergus carried Samuel up the
steps. He must have been drinking in the van while his sister
drove because he was in a good mood and he hummed a lullaby
to the boy and grinned at Gilly.

How could he think he'd get away with this? He and Jane
might be planning to leave the two of them shut up in this tower
house, collect a ransom and disappear. Their father avenged, a
fortune in their pockets as he and his sour-faced sister headed for
Australia to join their uncle. Had they asked Marc for a ransom
yet? If so, how much?

Samuel's high-pitched laugh brought her back to the
present. She opened her eyes as he stabbed at the book with a
finger. "Look here, Gilly. Look!"

She moved to sit beside him. It was an illustration of a Norman
keep with soldiers battling outside. A line of men hammered at
the door with a battering ram while inhabitants at the top of the
tower poured liquid down on them through a hole in the wall.

She read him captions from under other photographs and added, "That tower there has been restored, like this one."

Had Marc mentioned a wealthy American who owned the mill? It was possible he owned this castle as well. It would be easy for Fergus to get hold of the keys. Perhaps he was even paid a fee to keep an eye on the properties. If so, he would know them well. Had anyone found her shoe outside the mill yet? Jane had spotted that she had only one shoe but hadn't asked about it and didn't seem bothered that Gilly was only wearing a pair of socks.

Jane unlocked the door and entered. She tossed a paper bag onto the bed and Samuel rushed to open it. He held up a jam doughnut.

"Thanks," said Gilly.

Jane turned to leave.

"Where's Fergus?" Samuel asked.

"Asleep."

"How long will we be here?" Gilly took the doughnut Samuel offered her. She bit into it and jam ran down her chin.

Jane shrugged. "As long as it takes."

"Have you asked Marc for money yet?"

"You don't need to know that." She pulled the door handle.

"Well thanks, anyway," said Gilly.

"For what?"

"For the doughnuts."

Jane stared at her for a moment, her dark eyes suspicious. She pulled the door behind her and the lock clicked shut.

As the hours passed, the day grew hotter. Sunlight streamed in the narrow windows and danced across the floor, but the thick walls remained cool to the touch. The sky was a vivid blue and the wind had dropped completely, the sea without a ripple. Over on the right, a yacht sat becalmed, white sails limp.

"I'm bored," said Samuel and sat upright. "How long do we have to stay in this room?"

"Don't know."

She heard footsteps on the staircase and the heavy door unlocked and swung open. Fergus scowled at them, blinking. He looked hungover and weary.

"Out, out," he said, loudly. "Time for some exercise." He stood at the threshold and beckoned them towards the steps leading upwards. "Up there. Gilly, you go first."

Samuel ran towards the door and Fergus caught his hand and pulled him back. "Not you, it's steep up there. Gilly, get a move on, for God's sake, my head is throbbing."

She walked past him and onto the steps. "Do you expect me to feel sorry for you because you drink too much?"

He pushed her forward and pulled the boy after him. "Up to the top. Wait at the ladder when you get there." His face was flushed and sullen.

Gilly decided not to argue and moved up the circular staircase, gripping the thick rope for safety. Fergus followed behind, holding Samuel's hand tightly. The muscles in her calves ached and she stopped to take a few deep breaths.

"Where are we going?" the boy asked.

"You'll see in a minute," said Fergus.

Gilly reached a wooden ladder leading to an oak trapdoor. Fergus produced a large key from a back pocket in his jeans and handed it to her. He pointed upwards and Gilly climbed the ladder and fitted the key into the lock. It turned slowly and she pushed the trapdoor open. Bright sunlight dazzled her and she turned away, her hands over her eyes, as screams of herring gulls filled her ears. Fergus climbed up behind her and, grabbing her shoulder, pushed her forward onto a paved area surrounded by a waist-high limestone wall. Flagstones underneath her feet felt warm from the sunshine and a white wrought-iron bench stood in one corner. The top of the tower, a square space with tufts of grass and lichen on the walls.

She turned to Fergus. "Who owns this place?"

He didn't reply but pulled the trapdoor shut behind him and locked it. They could hear the sound of his shoes on the steps, receding as he descended.

Samuel ran over to the wall and reached up as if to climb onto it. Gilly sprang forward and gripped his arm to pull him back. "No, no, be careful. It's very high." She looked out over the wall and her stomach spun as the wall of the castle dropped down to the fuchsia bushes below. She smelled the sea and felt the heat of the stones under her palms. At least they were outside in the fresh air.

"I can't see over," complained the boy. "Can you lift me up?"

"Sam, it's a sheer drop down to the ground. I can't risk it."

"Please."

She looked around. "Try the bench. Climb up on that and look over but don't get onto the wall. If you do, I won't let you up on the bench again. Do you hear me?"

He was already running towards the corner. "Yeah, yeah."

She held onto his T-shirt to restrain him as he scrambled onto the metal seat. He put his hands on the wall and turned round to take in the view.

"Wow." He wriggled away from her.

"Remember what I said, Sam."

His dark eyes stared into hers. "Could we climb down and escape?"

"You must be joking. We'd fall and break our necks."

"We could tie the sheets together."

"No, Sam – too dangerous."

He jumped off the bench. Within seconds, he crossed the limestone flags and grabbed at the wall on the far side, which seemed a little lower.

Gilly followed him and put a hand on his shoulder. The horses stood below them, in the shade of a battered hawthorn tree, one of the grey ones rubbing its tail against the trunk.

"I'll let you go if you promise me you won't climb up on the wall."

He smiled his most charming smile, a wide grin, and nodded. "Okay, yeah."

"Promise."

"I promise."

Sighing, she released him and he was off again, running in circles on the stones, his arms spread out like a plane, loud engine sounds bursting from his throat. He was enjoying himself. It would do him good to burn off some energy. This was the first time he'd been outside since that dreadful day when he'd disappeared from the front steps of Glanesfort. It seemed like a month away though it was only a few days. How many days? Two or three?

Gilly sat on the seat and relaxed as the sun warmed the skin on her face and lower arms. Better here than in the dark, damp mill and, if they had to stay here for a week, it would be bearable. The middle of May and white flowers on the hawthorn below, like a bride's bouquet against the azure sea. She closed her eyes and rested her head on the wall.

A whistle made her spring to her feet and look towards the headland. Samuel climbed up on the bench beside her, pushed his little hand into hers and she closed her fingers tightly around it.

A figure in the distance stood at the edge of the cliff, looking down and waving his hand. Or perhaps it was a woman. A shout rang out. No, it was definitely a man, but too far away to hear what he was saying. Minutes later a brown and white spaniel appeared, obviously from some path up from the sea, and the man bent to pat it.

Gilly's heart skipped a beat. Suppose he came this way towards the tower. Would she be able to attract his attention and call for help? She muttered aloud, "Over here, over here."

"Who are you talking to?" Samuel frowned at her.

"That man over there with the dog. Can you see him?" She waved a hand and shouted, "Hey, hey!"

"Hey, hey!" echoed Samuel at the top of his voice. "Here doggy, good boy, here doggy!"

The figure seemed to turn and look in their direction and Gilly waved more frantically and yelled again. The spaniel bounded about in the grass, nose to the ground, before sitting down in front of the man who held up an object and threw it away from the cliff edge. The dog took off after it and its owner followed. He held what looked like a long plastic ball launcher.

"Damn." Gilly groaned. "He threw the ball back the other way. He didn't hear us."

"Hey, hey!" Samuel yelled. "Over here. Please, please!"

It was no use. The man headed off towards a gate at the far end of the field, stopping to scoop up and throw the ball every now and then, but purposefully walking in the opposite direction to the castle. The spaniel was a fanatic retriever with flapping ears. It jumped up and down in front of its owner, impatiently waiting for the ball to arc over the heather.

Still, it was a glimmer of hope. Perhaps this person brought the dog out here often, lonely and isolated though it was, and they might be able to attract his attention another day. She would just have to be patient. At least Fergus and Jane hadn't heard them. They were still downstairs in the castle and no hasty footsteps clattered up the ladder; no reprimand rang out.

After half an hour, Jane appeared to bring them down for lunch. This time she'd cooked food herself and it wasn't bad. Quite edible spaghetti bolognese, although the pasta was a bit soggy. Fergus was asleep in a room below them and they could hear his snores echoing up the steps when Jane opened the door.

Chapter 34

"Can we talk to Marc?" Gilly asked. "He will need to know that we're all right, won't he?"

"No." Fergus looked at his mobile phone. "He knows you're all right. I told him." He slouched in the armchair in their bedroom, a scowl on his broad features. "When he sends on the money, we're out of here."

"What about us?" Gilly sipped a mug of coffee and made a face. Making coffee was not one of Fergus's skills.

He drummed his fingers on his knee. "You'll stay here. Don't worry, we'll tell him where you are once he pays up."

"How much?"

"Enough to keep Jane and me going for years."

"Do you think he'll be able to pay it?"

Fergus shrugged. "You better hope so, Gilly, or you'll be here for weeks." He yawned and pushed himself out of the chair, walking over to the window. "I'm sick to death of this bloody place. The mobile signal is non-existent."

"What did you do with my mobile?"

"Chucked it into the canal along with mine. Can't have the Gardaí tracking us, can we?" He tapped the side of his head with a finger. "I'm not as stupid as you think."

"I never thought you were stupid, Fergus. It's just a pity..."

"What?"

"A pity that you chose this way... this plan, when you could have talked to Marc. He would have understood. I know he would. I'm sure he'd have helped you."

"You don't know him very well, if that's what you think." He swung away from the window and returned to the chair, slumping down in it with a groan.

"Don't you understand why he changed his name? He didn't want to be associated with his father's fraud – the man left him and his mother penniless. He had to leave college and work on building sites."

Fergus resumed beating out a rhythm on his knee. "Yeah, sure. My heart bleeds for him."

"No point talking to you if you're just going to be sarcastic."

"And you, sweetie pie, should keep your nose out of my business, if you know what's good for you."

"This is our third day here, Fergus. Can I call my sister if I can't call Marc? Please, let me call her. She must be worried sick about me. My parents must be worried sick."

He shook his head and took out his cigarettes, fiddling with them. He only had a few left and she knew he was trying to save them. Jane wouldn't let him drive to the local village as she thought the countryside was swarming with Gardaí now that they had been missing for so long. Too risky. Gilly had seen Jane going out in the black van, an auburn curly wig over her hair and she wore sunglasses. Easier for her to change her looks than her brother and someone had to go out to buy food. She was a master of disguise.

"Why did Jane dress up as the white woman, Fergus?"

His bloodshot eyes glanced at her. "Why do you think?"

"To frighten me? To keep an eye on me?"

"Yeah – and Marc."

"I suppose it amused her."

He grinned. "Yeah, I guess it did. You should have seen your face, Gilly, when she stared in the window. Jane said you looked terrified. She thought it was hilarious."

Somehow, she had to get him to agree to let them go out on the roof again. He'd refused the day before. Once on the roof, they might be able to persuade him to go below and they could try again to attract the attention of the man with the spaniel. If the man was there. She'd seen him again the previous morning, walking briskly along the clifftop as the dog bounced about in the heather beside him.

"Can we go outside, Fergus? We're getting cabin fever stuck in here."

He pushed the cigarettes back into the packet and sighed. "No."

"Why not?" asked Samuel, looking up from his drawing.

"The thing is," said Fergus, "you can't go out on the roof today because it's raining."

"It's not," said Samuel.

"It was a minute ago."

"It's not now."

"Just ten minutes, Fergus," said Gilly. "We need some air. We've been locked up inside for two days."

"No way. Jane said I wasn't to let you go up on the roof. She thinks it's dangerous."

"We won't fall off the wall," Samuel ran over to the window and looked out. "See, no rain. It's gone."

"I'm not talking about you falling off." Fergus frowned. "I'm talking about someone seeing you."

"Who's going to see us in this place?" asked Gilly. "It's in the middle of nowhere. There's no one to see us."

Fergus hesitated.

He ran a hand through his lank hair, watching Gilly pick up a sketchbook and a packet of crayons Jane had given the boy.

"We'll go up and draw a few pictures and get some fresh air." She drank water from a plastic bottle. "What harm can that do? Come on, Fergus, you know your sister has gone shopping. She won't even know about it."

She held her breath while he stood at the open door, undecided. Alcohol could often improve his mood, but it could also make him more volatile. "Oh, yeah, okay then. Just a few minutes while I have a smoke. I need a cigarette."

He led them up the spiral staircase, climbed the ladder ahead of them and lifted back the trapdoor. Samuel followed with Gilly behind, one hand on the ladder and the other holding the crayons and the plastic bottle of water, the sketchbook under her arm.

A sharp smell of the sea stung her nostrils as she stood upright. The fields glistened in a watery sunshine, emerald green against the bank of black clouds rising to the right.

White horses danced on the crests of waves that chased each other towards the shore. Wherever they were, it was a beautiful place.

Fergus sat on the bench and lit a cigarette, inhaled and blew out rings of smoke. "Yeah, it's good up here. Seat's a bit wet, though." He stood up and inspected the back of his jeans.

Gilly put her hands on the wall and hoped he would soon become bored and go below. No point distracting him with conversation. She twisted the cap of the plastic bottle and drank the rest of the water.

Samuel wheeled in circles on the flagstones, arms outstretched, flying his imaginary plane.

"You're very quiet," said Fergus after several minutes. He shuffled over to the wall where she was standing. "What's happened to you?"

She shrugged and moved away when he rested his forehead in a mock affectionate manner against her shoulder. "Nothing's happened."

He removed a piece of tobacco from a front tooth and peered at it. "It's nice up here, but I could do with a beer."

She rolled her eyes and muttered, "Then go below and get one." She swung away as a movement caught her eye.

A figure walked onto the cliff path from the road several fields away. The man with the dog. Fergus must not see them. She turned away and glanced at Samuel. She hadn't told him her plan just in case because he was only four years old and might blurt it out in excitement. She would tell him as soon as she'd got rid of Fergus.

Fergus rested his back against the parapet and yawned. "I'll go in a minute. It's good to get some sun."

Out of the corner of her eye, Gilly could see the dog bound along the cliff edge. It was the same one, brown and white, the springer spaniel, which darted here and there with its tail wagging enthusiastically when its owner swung the plastic launcher and tossed the ball into the air. She turned her back on the sea and looked at the trapdoor. How could she persuade Fergus to go back down?

He looked at her suspiciously. "What's up with you?"

"Would you get me a beer too?" She breathed slowly in an effort to calm her racing pulse. "Can I have one, please?" Her palms felt slippery with sweat.

She worried that Samuel might spot the man with the spaniel and alert Fergus without thinking. Gilly put out an arm to catch the boy as he ran past and handed him the crayons and book.

He took them from her and dropped on his knees on the flagstones.

"Are you going to draw with me?" he asked.

She nodded and bent down to turn over the pages. "Here's the nice picture of the rabbit we drew yesterday. How about a few baby rabbits? You get started and I'll help you in a minute."

She stood up, watching Fergus toss his cigarette butt on the ground.

Gilly slowly stepped in a circle, as if to check how Samuel's drawing was progressing, and she cast a quick glance towards the sea. The dog was bounding in circles, heading towards the castle, while the man stood looking out at the waves. They were only one field away now. Her heart thudded against her ribs as she bent over the boy. "That's lovely, Sam. How many babies do you want to draw?"

"Only five more minutes out here," said Fergus as he lit another cigarette and sucked hard on it.

"I thought you wanted to save your cigarettes? What about the beer?"

"Nah, I've only got two bottles left."

"Share one with me, please."

"I'm not that generous – though a beer up here in the sunshine sounds appealing."

Gilly knelt beside Samuel but still Fergus lingered, his back to the sea. What if he turned round and saw the man? Why wouldn't he go? She hoped he couldn't see her hands tremble.

"I'll finish my cigarette first," he said, as if reading her mind.

Gilly couldn't see over the wall from where she sat on the flagstones beside the boy. The dog might not come into the field and the man would probably then walk back the way he'd come. If she could only get rid of Fergus for a few minutes, she would wave to attract attention, or she would whistle to summon the dog. Dogs had good hearing, hadn't they? If she could get the dog to come, the man might follow. She glanced at the empty plastic bottle. If it was just the spaniel, she would write the message and put it in that.

Fergus's hair looked greasy in the sunlight, his skin blotched and reddish stubble on his chin. When she'd first met him, he had a lazy smile and amusing jokes, but he'd changed, become more angry and bitter since his father's death. He'd changed totally. And she'd changed too. A year before, she could never have imagined falling for a man like Marc Fletcher. Men in suits and ties were not her type at all. The suit brigade had always made a beeline for Vanessa and ignored her. A year before, she would probably have been taken in by Fergus and his lies and she would never have dreamed that someone like Marc would even give her a second glance.

Poor Marc. Where was he now? What was he doing about paying the ransom? Surely Fergus wasn't actually bad enough to harm her or the boy? If Marc couldn't or wouldn't pay, Fergus and Jane would be more likely to take Samuel away with them and leave her locked up here. Fergus had hinted that much. If he and his sister did that, would they bother to let anyone know where she was? Her heart began to thud against her ribs again. Best not to think about that. If only she could persuade Fergus to go downstairs. He watched her with a mocking smile and a hard expression in his eyes. She turned back to the drawing book and concentrated on that.

Fergus's shadow fell across the pages. "That's not bad, Sam, not bad at all."

"What about that beer?"

"You're very keen on beer all of a sudden, aren't you?" He bent down and gripped her arm. "What are you up to?"

"Nothing." She tried to pull her arm away and recoiled from his nicotine breath.

"Don't do that to Gilly." Samuel pushed at him.

Fergus laughed again, tauntingly. "Come on, big strong man. You defend the lady."

Samuel thumped him on the chest with a fist.

"Stop, stop it!" Gilly caught hold of the boy's hand. "Don't let Fergus upset you. It's not worth it."

"Don't let the nasty man upset you." Fergus mimicked her

voice. "Sam likes me, don't you, Sam?"

The boy leapt up and flew at him, hitting out with both fists clenched. "I hate you, I hate you!"

Fergus thrust him away and he burst into tears.

"Leave him alone," Gilly said. "You're too old to act like a pathetic bully."

She had done it now, pushed him too far. The words were out of her mouth and she couldn't retract them. Fergus reached out and squeezed the back of her neck with one hand and, when she tried to jerk away, his grip tightened. She cried out in pain and flailed her arms at him.

Samuel threw himself on Fergus and shouted. "Let her go, let her go!"

Fergus released his grip on Gilly's neck for a few seconds and shoved Samuel to the ground, where he fell in a heap. Gilly struggled to fight Fergus off, but he was too strong. She lifted a leg and tried to kick at him. Tears of pain sprang into her eyes. She could see Samuel lying on the ground, dark eyes wide in his pale face.

"You're a drunken bully. Let me go!" she screamed and scratched at his face. Her nails caught him beside his left eye and dots of blood sprang onto the skin.

He rubbed at it with the back of a hand. "You little cat! How dare you attack me like that." He raised his hand and she cowered down. His blow caught her on the side of her head and she stumbled backwards. He swiped at her again and hit her on the nose. She shrieked in pain and sank to her knees with her hands over her face, blood oozing between her fingers.

Fergus strode off towards the trapdoor and muttered over his shoulder, "Now you might have more respect for me. I'll be back in a few minutes."

Gilly heard the bolt slide into place and jumped up. "Come on, Sam, be quick. We only have a short time." She held the sleeve of her shirt up to her face, wiping the blood away.

The boy climbed to his feet, staring at her.

"Take off your T-shirt and wave it. Go on, good boy, go over to the wall. Take it off and wave it. The man and the dog are there. We've only got a few minutes to try to attract their attention." She dragged Samuel after her and looked out over the wall, searching. The man was still on the cliff edge but the dog was closer, its tail wagging as it nosed around the gorse bushes and circled among the horses that watched with ears pricked.

She helped Samuel pull off his T-shirt and showed him how to wave it from side to side, mopping away more blood that poured from her nose. Pain throbbed and the side of her left eye felt swollen. Had Fergus broken her nose? Couldn't think about that now, though. One brief chance to get help and all her effort had to go into that.

Samuel jumped up and down, his arms swirling the T-shirt. "Hey, hey, over here!"

Gilly ran back to the book and crayons and she scribbled frantically. What to say? Help us, we've been kidnapped, ring this number... she tried to remember Marc's number. So difficult to memorize numbers when all she did was press a saved contact on her mobile phone. Blood dripped onto the paper and she wiped it away. Vanessa. Yes, hers was easier to remember. Four eights and 333 at the end. Was that it? It would have to do. She stopped to listen. No sound from below yet. Better put Marc's name and address too. That would be a good idea. She scrawled them on top of a drawing of scarlet flowers.

"The dog is coming, the dog is coming." Samuel continued to wave, his voice rising in excitement. "Look, Gilly."

She tore the page from the book, stuffed it into the plastic bottle and ran back to the wall, leaning over to see where Samuel pointed. The spaniel was below them, snuffling at a clump of scarlet fuchsia. Gilly whistled and the dog paused. The long drop down made her head swim. She whistled again and this time the dog raised its head and looked up at them, a friendly expression with freckles on a white muzzle. The ground was slightly higher on this side of the castle, with a bank that sloped down to the river.

"Good dog," she called. "Good boy."

The spaniel wagged its tail cautiously.

"What are you doing?" Samuel asked.

"Shush, watch this." Gilly held up the plastic bottle, with cap firmly in place and her message inside. "See this, dog, see this bottle. Take it to your master." She waved it around to keep the dog's attention. Her heart pounded. Their only chance. If the dog ignored her and ran away, all would be lost.

The spaniel sat obediently and continued to stare up at them, its tail wagging faster. Samuel laughed with delight.

Gilly waved the bottle again. "Take it, take it." She threw the bottle towards the dog and hoped it wouldn't go into the river behind the fuchsias.

That was exactly what happened. The wind caught it and she groaned as the bottle plopped into the water. It was too light. She should have put a stone in it, or something else to weigh it down. She only had one bottle.

Samuel grabbed her arm. "Look, look, he's jumping in."

The spaniel landed with a splash in the river and swam towards the bottle. It took it gently in its mouth.

"Good dog!" Gilly shouted. "You're a great dog. Now go! Go away, quickly." She heard footsteps on the ladder leading to the trapdoor.

The bolt shot back and the door slowly began to lift.

Gilly sprang forward, put her arm round Samuel and propelled him back to where they had left the book and crayons, dragging him down beside her. She sat upright, her hands back over her bleeding and throbbing nose. The swelling had reached her eye and she could barely see out of it.

Fergus climbed out, shut the door behind him and walked towards them. He had a bottle of lager in one hand and a tea towel in the other. He tossed the damp cloth at Gilly, strolled over to the bench and said, "Get yourself cleaned up – you'll frighten the boy looking like that."

Chapter 35

Gilly looked in the bathroom mirror and lifted a finger to touch the left side of her face, which was purple and swollen, the eye almost completely closed. Blood covered her nose and matted the hair above her ear and her top lip had split open. Pain came in throbs as nausea swelled in her stomach. She put the tea towel under the running tap and dabbed at her face, wincing with pain. Her nose didn't look broken; for that she was thankful.

She walked back to the bedroom and Samuel glanced up from the book about tower houses. "Your face looks hurt."

"Sore, you mean. Yes, you're right. It's very sore."

"Gilly..."

"Yes, Sam." She sat on the bed and rested her head against two pillows. Would this pain ever go away? She was lucky Fergus hadn't knocked out her teeth. So much for thinking he and Jane wouldn't harm them.

"Do you think the dog gave the bottle to the man?"

"Hope so." She closed her eyes. Hope was all they had. Hope and perhaps a bit of luck. If the man had thrown the ball again, the spaniel might have abandoned the bottle, dropped it somewhere where no one would find her message.

Fergus had continued to sit and drink beer for another fifteen minutes with his back to the sea while Gilly and the boy lay on the ground. She ignored his taunts and answered his questions with a simple yes or no. Better be careful what she said to him in future. When he ushered them downstairs, she'd managed a quick glance towards the cliff and saw neither the man nor the dog.

"He was a clever dog, wasn't he?"

"Yes, let's hope he was clever enough to give the bottle with our message to his owner."

The boy nodded and returned to his book.

"Please don't mention the dog to Fergus or his sister."

He shook his curls. "No. I won't mention."

She smiled and drew in her breath. It hurt to move her face.

The lock clicked and Jane pushed the door open with a foot. She carried a tray with food on it.

Gilly glanced at her.

The woman put the tray on the bedspread beside her and let out a low whistle. "What the hell happened to you?"

"Your charming brother."

"He didn't mention it." Jane pointed at the food. "Lasagne."

Samuel got to his feet. "I'm hungry."

"I'm not," said Gilly. "I feel sick."

The other woman stared with her habitual blank expression, no feeling or sympathy in her cold eyes.

"My face is very sore. The pain makes me feel sick. Have you got any paracetemol?"

"Don't know."

"Isn't there a first aid kit or something in this place?"

Jane shrugged. "How would I know? I've never been here before. I'll ask Fergus." She peered closer at Gilly's face. "So, what happened?"

Gilly didn't reply.

"Fergus attacked Gilly," said Samuel, his voice rising. "He went crazy."

"Sam, stop!" Gilly warned.

The boy fell silent.

Jane stared at her. "What the hell?"

"I antagonized him, that's all."

The woman rolled her eyes and moved towards the door. "You probably deserved it."

"Paracetemol," Gilly called after her.

"I'll have a look." She locked the door behind her.

Gilly grinned at Samuel and screwed up her good eye. "Well, no sympathy from her. Typical."

"I hate Fergus," replied the boy. "And I hate that witchy woman."

Gilly pushed herself up and helped him to lukewarm lasagne. It was in a plastic container, shop-bought and obviously heated up by Jane in a microwave. Samuel liked it, ate his plateful enthusiastically and asked for more. The smell of the cheese made her stomach churn and bile welled up in her throat. She shuddered and groaned as she lowered herself onto the pillows.

The woman returned about fifteen minutes later with a couple of white tablets and a glass of water. "Here, try these." She held them out to Gilly.

"Are they paracetemol?"

Jane frowned. "Guess so. It said painkillers on the packet. Fergus found them." When Gilly hesitated, she added, "I'm not a bloody nurse, you know. Just take the damn things."

"All right, all right." Gilly swallowed them and sank back on the bed when Jane left the room. At this stage, she felt she didn't care what they were as long as they helped stop the pain, which ran up the back of her neck and across the top of her head. Her left ear throbbed.

"I think you should go to hospi... hospi... hospidal," Sam

suggested. "I wish we could see Alice. Alice is a nurse, isn't she?"

"She used to be and she's good at looking after people."

He looked sadly at her. "I miss Alice and Dad."

Gilly reached out to pat his hand. She closed her eyes and dozed for a while. She found it difficult to lift her head from the pillows as she reached out her hand to grip the glass of water. Very strong tablets to have such an effect so quickly. However, the throbs of pain were fading away and that was a relief.

She must have gone to sleep again because daylight had faded when she looked out of the window. Getting dark, so how many hours had passed? She turned to look for Samuel and saw him asleep beside her on the bed, one arm under his head. When she moved, he opened his eyes and smiled at her. She felt suddenly happy and longed to hug him. What a sweet child he was. She would never have believed she could like a boy so much. But her head was still too sore to move to embrace him and she lay still. It was relaxing lying there and she felt like humming.

"Do you think the man with the dog is going to rescue us?" Samuel asked.

She remembered seeing a dog sitting obediently below them. Such a long drop down, but she could see every little brown freckle on his face. She wished she could hug him too. She would never complain about dogs in clients' gardens again, even if they dug up her plants. She wouldn't complain about dogs, or children, or even clients. She would be nice to everyone. So nice that they would all like her. She tried to smile and the left side of her face felt stiff. Strange. What had happened to her? She touched her swollen eye with her fingers and let out a cry of alarm.

Sam sat up and stared at her.

"I feel really weird," she murmured and abandoned an attempt to sit up. "But I had a lovely dream about the sea and that we were on holiday in a castle..."

"We are in a castle."

"My face is very odd. It only moves on one side. What happened to me?"

"Fergus hit you," said Samuel in a matter-of-fact voice, as if answering a perfectly normal question.

Gilly shut her eyes because the boy's face was too close to hers and seemed to grow larger by the minute. There was a loud ringing in her ears. Tinni something. Tinnit... no, couldn't remember, but her mother had it once, whatever it was called. She longed to see her mother now. Mum would be able to give her a hug and all would be well. She yawned. So tired. She might as well just lie back, relax and wait for Mum to come.

"Gilly?" Samuel came closer and his eyes grew bigger. Bigger and bigger. Two huge, round chocolate eyes.

She held out a hand to keep them away. "Not so close, sweetie. I can't see very well. I feel a bit weird."

"Dad says never to take sweets from strangers," said Samuel.

"What?"

"Sweets. You shouldn't take sweets."

"I didn't eat any sweets, did I?" Gilly tried to remember. Someone had come into the room with food, definitely. The boy had eaten a lot of it. It had cheese on the top.

"She gave you two white sweets." Samuel sounded impatient. "The witch. She gave you sweets and you ate them."

This was really strange. She had no recollection of eating sweets. She hadn't seen any witches either. Very very weird. She decided to go back to sleep and wait until her mother came.

She must have only been asleep for a few minutes because it still wasn't quite dark outside. Two hands gripped her shoulders; shook her. She opened her right eye and found she couldn't open the left one. What had happened to it because it seemed to be glued shut?

"Gilly, Gilly." Samuel was breathing down on her face and had materialized as if out of a fog. "Wake up."

"Oh, Sam, hang on, I'm a... I'm a bit tired, honey."

"You have to wake up now. There are men here." His voice sounded muffled. A loud ringing sound in her ears. Difficult to hear as this fog muffled his words. Had she been dreaming about the sea? Maybe the mist came from the sea. Where was she?

"Men are banging at the door," shouted Samuel. "I think it might be the man coming to rescue us."

Man? What man? She tried to speak but the words were impossible to articulate. "I don't... I feel so..."

The door crashed open and thumped against the wall. Gilly jerked with fright and settled down again. If she could just go back to sleep until the fog cleared away.

Someone shrieked. She opened her good eye and saw hands snatch at the boy, who screamed and kicked out. They were big hands that came out of the fog and looked familiar. She'd seen them before. The hair on the back of them was a reddish blond.

"No, no, Fergus! Gilly, help me." Samuel shouted at her. It was definitely Samuel. She recognized his dark curls and his cute little face. Such a sweet boy.

She tried to sit up. The boy sounded upset and Fergus towered over her, his face screwed up in fury.

"What doing?" she slurred.

Fergus pushed her roughly back on the pillows and lifted the boy onto his shoulder, carrying him towards the door like a sack of potatoes. Samuel screamed and struggled as Fergus took him away into the fog.

Something wasn't right. She would have to follow them. It wasn't kind of Fergus to frighten the boy like that. She would stop him and give him a lecture. If he thought this was a joke, he had gone too far.

Gilly managed to get her feet off the bed and onto the floor. She paused to take a few breaths and heard distant shrieks and footsteps. The room seemed to vibrate with footsteps, but no one came in. Maybe they were outside on the staircase. She remembered a spiral staircase that led upwards.

She gripped the bedside table and slowly got to her feet. Her limbs were heavy and her head throbbed. She gasped and stood for a few minutes. The ringing in her ears deafened her. Then it drifted away and the clatter of feet on stone returned. Followed by shouts.

She groped along the side of the bed, held onto the post in the corner and tried to listen. Another shriek rang out and she remembered the hands that had hauled away Samuel. She would have to make the effort to follow, even though she longed to lie down on the mattress and go back to sleep.

Perhaps she was in a dream and would wake up in a minute. She pinched her arm, but nothing happened. It was strange that the pinch didn't hurt. Nothing hurt. She had injured her head, her nose and her left eye, but nothing hurt.

The fog around her seemed to numb everything.

Gilly let go of the bedpost and staggered towards the door. She fell onto her knees on a patterned rug and examined it carefully. Dark blue with swirls of pink and cream. She would have to try again. She got slowly to her feet, held out her arms to aid balance. The door looked so far away. If only she could push herself towards that and grab it before she fell over again.

She launched herself into the mist that swirled between her and the doorway and fell forwards. This time she didn't hit the ground. Arms reached out and she felt herself suspended in mid-air.

"Thanks," she muttered and wondered to whom they belonged.

Kind of someone to catch her or else she would have landed

on the floor. No rug now, just dark oak boards and stone steps outside the door. She felt mildly nauseous.

"Gilly, Gilly," a familiar voice said. It said something else, but she couldn't hear with the ringing whine in her ears that drowned out the words.

"What? Sorry, can't... can't hear too... hearing not too good," she managed to explain.

"What have they done to you, sweetheart?" A kind, worried voice. The strong arms held her up as she slumped forward.

"Am all right," she murmured. "Must find Samuel. Fergus..." She put her face close to the man who held her and recognized Marc. She attempted to smile. "Oh, Marc, it's you. I feel a bit weird... must find Samuel."

Marc's arms tightened around her as he held her against him and kissed her forehead. "Don't worry, it's all right now. Everything will be all right. I'm so glad to see you, but what happened to your face? Dean, Dean, come here and help me, please."

She felt herself passed to other arms and called out, "Marc, I'm sorry..." What was she sorry about? She had no idea.

Dean supported her through the doorway.

"Call an ambulance. 999. Immediately. Do you hear me?"

"Yes, Mr Fletcher."

"And take her downstairs. I've got to go up to the roof. Don't let her out of your sight."

Gilly opened her right eye again and tried to summon some energy. "Marc?"

"He's gone upstairs after Fergus. Fergus has taken Sam out onto the roof. You're to come downstairs with me." It was Dean's voice. Dean from the garden. He dialled a number on his mobile.

She stared into his face. "Dean. You've got to help Samuel. He was... was..."

"The cops and Mr Fletcher have gone after Fergus," said Dean. "They'll help Sam, don't worry. You come with me, Gilly. You're not well. You need to go to hospital."

She struggled in his arms. "No, no. Can't... don't want... not leave Sam. Fergus will hurt him."

"Emergency," said Dean into his phone. "Can you send an ambulance? Woman with... I dunno, maybe it's concussion. Her face is battered."

"I think Fergus hit me. Upstairs, Dean... got to get..."

"Yeah, Gilly, hold on. Can you send an ambulance to a castle near the sea? It's called Dunglas Castle near Skibbereen, near Black River, I think. An old castle that's been done up."

"Dean," Gilly gripped his arm. "Upstairs, help me get upstairs."

"But..."

"Upstairs!" she tried to shout but it sounded more like a squeak.

Dean's face lined with concern. "I dunno, Mr Fletcher said..."

"I will talk... speak... to him," said Gilly, as loftily as she could manage. "Upstairs now, please. Help me."

His arms steered her towards the steps. She lifted her elbow and hooked her right hand over Dean's shoulder. He was wearing a black shiny jacket, leather or some sort of fake leather.

They climbed more steps, never-ending steps that went up and up. She clung onto Dean's shoulder. So tired now and her legs felt stiff and wooden.

"Mr Fletcher is gonna kill me," Dean muttered after a few minutes. "He said to take you downstairs. Why won't you listen?"

Gilly laughed. "I'm gonna kill you too." It was a good joke, so she laughed again. Her laughter sounded high-pitched and echoed in the stairway.

Another man pushed past them.

"Sorry, Sergeant." Dean pulled her against the wall.

"Hey, watch... where you're going," said Gilly and felt braver now that she had Dean's support. She would get upstairs and out onto the roof and give Fergus a piece of her mind for the way he was treating poor Sam. The bully. "Fergus... bully," she told Dean.

"I know that."

"Big, big bully. He hit me... I think."

"Yeah, yeah, you really need to go to hospital. You're not making any sense."

"Not now," said Gilly. "Up..."

Dean sighed.

"Get me up."

"OK, OK. Hold onto me. This ladder is gonna to be difficult."

Dean was sweating now. She could smell the sweat and she could feel it on his neck. He often sweated in the garden at Glanesfort when he was doing hard work like digging. Yes, Glanesfort was where Marc lived and he had a lovely garden. It was all coming back to her so there was nothing wrong with her memory, no need to worry.

It took a long time to get up the ladder. She was several rungs up when she fell back down on top of Dean who tried to hoist her from below. She laughed as she slipped sideways. "Oops. Nearly gone..."

"Gilly, try to lift your foot when I say so. Do you understand?"

"Which foot?"

"Right foot, then left foot."

"OK."

She obediently placed her right foot on the rung and Dean pushed. She swung to the left and laughed again. No control over her limbs. She thought she might be drunk, but she couldn't remember anyone giving her alcohol. Difficult to remember anything that had happened when her mind was playing tricks on her. Snippets of memory swept up and retreated like waves on a beach.

A hand appeared from above and a voice ordered her to hold onto it. She grabbed it and felt herself pulled upwards. Fresh air outside, cold wind on her face. She staggered forward.

"What are you doing up here?" Marc's face was close to hers. "I told Dean to take you downstairs."

"She won't listen, Mr Fletcher, I tried, I tell you, I tried."

"Fergus... Sam," said Gilly.

"Yes, they're over there." Was Marc smiling at her? He had a kind smile and his eyes crinkled at the corners. She loved him. She wanted to tell him that she loved him, but he vanished into the fog.

"Where is Sam?" Gilly asked as she stepped away from the trapdoor. Must have been the sudden movement made her feel dizzy. She clutched at the nearest arm and managed to steady her legs. Why was she so weak? Flu. Must have flu.

"I'm worried about her, Mr Fletcher, she's talking garbage."

"Did you call the ambulance?"

"Yeah – it's on the way."

Gilly listened to this conversation with interest. She was ill, had flu. Why didn't they understand? And Fergus had hit her, but she couldn't remember why. "Not garbage," she said. "Don't need ambulance."

Marc instructed Dean to hold onto her. She couldn't see where he went. Voices spoke around her but the words were indecipherable, a continuous mumble.

"Sit," said Dean. "There's a bench here. Sit down."

She lowered herself onto the iron bench. The voices sounded louder, but the ringing in her ears confused her and her stomach swirled like the mist in front of her eyes. Sick. Flu. She should have stayed in bed and waited for her mother to come.

She rested her head on Dean's shoulder for a few minutes

until the dizziness eased and she could see more clearly. A figure on the wall advanced towards them. Two figures. One was small and the other tall. A few men stood nearby and one looked like he was trying to coax the man on the wall to climb down. She strained her ears, but still couldn't hear.

Gilly realized the smaller figure was Samuel and cried out. "No, Sam! I told you not to get on the wall."

Dean squeezed her arm. "Shush."

"But Sam's on the wall..."

"Yes, I know. Shut up, Gilly – give the detective a chance to get him down."

Dread paralysed her. Fergus and Sam on the wall. Fergus had hit her. He would hurt the boy. The man talking to him moved a little closer and Fergus suddenly swept Samuel off his feet and lifted him out over the edge. No, no! Big drop down, she remembered the dog as he sat below, brown freckles and wagging tail. Long, long way down. She attempted to call out, but Dean put his hand over her mouth. She tried to wriggle out of his grip.

Fergus stepped along the wall, moved away from the two men who followed him, the boy dangling in his arms. The mist in front of her eyes lifted and she could see the anger on Fergus's face, she could hear Samuel's screams. She wriggled again and Dean removed his hand from her mouth.

She clutched his arm. "Fergus has Sam. Look!"

Dean's face was white with sweat on it. Sweat everywhere now. Her own hands covered in sweat. Her nose started to bleed and blood dripped onto her palms. She covered her face with her hands and peered through her fingers. Nausea swelled inside her and she shivered. The cold mist descended again and her skin felt icy.

"Feel sick," she whispered to Dean.

Fergus tripped and recovered when Samuel cried out again.

Fergus was close to her now and yelled, "Get back, get back or I'll throw him over."

Gilly heard his words ring out as she struggled to her feet and her stomach heaved. "Going to be sick..."

Dean put his arm round her to pull her down and she heard him breathing heavily. The fog swirled and thickened and she no longer saw Fergus, but could just about glimpse the boy's frantically kicking legs. The parapet began to spin; the murmuring figures revolved in front of her eyes, faster and faster. She fell forwards and landed on her knees. She looked up and saw Fergus topple backwards into darkness. She screamed and Dean's hands landed on her shoulders, but it was too late. Blackness surrounded her, cold enveloped her, as she sank onto the flagstones and her consciousness ebbed away.

Chapter 36

Bright light shone beyond Gilly's eyelids. Her head lay on a pillow with a sheet and cotton blanket covering her. She was on a narrow bed because she could feel the edges with her hands. She opened her right eye. One side of her face ached when she tried to move it. Overhead a white ceiling with a florescent light; blue check curtains surrounded the bed.

A slim woman in a navy uniform adjusted an object beside her, a plastic bag that hung on a metal stand, and switched off a bleeping sound.

Someone sat beside the bed, someone familiar whose face slowly came into focus. It was Alice.

"Oh, you're awake. How are you, dear?" Alice said, concern in her eyes. She reached out and touched her hand. "You've had a good sleep."

"Where am I?" Her dry tongue seemed to stick to the roof of her mouth, the words difficult to push out.

"In hospital. How do you feel?"

"I'm very thirsty."

The nurse examined the tube that led to her hand and pointed at a jug on a nearby locker.

Alice released her hand and poured water into a glass.

"You'll have to sit up. Can you sit up?"

"I'll try. What's this thing for?"

"Just an IV drip, that's all," said the nurse. "We put it there in case you were dehydrated." She helped Gilly to shift into an upright position. "Here, try to drink a little water." She handed her the glass.

"I feel weak."

"I'm not surprised," said Alice. "You've had a very shocking time."

Gilly sipped the fluid.

"Would you like painkillers? Any headache?" the nurse asked.

"A bit of a headache and my face feels sore."

"I'll get you some pain relief to help. You lie back there on the pillow and relax." She swept the curtains aside and disappeared.

"Your family will be so pleased to see you." Alice placed the jug back on the locker. "They've been here all night – we all have – waiting for you to wake up. They're in the restaurant having a bite to eat. I said I'd wait here until they come back."

"What time is it?"

Alice consulted her watch. "Almost nine thirty. You were admitted at about three in the morning. Can you remember anything?"

Gilly shook her head. "Not much."

"Perhaps that's just as well."

Gilly closed her eyes and groaned softly. "Where's Marc?"

"He was here too, most of the night, in fact. He's driving Samuel home."

"Sam? Is he... is he all right?"

"He's very shaken, naturally, after that ordeal, but he'll be all right."

Gilly shuddered. "Oh Alice, it was terrible. So frightening for poor Sam." Fergus had snatched him away from the bedroom and there had been something terrifying. What was it? Outside, on the roof. Yes, they'd both been on the wall of the parapet before she'd passed out. Fergus had threatened to throw the boy over the edge. All coming back to her.

"Poor little boy, he'll need a lot of rest. He spent the night here in the hospital, but he was keen to get home. The doctor was happy with him, said there wasn't any need to keep him in."

"I'm so glad to hear that." Gilly touched her swollen eye. "Do I look terrible?"

"You've got a nasty bruise and your left eye is very swollen. We were so... I know this might sound... but Marc and I were so thankful that you were with Samuel. The thought of him there on his own with those two... those two hateful people, it fills me with dread."

"I feel so tired. I can't remember much. It all seemed to be happening in a thick fog."

"You were drugged," said Alice. "A strong sedative of some sort and it seems as if you had a bad reaction to it. Marc told us you were staggering around talking nonsense. He said you turned as white as a ghost before you collapsed."

"The woman, Jane, gave me some white tablets when I asked for paracetemol."

"Tranquillizers. That woman has been arrested, thank goodness. She deserves... well, at least they've caught her."

"What about Fergus? What happened to him?" Did she remember him toppling backwards? Nobody could survive that fall. Perhaps she'd imagined that, though, because she might have been delirious, hallucinating.

"I can't understand how Fergus could do such a terrible thing to Samuel and to you... he must be deranged."

"Did he...?"

"Well, he's alive, believe it or not. He survived the fall from the top of the tower, goodness knows how, but he survived it.

Marc said he's unconscious still and in intensive care."

Gilly glanced at the door. "Not... here?"

Alice bent to search her handbag on the floor by her feet. "I'm not sure, but I doubt they'd bring him here after what he's done. I imagine they'll keep him somewhere secure. I'll call Marc. He said to let him know when you woke up. He spent the night walking from your bed to Samuel's – the poor man is worn out and now he has a three-hour drive."

"I'd love to see him."

"He'll be so relieved to know you're all right. He's not answering his mobile so I'll send him a text. What happened to your face?"

"He hit me... Fergus hit me."

Alice uttered a small cry; put her hand to her mouth.

"How did they find us? How did they know where we were?"

"Marc found a list of holiday houses in Fergus's apartment. Apparently, he looked after them for a wealthy American and Marc knew about the mill, but not the others. They found your shoe outside the mill, you see. There was a brochure of about fifteen properties, holiday rentals and suchlike. The Gardaí worked their way through them. They sent men to check them out and last night Marc got the phone call from your sister."

"Phone call from Vanessa?"

"Yes, she'd received a call from a man who lives near here in West Cork. She said she didn't know what to think when he told her that his dog had brought back a plastic bottle with a message inside, a scrawled message splattered with blood. The man thought it might have been a joke at first, but decided to ring the number you'd written down... Vanessa's number. It was you who wrote that, wasn't it?"

"Yes, it was. I'm so pleased to hear that – and Sam must be delighted. We were rescued by a dog." She twisted her mouth, tried to smile and winced as the curtains parted and the nurse reappeared with painkillers.

Chapter 37

Gilly stood on the gravel at the front of Glanesfort with her mother and sister, while Ken revved the engine of his Audi and hooted the horn with playful impatience, like a big child with his shiny red car. The novelty still hadn't worn off. Behind her, Samuel hummed to himself and hopped up and down the steps.

"Thanks again for my birthday lunch and I loved the chicken dish. I nearly believed you when you pretended you'd made it yourself." Vanessa pushed her sunglasses back on her head. "Say hello to Marc from us. We were sorry to miss him, weren't we, Mum?"

Gilly kissed her on the cheek and turned to hug her mother. "Thanks for coming."

Her mother's soft face creased into a smile. "It was fun, darling. So glad to see you and know that you've recovered after your horrible experience. You gave us such a fright."

"I know, Mum, I'm so sorry."

"You've done a great job – the garden is wonderful." Her arms encircled her as she squeezed affectionately and Gilly smelled her mother's rose-scented perfume. "I don't suppose Marc would give me a job too?"

"He might. Will I ask him?"

"Don't encourage her. She'll want to move down here next." Vanessa's mouth twitched. "We'll bring Daddy next time. He said he'd like to have a proper look around this place."

"Is that a threat or a promise?"

"He wants to see you, too, not just the house and garden." Vanessa gestured to her mother. "You go to the car, Mum, I won't be a minute." She waited until she was out of earshot before she nodded towards Samuel and whispered, "How is the little boy doing?"

"He's all right considering what happened to him, but he gets frightened at night." She linked arms with her sister as they strolled towards the Audi. The afternoon sun still felt warm. "I'm glad you came. It has been... well... difficult to say the least. Poor Sam hates sleeping in his own bed now and spends all night with his father. Marc told me to keep an eye on him today – not to let him out of my sight."

"Give him time. I'm sure it will just take time for him to get his confidence back."

Gilly nodded and glanced back at Samuel who was sitting on the gravel, pushing stones into a heap between his feet.

"What happens when your work here is finished?" Vanessa gazed into her eyes. "You need to think about this. Where will you go? You can't stay here forever."

"I know that."

"You'll have to decide what you're going to do. What have you done about the hotel garden in Galway?"

"I've told them I'll take that job."

Her sister smiled and leaned forward to kiss her cheek. "That's good news. I think you need to ask Marc to make a decision about your future. I mean, does he want you to stay with him or not?"

"Vanessa, I can't, please don't suggest that. I don't want to put him under pressure at the moment."

"Just don't put it on the long finger. Most men need a subtle nudge, believe me." She bent to get into the passenger seat. "Take care."

Gilly waved as they drove away and turned to beckon to Samuel. "That went well, didn't it? A good day, I think."

He seemed happier today, poor little boy. Saturday, the fifth of June. Only two weeks since they'd been rescued.

"Where's Dad?"

"He's still in Dublin, but he'll be home soon. I got a text from him about twenty minutes ago. Shall we go back to the garden and look for the goldfish?"

The boy agreed enthusiastically. He loved looking for fish under the young lilypads and enjoyed poking his fingers into the clay at the bottom of the pool. He led the way and skipped ahead of her down the path.

Marc had gone to visit Fergus, who was still in intensive care, still lying there in a coma. Why did he bother? She never wanted to see Fergus or his sister again.

They reached the pool and she bent to stir the water with her fingers, squinting at Samuel in the sunlight. She was still getting occasional headaches and should be wearing her sunglasses. Had she left them in the car?

"Can you see the goldfish?" he asked as he bent over the stone edge. "I'm gonna pretend it's a big orange shark."

"Careful," she warned. "If it's a shark, it might bite off your hand."

He giggled and frowned with concentration as his fingers probed for fish that darted about under the safety of a wire mesh, lost now in his own four-year-old world.

She wondered how long Marc would be. The water shimmered in the sun and little wavelets caused by the boy's antics lapped over the lilypads.

"When is Alice coming home?" Samuel asked.

"Not for a few weeks. Your dad has given her a holiday. She's staying with her brother and his family."

"Will she remember me when she comes back?"

"Of course she will. Alice will never forget you."

She glanced around. The yew hedge had improved and, although a slow grower, the plants looked strong and healthy. Shrubs inside the hedge already reached out to touch each other. Buddleias, *Ceanothus* 'Gloire de Versailles' and mock orange blossom, *Philadelphus* 'Belle Etoile' with its heady scent, swayed gently in the breeze.

The boy pointed and shouted, "Hey, look, there's the big one." He treated her to one of his brightest smiles.

Gilly grinned back. How much did he remember of what had happened? During the day, he seemed happy and carefree; memories of the nightmare returned only after dark.

The door to the yard swung open and she turned to see Marc walk in, wearing his suit trousers and a pale blue shirt. He came towards them with a lighter step – definitely a lighter step.

He leaned over Samuel and placed his hands on his shoulders. "Well, young man, what are you looking for?"

"Do you know something, Dad? Gilly put ten goldfish in here and I can only find eight."

"You keep looking, sweetheart. Perhaps they're hiding under those lilypads." He gestured to Gilly. "Let's go for a walk."

The boy sang to himself as they left him alone to search for fish and they walked out through the gap in the yew, turned right along the path towards the beech arch. She shaded her eyes from the sun, felt its warmth on her face as she waited for him to speak.

"Samuel seems happier, doesn't he? I'm going to get him a dog, Gilly. I think I'll try to find a rescued one that might appreciate being hugged to death by my loving son."

"Oh, he'll be thrilled. What breed?"

"A big black shaggy one that will probably leave mud and hair everywhere and drive poor Alice to distraction. That's how Sam always described Wolf, isn't it?"

"It's a great idea. He deserves a real Wolf. So what happened at the hospital?"

He didn't reply, but took her hand and they strolled under the arch in the old beech hedge, where new leaves already sprouted from the wood she'd pruned back.

Marc stopped to admire it. "I can't believe it's the same hedge – it's amazing what you've done to this garden, you and Dean."

"His granny is very proud of him. She thinks he's found his vocation."

They moved on towards an antique sundial, opposite the wall with the recently planted fruit trees: pears, plums and greengages.

"I've offered him a job here, a permanent job maintaining the garden, seeing as you will probably move on somewhere else and leave me in the lurch."

"Did he accept it?" She ignored the second half of his sentence.

"Only on condition he gets an apartment for his grandmother as part of his wages. He wants to get her out of the city apparently."

They ambled along the mown grass path towards the rose garden, getting closer to the subject that they both seemed to be avoiding. Dean had worked hard and deserved a steady job. Above them, fluffs of cloud scattered across the vivid sky. Some shrub roses were already in flower, pink and white heads weighing down the young stems.

"I should have snipped some of the blooms off, I suppose, to give the plants a chance to get really strong," Gilly said. "But

I had to leave them. They're so beautiful and it seemed a shame to cut them." She lifted one velvety blossom and bent to breathe in its sweet, heavy scent. "This one is called 'Madame Isaac Pereire', a Bourbon rose from 1881. Just smell that perfume."

"*Magnifique*," he muttered. "*Elle est tres belle.*"

"I believe she's named after a French banker's wife, like your mother."

"Louise will be charmed, I'm sure." Marc still said nothing about Fergus.

She couldn't go to the intensive care unit to see him, with machines attached to him that whirred and bleeped, but Marc had been several times.

As if reading her thoughts, he said, "I know you told me I shouldn't go to the hospital, that I should let the Gardaí deal with Fergus, but I felt I had to be there when he woke up – to talk to him."

She waited.

"I wanted to know why... why he did what he did, why he treated you and Sam so badly. There was no need... if he had come to talk to me before, I would have been sympathetic... but to put us all through that."

"Obsessed, he was obsessed. I tried to tell him you would have listened to him, but he couldn't understand, or wouldn't."

He pointed at a new bench under the arch where the thornless rose, 'Zepherin Drouhin', had only recently begun to climb up the wooden trellis, delicate new leaves with pink buds that would soon open into fragrant old-fashioned flowers.

They sat on the seat, close but not touching.

She looked around at the young box hedging that framed the shrub rose beds. "I will never forgive him."

"I know Fergus thought I'd used the money that my father embezzled to build up my business," Marc said, "just like I told you in London. He mentioned that, didn't he? It's only natural people would think that."

"But how can anyone know for certain what caused his father's stroke? Perhaps it would have happened without..."

"Without losing his life's savings? Maybe, but Fergus and Jane would never accept that." Marc sighed and leaned towards her, ran a finger along her nose. "It's better, isn't it? How are the headaches?"

"Nearly gone."

Still the serious expression in his grey eyes. "Gilly..."

"Yes?"

"I've something to tell you."

She glanced at him. "What?"

"He died, Gilly. Fergus died this morning." He went on quickly. "The doctors decided to turn off the life support machine, you see. He was never going to regain consciousness or, if he did, he wouldn't be able to..." His voice trailed away and he shrugged in that French manner he used when he didn't know what to say. A shrug that implied more than any words could.

Her heart made a little flip. "I... I suppose it's for the best if the doctors thought that... but his mother... I feel sorry for her."

"I didn't see her this morning, but I'll go to visit her."

"What a waste of a life, Marc, when he could have... I liked him in the beginning. He could be amusing, but he changed so much after his father died."

"The tenants always liked him too."

She took a deep breath. "I don't know what to say. I'm sorry, I suppose, but..."

"The way he treated you and Samuel was unforgivable. I wanted an explanation from him and now... now I'll never get one."

Gilly watched the sunlight flicker on the glossy leaves of the rose. "And Jane? Will you talk to her?"

"No, I don't think so. There'll be the trial, of course, and you will have to be involved, I suppose. I'm not looking forward to that. No, I won't bother with her."

"I'm not looking forward to it either. What will happen about their uncle?"

"Nothing, unless he comes back and they find him. My guess is he'll stay away, wherever he is. How did your sister's birthday lunch go?"

"It went well. My mother loved Glanesfort."

"You've done wonders here. Just look at this walled garden – I like the way you've laid it out like rooms, each section with a different theme. What's this pure white rose?"

"It's 'Blanche Double de Coubert'. It will grow tall and give you privacy in the summer months."

"I like the sound of that." He took her hand, glanced around. "Where's Sam?"

"He's still over by the pool. Marc..."

"What is it?"

"What will happen when the garden's finished? It's probably only three or four weeks away. You won't sell Glanesfort and move back to London, will you?"

"You told me you want to take the job in Galway."

"Yes, I will take it. It's a big project... would be a good experience, another big project to add to my CV. You must realize it will help my career."

He didn't reply.

"I'm gaining confidence," she said. "I really feel I might be a successful landscape designer now. You're not going to leave Ireland, are you?"

He squeezed her hand. "I had one piece of good news this morning. While I was waiting in the hospital, Michael rang from London. He told me that Kiu Fat and his investment company have made an offer for my offices."

"That's great."

"Twelve per cent lower than the Japanese, but at least it's a definite offer and it's also cash, which should please the bank. I would like to get Michael to handle this. If he could manage the Cantonese in Hong Kong for Mr Azuma, he will cope very well with Kiu Fat and his team of Chinese speculators." He sat upright. "I would like to go away for a while... to take Samuel with me on holiday, a real holiday." He turned to face her, as if to check her reaction, as a flicker of amusement danced in his eyes.

"So you are going away?"

He touched her arm; his fingers stroked her skin. "Well, I thought you'd be busy, you know. That garden in Galway is going to take up a lot of your time and it's very far from Glanesfort."

"Barely three hours drive away."

"We'll hardly see each other. I don't want you to feel you have to come and visit me every weekend. I don't want to cramp your style."

She stared at him, incredulous. "Cramp my style? I thought you'd want to come and see me sometimes."

"Did you?" He looked away so that she couldn't see his expression.

"Yes, I did. Is that so unreasonable? Where are you and Samuel going?"

Still he kept his face averted. "France. My mother has asked us to stay with her and François."

"To France?"

"Alice rang this morning. She wants more time off to go to Devon with her brother and his wife. They booked a house down there and if anyone needs a break, poor Alice does. We can stay with my mother and her husband in their villa on the Côte d'Azur."

Gilly pulled away her hand and stood up. "I hope you have

a lovely time."

He also rose to his feet. "Oh, I intend to. Sam and I will enjoy the sun and the sea. The food is very good there too and my mother is an excellent cook."

She couldn't believe how relaxed he sounded and he actually had the cheek to smile at her. Gilly swung away in exasperation, but he caught her arm and pulled her round to face him.

"I had hoped..." he began.

"What?"

"I had hoped that you might put off your job in Galway for a little while, not forever, of course, but long enough to..."

"Long enough to what?"

"To come with us to France." He raised his eyebrows.

"Marc, have you been winding me up all this time?"

He put his head to one side. "Possibly."

She couldn't quite suppress a snort of laughter. "I thought you were being serious. But will I get on with your mother?"

"I hope so. She can be difficult sometimes, but her heart's in the right place. I'm sure she'll take to you. Just remember to brush your hair every morning. You'll like François, my stepfather. He's very charming. He has a teenage niece who will be happy to look after Samuel so we can spend some time on our own." They sat on the seat again and dappled light played on his face, the sun filtering through the squares of trellis. "We'll be able to go out to dinner, go for walks, enjoy the sun – whatever you like – all those things we've never done."

"I'd love that. It sounds wonderful, thank you." She added, "The worst thing Fergus said was that you mightn't think I was worth... that you mightn't want..."

"Do you think I wouldn't pay a ransom for you?"

"Would you, though? I'm glad it never came to that but, just out of curiosity, how much would you have paid to get me back?"

The lines beside his eyes creased. "I'm always amazed by the questions you ask. Let me see, I would need to calculate your long term resale value, plus rental income in the short term…"

She pushed against him, rolled her eyes.

"I'd have to consider such an investment very carefully."

"Seriously, though," she said, "I'll need a reference for the Galway hotel project. Will you write one for me?"

"Of course, my love. I'll tell them that you're impatient and impulsive and you never listen…" He waved a hand to include the garden. "But you're also loyal, brave and a hard worker. I'll spin them a good story, don't worry. No one will be able to resist you. I know I can't."

"You can't what?"

"Can't resist you."

"So you think I'm an asset then, worth paying for?" She threw her arms round his neck.

"Most definitely an asset." He drew her to him, bent to kiss her.

"Daddy, Daddeee…"

Over the shrub roses, Gilly watched the little figure turn the corner by the sundial, his arms out wide as he scampered along the grass path towards them, uttering loud, explosive engine noises.

Marc stood, lifted her up and swung her to her feet. "I think we'll all go for a drive and buy ice creams – and then we'll tell him about the dog."

To the reader

Thank you for reading *The Neglected Garden*. I hope you enjoyed it and, if you did, perhaps you would be kind enough to leave a review. This makes a big difference to authors these days and it can be as short as you like. Your help is much appreciated.

If you are interested in receiving the occasional notification by email about other novels and special offers, you will find the form for my newsletter at www.suzannewinterly.com.

You can also find me on the following social media platforms:

Facebook
www.facebook.com/suzannewinterly

Instagram
www.instagram.com/suzannewinterly

Pinterest
www.pinterest.ie/suzannewinterly

Acknowledgements

Thank you to my family and friends and especially to my husband William who always encouraged me.

I couldn't have written *The Neglected Garden* without the expert advice of horticultural friends. Many thanks go to garden designer Arthur Shackleton for creating Gilly's plan for the walled garden at Glanesfort. Thank you to Jenny and Andrew Glenn-Craigie of Landscape Restoration for their input and plant knowledge. They stopped my heroine putting plants in the wrong places and gave her plenty of ideas.

Thank you to Marjorie Quarton who first put me on the novel writing path. I'm grateful to the Hilary Johnson Authors' Advisory Service for editorial and copy-editing help and am certain their suggestions made this a better book. My thanks go to all at SPF 101 and especially to Mark Dawson and James Blatch. I've learned so much from them and from the generous advice in the authors' group.

The cover was designed by Stuart Bache of Books Covered and it was a great thrill to see my story come to life visually. I'd like to thank Bryan Cohen of Best Page Forward for his book description skills.

Thank you to Michael who put a lot of effort into making the Japanese scenes authentic. He even offered advice on what wine they would drink.

Many thanks to my former boss Cahir, who gently urged me on, and to Louise who produced copious cups of tea and helpful advice. I can't neglect to mention Nicola, Tara and my sisters, Jill and Rosemary, who made suggestions when called upon.

About the author

Suzanne Winterly was born in County Tipperary, Ireland. She has an English degree from Trinity College, Dublin and has written articles for specialist newspapers and magazines about horticulture and horse racing.

She has two sons and lives in the country with her husband and a variety of four-legged friends.

The Neglected Garden is her debut novel.

Website
www.suzannewinterly.com

Facebook
www.facebook.com/suzannewinterly

Instagram
www.instagram.com/suzannewinterly

Pinterest
www.pinterest.ie/suzannewinterly